LINDSEY

LINDSEY
LOVE AND INTRIGUE

Kimberly Kolb

iUniverse, Inc.
Bloomington

LINDSEY
LOVE AND INTRIGUE

iUniverse books may be ordered through booksellers or by contacting:

iUniverse
1663 Liberty Drive
Bloomington, IN 47403
www.iuniverse.com
1-800-Authors (1-800-288-4677)

ISBN: 978-1-4759-8790-4 (sc)
ISBN: 978-1-4759-8791-1 (hc)
ISBN: 978-1-4759-8792-8 (e)

Library of Congress Control Number: 2013907555

Printed in the United States of America

iUniverse rev. date: 6/3/2013

To

my mother, Barbara, for always making the time;
my father, Donato, for making me believe every problem can be solved;
my husband, Jeff, for countless moments that were
better than I ever could have imagined;

and to the sixteen-year-old in each of us, for your unending capacity to dream.

CONTENTS

ACKNOWLEDGMENTS

I would like to thank my mom, Barbara Cantalupo, for being the first to read my initial rough draft and for her long hours of skilled editing of those early versions. I would also like to thank my dad, Donato Cantalupo, for always believing in me and the paths I choose.

I am grateful to my husband, Jeff, for supporting me in this, and all my endeavors.

I want to thank my uncle Jack Hess for putting words to this project when I couldn't, and Jack and his wife, Pat, for reading an early draft and encouraging me through to publication.

To my dear friend Michelle Kilbourne—we walked together for hours and sat in many coffee shops over the course of several years. At the end of the journey, you received your PhD and I have published my book. I can only hope my kids have friends who encourage and challenge them as much.

And to everyone who has believed in me—teachers, coaches, colleagues, friends, and family—I thank you. I am indebted to you for your kind words of encouragement.

1 THE FIRST DAY: *I CERTAINLY HOPE SO.*

FIRST DAY OF SCHOOL. I wonder who'll be in my classes.

As I shower and start getting ready, my mind begins to wander. What will this year bring? Will I have girlfriends—*real* girlfriends—or will it be like it's always been, me as mostly a loner? I've always had friends, but not *good* friends. Not the kinds of friends you read about or see girls have in the movies. I tend to get along better with guys. Girls are so much trickier. Well, at least for me. I think I'm the only fifteen-year-old girl in the world that doesn't have three BFFs.

Looking in the mirror, all I think is *ughh*. I wonder who'll be in the cool crowd this year. Mostly I like not being part of a group. I'm just me. I hang out with the kids I like, regardless of whether they're popular or not or which group they're a part of. Truth is, I wish I was more outgoing and social. The kids who are outgoing seem to be friends with everyone. I know most of the kids in high school think I'm shy. Maybe I am. More than anything, I think most of what they talk about is ridiculous, so I choose not to join in.

It would be so much easier to be a guy. Wake up, two minutes in the shower, throw on a pair of jeans and a T-shirt, and show up at school—instant cool. Instead, I'm faced with an endless array of decisions like, should I straighten my hair or curl it? Should I wear eyeliner or just blush and lip gloss? Then there's the annual challenge of selecting an outfit for the first day of school. The judgment girls place on that first-day-of-school outfit is tangible. I guess the guys are judging too. Who gained weight over the summer? Who got taller? Who changed their hair? Nightmare. At least Mom has taken me shopping so I have plenty to choose from, but walking into my closet now, suddenly nothing seems right. What will the girls wear this year?

Staring at my organized closet, I decide on jeans that I know fit well, with a new pink top. Grabbing my backpack off one of the built-in hooks, I head downstairs. Of course, I'm the only one left in the entire junior class who's still fifteen and can't drive yet, but luckily my neighbor Isabella will give me a ride to school.

ೞೋೞ

As I ring Isabella's doorbell, I wonder if it's really Tuesday. What if it's actually Monday, Labor Day, and I wake up her whole family on the wrong day? Stop it. Of course it's Tuesday. No one's home at my house, right? Mom and Dad already left for work, so it must at least be a weekday. Wonder if I'll ever stop questioning myself as to what day of the week it is. Do other people do this? Some probably do, but they likely live in a different kind of "home." Smirk. My mind turns to Isabella. I'm sure I'll get an update on everything she and Rick, her boyfriend, have been doing. They'll go to the homecoming dance together. I wonder if anyone will—

"Hello, Lindsey!" beams Mrs. Castiglioni. Isabella's mom is like chocolate chip cookies, warm and inviting.

"Hi," I say as she gives me a hug and a kiss on the cheek.

"How was your vacation out east? Must have been wonderful;

you got plenty of sun!" she continues while holding my arms, which are pale in comparison to her natural olive tone.

"It was great, thank you."

"Hey," Isabella says as she comes in, looking ridiculously pulled together. "Ready?"

"Yep."

We step through her foyer and into the garage, and I wonder which guys got cuter over the summer. Guess I'm as judgmental as the rest. Will *he* be in any of my classes? As we slide into Isabella's car, the music is already on. We head out and drive around the lake.

Isabella and I are not really close, but then again, am I close to anyone? I consider Elena and Melissa friends, but am I really close to them? Isabella's family has lived in the area for a while, and ever since I moved here, she has been nice to me.

And she's willing to drive me to school, so I figure I should at least try to be social. "How's Rick?" I ask.

"Terrific. We're doing great. It's been eight months—can you believe it?"

"That long?"

"I bet we stay together forever!"

"Hmm." *Forever?* Seriously, this is exactly why I don't get girls. Forever. Right! Why would you *want* to be with him forever?

Glancing around our small town, I remember riding through it for the first time. Nervous, excited, and mad that we had moved! Again!

We moved here, to Emit, Michigan, from the suburbs of Chicago the summer between my seventh- and eighth-grade years. I remember my dad and I were on one of our walks when he told me that he would be leaving his office at the end of the school year to start his own practice and that we would be moving to Michigan. My dad had started his career as a lawyer working for the New York District Attorney's Office prosecuting some of what he calls "the-most-violent-criminals." He says it like it's one word. Then we moved from New York to Chicago, and he worked as a lead prosecutor for their state attorney's office.

3

We moved from New York because of what our family knows as "the Case"—the Case that changed things. I still don't know much about the Case because it's one of those things you just don't bring up. Whenever I mention it, my dad's face tightens. He cracks his neck and usually answers in curt responses until he or my mom changes the subject. What I do know is that he had been preparing to go to trial to prosecute a sixteen-year-old who had apparently sexually assaulted and brutally beaten a couple of young girls. My dad was planning to try him as an adult. Before the trial even started, my dad received an anonymous letter letting him know that the author hoped my dad was successful in prosecuting this kid and sending him to jail for life. The letter said that if my dad was the prosecuting attorney and the kid ever walked free again, the writer would ensure *I* would understand what pain was before burying me alive.

Dad was brought up by parents who had immigrated to the United States, and he was raised with very strong family values. His Italian father died young, but my mom once told me Dad knew what his father would have said to him about caring for me. Hearing his father's advice in his head, Dad immediately transferred the case to another attorney.

My father refers to the kid who was accused as the Animal. The Animal cut a deal with the new lawyer and only served nine months in a juvenile facility. In the year following his release, three girls were brutally murdered in New York. There was no physical evidence at the crime scenes, except one thing, the same at each. My initials, LB, were carved into a tree within a few hundred feet of each of the girls. My dad, and all the authorities, are convinced the Animal killed all three of them. These remain open, unsolved cases.

I know Dad thinks he would have been able to try the Animal as an adult, won the case, and sent him off to a real jail. I think Dad has always felt responsible for those three girls killed in New York. He's never given up a case since. After the Case, I think my dad felt like he needed a fresh start, so we moved to Chicago.

After a few years in the state attorney's office in Chicago, Dad took a position at the US attorney's office in Chicago. I guess he has always been a good courtroom attorney, but he really built his reputation during his years as a prosecutor in Chicago. He had several major cases that gave him a lot of national notoriety. He told me once that with his record, he should be able to build a strong private practice on his own, and my mom had always wanted to live in a bit more rural area. He started building the business when we were in Chicago, and he must have gotten some good clients because my mom built her dream home on the lake when we moved here to Emit.

Now he has a thriving practice. He says it's much better because he gets to pick his clients and his cases, whereas when he worked for the government, he had to take whichever case they gave to him. I think he still likes to be involved in criminal work, but now he also gets to work with clients like our neighbor, Mr. Kirkwood, in corporate law. Truth is, Dad still seems to get asked to consult on some of the high-profile cases being prosecuted by his old government offices in Chicago.

As Isabella and I pull into the student parking lot, my thoughts are interrupted. I see *him*: Chris Buckley. *Sigh*. He waves at us, so of course Isabella waves back. Wow, he always looks … Wait, is he looking at me? He spent last spring semester and the summer studying abroad in London, so I haven't seen him since the fall of our sophomore year. As always, he looks terrific. I glance over at Isabella, as I assume he's eyeing her—and realize she's on her phone and totally engrossed in conversation with someone, probably her boyfriend, Rick. Turning back, I think Chris looks my way for just a second, then he turns to grab his backpack. Maybe he'll be in one of my classes again this year. I certainly hope so. If not, maybe he'll try out for the fall play; he's clearly one of the reasons I've enjoyed being part of the school's productions. Wonder who he's seeing. I've had a crush on him since eighth grade, when my family moved to town. We had a fleeting moment of romance back then, and ever since he's always been nice to me, but, sadly, I'm not even sure he knows I'm a girl. Maybe this'll be the year that things change. Who knows?

I've daydreamed about him more than I want to admit—even to myself.

Shock, Rick parks right next to Isabella.

"Hey, Lindsey."

"Hey, Rick. Thanks for the ride, Isabella."

"Sure. See ya!" she says as she walks off with Rick's arm around her. I wonder what she sees in him. I guess he's cute enough, but he's definitely not one of the smartest guys in the class. What have they talked about for eight months? Seriously. On the other hand, I bet I could think of eight months of things to talk about with Chris.

Next thing I know, Rick's brother, Kevin, is standing next to me. Kevin is a senior, towering over me at six foot one. He's in the honor society, plays soccer, and has been dating the oh-so-perfect Andrea for the past year.

"Hi, Lindsey, nice tan."

"Oh … um, thanks." *Why are you talking to me?* "How, uh … how was your summer?"

"Pretty good; I didn't see you around much."

"Oh, yeah, well, I guess I spent a lot of time at gymnastics practice, and I was visiting family the last couple weeks in August." Nervously I keep looking down and playing with the zipper on my backpack. As I glance up, I notice in the split second that we make eye contact, he's smiling at me. He pulls his backpack over his shoulder, grabs his gym bag, and starts to walk toward school. I start to dig out my iPhone so when Kevin starts walking in with someone else, which should be happening any minute now, I can at least listen to my tunes and look normal even though I'm alone. I quickly look around the school grounds to see where Chris has gone. No sign of him. Oh, well.

Just then Kevin turns back and asks, "You are coming to class, right?"

"Huh? Oh, um, yeah." As I start across the student parking lot, I can't help but notice that he seems to be slowing down. Is he waiting for me? A lowly junior? Should I catch up with him? He must be waiting for Andrea. I decide to walk in his general direction, which, after all, is in the direction of the school entrance, so that way I can either meet up with him, if by some strange twist of fate he does want to walk with me, or I can just head to the building, in the more likely case that he barely knows my name and I'm hallucinating this entire interaction. I probably imagined Chris noticing me too. Great start to the year, Lindz.

As I continue to walk in Kevin's general direction, in a deliberately slow manner, I see Andrea wave at him from across the lot in an overly enthusiastic way. Okay, hallucination officially over. Cue Kevin eagerly walking over to Andrea and putting his arm on her shoulder.

Wait a minute. Did he just nod at her? What does that mean? Well, she is walking with some friends. I keep my steady, slow pace and approach Kevin.

"So, what's your first class?" he says as he seems to be matching my stride.

"Oh um, chemistry, with Lyons," trying to seem casual on the outside as I am totally dying on the inside. *Why are you walking with me?*

"I had him last year—good luck with that."

"Thanks." As I try to focus on what he's saying, I can't help but notice that he continues to walk with me. Okay, so he's just being polite. His mother works at our school and is so nice. She would be proud of his good manners.

As he heads down the hall, he says, "My locker's this way, but maybe I'll see you later."

"Sure." Heading to my locker, I nod at a few kids I haven't seen since the end of last year. I wonder why Kevin didn't walk in with Andrea.

There's the Fab Five gabbing it up. Jennifer is across their circle from me and is nice enough to call over to me as I pass the group in the hallway, "Hey, Lindsey!"

It's fair to say that I have a soft voice, so I try to call back loud enough so she can hear me over the general din of students starting the year, as well as the Fab Five discussing … who knows what, "Hey, Jennifer."

"You going to practice today?" she says with genuine enthusiasm.

"Oh yeah! I'll be there."

"Great. See you then." Jennifer and I have been on the same club gymnastics team since I moved here. It's nice of her to acknowledge me while the Fab Five is holding court. The others do not even seem to notice. Shock. Those are the kind of friends I don't need.

As I turn the corner to get to my locker, I see Jon. I can't help but smile, although I consciously control it to a small curl. I must admit a part of me is seriously hoping that his crush on me is still in full throttle. It was nice last year to at least have one guy notice me for more than just the fact that I'm still considered the "new kid." Jon is a sophomore, and a rather cute one. I'm not really interested in Jon. At least for me, there weren't any feelings last year, but if I'm honest, I get a huge surge from the attention he gives me.

"Hey, Lindsey. Good to see you," he says as he hooks one arm over the top of his locker in a smooth, but deliberate, attempt to look casual.

"Hey, Jon, how was your summer?" I give him a sideways glance, and although I'm actually shooting to look him in his eyes, I realize he grew a good two inches and I'm looking at his dimpled chin.

"Good. My trip with my folks to London and Paris for a few weeks was great. How 'bout you?"

"Cool! Oh, you know, the usual." I throw my backpack into my locker, and slam it shut. He slams his as well. I suspected he was already done with his locker when I had turned the corner, but now I'm pretty sure he still has a crush on me. And I'm selfishly thrilled at the prospect. As I look up into his gray-blue eyes, which don't seem to leave me even as his friends are greeting him, I ask if he has chemistry first period.

"Yep—shall we?" he says with that familiar glint in his eyes. It's our traditional greeting. Last year we had first-period biology together, and he always said, "Shall we?" and I would reply, "Surely," which I do again this morning.

I feel a little guilty walking down the hall with Jon, because I know I'm probably not going to go out with a lower classman. I wonder … does Kevin, who's a senior, have the same rule? Happily, Chris and I are both juniors, so the dream lives on. But Jon seems to know I'm not really interested in him in that way, and he doesn't appear to care. No idea why—but I figure why not enjoy the attention from Jon since Chris isn't giving me any?

Walking down the hall we hear the first bell, and we both quicken our pace. I'm always glad to have someone to walk with down the back hallway—the so-called "burnout" hallway. I hate going down here alone. All the kids that smoke hang out back here. Why do they all wear black?

I see Mark tossing out his cigarette butt in the courtyard and smile. Mark is such a rugged outdoorsman. Always going camping, or rock climbing, or something outdoorsy. I admire how comfortable he is out in nature.

"Hey, Mark," I say, and with this, Jon looks over to see who I know in this particular hallway.

"Hey, Lindsey, how's it going?"

"Good. When do you have lunch?" I ask, and I'm glad we still seem to be friends.

"Third—you?" he asks.

"Fourth, but they overlap so maybe I'll see ya later," I say as I pass by, still walking with Jon. Fortunately, no one else talks to us as we turn into the chemistry lab, because, except for Mark, the rest of the crowd looks way too tough for me. The usual array of kids are in chemistry, and Mr. Lyons is already projecting his tablet on the screen. I'm hoping that Jon will sit with me at a lab table. Given that he'll likely be salutatorian or valedictorian for his class, being his lab partner will just about guarantee an "A" for me in the class. So I turn to him and ask, "Lab partners?" The prospect of flirting with him for the year is also exciting in a ridiculously giddy way.

With a broad smile across his face, he responds, "Definitely," as he guides me to a table in the back corner by the window. And the Crush lives on. I know I shouldn't enjoy the attention as much as I do, but I just can't help it.

&OCB

For third-period English, I choose a seat toward the back, but most of the seats are still open as we still have a few minutes before the class bell. I assume most kids already know who will be in their classes and will walk in with a friend. Almost everyone at school posts their schedules online in a "private" area, which ironically they give most of the school access to. My dad won't let me join any of those websites, let alone post any information about myself online. Both of my parents are attorneys, but they work in very different areas of the law. One of the many benefits of my dad having been a district attorney for many years is his general distrust. Rather than the typical American perspective of innocent until proven guilty, my dad works from the perspective that everyone I meet is a criminal until proven otherwise. I always kind of knew this, but it really hit home when I made the mistake once in fourth grade of telling my folks about my day at school and mentioning that a boy was picking on me.

At that dinner I think I learned what an inquisition is. Dad went completely crazy. Asking me all kinds of questions, over and over again. "Did he touch you? Has he ever hurt you? What exactly do you mean 'picking on you'? How long has this been going on? What did the teacher say?" I don't think he even knew my teacher's name before that. Next thing I knew he was scheduling meetings with my teacher, the principal, and the kid's parents. He blew the entire situation completely out of proportion. The truth is the kid would just say mean things to me at recess and lunch, basically anytime he saw me when a teacher wasn't around. But after my dad's string of meetings, not only did that kid tease me, but so did all his creepy friends. I learned very quickly to be careful what I said about other kids at school.

Then Chris Buckley walks in, and I'm instantly thrilled. I see him and my mind can't think of anything else. Chris has perfect hair, shiny and brown, with subtle blond highlights that seem to spike and fall in a casual precision around his face. He is about six feet tall and has a completely adorable, dimpled smile that lights up his eyes, making it impossibly contagious. I don't think he has ever really had a girlfriend, but he always seems to have a date. He's one of those guys who are so handsome and cool everyone likes him. All the girls want to date him and hope to be the one he actually chooses as a girlfriend, and the guys all want to hang out with him. To me, he is simply devastating: bright blue eyes framed with long, dark lashes; broad shoulders; and a lean muscular build. Unattainable perfection realized.

Chris says, "Hey, Rob! Hey, Jason!" Jason gets a knuckle bump as his greeting from Chris. I'm, of course, still looking at him, as I assume is most of the room. Does he even notice that girls stare at him all day long?

"Hey, Chris!" bursts out Amanda. Amanda is another member of the Fab Five, the most popular group of girls in our class. Whatever "popular" really means. Nightmare. They will, of course, all be on homecoming court next year. Amanda is okay. Maybe not the worst of the bunch, but clearly she figures Chris is in her league. Isn't that how it always is? The best-looking, most-popular guys, all seem to be taking turns dating the best-looking, most-popular girls. Nightmare.

"Amanda," Chris responds with an easy smile.

Amanda continues to glow in his direction. "I forgot you're in Ms. Lowen's English class. This is gonna be fabulous." *Right. You forgot he's in your class.* He slides into the desk behind Jason, just in front of me, the seat next to Amanda. *Great. I'm sure she won't be chatting him up all year.* I know I'm not an outcast, but I'm also not in the "in crowd." *I wonder what this year will bring.* But my thoughts are interrupted when Chris turns the full force of his killer dimpled smile on me, "Hey, Lindsey! Wassup?"

Time changes pace, seeming to both slow and quicken simultaneously. These are the moments when I wish I wasn't so quiet. All the other girls seem to always have something clever to say and deliver what seem like their scripted lines in such an engaging way. The guys flock to them like bees to honey. That's just not who I am.

Stealing a quick glance in his direction, I say, "Hey, Chris."

He raises his eyebrows and starts to ask me, "Hey, are you …" only to be interrupted by Ms. Lowen starting class, "Welcome back from summer vacation, ladies and gentlemen." Chris rolls his eyes as he turns back to face Ms. Lowen at the front of the classroom.

Am I what? Aware something is on my face? That my hair is sticking out? That my fly is open? Unconsciously I check my fly. Everything fine there. Next I run my hand through my hair; seems fine. What is Ms. Lowen saying? She spends the first half of class explaining how our grade will be calculated. The second half of class, we jump right in and start a poetry unit.

೮೦೦೪

Class bell. Lunch is next. I hope there are kids I know in my lunch period. I already know that Melissa has lunch with me, so at least I can look for her. As we all start leaving English, Chris is chatting with Jason and Rob, so I make my way to the front of the room to head toward my locker before lunch.

"Bye, Lindsey."

"See ya, Chris." *Huh?* No idea what he was going to say earlier, but at least he acknowledged me before leaving the room. Take that, Amanda!

ൽൽ

Walking down the hall, I see Joel weaving through some kids to walk with me.

"Hey, Lindsey."

"Hey, Joel." Looking at the lake we live on, Isabella is my neighbor on the south, or right, side of our house, while Joel and his brothers are our neighbor to the north, or left, side.

"How was your vacation?"

"Good, thanks."

"We missed you out on the lake the last few weeks."

"Thanks, but I'm sure you found plenty to do."

"I guess. Hey, Mike and I are having a party next Saturday after the football game."

"Really? Cool." Mike is Joel's fraternal twin.

"You should come over."

"Sure, I guess."

"There'll be a lot of kids there. Anyway, I should get to class before the bell. Hey, when do you have chemistry—maybe we have it together?"

"I had it first, too bad. I'll see ya."

"See ya."

Heading into the lunchroom, I'm hoping that Melissa is already here and saving me a seat. Looking around for someone I know, I see Chris coming out of the lunch line. Smiling at him, I turn toward where Melissa and I sat last year and am glad to see her there.

"Hey, Melissa," I say softly, hoping the seat next to her is for me.

"Hey, Lindsey! Here, sit here."

"Thanks, I'm gonna go get some food, I'll be right back." Whew. Someone to sit with at lunch.

ൽൽ

Last period is study hall, which I can take in the cafeteria or the library. I opt for the library in order to avoid all the inevitable socializing I will be left out of in the cafeteria. I head to a large corner table and sit alone, in hopes of getting my history homework done before gymnastics practice. I'm so lost in my own thoughts I don't even realize that Kevin Walker is standing next to me until he deliberately clears his throat. Is that the second time he cleared his throat? Oh, man.

As I look up and say hi, he gestures to the obviously empty table I'm at and asks if I'm sitting with anyone.

I stammer, "Well, um, no. Oh, I'm sorry. Do you need the table for a group? I … I can move to one of the cubes," and I start to gather my books and papers.

"No. No, I'm just wondering if I can join you." He just oozes confidence while mine seems to be draining away.

Oh sure, I'd love to sit with you and Andrea, I think as I hear myself mumble, "Sure, no problem." Pushing my backpack out of his way, he sits right across from me. I rest my head on my hand as I force myself to return to reading so as not to look at him, although I have the distinct feeling he's watching me. Or is it the rest of the room staring at *us*? They're all probably wondering the same thing I am—why is *Kevin Walker* sitting with *her*? Shouldn't he be with Andrea? Or some other knockout senior?

"So, what are you studying?"

Is he still talking to me or did he call someone? As I tilt my head slightly and look over to him, I realize he is talking to me with his eyebrows raised and half a smile, as if he's amusing himself.

"Um, history."

Sarcastically he comments, "Must be fascinating."

"Completely," I say, and much to my own surprise, I hold his gaze rather than look away.

"Did you get a lot of homework?" he asks, and keeps his eyes fixed on me.

"Uh, not much, you?" *Is this really happening?* Nervously I look away.

14

"Nah, just the usual first-day stuff. You have practice tonight?"

"Yeah, first practice here for the high school team. You?" I manage to say, but I'm still consumed with the question, *Why are you here?*

"Yeah," he says.

The librarian starts to take a stroll around the room as a not-so-subtle reminder that we aren't supposed to be talking.

As I glance around the library, I see three guys from Kevin's soccer team at another table; and, oh great, two of Andrea's friends are in the back. Did they just look at me? Man, she is going to be ticked. *He* sits with *me,* and somehow I know *I'll* be the topic of their text messages.

Turning back to my homework, I try to study. I must have read the same sentence five times—I can't even grasp the meaning. How much time has passed? Kevin has a book out that he seems to be reading. As I try to sneak a peek up at him … *Oh damn!* I shoot my eyes right back down at my book—*is he still looking at me?* I look back at him more deliberately; is there something in his eyes?

"What?" I whisper.

In his own hushed tone, "Nothing. What? Just studying."

"Studying what?" I ask.

He just smiles and raises an eyebrow in response. Like a fool, I smile uncontrollably and feel the blush building. Humiliating. Back to history. I promise myself I will actually read the rest of this section without letting him distract me. Focus. *Focus!*

The last bell of the day rings. Thank goodness. I expect Kevin to go meet up with his soccer friends and that will be that, but as I pack up, I notice that he's waiting for me. I know he's waiting as he has only one book out and has it in his backpack in a flash. I'm so distracted that I drop my notebook, which he picks up and starts to put into his own bag. "Hey!" I say quietly with a smile.

"Just kidding," he says, handing it back to me.

"Ready?" he asks as I swing my backpack over my shoulder.

"Sure," I say in an obviously timid manner, which prompts a smirk across his square jaw.

As we walk toward the locker rooms, he asks when our first meet is.

"We have a mock meet here two weeks from Wednesday—but there aren't any judges."

"My first soccer game is next Thursday," he says as he looks down at me with that same smirk.

We approach the guys' locker room first. As he turns to open the door, he looks back and in an unusually quiet voice says, "See you later," with a look on his face that made me think of one of my grandmother's many sayings—he looks like the cat that ate the canary. And I can't help wondering why that came to mind. I should really call Grandma. Anyway, no time now. I need to change and get up to gymnastics practice.

2 GYMNASTICS: *FIRST PRACTICE.*

ALTHOUGH I'VE BEEN COMPETING in club gymnastics since I was six years old, for the longest time I didn't think I would ever enter this locker room as a member of the high school gymnastics team. When we moved, one reason we picked Emit, Michigan, was because there's a good gymnastics club in town with a great coach. I've been a level ten gymnast for the past three years, which is the highest level of competition before you enter the elite ranks. I'm not good enough to be a contender at the elite level, so years ago, we decided that I wouldn't move to an elite training schedule, but instead would remain a competitor in "club." Sometimes I wonder if I could have made a run for it, but the reality is that you have to give up so much and I would not really have been a contender at the international level anyway. Elite girls typically work out thirty-five to forty or more hours per week. As it is, I'm in the gym about eighteen or twenty hours a week. Deciding to stay at the club level was the only choice I'd had to make in gymnastics until I was getting ready to enter high school.

When you get to high school, gymnasts face a tough choice. For most girls, you either leave the club you've trained and competed for since you were little and join the high school team, or you stay at club and give up the opportunity to be part of a high school sport. Virtually all the good clubs won't let you do both. I'm sure this is always a hard choice, but I think it was especially hard for me because we moved here in eighth grade, so I had only one year at my club. I knew joining the high school team would have been a great way to meet a bunch of girls, maybe even gain a few friends, but then I got to know Coach Dave and Jennifer.

Coach Dave is a great coach. We first met at a summer gymnastics camp years before I moved to Emit. Now he works to make me both a better gymnast and a better person. Not only has he improved my technical skills, but he's made me a much more confident gymnast. He invests so much of himself into the team. The first time Coach Dave met with my parents and me, he wanted to know which colleges I was interested in attending. I was in seventh grade. Needless to say, my parents were ready to sign up. The only drawback to his club was that it's across town from our house and in an industrial park my folks would rather I not hang out in.

Jennifer is really the first person I met in Emit. When I came to visit the club, Coach Dave asked her to show me around. She's a level ten gymnast as well, but since she is one of the oldest juniors and I am the youngest, we're in different age groups the way they split up club meets, so we're usually not in direct competition. Having become friends while working out together almost every day, I'm thankful we don't compete against each other often. I have always hoped that if we did compete in a big meet, we would still support each other, but I'm sure the competition would put pressure on our friendship. We are completely different gymnasts. Jennifer is more muscular and powerful. Most people describe me as graceful, and I'm clearly more of a slight gymnast. When I was younger, Mom made me take eight years of ballet, which I think I whined about before every practice. But the truth is she gets credit for any level of grace I bring to the sport.

So I decided, much to my parents' delight, to stay at club through high school. I'm not one to cry much, but I did have a few bad nights when I was trying to make that choice. But once I made my decision to stay at the club, I never looked back. What's the point? Freshman and sophomore year I competed in club, and as it has been since the first day I stepped into a gym, I loved every minute of it.

Then at dinner one night about a month ago, Mom says that Coach Dave had offered to allow Jennifer and me to compete on the high school team for our junior year, on a trial basis. I was shocked and so excited! Mom had already talked to the high school coach and he agreed to Coach Dave's proposed schedule, so we could give it a try. Our schedule would be Monday, Friday, Saturday, and some Sundays at the club, and Tuesday, Wednesday, and Thursday in the high school gym. Since high school doesn't practice on Fridays or the weekend anyway, we would only be missing one high school practice a week. Coach Dave also said we could only work out with the high school team from the beginning of school through the high school state meet. Hearing that both coaches had come to an agreement and that I could be part of a high school team, I practically burst with excitement.

I was thrilled that I would get to be in a high school sport and meet more girls in my high school, and now the kids at school might actually find out what I do all the time (as I'm hardly ever free after school). Club gymnastics teams only compete in USGA events and high school teams compete exclusively in the high school meets, so there's no inherent conflict in representing both teams, but most coaches just won't let you work out anywhere but in their own gym. Coaches have that in common with lawyers—they like control.

This was huge. As soon as my parents told me, I ran to call Jennifer, who had apparently just found out as well. We were both so excited we were practically screaming at each other on the phone.

80 03

As I change in the locker room, I'm excited and a bit nervous as this is my first high school gymnastics practice. The few clubs I've been a part of all had a specific format for both daily warm-ups and workouts. Clearly at this point, I have no idea what the protocol here will be. I came by the gym once before with Mom to meet with Coach Parker, but no one was in the gym at that time so I haven't even seen the other girls work out. Granted, I've been going to high school here for two years, but since I never thought I would be able to join the high school team, I never really paid much attention to their workouts. I did go to one of the high school meets my freshman year, but honestly, that was more to check out the talent level. Needless to say, I was shamelessly pleased that I knew I could beat anyone on the team in a competition.

Carrying my grips in a small bag, I enter the spacious gym. There is not much to hide behind when all you are wearing is a leotard. The gym overlooks the basketball court below, and is shared by both the boys' and girls' teams. I see most of the girls are already stretching out on the floor. The entrance I came in is just up the stairs from the girls' locker room, and is close to the two sets of uneven parallel bars. I set my grip bag down on the floor near the first set. I assume some of the girls are freshmen as they seem to be wandering around the gym a bit.

Stepping over some stacked mats, I walk self-consciously over the floor exercise mat to sit and stretch near the other girls. The chill of my reception is not entirely unexpected, but still a bit disappointing. I try a slight smile when I make eye contact with a few of the girls. Most smile back, but that is the extent of our greeting. Elizabeth, a clear member of the Fab Five, whispers something to Peggy. I can only guess what it's about, but I'm confident it's not good. Oh, well. This may be *your* gym, but we're on *my* turf.

Thankfully, Jennifer comes in next and sits down next to me.

"Hey, Lindsey. Hi, Peggy. Hey, Elizabeth."

"Hi, Jennifer," I reply but am drowned out by Elizabeth. "Hey, Jennifer. Welcome to high school gymnastics," Elizabeth responds, and then, like it's an afterthought, adds, "You too, Lindsey."

"Thanks," I say cautiously as the words were kind, but the tone was a bit acid.

"Well, we do warm-ups as a group, and we all do the same stretches together—okay?" Elizabeth says.

"Sure," Jennifer replies after looking at me; I had nodded.

Coach Parker walks in and calls all the girls to the floor for an initial meeting.

"Hello, girls. For those of you who don't know me, I'm Coach Parker. Welcome back to all our returning gymnasts, and welcome also to all the new faces." So here we are. Day one. First practice. Coach Parker continues, "Freshmen, don't be intimidated. There's a lot of talent in the room, but everyone had a first day in the gym. We will all do warm-ups together, and then I will split you up for our workouts. At the end of practice, we will all come back and do strength training as a group. Okay? Well, then, why don't we have one of our seniors lead the warm-ups? Let's make it a great year!"

Warm-ups are uneventful except that I feel like Elizabeth and Peggy are scrutinizing everything I do.

When we're done warming up, Coach Parker returns to the floor to talk to the team. "Okay, ladies, I'd like to start with varsity vault. Let's have the JV team and the freshmen go with Coach Wilson to beam. Jennifer and Lindsey, come with me and show me where you want the board set."

Jennifer and I have an agreement with Coach Dave not to throw anything too risky in the high school practices and competitions as he can't be here to spot us and we shouldn't really have to in order to place in any of these meets. Generally speaking, the better gymnasts stay and compete in their clubs. Jennifer should really be my only competition. Given this agreement, practice is pretty easy and runs relatively smoothly.

At five thirty, Coach Parker whistles, which is apparently the signal to stop working out and come back to the floor for strength training.

"Okay, as I said earlier, for all you new girls, we spend the last twenty to thirty minutes of each practice stretching and doing some strength training. We'll have the varsity team take turns running this part of our workout. Who wants to go first?"

"I will," Elizabeth announces. "Let's start with thirty V-ups."

Rolling my eyes, I stretch my legs out so that I'm lying on my back ready to do the exercise, which requires you to lift your legs and upper body at the same time so you look like a "V" at the top of the exercise. It quickly becomes apparent that whoever is leading the strength training doesn't need to actually do all the exercises, but rather judges the rest of the team on how well they are doing each movement.

Elizabeth tells a sophomore that she needs to start over because her legs were bent.

"Great job, Peggy!" Shock.

"Oh, I'm sorry, Lindsey. Those legs look bent. I think you need to start over," Elizabeth says in a sickeningly sweet tone.

I know my legs were straight, and I know she did this just because I was almost done. Oh well, a few more V-ups can't hurt.

All in all, practice is good. I'm always very focused in the gym, and even if I wasn't, there's rarely time to chat with my teammates anyway. Plus, I can already tell that Coach Parker is excited by what Jennifer and I add to his team. Knowing that he is pleased helps me relax a bit.

3 A RIDE HOME: *THIS CHANGES EVERYTHING.*

AFTER PRACTICE I'M SUPPOSED to text Isabella and meet her near her car. It's nice of her to wait since her volleyball practice isn't as long as my gymnastics practice, but she agreed to wait for me for these first few weeks of school until I get my driver's license. Mostly I think Isabella is nice to me because we are neighbors. I'm not sure if we would be friends if we weren't neighbors.

As phones aren't allowed to be used inside school, I wait until I step outside to check my phone. I notice I have a text message from Isabella. Only one text message—I bet everyone else gets like ten a day. I hope she hasn't been waiting too long for me.

5:12 P.M.   Hey. Change in plans. Walk 2 student lot. Your ride will be waiting. :-)

Okay, what does this mean? Didn't she wait for me? Who is taking me home? Who could it be? Oh, man. Walking cautiously, I head over to the student lot, which still has a number of cars from all the athletes at practice for various sports. As I enter the lot, I don't see Isabella or

23

anyone else who I think might be driving me home. I turn to look around and see a car pull up to me. I step back and notice Kevin is driving. He has this sly grin on his face as he stops next to me.

"Need a ride?" he says.

I bite my lip and reply, "Um, I'm … ah … I'm not sure."

"I am; get in," and then the grin turns into a big smile. "I told Isabella I would drive you home so she could take Rick home."

"Oh, okay." So whose idea was this? Isabella's? No, I don't think she would do that. But then again, girls do anything to get more time with their boyfriends.

I'm still pondering this as I get into his car.

"Ready?" he asks.

"Sure." In an attempt to be helpful, I say, "I live right …"

"You're next to Isabella, right?"

"Yeah."

I thought I would try to figure out what's going on, so I say, "I'm sorry Isabella put you up to this." I say this in a timid voice, hoping to unearth the truth. As we turn out of the student lot, we pass Jon, who did a bit of a double take to see me with Kevin—captain of the soccer team, vice president of his class, and of course, dating Andrea. Great.

"Oh, no worries, she didn't." *Okay, so what does that mean? Why aren't you driving Andrea home? Are you flirting with me?*

We both sit listening to the music for a few minutes as we drive through town and around the curve of the lake toward my house. Oh, what the heck. "So, um … how's Andrea?"

"I wouldn't know," he says as he looks at me. "We broke up about a month ago."

A month ago! Wait a minute. This changes everything. As this news starts to settle in, I realize I'm still looking at him, and he just caught me. I quickly turn away embarrassed. *So are you driving me home because Rick wants time with Isabella?*

"How was your first day?" he asks casually.

"Oh, fine—how about you?" Fine—until now … when I am a bit freaked out that *Kevin Walker* is driving me home.

"Good, I guess. Did you see Mrs. Brady's hair?"

"Yeah, I did," I say, smiling.

"What a color—I mean, seriously, did she do that on purpose? It's purple, right?"

Laughing a bit with him at Mrs. Brady's expense, I look over and see Joel and his brother Mike turning into their driveway. Wonder what they think seeing me with Kevin Walker. I'm still trying to figure all this out as he turns into our long driveway. The leaves on the trees along the drive are starting to turn colors. New school year, new season, new driver—wonder what else will change this year. I reach down to grab my backpack as we near my house.

"See you tomorrow, Lindsey," he says, turning toward me.

"Thanks again for the ride," I reply as I open the door and get out.

Walking in front of his car, I am totally self-conscious of him watching me walk, so I turn and give him a little smile. Smiling, he waves with one hand and then drapes it on the top of the passenger seat to back out of our driveway.

∞∞

Mom and I have a nice dinner together. We have fun making pizzas and talking about our days. Mostly we talk about my day as it was the first day of my junior year.

"Is Joel in your science class again this year?"

"No, but Jon and I are lab partners."

"How nice."

"Chris Buckley is in my English class."

"Oh, very nice." Yes. It is very nice.

"Thankfully, Melissa is in my lunch period so we sat together. She was telling me about a couple of the books she read over the summer, which reminds me—Mom, when you're in town tomorrow, can you pick up another mystery for me?"

"Sure. Do you want another one from one of your favorite authors?"

"Yeah, and grab me one of their recommendations so I can try a new author."

"You got it. Do you have much homework?"

"Not much, but I want to get ahead."

"Okay, well, go on up. I'll clean up."

"Thanks, Mom."

∞ℝ

As I lie in bed thinking about the first day of school, I'm so pleased that Chris and Jon both are in one of my classes this year. I wonder if Chris just hangs out with me because he knows I have a huge crush on him, and in some small way, my crush thrills him the same way Jon's crush thrills me. Probably. So sad.

I wonder if Kevin will sit with me again tomorrow in study hall. If nothing else, that prospect is giving me a nice wave of excitement for the year ahead. On some semisubconscious level, I figure that being seen with Kevin, a cool senior, puts me into a whole new category at school. Even though he broke up with Andrea, I don't know if he's already seeing someone else. Dating a senior seems like too much to hope for. But that would be *cool*. Sure, I continue the dream that Chris will notice me, but if I can't have perfection, it would be nice to at least not be home every Saturday night.

Here I am a junior and have never been asked to one of the all-too-heralded high school dances. Rather depressing at times. Most of the time, it doesn't bother me; it's just a fact of life. Well, at least it's a fact of my life. Only totally popular kids or kids who are in relationships go as lower classmen. But now I'm a junior. What if I'm the only girl I know who isn't asked to the dance? Clearly, the Fab Five will be asked and will continue their perfect attendance at school dances. How do they do it? I get that they are pretty, but how is it that all the cool guys and cool girls go to every dance even if they're not "going" with anyone? Guys don't call me, but since they never have, I guess I really don't know what I'm missing. Most of the time I'm so busy at school, the gymnastics club, or studying, I don't think about it. But there are moments when it bothers me deeply.

As a result, I have grown to try to mentally ignore certain traditions in high school as much as possible. Traditions like the all-too-public popularity contest conducted twice each year called "Flower Day." Every fall and spring semester, there are a few days when kids sit outside the cafeteria taking orders for carnations to be sent from one student to another. Then, on another day later that week or the next week, kids deliver flowers throughout the day to the popular students. Getting flowers is a clear and very visible sign of one's popularity. I'm sure it feels great. I wouldn't know. I'm a card-carrying member of the "Never Been Sent a Carnation Club."

I seem to be a bit jealous lately of all the attention some of the girls get from guys. From where I stand, these girls have everything. They always know the perfect thing to say to sound cute and coy, they have a great sense of style, and both the girls and guys constantly call and text them. It's so unfair. Jealousy is a powerful emotion. I might as well use the strength of it to fuel a good workout tomorrow.

I would be so happy for Melissa and Elena, my two girlfriends at school, if they get asked to the dance. If no one asks me, the truth is, I'll feel sorry for myself. But if someone does ask me—I'll freak out! What exactly do you do at a dance? What would I wear?

Not problems I will likely have to solve anytime soon.

⁂‽

The rest of the first week of school went about as expected. Now it's the second week of school and Kevin is sitting with his soccer buddies today in study hall, so I try to get some work done. With only about fifteen minutes left in the period, Kevin comes over to sit with me. *Interesting.* Sadly, we can't talk at all as the librarian is making constant rounds to keep everyone quiet. When the bell rings, he gets up with me and I half expect him to go back to meet up with the guys, but he starts to chat with me about the day. As we pass kids in the hall, I'm sure they're trying to figure out why Kevin Walker is walking with me. Little do they know, I have no idea either. But I have hope. Last week I was feeling a bit jealous. I'll take hope over jealousy any day.

"Can I give you a ride home?" Kevin asks.

"Sure," but a whisper is all I can seem to muster. Why am I so nervous with guys? They all seem so confident. It seems like they know exactly what to do. How is that possible? Are they only like that with girls they *really* like?

"Good, I'll see you in the student lot at about five thirtyish." And as he walks into the locker room, he calls over his shoulder, "And don't worry. Isabella already knows." Great. Confirmation of how pathetically predictable I am. I don't even remember practice. It's a blur of strength training, girls on my periphery whispering and giggling, and thoughts of my ride home.

After practice, I walk over to the student parking lot and see Kevin leaning against the passenger side of his car. He is the picture of composure: shades and headphones on with music playing. Of course, he has showered and changed at school. So glad my hair is in a ponytail and I'm in sweats. I'm suddenly conscious that I probably still even have some chalk on my hands. Great.

I desperately try to minimize my pathetic smile so I don't look like a complete idiot walking over. For someone who doesn't smile a lot, I'm suddenly having a hard time controlling mine.

As he pulls one earbud out, he calls over to me, "Hey."

"Hey."

"You should hear this song," he says as he hands me an earbud.

Smooth. He knows I need to step close enough to him to get the earbud in my ear without pulling the other one out of his ear. So I step toward him and lean on the car next to him, popping the earbud into my ear.

As I listen to the pull of the violins and harp with a rock beat behind the strings, I must admit, "Very cool." I have always loved the sound of a harp.

"Yeah, it's a group out of France."

"France? How did you hear of them?" How do guys find the time to find music groups in France? The longer I listen, the more I like it.

"Oh, I don't know, just found it on the web."

When the song finishes, he stands up from the car so I pull the earbud out. He opens the passenger door.

As I sit nervously in his car, I wonder if he's just having fun toying with me or if he actually likes me. Part of me doesn't care, and part of me is wondering if I'm setting myself up to be disappointed.

"What are you up to this weekend?" he asks without looking at me.

Ten thoughts leap into my mind at once. Am I a loser if I don't have any plans? If I have plans, does that mean he won't ask me out? Do I want to go out with him? I start out on what I assume to be safe ground: a family commitment.

"Well, my dad gets back in town Friday so we're all going out to dinner." Will he notice that I've not said anything about Saturday night?

"Cool. My mom said that your dad was mentioned in the paper in an article about one of his cases."

"Yeah, he always has some crazy case going on."

"Are you going to the football game Saturday?"

"Yeah, I think I'm going with some of the girls." Oh, man. I hope Melissa and Elena still want to go together.

"Maybe I'll see you there. It should be a great game." Maybe? What does that mean? "Are you guys going to Joel and Mike's after the game?" he continues.

"Um, I think so. I guess so. Joel mentioned it." What did I say?

"You guys should go. I hear they're going to set up a bonfire on the beach."

When we pull into my driveway, I'm as confused as I was a

week ago. Is Kevin just trying to help his brother get more time with Isabella? Does Kevin like me? Do I like Kevin? Do you want to see me this weekend? Trying not to sound too appreciative, I say, "Thanks for the ride," and step out of the car. He gets out to walk me to the front door.

"Looks quiet. Anyone home?"

"Oh, probably not. My Mom'll be home in a while." Oh … maybe I shouldn't have said that. Am I supposed to invite him inside? What would a senior do in this situation?

"You okay?"

"Oh yeah, I'm alone a lot." Truer words were never spoken.

"Okay, well, I'll talk to you later."

"Bye," I say as I turn to unlock the door while my mind is preoccupied with questions. Talk to me later? Later when? Are you calling me later tonight? Or later like maybe I'll run into you one day sometime in the future? I'd rather get a call from Chris. Will Chris ever call me?

⁖⁗

The next day I enter the library for study hall and sit at the same table I sat at yesterday and choose the same seat, hoping it will bring me good luck again. Any advantage is worth a shot. As other kids walk in, I try to study chemistry while I steal glances at everyone coming in. I hear the soccer guys call Kevin over to their table. Terrific. No doubt who will lose this match.

Sure enough, Kevin heads for his soccer buddies and sits down with the team. Oh, well, back to chemistry. Back to reality. Once again, I find concentration is an elusive goal. I reread the same paragraph so many times, I finally turn the page out of pure embarrassment that someone may have noticed that I apparently can't read. *Focus.*

Finally I manage to force myself to concentrate long enough to at least grasp that I'm supposed to be learning about atomic theory.

My peripheral vision picks up someone walking across the library toward me, so I force my eyes to stay on the page. *Do not look up! Do not check to see if it is him. Oh, please, let it be him.* As Kevin sits down in the chair opposite me, I sense that he's smiling.

4 FIRST FOOTBALL GAME: *THE FOOTBALL TEAM WON, BUT I SEEM TO BE IN THE LEAD.*

FIRST FOOTBALL GAME OF the year. As I wake up, part of me can't wait to get to the game. But part of me dreads these kinds of events. I'm always nervous that no one will want to talk to me, or even want to sit with me. What if I can't find a seat in the stands? How embarrassing would that be? Everyone else will have friends waving to them and calling them over to sit together in the stands. I even worry that my "friends," Melissa and Elena, don't really want to hang out with me. In eighth grade, we all had homeroom together, and they were nice enough to invite me to sit with them at lunch that first day in my new school. They are both nice, and we have been hanging out together at lunches and recess since. I think they like me, at least I assume so, given that they hang out with me, but what if they feel like they have to? What if I'm sitting with them, and Chris or Kevin wave at me? Will they be annoyed if I go talk to one of the guys for a few minutes? Maybe they'll be jealous. On the other hand, maybe they would be happy for me. That would be so nice. I wonder if Kevin would consider sitting with juniors. If he did, would he think we are all so incredibly boring he would stop talking to me? I bet Chris will go with the twins. What am I going to wear? Ugh. Nothing is easy. I hope Melissa or Elena call me before I have to call them. I hate being the one to call. I hope they call by eleven. Kickoff is at one o'clock, and I really want to go with them to the game.

At eight in the morning, Mom takes me to my gymnastics club for practice, which goes well. As soon as I'm done with my workout and get in the locker room, I check my cell phone. Thank goodness! Melissa sent me a text asking me to call her back to confirm when she can pick me up for the game. I get in the car with Mom and call Melissa to finalize our plans.

⅘⅗

I hurry to get ready, as there is not much time before the girls will be here. I barely finish my hair and makeup when I see Melissa's car through my front bedroom window. Grabbing my phone, purse, and a jacket, I head downstairs. Here we go. I hope I'll get a chance to hang out with Chris.

I walk into the family room, where my folks are watching TV.

"Okay, I'm heading to the football game."

"Have fun," is Dad's response as he looks up from his iPad.

"Will you be home for dinner?" Mom asks as she turns away from the football game.

"Yep, see you then."

"Hey, guys," I say to Melissa and Elena as I climb into the backseat.

"Hey, Lindsey."

Elena turns around in her seat and starts to talk about her latest crush, Robert. They have math together, and she can't get enough of him. She's going on and on about everything he said this past week in class. I agree with Melissa that the fact that he talked to her twice this week means he probably does like her. We all think that he will ask her to the homecoming dance. I wonder who Chris will ask.

How many times did Kevin talk to me this week? Does Chris talking to me in English count? I wonder who else Chris is talking to. Chris will definitely go to the dance; the question is with whom? The attention from Kevin is exciting, but the thought of going to a dance with Chris is heady.

വൽൾ

As we approach the front of the school, I can see the entire campus is busy with kids parking their cars and walking over to the football field. I feel a surge of excitement at the prospect of what the day will bring. It is early in September and the weather is still nice, but I put on my jacket as I'm sure it will feel cooler sitting in the stands all afternoon.

I see Jennifer and Peggy walking together. Peggy is a member of the high school gymnastics team even though she must be five foot ten, which is tall for a gymnast. Technically, she is not part of the Fab Five, but she is very popular. Usually she dates upper classmen. Her parents are divorced, which must be hard on her because she has to split her time between her mom and dad's places. I heard that her dad is dating someone in our small town. That has to be weird—watching your dad date. Nightmare.

I see Jon, who is walking with a group of sophomores, and wave to him. Melissa catches my eye and nudges me in the ribs with her elbow. "You should go talk to him."

I look at her and roll my eyes. She looks at me, raises my eyebrows ever so slightly, and tilts her head.

I look in Jon's direction again and see that he and his friends are headed our way.

"Hey, Lindsey. Melissa. Elena."

"Hey, guys." I doubt I can remember everyone's name so I play it safe.

"It's a great day for a game," Jon says with enthusiasm.

"Yeah, it's perfect out here," I reply, happy to be in a group.

As one of Jon's friends says something about how we should kill the other team, I see Kevin pull into a parking space and notice as he and one of his soccer buddies get out of the car. Is the fact that Kevin might see me with Jon good or bad? Will he think I'm interested in Jon and ignore me? Or will he think it is cool to like a girl that someone else is interested in enough to talk to? Hmm. Jon is only a sophomore. Would he feel a spark of jealousy? I decide it's a good thing and try to focus back on the conversation. When there is a break, I ask Jon, "So, you guys want to go in?"

"Yeah, let's go," Jon says with a grin. Gotta love the Crush.

Walking in, Melissa matches my pace on the left and Jon on my right. Jon's friends are still talking about the game and how good our team is this year. As we circle the field and pass the concession stand, I notice the high level of energy and excitement everyone has as the game is about to begin. The cheerleaders are bouncing and chanting in unison, and the stands are quickly filling. I follow Jon up the steps to try to find a seat. The band, which has filled most of the left side of the stands, rises to play a song. Jon asks if a spot about halfway up the middle section will work. I turn to Melissa for her thoughts. "Yeah, great—let's grab them before they're gone." Climbing past the first few rows, I see the Fab Five and all their hangers-on with their perfect outfits and perfect hair in the lower section. Isn't it nice of them to hold court at the game? Guys, of course, are surrounding them like a pack of wolves waiting for their prey to show a moment of weakness.

Football games are so long you want to sit next to people you like. Finding the right seat is always tricky. Some of Jon's friends take the row in front of us; Adam and Jon slide into our row. Adam and Jon are good friends, which makes sense as they both are so smart, especially with all things mathematic and technical. I follow Jon as he slides down the row to sit.

I've lost track of Kevin, but I see Chris climbing up the steps looking for a seat with his friends, Mike and Joel Kirkwood. The three of them are always together. I'm envious of how close they all are with each other.

"Hey, guys," Chris shouts over the band playing our school song. Melissa, Elena, and I all say, "Hey." I can't take my eyes off him.

"You guys going to the twins' party later?" he asks, looking right at me.

"Yeah, I think so. You?" Sigh.

"Oh yeah; it should be great!"

Great. "What time is everyone going?" *Maybe you'll talk to me at the party.* A real high school party. That means beer. I've never had an alcoholic drink. I'm sure I'll be the only one not drinking at the party. Then Chris says something I can't quite hear.

"What time?" I shout over the band, which is getting louder and louder.

With a shrug, he yells back, "I don't know. I guess about nine. I'll look for you there. We're gonna go sit down. I think they're about to kick off."

"Bye." He is so cute. I hope I do see him there. Maybe, just maybe, he will ask me to the homecoming dance. Most people will be asked this weekend, as the dance is three weeks from tonight. Maybe Chris has already asked someone. I see a couple of Kevin's soccer teammates walking up the stands. I wonder where Kevin is. He's probably making up with that witch Andrea.

The game is fun, chatting with friends, watching a few plays. When the entire crowd stands up, I do as well, as I figure something good must be happening. Jon and Adam talk to me off and on between plays about a recent movie or when my next meet is. I find myself wondering which sophomore that likes Jon thinks I'm the witch for taking up all his time. Oh well, nothing I can do about that.

Halftime I decide to get a soda and hot dog. I haven't eaten all day, and my workouts always make me hungry. Elena says she'll go with me, so we head to the concession stand. Standing up, I feel a rush of lightheadedness and realize I really do need some food. The line is pretty long so we chat about her crush on Robert some more while we wait. After placing our order I hear, "Hey," from behind my right ear. I turn around and look up to see Kevin looking at me. Awesome.

"Hey," is my brilliant reply as I reach back for my hot dog and soda.

"Good game," he says, cool as a cucumber.

"Yeah, and the weather is great." The weather? Am I seriously talking about the weather?

"Yeah, should be perfect for the Kirkwoods' party tonight," he says while Elena pays for her food.

"Yeah," another brilliant response while I look like an idiot holding the waxed paper-wrapped hot dog and an ice-cold Diet Coke.

"Are you going with the girls?" he asks.

Glancing at Elena, I'm thinking that I've had no other offers so I say, "Yeah, I think we're planning to go later tonight."

"Cool; maybe I'll text you later to see what's up."

"Great."

"See ya," he calls as he heads back to the stands.

Elena turns to face me completely and says with one hand on her hip, "Are you kidding me? Spill it!"

"Not now. Later. Let's go back to our seats."

As we walk back, I'm biting my lip, fighting a smile. Reaching into my jacket pocket, I check the battery on my cell phone.

Climbing the stairs, I whisper to Elena, "Not at our seats, okay?"

She turns with a smirk and says, "Sure. I would hate to see Jon melt right here in the stands." Sharing an old joke and mocking the wicked witch of the east from the Wizard of Oz movies, she adds, "What a world, what a world!"

"Nice," I shoot back at her.

"No, what is *nice* is Kevin. I mean, are you kidding me? A senior!"

Fourth quarter, and we are up by ten. I can hardly wait for the party tonight. What will I wear? Will Dad let me go?

"Hey, Elena, what are you wearing tonight?"

"Um ... jeans, I guess. I think it's supposed to get pretty cool," she says with a huge smile and raises her eyebrows and widens her eyes for emphasis.

"Okay," I reply, rolling my eyes.

"What's going on with you two?" Melissa asks.

"Nothing," then I lower my voice and continue, "I'll tell you later. Not here, okay?"

"I'm dying, but okay. Don't forget what it is, okay?"

"Oh, I won't forget."

As soon as the game is over, we all head back to the student parking lot. I'm in a ridiculously good mood. What a great day it has been already. Jon and I are walking out together when I feel my phone buzz. I quickly take it out and check to see who it is—just in case. I contain a smile. It's a text from Kevin.

> **3:32 P.M.** Hey. Want a ride home? I'm at the east side of the student lot.

Yes, I want a ride. Luckily, Jon parked on the far west side, so as we near the lot, we say good-bye to him and his friends. I can't help but feel a little guilty when we say we'll see him later at the Kirkwoods' because all I want to do is send a reply to Kevin's text.

Immediately Melissa turns to me with an intense look. "Okay, spill it. What's going on with you two?"

"Oh, it was not both of *us*," Elena replies with a knowing look.

I say, in the most unassuming tone I can muster, "I'm so sorry, but is it okay if I catch a ride home with Kevin Walker?"

"Are you kidding?" Melissa exclaims too loudly.

"Shhhh!"

"Absolutely—when did he ask you?" Melissa says with what seems like a genuine smile.

"He just sent me a text," I reply, holding up my phone.

"Okay, seriously you need to fill us in. Are we still on for tonight? Or are you going with him?"

"No, no, it's not like that." *Is it?* "We're on—what time?"

"I'll be at your place at nine thirty."

"Sure, okay, wish me luck."

"From what I saw, you don't need it!" Elena says with a laugh.

I'm so nervous walking across the lot. I don't know what to do with my hands, so I put them in my jacket pockets.

I see Kevin and a couple of guys talking to some senior girls. Great. Am I supposed to walk up to that group? I slow down in hopes that he'll see me before I reach everyone. As I get closer, I notice that one of the girls sees me. Did she just step in front of him to force him to look at her? I approach the group slowly and realize he has definitely seen me as he turns to open the circle. *Are you kidding? I don't want to talk to this whole group. Can't we just go?*

"Hey, Lindsey," Kevin says as the girls and his friend Andrew make room for me in the group.

"Hey."

"You ready?"

"Yeah, I mean if you are."

"Yep. Bye, guys. Andrew, I'll talk to you later."

"Okay. Better text me. I'm going to the club with my folks for dinner. Hey, Lindsey."

"Hey, Andrew," I say, but am surprised Andrew has spoken to me. I'm pretty sure he has never talked to me before.

"Let's go," Kevin says as he turns toward his car and pulls the keys out of his pocket. As we walk together, I can feel all those senior girls burning a hole in my back.

Then I see Chris walking with a large group of guys and girls and catch his glance. Oh, man. I really wish he wasn't seeing me with Kevin. But then again, maybe he will see me in a different light if he thinks I'm hanging out with a senior. There are land mines everywhere.

On the ride home, all I can think is … The football team won, but I seem to be in the lead. But the lead of what? What is Kevin thinking? Why does he keep giving me rides home? The truth is I'm enjoying the attention, but I'd rather be getting a ride home from Chris.

5 THE PARTY: *SORRY NIGHT WAS CUT SHORT.*

6:00 P.M. TOO EARLY to get ready so I decide to watch TV.

6:30 p.m. Still too early; check e-mail.

7:00 p.m. Ugh.

7:05 p.m. Is time standing still?

7:30 p.m. Elena and Melissa keep texting me asking about Kevin. I put them off until we get together tonight. But it is nice to actually receive some text messages!

8:00 p.m. Okay. If I move slowly, I can start to get ready, so I take a shower.

8:30 p.m. What to wear? Wonder what the Fab Five will wear?

9:12 p.m. Ready early. Back to TV.

9:20 p.m. Mom stops by my room and says I look nice. I'm not really in the mood to chat it up with her as I'm getting nervous about the party. She also says that she and Dad don't want me to walk home; they want me to get a ride with Melissa. Fine. At least he's letting me go.

9:40 p.m. I finally see the headlights of Melissa's car pull down the driveway. I grab my phone (and check for the tenth time that it's on and fully charged), my purse, and my jacket. I check how I look one more time. As I leave my bedroom and head downstairs, I can hear an Italian opera coming from Dad's office. He's on another case. He never works all weekend for his corporate clients, and he always listens to opera music when he is preparing for a big case. When I was younger, I used to get ice cream if I could name the opera and composer. Everything has a goal. This section is easy. *Rigoletto* by Verdi. He loves Luciano Pavarotti. I call "See ya later" to my folks.

"Be back at midnight," Dad calls back. Never one to miss an opportunity to set a boundary.

"Yep, bye."

I jerk the front door to pull it shut, and let the storm door swing closed. Stepping down the stone front steps, I head toward the bright headlights. As I open the car door, something in the woods catches my eye. I pause, one foot in the car and one still on the driveway, and hear Melissa and Elena greet me. I see something. Or did I? Was that a flicker on something or just a shiny leaf? Is something … someone … in the woods?

"Come on, Lindsey!" Elena says from the passenger seat.

"Yeah—" Sliding into the car, I can't take my eyes off the trees between our place and the Castiglionis'. Is that …

"Okay, spill it. And I mean everything!" Melissa starts, interrupting my thoughts.

"I can't believe you got a ride home with Kevin Walker! Seriously, what's going on?" adds Elena as she bounces a little in her seat with excitement.

Playing down my own excitement I say, "There really isn't that much to tell."

"Are you kidding?" asks Melissa.

"Yeah, I mean how did this all happen?" follows Elena.

"Nothing's happened. He just sat with me in study hall a few times."

"I heard he broke up with Andrea," Melissa adds over her shoulder.

"Yeah, he told me that they broke up about a month before school started," I add.

"Do you think he'll ask you to the homecoming dance?" Elena adds with emphasis.

"Oh yeah, sure. Why not go with a junior when half the senior class is literally hanging on your every word? Those girls were like vultures after the game," I reply, still hoping to go to the dance.

"Well, I think he will—*that* would be so cool! Is he going to be at the Kirkwoods' party tonight?" Melissa says as she pulls off the road to park at the Kirkwoods' well-lit home.

"He said he would be."

"Well, maybe I'll only be taking Elena home tonight."

As they are both giggling, I say seriously, "No, please don't leave me there." I only tell them about Kevin because it is fun that someone is paying attention to me and they already pretty much know since he gave me a ride home. Going to a dance with anyone would be cool, but Kevin is a senior, which makes it just unbelievable.

"Oh, what do you care? You can walk home from here."

"I know, but my folks just made me promise to get a ride—please?"

"No problem. If you need a ride, you got it. But if you get a better offer, feel free to take it!" and with that we all climb out of the car.

I've never mentioned anything to them, or anyone else, about how much I really like Chris because I didn't want to jinx anything. But going with Chris would be—too much to hope for, I'm sure. But maybe, just maybe I'll at least get to go to a dance—finally.

The Kirkwoods' home is just down the road from mine, but like most of Emit, their house is set in a dense forest. Behind the large main house is a pool, a large pool house, and a beautiful dock where they keep their boats and Jet Skis. Already there are plenty of cars along their long and winding driveway, as well as on the street outside the stone and iron gate.

Even though I'm with my friends, I get tense walking in, as this is really my first high school party. I'm worried that no one will want to talk to me, or worse, that they won't even remember my name.

The Kirkwoods' property is one of the largest on the lake, second only to the estate where Chris and his family live. I'm not really sure what Mr. Kirkwood does, as every time I turn around, I learn about a new business he owns. As we round the main house, we start to hear the beat of the music and the laughter and chatter of the crowd. I hope that there are at least a few people I know so there will be someone to talk to.

Since it's still pretty nice out, the twins have opened all the French doors on both the pool and lake sides of the pool house so we can see straight through to the bonfire. The lights inside the pool are turned on, giving off a beautiful blue shimmer of light onto the kids on the pool deck. In the pool house the lights are dimmed, and the crowd seems to bounce with the beat.

Another group of kids are down by the beach around the bonfire, which appears big even from this distance. Mr. and Mrs. Kirkwood must be out of town this weekend or at least for the night.

I'm relieved to see some friends of ours in the pool house. Melissa takes the lead as we weave through the dense crowd. Moving through the main sitting room, I feel someone grab my arm. I turn to see who is trying to yell "Hey" over the crowd.

"Hey, Jon."

"Hey, you want something to drink?" he asks loud enough for me to hear.

"Sure."

"Beer?"

"Uh, no. How about a Diet Coke?"

"Sure."

I don't want to have any booze. Life is complex enough. I've never considered drinking because I know that would mean stepping into the unknown.

Jon hands me a plastic cup of ice and soda.

"Thanks. Have you been here long?" I say, trying to speak loudly enough.

"No, we got here about a half hour ago."

"This place is packed," I yell back.

"Yeah, I know."

Then Melissa and Elena come back, each with a plastic cup filled with beer that must have come from the keg. How do Joel and Mike, who are both juniors, get a keg?

"Let's go to the bonfire," Melissa yells over the crowd singing to the latest hit by a young pop star; she nods toward the back.

"Okay," I agree, and I start to follow her and Elena through the crowd again.

"Come on," I encourage Jon.

"I'm gonna hang with the guys; I'll go out later."

"Okay."

As we make our way through the crowd, I realize that most of the junior and senior classes are here. The bonfire is pretty big, with sparks popping over the music. Joel and Mike and their friends must have piled up a group of pallets, which are glowing a deep red with heat. Flames are licking up at least six or seven feet into the dark night sky. As I look back down from the stars, I notice Kevin about twenty feet away from the bonfire talking with Andrea. Wham. Elena and Melissa follow my eyes and notice as well. They pull me over to a group. I'm sure they both know I'm not happy, although I'm not even sure why.

"It means nothing. She's probably stalking him," Elena whispers to me with a sympathetic smile.

"It's fine."

As if on cue, Chris and a few other guys join the group we're standing with. Okay, so Chris is one great distraction from the drama on the beach. I realize that in an effort to look like everyone else, I must have been constantly sipping my soda because it's empty except for a few pieces of ice. Chris seems to notice and downs the last third of his beer. He asks if I want a refill.

"Sure."

"Come on." Sure. I would follow you anywhere.

Chris leads me back to the pool house. We squeeze our way into the kitchen area and get refills. I appreciate the fact that he doesn't push beer on me and, instead, immediately offers a Diet Coke from a cooler without any pressure. Then I wonder how he knew I wasn't having a beer. A group of guys are calling him over, so I say thanks and turn to head out back again.

"Where you going?" Chris asks over the crowd.

"Just back to the bonfire, I guess." Unless, of course, you have another idea?

"You'll be here for a while, right?" he asks.

"Yeah, sure."

"Okay, well, look for me before you leave, okay?"

"Sure." Absolutely. How about if I continue to watch your every move tonight? Just like I've been doing since I first saw you in eighth grade.

"See you later," he calls as he merges into a group of guys.

Stepping onto the back deck, I look around for Elena and Melissa, or anyone I can walk up to and not feel like I'm intruding on them. It's really dark out and hard to see anyone unless they're right near the glow of the bonfire. I see Elena's jacket and move around to that side of the circle. She sees me coming and thankfully moves to make room for me in the group. Truth is, I really don't have much to say, so I start to wonder why we all looked forward to this party so much when mostly all we are doing is standing around. Someone squeezes my waist on one side from behind so I turn quickly around to come face-to-face with Kevin.

"Hi."

"Hi." So where is the lovely Andrea, I wonder. Probably watching this little exchange.

"Want a s'more?"

"Um, sure, they have 'em here?"

"Yeah. They have all the stuff over here. Let me get a couple of sticks," Kevin says as he walks over to the edge of the forest. He comes back with two, pulling off all the small branches. "Here you go."

"Thanks."

I put a marshmallow on my stick. As we walk back to the bonfire,

I can't help but wonder what he's thinking. There are two couples sitting on tree trunks toasting marshmallows near us.

"Having fun?" he asks while twirling his marshmallow.

"Yeah, it's a great party." *What a dumb response.*

"You have practice tomorrow?"

"Yeah, over at the club; it's optional, but I'll probably go."

"This is your first year competing on the high school team, right?"

"Yeah, it's so nice this year to be able to compete both at club and high school. How about you? Soccer practice tomorrow?"

"Nah. Not on Sunday."

"Can you believe this is your last year in high school?"

"I know. I need to start my college applications."

"Oh, I'm sure you'll get in anywhere you apply."

"Thanks," he says as he glances at me. Our eyes meet briefly; briefly, of course, because I immediately look away. He continues, "But I don't think it'll be quite that easy. Hey, maybe I could ..." Kevin starts, and then we both turn as we hear some of the guys around the pool yelling something. Then Kevin grabs his buzzing cell phone.

"Cops," is all he says as he reads the text.

"Oh God" is all I can think. Dad is going to freak if he sees cops at the Kirkwoods' knowing I'm here.

Kevin must have seen my face go pale because he says, "It's fine, nothing's gonna happen."

Over his shoulder I see the crowd from the pool house start to break up and notice Chris looking my way. Great, I can't get a date with anyone, but anytime I actually talk to a guy, the one guy I'm interested in has to see me. In just a few seconds, the crowd blocks my view, and I lose sight of Chris.

"You don't understand. My Dad ..." I say with concern.

"Oh, yeah, okay, come on," he says as he grabs my arm and starts walking toward the pool house with purpose. Just then I see Jon and a small group running over.

"Hey, Lindsey. Kevin. You guys heard? Cops are pulling in. I came here on my parents' boat, you want a ride? I can take a couple more."

Kevin immediately says, "Yeah, can you take her?" then turning to me, "I'm sorry, but Jon can get you home on the lake, and I need to get my little brother out of here. He's only a freshman and probably freaking out. You'll be okay with these guys. Thanks, Jon—now make *sure* she gets home," he orders in a very authoritative tone.

"Sure." Looking around at the diminishing crowd and the blue and red flashing lights from the police cars, Jon says, "You ready, Lindsey?" but I just stand there a bit stunned. I'm wondering if I should be happy to get out of here or put off that they are telling me what to do. But there's no time for an internal debate. Jon's friend, Adam, grabs my arm firmly, and practically drags me to the dock.

"I need to check on Elena and Melissa," I say softly as I'm torn between not meeting the cops, ending my conversation with Kevin so abruptly, and feeling guilty for Jon's kindness. Taking my other arm, Jon tells me that he saw Melissa and Elena when he was coming over and that he told them he would be sure I got home. As the guys help me climb into Jon's boat, I realize my phone is buzzing. It's a text from Elena:

10:18 P.M. Hey. Cops here. Jon said he would get u home lake side. So we left. Txt me back so I know u Ok.

At least my friends are okay. I hope the twins don't get in trouble from the cops. The fact is, I have never heard of the cops really doing anything at a kegger except breaking it up, which is a goal they seem to have accomplished this evening.

As my place is so close, Jon takes me home first.

"Thanks so much, Jon. I really owe you."

"No problem. You want me to walk you up to your house?" he asks a bit sheepishly.

"No, I'm fine. Thanks again," I call back as I step onto my family's lit dock. I text Melissa and Elena that I'm home as I walk up the winding stone path toward my house. They text back saying they heard the cops just drove off when everyone was leaving. I walk around to the front and open the front door in hopes that my parents are asleep so they won't realize that a car didn't pull into the driveway. Then I notice a text from Kevin:

10:28 P.M. Hey. U get home Ok? Pls reply.

10:29 P.M. M home. Thx. U Ok? No trouble I hope.

10:31 P.M. Yep. All good. Sorry night was cut short.

I wonder what the night would have been like if it hadn't been cut short. Would Kevin and I have spent more time together? Would he have taken me home? Not likely; Andrea still seems to have him on a short chain.

I wonder if Chris has anyone on a chain.

I wonder if anyone has ever had Chris on a chain. Doubt it.

6 MY RIDE: *FADE TO BLACK.*

IT'S MONDAY, SO I have practice at the gymnastics club after school. Jennifer drove me from school to the club.

After practice, I grab my stuff and check my phone as I head out of the locker room. Unfortunately, I have a voice mail from Mom, who is supposed to pick me up and bring me home. She is running late at work so she called Mrs. Buckley to see if Chris could pick me up after his hockey practice. Of course Mrs. Buckley said he would be happy to and apparently left him a message telling him to do so. I must admit I am excited to see Chris. With the homecoming dance just two weeks from Saturday, a little time with Chris when I don't have to compete with anyone else may be just what I need. I'm done at six, but Mom said that Chris would pick me up around six thirty when his practice is over, so I should wait for him at my club. Since it is still pretty nice out and I know the long, cold winter will be here soon, I decide to walk over. The sun is setting but it's not quite dark so I head out. Walking through the industrial park is not my favorite place to be, but there aren't many people around. I see only

50

a few guys down the street who appear to be on break as they stand outside smoking.

I decide to wait outside when I get to the hockey arena. In about fifteen minutes, Chris walks out with the twins and a few other guys, and looks surprised when he sees me.

"Okay, I'll see you guys later," he says and then walks over to me. "What are you doing?"

Immediately I realize he doesn't know he has been stuck with driving me home. "Oh, I'm so sorry, I thought you knew," I start, but am cut off.

"No, I got the message from my mom; I know I'm taking you home. It's no problem, but why did you walk over? I was going to pick you up."

Embarrassed, I reply, "Oh, I just thought I would save you the trip."

"Are you kidding? You can't just walk around this area. You don't know who's around. If my mom finds out you walked over ..." he trails off, shaking his head.

"Sorry."

"It's okay. Come on; let's go," he says, smiling, and rolls his eyes.

His plates are so cool—HATRIK. Chris is as into hockey as I am into gymnastics, and I can't believe no one else in Michigan had requested "hatrick" for their plates. I googled it the first time I saw it, and when I realized it meant three goals in one game, it made me wonder if Chris has had many hatricks in his games. He loads his hockey gear in the trunk of his silver sports car. I'm surprised to see all that stuff fit in his car's trunk. I climb into the deep bucket seat in the front and notice that the car smells new and is as beautiful inside as it is outside.

As we pull out, he turns the radio on, and for a minute we sit in silence.

"You have a lot of homework?"

"Not too much. You?" I reply.

"No."

Silence.

Awkward silence.

"Too bad the twins' party got cut short," he says.

"Yeah, there were so many people there."

"Yeah, so I guess you're going to homecoming with Kevin Walker," Chris says without looking at me.

"No," I burst out too quickly. *What? You think I'm going with Kevin?* Here I am foolishly hoping maybe you might ask me.

"What?" he says, looking right at me.

"What do you mean 'what'?" and then I'm suddenly embarrassed.

"I heard ... and then I saw you both ..." he says, looking alternately at me and then the road while his voice trails off.

Sigh. Fighting to keep my composure and turning to look out the passenger window, "No. I'm ... I'm not going," I sputter as my voice cracks with emotion.

"What do you mean you *aren't* going?"

Now I realize how pathetic this all really is. "I'm ... I'm not going. Kevin and I are just friends."

I can feel him staring at me.

"Lindsey, I heard from ... I mean, everyone thinks that ... I'm sorry."

I glance in his direction and then turn away as I begin to choke up; I don't want him to notice the tears building in my eyes. We must just be friends too, but he can see I'm overreacting for us to be "just friends." I realize that he is right to feel sorry for me, as I'm the loser junior who's not going to yet another high school dance.

Suddenly, in my peripheral vision, I notice the car ahead of us has slammed into the car in front of them, which has stopped. We are moving too fast toward the car ahead of us. I scream *"Chris!"* and turn to face the front of the car. In one motion he downshifts, pounds the brakes, and throws his right arm across my stomach, forcing me to slam back into the seat. The car responds with a quick smooth stop, but the bumper in front of me is so close, I can hardly believe we haven't hit them. Up ahead a car cut off the one directly in front of us, and they crashed. Chris stopped with an inch to spare.

As I realize we almost had an accident, I become aware that I'm having trouble breathing. Chris is saying something to me, but the wind is completely knocked out of me. I start to see stars. No, no, *no.* Do not pass out! Not again. I can't hear anything. He's saying something. I see more stars. I have tunnel vision. Fade to black.

ᘓᘔ

I hear Chris urgently saying my name. Why does he keep saying it over and over? Are we moving? Oh, man. I did pass out. Open your eyes. *Now.* Okay, *now! Open your eyes!*

My eyes begin to open, and I realize I'm still struggling to breathe. Chris is saying something. Whoosh. I get a gush of air. Okay.

"Lindsey? Lindsey, are you okay? Lindsey, can you hear me? I better call ..."

"I'm ... I'm fine." Oh, man, this is embarrassing. He gets stuck giving me a ride home, and then I faint in his car. Terrific. That won't be all over school too quickly! As I gain my composure, I realize I'm shedding a few tears. Nightmare. It happens every time I faint.

"Lindsey, what's wrong? Did you get hurt? What is it?"

"No. No, I'm fine; I'm just ... I'm just startled."

"Are you sure?"

"Yes. Yes." And in a moment I'm breathing again and am wiping the tears off my humiliated face.

Chris pulls back into traffic as we continue to my house. Then it happened. He wraps my hand up in his. Not one of those tentative brushes like in grammar school or a quick squeeze and release to gauge my reaction—he *grabbed* my hand. I turn to look at my hand in disbelief and then unconsciously look up at him.

"Are you sure you're okay?" he asks again, with genuine concern.

All I can do is nod. I could just die. Then I sputter, "Sorry."

"Sorry? What are you sorry for? I'm the one that should be sorry. You sure you're okay?"

"Yes, just completely embarrassed." Then his phone rings, and as it is connected to the car's sound system, I can see on the console screen between us that it's Elizabeth, card–carrying member of the Fab Five. Because fainting in his car isn't humiliating enough, a girl has to call him. And although I realize in this moment that I had been hoping he had wanted to drive me home, I find myself saying, "Oh. Uh, you should get that."

Something I can't quite read momentarily runs over his expression, then he looks away. "No, I shouldn't." He quickly looks back at me and realizes my confusion. He must have hit a button, because the screen says the call has ended and the music is playing again. He gently squeezes my hand and gives me half a smile. Oh my God.

We are quiet the rest of the way to my home. He holds my hand till we pull up to my house. I don't want him to let go; I'm just so thrilled that he's holding my hand. I can't even think straight.

"Well, thanks again for the ride," I say in a sheepish voice, not sure what all this means.

Still holding my hand firmly, he turns to face me and says, "Yeah, I'm sure you appreciate my almost getting you in an accident. I'll do better next time," he says with a smile looking right at me. "You sure you're okay?"

"Yeah, completely," and I can't help smiling at the thought of a next time, even though I cannot get myself to look at him.

"Thanks again," I whisper as I grab my backpack with my right hand. Suddenly my breath is gone again.

Still holding my left hand firmly, he takes a deep breath and says, "Look, Lindsey, I don't know what to say. Some of the girls said you're going to the dance with Kevin, and I've seen you with him a couple of times so it made sense. And the dance is only in like a week or two, so I asked Elizabeth."

I want to die. I let go of his hand and grab the door handle as I turn away.

"No, Lindsey, wait," he pleads.

Looking out the passenger window I mutter, "I'm sure you'll have fun." Opening the passenger-side door, I feel so sad.

"Lindsey, please look at me."

"Thanks again for the ride. Bye," is all I can say as I get out and slam the door. As I'm walking around the front of his car, I refuse to look at him. Heading up the path to my house, I hear a muffled bang, but I'm determined not to look back. Did he bang the steering wheel? Did he bang his head on his headrest?

I head up to my room and start my homework. In a little while I hear my phone buzz, so I check my cell. Chris has sent me a text message.

6:36 P.M. Hey L. U Ok? Feel terrible.

So I decide to make him wait a while. Later I reply:

8:32 P.M. Hey. M fine. Np. Thx.

I stare at it for a while and finally hit send.

8:33 P.M. Glad to hear it. Can give u a ride anytime. C u in English 2morrow.

Great, can't wait.

෴

For two weeks I have looked forward to seeing Chris in English class each day. Today, I'm dreading it. We have now been assigned seats, so he has to sit directly behind me. As he walks in, I glance up and see him through wisps of my blonde hair. Looking at him, I can't help but smile. With a sideways smile and the lift of an eyebrow, he drops a note in my book:

> *I just told all the guys that you caused me to almost total my car yesterday, and then you fainted.*

What? Before I can even process this, my head snaps up, my eyes grow wide, and I hear myself give out an audible gasp. Oh ... Wait ... Then it hits me. Nice. Two can play at that game.

> *That's funny because I spoke to my dad last night; he would like to discuss your reckless driving, especially while you have his only daughter in your car.*

In an attempt to look unshaken by his mere presence, I slide the note back to him without moving my eyes off my book.

"Nice!" is all he can whisper to me while Ms. Lowen lectures to the class.

⊗⊗⊗

When class ends, I gather my books and notice that he has tucked our note into a pocket of his backpack. Now, clearly I would have kept that note, but he is probably just ensuring that any evidence of our interaction is destroyed.

"How's your day going?" he asks with what I think may be a touch of genuine interest.

"Oh, fine, you?"

"Good." I bet it was good. Must be tough having all the guys jealous of your talent and all the girls drooling over you. As we walk down the hall, he says hi to the kids he knows well.

"See ya later," he says, looking right at me.

"Bye," I spit out as I head to my locker. I know he's trying to be nice to me. He must feel sorry for me, but I really don't want anyone's pity.

7 PAIRING UP: *JUST LOOKING AT HIM MAKES ME NERVOUS.*

LATE SEPTEMBER, AND EVERYONE is in the full swing of school. Autumn is creeping in as the leaves start to fall and the humidity disappears, leaving the air fresh and cool. It's my favorite time of year. I love the crisp air, rich colors, and fall clothes.

My first high school mock gymnastics meet went well last night. Today's practice went well too. I hit three beam routines in a row. Mom picked me up after practice, dropped me at home, and then went off to run errands. I recognize Mozart's opera *Le nozze di Figaro* pouring out from under the office door, which means Dad's working, so I'm happily on my own in my room.

I decide to check e-mail to see if anyone is online. I have a few e-mails from kids asking questions about homework. I like to help out when I can, so I respond to them. Then I get a chat message from Chris.

Chris: Hey

Lindsey: Hi
Chris: Did u c that tryouts for the play are in a few
      weeks?
Lindsey: Y
Chris: Are you trying out?
Lindsey: Think so. U?
Chris: Y – I'm planning to go 4 one of the larger parts.
      Need to try out as a pair for the leads – you want
      to try out together?

Oh, boy. A lead character? I'm not so sure I want to have a big part. Sure, I have had some decent parts in the past, but not a major role. What should I write? He knows I'm online—I don't want to hesitate too long, or he'll think I don't want to work with him; working with him would be awesome.

Lindsey: Would be fun but I'm not sure I'm good
      enough 4 a big part. Don't want 2 drag u
      down.
Chris: Your kidding right? U will definitely get a big role.
      We should try out together. Can I sign us up?
      Think all rehearsals are in am during week.

Since our high school is not huge, a lot of kids who play sports are also in the school plays, so the drama teacher, Mrs. McKnight, runs most of the tryouts and rehearsals before school or on the weekends. That way kids can do both, which is great. I know a lot of schools where you have to choose.

Lindsey: If we try out together can one of us make it?
      Or if I mess up are you out too?
Chris: You are crazy. We will both make the show; we
      did as frosh & sophs, signing us up ;-)
Lindsey: U sure?
Chris: I asked u. Done. When can u practice?
Lindsey: Do u know the play?
Chris: Y
Lindsey: Well?????

Chris: LOL I will get copies of the scripts. Can you
      rehearse at all next week?
Lindsey: Morning?
Chris: Y
Lindsey: Let me know what day so I can check my ride.
Chris: I can pick u up – how about M, W, F?
Lindsey: U don't need to pick me up, my mom can
      bring me. 7?
Chris: U live just around lake, will get u (unless not Ok w
      ur folks?) truth!
Lindsey: U sure?
Chris: Done. Be there @ 6:45 M.

How should I respond? It feels like the chat is ending, but I wish I knew what he is doing this weekend. In the end, I just let it end.

Lindsey: Ok c u then. Bye.
Chris: bye ;-)

 ∓

Monday morning I see Chris pull into my driveway. I grab my backpack and coat and head out to his car.

"Morning," Chris says with a big smile as I get into his car.

"Morning. Thanks again for the ride."

"Never a problem."

"So, are you gonna let me know what the play is?"

"Oh, I'm sure you've never heard of it, I mean at least I hadn't, but I picked up two copies of the script for us. It's by some guy named Bram Stoker."

I gasp and with huge eyes turn to Chris, "*No!*"

"Yes, *Dracula,*" he says with a Transylvanian accent that morphs into a huge smile.

"You're just teasing me." Chris must remember how much I loved the book from when we read it freshman year for English. "It's perfect. It'll be a great show. Which part are you going for? Dracula would be so cool!"

"Van Helsing," he says with his over-the-top accent again.

So what does he think I'm going to play?

"Oh, you'll be an awesome Van Helsing, but what do you think I'm reading for?" I ask with concern.

"You'll be Mina, of course."

"Of course," I reply thick with sarcasm. "You will definitely get a lead part, but I ..."

"Would you stop? First, I will not '*definitely*' get anything, but I do think we have a shot to be Van Helsing and Mina if we work together."

"Are you sure if we try out together that we'll be judged separately?"

"Yeah ... yeah. No worries. What'd you do this weekend?"

Nightmare. How is it going to sound when I admit to the reality of my boring life? "Oh, you know, not much. Homework. Practice."

"Didn't you go out?"

"Oh, no, not really," I reply as I turn to look out the window to avoid his eyes as he realizes what a lame audition partner he has.

"Oh," is all he says.

Yeah. "Oh" is all I can think. I figure I might as well hear about his fabulous weekend. "How about you?"

"Oh, Friday some of the guys got together and kind of raced our boats before we have to pull them out of the lake."

"That sounds fun." And you only mentioned the guys.

"Yeah. It got a little crazy."

I'm only half listening now as I start to replay in my mind the scenes in *Dracula*. Is there a kiss in the book? Why can't I remember? Could I kiss someone on stage? Would they know how little experience I really have in that department? Stop it. You aren't getting a part anyway.

We get to school and find an empty classroom to practice our lines. As Chris hands the script to me, I can't help but notice on the cover that there are only seven characters in the play.

"Chris, I'm happy to try out with you, and I'm flattered that you thought to ask me to work with you, but there are only three parts for girls."

"Yeah. So? There are only four parts for guys. So what? We have both been in every production we have auditioned for since we first tried out freshman year. We have a great shot."

"You know they are probably going to give all the parts to the seniors trying out," I say, a bit more deflated as the truth of my own words sinks in. With that, Chris drops the script on a desk in the front row and comes over to sit next to where I'm leaning on the teacher's desk.

"Would you rather try out with someone else?" he asks, looking down at me.

"No," I say a bit too forcefully as I turn to look at him. With a slight shake of my head I say, "I ... uh ..." Oh, boy. Just looking at him makes me nervous. "You are always great to work with. It's not that. I just don't think I have a real shot," I admit.

"Well, if I want to work with you," he starts, while looking straight ahead, and then getting up turns to look right at me, "which I do. And if you want to work with me ... then what's the problem?"

That seems like half a statement and half a question, so I just smile and nod slightly.

"Then that's that. Let's get to work, okay?"

"Sure." Sure, work with me and date Elizabeth. Perfect.

He had marked the sections we have to deliver for auditions. I'm dying to read the entire script to see what I'm really in for. Depending on how they wrote the play, there definitely could be a few intimate scenes. We have to memorize about five pages of lines for rehearsals. We both agree we should be familiar with the lines by Wednesday and have them memorized by Friday, so we can spend next week focusing more on the delivery and staging.

There are three scenes we have to use in the tryouts. The first one takes place at dawn in Lucy's tomb. Van Helsing drives a stake into Lucy's heart at the start of the scene. It is a fairly straightforward scene, and we run through it easily.

The next scene we need to practice is in Mina's bedroom, where Van Helsing hypnotizes Mina while Arthur, her husband, watches. As we start to read that scene, Chris tells me that Mrs. McKnight will read Arthur's lines during the auditions. The scene is intended to be a moment of tension in the play. In a previous scene, Mina has already drunk the blood of Dracula, and so, according to Van Helsing, she is part of him and is inextricably connected to him.

Part of me is thinking that I should be perfect for a part where I have to play a woman who is in a trance from being hypnotized—how hard can that be? I start to read my lines, but Chris interrupts and we begin to discuss whether I should be sitting up or lying down. It is a hard scene for me to run through since I haven't yet memorized my lines, and as I'm playing a woman in a trance, my eyes should really be shut.

The final scene we need to learn is on the train in Transylvania. This scene includes one line from Arthur. Mina is pleading with Van Helsing to drive a stake through her heart if he thinks there is no hope for her.

"I think we should read this scene standing," Chris suggests.

"Okay, I think that'll work," I say as I get up. I look at him as much as I can while still reading the script. Chris is still holding his copy, but it seems like he already knows his lines. I'm feeling guilty for not knowing my lines yet, and decide I need to study hard in the next few days.

After I deliver my line "I want you to promise me something," Chris suggests, "Hey, I think since you are pleading with me here and in the last scene you are hypnotized and don't really get to do much, I think you should grab my arms and really plead with me."

"Oh, okay. That's a good idea."

"Let's try it again."

```
Mina: "Doctor?"
Van Helsing: "Yes, Mina?"
```

I deliver my line and gently grab Chris's left arm with my right hand.

> Mina: "I want you to promise me
> something."

"Okay. Lindsey, if you are pleading for your soul, is that really how you get my attention?"

"Well, if it's my *soul*." I smirk.

"Okay, then *grab* my attention," he says, emphasizing the words by bending his knees and slanting his upper body back.

So we try it again. I drop my script as there are so few lines in the scene I figure I can remember most of them. As soon as mine hits the floor, Chris raises an eyebrow and drops his as well, with a smirk of his own.

> Mina: "Doctor?"
> Van Helsing: "Yes, Mina?"

Chris says in a bit of a distant way, which makes sense given that he is playing the older professor.

As I deliver my line, I grab both of Chris's arms with both of mine and really begin to feel the character. Forcing myself to look into his eyes, I plead with him,

> "I want you to promise me
> something."

Chris hesitates in delivering his lines just a second, and something seems to have shifted between us. The bell rings. Smiling, we both break from the scene.

"Saved by the bell," I say as I abruptly let go of his arms and step back.

"Yeah," he says, hesitating a moment before packing up his books.

"I have to run; I have to get all the way across the building. See you in English."

"Okay. See you later," he calls after me.

&#8D%&#8DM

The rest of the day, I find myself wondering what shifted between Chris and me. Was there something there? Did his eyes focus on me, not Mina, but me? Or am I seeing what I want to see?

There was something.

Wasn't there?

8 EMPTY: *EVERYONE PEAKS AT A DIFFERENT TIME.*

IT'S WEDNESDAY NIGHT, TEN days before homecoming. Chris and I had a good rehearsal this morning, but I'm even more convinced he'll get the part playing against someone else. Today Kevin sat with his friends in study hall, which he has been doing a few days each week. A few days each week, he sits with me. Classes went well and practice was fine. I'm confident Jennifer and I will do well at the invitational tomorrow.

Isabella gave me a ride home again tonight. She offers me a ride most nights—certainly on all the nights when Kevin has a game or simply doesn't ask to take me home. Which makes me wonder who he's driving home on those nights. I guess we are just going to be friends. Better to be friends with all the cute guys at school than to have them not even know my name.

On my way home from school with Isabella, she is going on and on about who's going with whom to the homecoming dance. It seems like everyone has already been paired up. I keep trying to be polite and pay attention, but I just want to get home. What is she saying? Oh, she is talking about her dress, which she bought over the summer because, of course, she knew she would be going to the dance with Rick. I'm lost in my own thoughts and then suddenly realize we are at my place.

I ask Isabella to drop me at my mailbox because I can't take any more of her chatter today. After getting the mail, I start to walk up our winding driveway toward the house. Flipping mindlessly through the mail, I hear something rustling in the woods and look for a deer or rabbit moving through the leaves on the ground. I hear a car and turn toward the road and catch a glimpse through the trees of the tail end of a pickup truck going past our house. Turning back, something else catches my eye in the woods. I walk into the woods and see it again. Looking back at my house, I decide to go see what it is.

About twenty more steps, and I can start to see the Castiglionis' house as I approach the stark white object that I realize caught my eye: a couple of cigarette butts are scattered in a clearing. Four to six inches of leaves are all around except on one side of a large tree, where two or three cigarette butts have been dropped. Must be from one of the landscapers. I push the butts under some leaves with my shoe. "Click." I jump. The click must have been the sound of our exterior lights coming on for the night. Laughing at my own jumpiness, I head to the house.

I walk into my empty house and head up the wide wooden curved staircase to my room. Although I just worked out, I'm not hungry. I enter my room and go through the options of turning on my computer, pulling out my homework, or changing clothes. But I'm simply in a funk. Still not going to homecoming.

I sit down to study and hear Mom arrive home downstairs. I get up, and as quietly as I can, I shut my door. Mom comes upstairs to change and calls down the hall, "Hey, Lindsey. How was your day?"

"Good, thanks," rolling my eyes to no one but myself.

"What do you want for dinner? Dad's staying in the city again for a case."

"Sorry, Mom, I already ate—and I have a lot of homework." I just can't sit through dinner tonight.

"No problem. Let me know if you want something later."

Whew. I get the night to myself.

I force myself to concentrate for a couple of hours, long enough to finish all my assignments. Then noticing the time, eight fifteen, I finally allow myself to think about it. The tears start to build. It is only a week before the homecoming dance, it is after eight (which is, of course, the outside limit of the appropriate time to call someone), and I have exactly no date.

The first two years of high school, it really didn't bother me that I had no dates, but suddenly I feel like I can never show up at high school again. Why doesn't anyone ever call me? What's wrong with me? I wish I never had to go to that place again. What if I never get asked to a dance? What if I don't even get to go to my own prom? *Nightmare.* I am so frustrated I get up and turn off my cell phone and computer. I throw all my homework in my bag and flop back onto my bed.

I'm consumed with thoughts of everyone else spending the next week talking about their dresses, how they will do their hair, which couples will go to dinner together. I can't bear it. The tears start to flow freely. I feel sick to my stomach. Isabella is going with Rick, Melissa has been asked by Gary, and Elena is going with Robert. It's so depressing. And Chris. Chris is going with Elizabeth. I want to hurl.

I hear a knock on the door. *Mom.* Not now. Just because I don't have my own place, aren't I entitled to some level of privacy?

"Lindsey? You okay?"

I try to hide how upset I really am by steadying my voice and wiping my face off. "Yeah, I'm fine. I just had a long day."

"Can I come in?"

I would rather you go out to dinner and leave me alone, but instead I just say, "Um, uh huh."

And she walks in. I can see her face shift when she sees me, which just makes me feel even more helpless. She knows I don't cry much, so I can see her pain in seeing me completely fall apart.

"What happened?" she asks in her caring and kind voice. And I just can't hold it together anymore. The tears are flowing, so I sit up and grab a handful of tissues to wipe my nose.

"Nothing."

"It doesn't look like nothing," she says in a concerned tone, and for some reason this sends me over the edge.

"*Nothing* is exactly what happened. Everyone has been asked to the homecoming dance; everyone that is, but me! What's wrong with me? Is it so much to ask to want someone to ask me to one stupid dance? I'm not even sure I want to go, but why isn't there one stupid guy in the entire stupid high school who wants to ask me?" It is very uncharacteristic of me to act like this, especially in front of my parents, so a small part of me is hoping she will get upset, yell at me, and leave. But she doesn't. Of course not, because the *entire* world is against me.

"I'm so sorry. I wish there was something I could do or say to make you feel better. You have so much going for you."

At which I completely cut her off. "Mom," with a dramatic roll of my bloodshot eyes.

But wisely she ignores me and keeps going, "You are smart, kind, a good student, a wonderful gymnast, and so pretty."

"Great, shocking news, you think your daughter's pretty. Wait, do you hear that?" and I wait for a dramatic impact. "That's the sound of the phone not ringing."

She continues as if I'm not even talking, "and one day the right person will notice all those things and more, and you won't even remember this one dance. I know it seems important now, but in the scheme of life, over time, you'll see it in a very different perspective."

Now I'm angry at Mom. "Are you kidding me? You want me to feel okay because when I'm seventy, I won't remember that I never went to a dance in high school? I'm sorry, but it does bother me." And the tears win again. The anger is brief, but the sadness feels endless. Even though Mom is sitting right next to me, I feel so alone.

Mom remains completely unshaken by my mood swings and continues, "Your time will come. Maybe not this dance. Maybe not today, but one day you'll see."

"I just don't get it. Why is it that the same kids have everything—all the friends, all the guys, they're beautiful, they're all on the class council, good at sports, it's just so …" The words escape me. I feel so sad. I feel empty.

"Everyone peaks at a different time. For some people, high school is the best time of their entire life; for others, it's college. But that's it. They peak early, and then the best days in their lives are just a memory. Your best days are still ahead, and I believe they will last much longer than a year or two in high school."

I can't even respond. A door opens somewhere inside, and I know she's right.

It is a profound moment that I know I will never forget. It feels like she reached into a box of truth and pulled out a ribbon from my future for me to see. I somehow know in this moment that my best days *are* ahead and that this is all just practice.

Mom gets up off the bed looking sad and as heartbroken as I feel, and suddenly I feel guilty about that as well. As she is about to leave I say, "Thanks, Mom."

"Sure, can I get you anything?"

"Um, no. But, I just can't drive in with Isabella tomorrow and listen to her go on and on about the dance. Can you drive me to school?"

"Sure, I can go in a bit late."

"No, no, you can take me early; I have lines to study anyway."

"Okay, and then I'll meet you at your invitational in the evening. I can take you home from there. Okay?"

"Okay, thanks." And my voice cracks.

⊱⊰

Better days may be ahead, but I wish today was a little better. I promise myself that I will not let anyone know I'm so sad about one silly dance.

But tonight I'm alone. For the first time in a very long time, I cry myself to sleep.

9 IN PERSON: *I'M GONNA KILL MY ROUTINES.*

I WAKE UP EARLY on Wednesday and get dressed. I grab my cell phone and coat to take our Airedale terrier, Baron, for a walk while Mom gets ready. Baron is so happy to have me talking to him and scratching his ears, I actually forget my own drama and open the back door before turning off the alarm. Damn. I run over to the panel and enter the code while the warning sound is still going off. Whew. Another thirty seconds, and Mom would have been shocked by the deafening scream of the alarm.

As Baron runs to the forest between our place and the Kirkwoods' property, I tug on his leash and pull my cell phone out to text Isabella and to let her know Mom is taking me to school.

What's this? I've missed three calls from Kevin, but I have only one voice mail. He called at 6:30, 8:15, and 9:00 last night. I tap my voice mail to pick up the message and hear, "Hey, Lindsey, it's Kevin. If you get this tonight, can you call me? Sorry it's late. I tried you earlier, but I guess you were busy. So, um, anyway, give me a call."

Huh? I wonder what he wants. I can't believe I missed his call.

I certainly can't call him this early. Should I text him? No, it's way too early. I'll look desperate. If he really wants to reach me, he can find me; he'll be in study hall.

Baron suddenly pulls on the leash, and I look up to see a bunny hopping through the early shadows in the ground cover. I bring Baron back to the house, and find I have a new bounce in my step.

The day is fairly uneventful, except, of course, the daily treat of seeing Chris Buckley in English. As the day progresses, I'm getting more and more anxious about study hall.

I enter the library for study hall and sit in my usual spot. I don't see any of the soccer guys around. Now that it's the last period of the day, I let myself consciously think about the fact that I'm hoping Kevin called to ask me to the dance. Why didn't he show up to study hall? Maybe he has practice, but wait, two guys just popped up from cubes that I didn't see before and they are on the soccer team. Why else would Kevin have called? Oh, well, no time to think about that now; I need to focus for my first high school gymnastics meet tonight.

With study hall over, I head to my locker to collect my books and gymnastics bag. I kneel on the ground to organize my backpack and try to block out all the noise of the kids in the hall. Then I see a pair of shoes between me and the next locker. As I look up, I see Kevin sliding his back down the lockers to where I am.

"So, I guess you were pretty busy last night, or maybe you don't want to talk?" he says with a smirk.

"Oh, um … I'm sorry; I was, um, well, I was with my mom all night." I'm so flustered at recalling my evening, I lose my mental footing. *I can't believe you came to my locker.*

"Oh, no problem."

"I didn't see you in study hall," I say.

"Yeah, sorry about that. I met some kids I'm doing a group project with in the cafeteria. Do you have some time?"

"Um, yeah. I have an hour or so before I need to be on the bus for my meet."

"Perfect; let's go."

"Let's go? Where are we going?"

"Come on," he says with a grin as he picks up my gym bag.

"Thanks." We walk out together to the student parking lot, and I start to wonder where we are heading.

"Are we leaving school?"

"No problem—your bus is at four, right?"

"Yeah."

"Do you have everything you need? Or do you need to go by the gym or something?"

"No, I'm set," I say, wondering what is really going on.

As we walk over to the student lot, I see Chris walking in that direction too. Depending on where his car is and where Kevin's is, we might cross paths. I would rather not have this little rendezvous if possible, but there is nothing I can do. It becomes clear we will, in fact, cross paths. Terrific.

"Hey, Lindsey," Chris says, looking me right in the eyes. Then, in a more tense voice, "Kevin."

"Chris," Kevin says, and I'm not sure, but I think he stepped a little closer to me as he said it.

"Hey, Chris," I say and am obviously uncomfortable.

"Lindsey, we still on for practice before school tomorrow?" Chris says, stopping right in front of me.

"Yeah, sure. See you then." Oh, boy. Is this good or awful? Will a bit of jealousy motivate Kevin or turn him away? Why would he even be jealous? What is Chris thinking?

"Practice for?" Kevin asks as we continue to walk toward his car.

"We're trying out for the play."

"So you're practicing with Chris?"

"Yeah, um … for certain parts this year, you have to try out in pairs, so Chris and I are working together."

"His idea?"

"As a matter of fact, I think it was." He doesn't seem jealous, but something is definitely in Kevin's tone.

"Yeah, I bet," Kevin says under his breath.

We are quiet till we get to his car, where he opens up the passenger side to let me in.

"I'm sorry, I um … I don't think I should leave campus before a meet," I say timidly. I can't believe I'm such a wimp. Kevin walks around the car and gets in the driver's side.

"Don't worry; we aren't going anywhere, I just want to talk."

"Oh, okay," I say as I glance quickly at him but am too uncomfortable to hold his gaze, although he seems to be looking at me the entire time while he gets in the car. I want to look and see where Chris is, but force myself not to as I know it would be rude to Kevin.

"So, I've been trying to get in touch with you for a few days," he says as he turns in his seat to face me.

"You have? When? I mean, I know you called last night, but …" I stammer.

"Well, I looked for you before school a few times, but I can't seem to find you. I guess you have been rehearsing with our friend Chris."

"Oh, sorry. Well, uh, where have you been for study hall?"

"Soccer practice starts early for us most days. That's why the whole varsity team has last period off."

"Oh, sorry," I stammer. Hmm. Of course, the school gives all the guys seventh-period study hall if they are in a sport. Ridiculous. Do all the girls on gymnastics team get seventh period off? No. Nice double standard. "Why didn't you just text me?" I ask before I realize that I'm probably being too forward.

"Well, I think some things should be said in person."

"Oh," I say, looking over at him for a second. I feel so tense, and I'm not sure why.

"Lindsey, do you want to go to the homecoming dance with me?" he says, looking right in my eyes.

I can't believe the immediate sense of relief I feel. "Sure," is all I say in a soft voice.

"Great. You okay if we go to dinner first?"

"What? Oh, sure, yeah." *What is my dad going to say?*

"Good, is it okay if we go with another couple? Maybe we could go with Andrew and his date?"

"Sounds great." *I'm finally going to a dance!*

"Good, then that's settled. So you ready for your meet tonight?"

"Yeah," I say, biting my lip to contain my big stupid grin. I feel like I already won All-Around.

"What time will you get home tonight?"

"Oh, about eight, I guess."

"Will you text me when you get home?"

"Oh, um, I guess."

"Cool," he says as he starts the car.

I jump a little as I don't understand where we're going.

"Don't worry; I'm just going to drop you back on the gym side for your meet."

"You don't have to do that; I can walk."

"We're already in the car. I'll drive you."

Before getting out, I force myself to turn and look at him. "Thanks," I say with real excitement.

"Good luck. I'll text you later to see how the meet went, okay?"

"Sure."

80C3

I may be only five foot four and around a hundred pounds, but I feel invincible. I'm gonna kill my routines. Yesterday I was in a complete funk. Today I feel powerful. What a difference a day makes.

80C3

Lying in bed, I start to think about the last few days and the months ahead. I actually got asked to a dance! And Kevin sent me a text earlier to see how my meet went. It feels so good to have a guy texting me for once.

I think Mom was right. These are the best days for some kids, but who? The Fab Five? Kevin? Not for Chris. Cool as he is in high school, I bet great things are ahead for him. Somehow I know Mom was right about me. Strange how one thought, one idea can completely change your perspective. I just know Mom is right, that for some kids their best days are in high school and for others it may be years later. They say that knowledge is power; I guess that's true. But insight. What Mom shared with me was insight. Insight into life, and who I really am. True insight can change you from that point forward. No one else may see the shift, but I can feel it.

10 NORTH MEETS SOUTH: *ALL'S WELL THAT ENDS WELL.*

"HEY, I JUST HEARD about a party some guy from South High is having tonight. We should go," Melissa says to me at the lunch table on Friday.

"Are you sure? I mean, what if they don't let us in?"

"Oh, everyone who goes gets in," Melissa says, dismissing my concern.

"Really? But they don't even know us." Having only been to a couple of high school parties in my life ... well, actually, as I think about it, I have only been to one at the Kirkwoods' house, so I'm not really sure how all this works. Wonder what my folks will think if I go to a South party. I think the only reason I got to go to the Kirkwoods' is because Dad's firm represents Mr. Kirkwood's companies, and from what I can tell, Dad seems to be his preferred counsel.

"They aren't going to know hardly any of us from North, but that's what a party is for. Come on, it'll be fun."

77

"Do you even know where it is?" I ask, throwing up another roadblock.

"Kind of, but I promise you, I'll find out by tonight. You in? *Come on.* I can pick you and Elena up."

"Are you sure about this? I mean, what if we don't know anyone at the party?"

"Would you stop? You're going. I'll find out where it is and text you later, okay?" Melissa says just before the bell. Without waiting for my reply, she stands up and grabs the wrappers and juice carton left from her lunch. "Great; that's settled. I'll call or text you later. Bye, Lindsey. Enjoy study hall," she adds to tease me about Kevin.

In the afternoon, it occurs to me that I've been to one party, the same one as Melissa, so how is it she's so certain how all this works? Maybe she is just more confident in her ability to get into parties hosted by strangers. I wish I had her confidence. I am a social wimp.

∞∞

"Hey, Lindsey, you headed out?" Chris calls after me as he catches up to me leaving the cafeteria.

"Yeah."

"Chris, do you have a minute?" Amanda asks, stepping right in front of me. Stepping around her, I look down and keep walking.

Heading down the hall, I hear someone calling me.

"Lindsey, Lindsey, wait up." Looking back, I'm pleased to see that it's Chris. "Sorry about that."

"No problem."

"Hey, are you going to the party at South tonight?"

"Oh, um, I don't know. I guess so."

"You should. Everyone'll be there."

"Really?"

"Oh yeah, I'll look for you."

"Great. I need to stop by my locker."

"Okay, see ya later, Lindsey."

"Bye." Sigh.

ଚ୦ଓଃ

"Hey, Lindsey," Isabella says as she sees me approaching her in the student parking lot.

"Hey."

"You ready?"

"Sure."

"Okay, guys, I'll talk to you later," she says to the two girls from our class she was talking to before I approached them.

As she pulls her seat belt on, she starts, "Did you hear about the party tonight over at South?"

"Yeah. Some kids were talking about it at lunch. Are you going?"

"Definitely, everyone's going—it's gonna be huge. And besides, there are no parties at North tonight."

"Right. Who are you going with?"

"Oh, you know, a couple of girls from volleyball. How about you?"

"Melissa and Elena are going, so I guess I'm going with them."

"Cool."

"Is Rick going?"

"Oh yeah, a bunch of the guys on the soccer team are going. Kevin's going, right?" she asks.

"I'm not sure. I mean, I hear a lot of people are going, so I assume so, but I don't know." *We're going to homecoming together, but I still hardly talk to him. He wasn't in study hall again today.*

"You know Andrea is still after him," she says and glances at me again. I think she is trying to gauge my reaction. This instinctively causes me to try not to react. I wonder if she passes on information from any of our driving chats to Rick. If she does, then I'm sure Rick would tell his own brother, Kevin. Hmm, better be more careful with what I say. Fortunately, we sit silently, enjoying the music for a while, and soon we are at my house. So I pick up my backpack and leave with, "Thanks for the ride. I'll look for you tonight."

"Great, see you there."

ᎭᎮ

During dinner, I decide I'd better clear the evening's plans with Mom and Dad.

"So, where exactly is this party?" Mom asks.

"Well, I'm not sure 'exactly,' but I know it's in the subdivision right across from South High. One of the South football players is throwing it."

"And I suppose his parents will not be home."

"Mom," I say, pleading with her.

"I know, I know. Well, who are you going with?"

"Melissa is driving, but Elena will be with us, and everyone will be there. Isabella is going with a bunch of friends too."

"Okay, but home at midnight."

"Thanks!" I say as I jump up to clear my plate before anyone decides to probe any further.

"Lindsey," Mom calls as I'm at the sink.

What now? "Yeah," I say without looking at her because I'm worried I may lose the party after all.

"How about I take you shopping tomorrow afternoon for a dress for the homecoming dance?"

I spin around, "That would be great. Can I get shoes and a purse? Please!" At which Dad looks up from his dinner. I know he is trying to keep his own excitement about my going to the dance down, but I figure I'll get whatever I want for this dance as it's my first. Mom looks at Dad and says, "Well, we have to finish the look, don't we?"

"Yes! Thanks, Mom. Thanks, Dad."

"I expect to meet this young man before the dance," Dad says, like he comes from a country where we presume guilt instead of innocence.

"Yeah, I'll ask him to come in before we go to dinner next Saturday, okay?"

"I'm sure we'll have a nice little chat," he says, raising an eyebrow at me as he gets up to clear his plate.

"Thanks, Dad," I sarcastically reply. Best to go upstairs and quit before this gets worse.

As I'm getting ready, I hear my phone buzz. It's a text from Kevin—fantastic start to the weekend.

6:32 P.M.   Hey Lindsey. U there?

6:33 P.M.   Hi Kevin.

6:33 P.M.   Sry about study hall. Had practice. U going to south party 2nite?

6:34 P.M.   Y

6:34 P.M.   Gr8. Will look 4u. Wud b good 2 c u.

6:34 P.M.   Sounds good. C u there.

꧁꧂

Melissa picks me up right on time at nine o'clock. I'm so looking forward to the party, and, of course, I'm also nervous about going.

We pass South High and continue to follow Melissa's GPS toward the address she got from someone at school. As we pull around the next corner I gasp, "Wow, look at all the cars. Looks like all of North and South are here."

"Right! It looks like the house is up on the next block," Melissa adds as she points to the destination indicator on the GPS screen.

I get a sudden rush of nerves. What if I lose Melissa and Elena? What if no one talks to me? Maybe I should have stayed home and watched a movie. Kevin did say he was coming, so it could turn out to be a good evening. I hope he comes up to me and wants to talk. I would hate it if we both see each other and he expects me to go over to him. I wonder if I will get a chance to talk to Chris.

Melissa squeezes her car in between two others I don't recognize. As we start to walk up the block, we can see other small groups of kids arriving for the party. A pickup truck guns by us too quickly given how close it was to us and all the cars parked on the road. Why aren't they coming into the party?

"Hey, guys, keep your phones on in case we get separated, okay?" I can't help but ask Melissa and Elena.

"Right, like Melissa has *ever* turned off her phone. This looks like it could be huge. I'm so excited," adds Elena.

The houses are smaller and don't look as well kept as in our neighborhood. I begin to wonder how all the kids that came in all these cars are going to fit in one of these houses. I'm glad I brought my coat as I feel the beginning of winter in the night air. My nerves increase as we approach the noise and bustle of the party. Cars are parked from one end of the street to the other, on both sides. In two driveways near the party, the cars are so close that they are bumper to bumper from the garage straight over the sidewalk to the street. I had heard that South was a rougher high school than North, but this was my first exposure to anything except a football game that was held there during my freshman year. At the football game I sat with my friends from North, and so I guess I really didn't notice anything else.

Three guys are standing near a car as we pass, each drinking a beer. They watch us walk by, but fortunately don't say anything to us, as I don't recognize any of them. We can hear music from inside the house as well as from the backyard. There is only one light by the front door, so it's hard to see more than shapes. The closer we get, the more I hear sounds from the crowd I assume has gathered in the backyard. As we walk up the driveway, I'm determined not to be the first in our little group to walk in, so I start to slow down. Melissa turns to me with a smile and takes the lead without saying a word. Elena's in the middle, but we start to bunch up closer and closer together as we approach the storm door.

Two guys bang the door open as they fall out of the house, doubled over laughing. One of them stands up straight, and in a much exaggerated and clearly a bit buzzed manner, holds the storm door open as he says to Melissa, "Right this way. Come on in, ladeez."

"Thanks," Melissa says like she was just here yesterday. I grab Elena's arm, and she and I share a smile as we walk in. The house is packed with kids; there is hardly room even to move into the house. Melissa manages to slip through the foyer toward the back of the house. As I'm not that tall, I'm mostly looking at the shoulders of all the guys around me and can see only a few people on each side. So far, I haven't seen a single face I recognize. Some guy starts chatting with Melissa, but I can't hear what they are saying. Melissa turns back to us and yells over the crowd and the music, "Come on, the keg is in the back." I try to squeeze through the crowd and follow her.

"Excuse me. Sorry. Excuse me," I keep saying as I try to press forward without taking an elbow to the chest.

"Look out, Jim. Comin' through," some guy says as he shoves two other guys against the wall so we can navigate through the crowd. Then he turns to say something to them under his breath.

"Thanks," I say, but I'm convinced they are still talking about Melissa, Elena, and me.

We finally make it down the hallway, and I notice a small kitchen on the right. We continue down a half flight of stairs into a larger family room. Going through the family room and out the sliding glass door, we find ourselves on a very crowded patio and see the keg. I wait in line with Melissa and Elena so that they can each get a beer.

Melissa turns to me and says, "Don't worry—I won't actually drink any."

"Oh, I know." As she is driving, she wants to reassure us that she will not actually drink any. I guess she thinks it will be easier to always be holding a beer. That way no one asks if she wants one. I don't think Melissa or Elena really like drinking, but we each need to find our own way to deal with booze at parties.

Similar to the twins' party, we stand around talking to each other mostly. We run through all the people we know who are going to the homecoming dance and talk about who is going with whom. I keep glancing around, but there are so many people I can't find Chris, Isabella, or Kevin anywhere. Soon the backyard is as crowded as the house was when we arrived. I'm sure there are lots of people I know here, but it is so dark I may not recognize them even if they are only a few feet away.

After about an hour, I'm starting to get really cold and decide to go back inside the house for a minute to warm up. "I'm gonna go in the house and get some water or soda or something," I say to Elena, hoping she and Melissa might come with me as I'm still paranoid that I'll get separated from them.

"Okay, I just saw Gary so I'm staying here and hope he comes over—okay? But I promise we'll be right here. Come back, okay?"

"Okay." Great, on my own. I take a deep breath and start to weave through the crowd. Because there are only two lights in the entire backyard and the place is jammed with kids drinking, I'm struggling just to get through the crowd. I begin to recognize a few kids from North now, which makes me feel a little better. Unfortunately, everyone in the group I recognize is smoking, and no one is in the same crowd as me so we barely acknowledge each other. Then I see my outdoorsman buddy, Mark, and work my way over to him.

"Hey, Mark."

"Hey, Lindsey, how are you?" he says while blowing the smoke from his cigarette up and away from me.

"Good, how about you?"

"Never better," he says with an easy smile as he toasts his beer to no one in particular. "You want a beer, Lindsey?"

"No, I'm fine. Thanks, though." And then two girls come up and I'm pretty sure Mark likes one of them, so I give him a wave and move on.

"I'll see you later, Mark."

"Okay, Lindsey—I'll look for you later."

"Okay, see ya." And he is quickly engaged with the other girls. I'm sure he already has a homecoming date. He never seems to be without some girl or another.

I finally make it up to the back door. Much to my disappointment, it is almost as dark in the house as it is outside. Entering, I pass a couple sitting on the couch making out. Seriously? What are you doing? There are fifty people in the room. I check my watch, and it is already 10:38 p.m. Only about an hour left. I wonder if I will get to see Chris or Kevin.

Trying my best to go unnoticed through the family room, I head to the stairs that lead to the kitchen, where I figure I can get a soda or water to hold in my hand. At least then I would have something to do with one hand. I get to the stairway, where some huge linebacker-looking guy moves his whole body in front of my path and leans on one arm on the wall over my head and says, "Hi."

"Hi. Um ... Excuse me."

"Sure thing. Can I get you anything?" he says without moving an inch.

"No, thanks. I'm fine," I reply.

"Yes, I can see that." *Great.* "Now, what can we get you to drink?" he asks, still blocking my path. Fortunately for me, some guy trying to get down the stairs shoves the linebacker guy to the side, so I squeeze through saying, "Oh, no thanks, I'm fine." I head to the kitchen. Turning the corner, I'm relieved to see that one kitchen light is on so the room is a bit brighter than the family room, but it is still rather dimly lit. As I move in, I realize that there are about fifteen guys jammed in this tiny kitchen, some standing around and some playing what I can only assume is a game of beer pong on half the kitchen table. The other half is covered with a mix of empty and full bottles of beer, bottles of liquor, and—I'm hoping—some soda. There is also a huge outdoor trash can wedged in the corner, which is almost full of beer bottles and plastic cups. Working my way over to the table, I'm shoved by somebody from behind and hit the kitchen cabinets pretty hard as I fall forward. When I turn back toward the room, the linebacker is directly in front of me holding a cup of beer.

"We meet again."

"Uh, huh." My lucky day.

"Hey, Ritchie, give me a beer for the little lady here," he calls over to one of the guys behind him.

As I reply, "Oh, I'm fine, thanks though," I see a guy who must be Ritchie pull a bottle of beer out of the fridge and hand it to the linebacker with a grin. "Sure, here you go. Need any help, Rock?"

The linebacker laughs a bit and says, "No, I got this one covered." Total nightmare. The last thing I want right now is to have my first beer. He opens the beer and offers it to me.

"Oh, no thanks, but, um, thanks anyway."

"No beer? Okay, well, as you can see, we have anything you want," he says, gesturing to the table of booze.

"Oh, um, I'm fine. Thanks," I say as I turn back toward the kitchen door thinking I will just forget the drink and try to find Melissa.

Deliberately, he raises his left arm as high as my head and puts his hand on the cabinet behind me, blocking my escape path. Then he leans his huge chest and face down toward me and says, "Oh, come on now, I'm sure there is *something* here you want." He says it with such emphasis and slurs each "s" so much, I'm confident he's already had too many. Not sure what to do, I just stand there in his shadow, feeling flustered.

"How about just one beer? For me?" he urges while he moves an inch closer. I realize that the other guys in the room are now laughing. *Are they laughing at me?* My body is still cold from the night air, but I feel my face start to flush.

"No, no thanks," is all I can manage to stammer. Then I see Kevin's friend Andrew in the hallway. I figure he's my best bet to get away from this beast.

"Andrew!" I yell over the noise of the crowd, surprising myself a bit. Andrew immediately turns to see who is calling him.

"Hey, Andrew." I can't quite see his face now as the guys in the kitchen keep moving around, but I think he is scanning the kitchen looking for whoever called him. Luckily he ducks down a bit so he can see me under the gorilla arm between us. Then he turns to look down the stairs in front of him. Are you kidding? You talk to me when I'm with Kevin, but now you look away? I have a glimmer of hope as he looks back at me. He does another double take looking down the stairs and then back to me. At this point, I'm doing my best to plead with him, with my eyes, to please come over.

Instead, he pushes his way down the stairs and is out of sight. I look back at the linebacker, who is taking a long drink he does not need, from his beer. Okay, so I'm on my own. I should have stayed home. I try to squeeze farther into the small kitchen on my left without him noticing. As soon as I inch to my left, his right arm comes down to slam the counter behind me with his empty cup.

"So, where were we? Oh, yes, we were discussing what it is you want to drink. Ritchie, give me two shots of tequila."

"Oh, yeah," I hear someone yell across the kitchen as several guys start to hoot and holler. I'm suddenly really nervous and my face is burning. My stomach starts to turn. I am completely alone in a crowded room.

I muster up my courage and try to look the gorilla in the eyes, ready to say something. Ritchie reaches over and hands him two plastic cups, each with two inches of what I assume is tequila. "Here you go, Rock," he says, looking down at me with a devilish grin.

"I'm, uh, gonna just go back and meet my friends," I say in a frail voice.

"I thought we were friends? I'm Rich, but everyone calls me Rock. And you are?" But like a fool, I just stand there. I can't think of anything to say. I know other girls would have some clever and biting comeback to put this Neanderthal in his place, but I have nothing.

So he continues, "You do have a name, right? I could think of a nickname for you, if you prefer."

This is a terrifying thought. "Lindsey, I'm … I'm Lindsey."

"Okay, Lindsey, friends help friends have fun, right? I just want to have some fun with you," he says as he puts his left hand on my waist, making me cringe even more.

"I'm sorry," I start to say as he leans even closer so I can smell the stale beer on his hot breath. Instinctively, I pull back—and hit my head against the cabinet behind me.

"Hey! *Hey!*" I hear from the direction of the hallway. We both look over to the kitchen doorway. It's Chris Buckley. Looking furious and shoving two guys out of his way to get in the kitchen. Behind him, Joel and Mike look equally upset, and then I see a group of other North guys behind them in the hallway who look keyed up. I feel like I can breathe again. Just as quickly, I realize that maybe this is about to get worse.

"Problem?" Rock says, but he doesn't move an inch as he turns back to stare me in the eyes, which are all of about four inches from his face.

"Yes! Lindsey, let's go," Chris snaps, moving next to me.

"Do you mind?" Chris growls looking right at Rock, with Mike stepping up and glaring at Rock as well.

"Just having a little chat," he says, looking straight at me. He finally stops leaning on his hand and stands up, throwing back his tequila. While he is slamming the shot, I squeeze past him and Chris pushes me on toward Mike. As I pass Chris, he whispers in my ear from behind, "Did he touch you?"

I shake my head as I say, "No, no, just being … you know."

"Yeah, I know," he says, turning back to Rock.

Mike pushes me farther through the group of North guys to his brother Joel.

"So, I take it that's your piece of tight ass?" Rock says, looking nose to nose at Chris as they stand only inches away from each other in the tight space. I snap my head around to see what's going to happen next. Everyone in the room tenses up, and the game of pong suddenly stops. The only sound for a moment is the backdrop of the music. Mike grabs Chris by the collar of his jacket and pulls him out of the kitchen saying, "Okay, that's it. Let's go." Then he says in a very authoritative tone looking at Chris who is pulling away from him and back toward the Rock, "*Hey*, not worth it. Let's get out of here." Chris shoots Rock one more look, pressing his lips together, and then takes a deep breath and moves past Mike to grab my waist and shove me out into the hallway heading for the front door.

"Let's go," he says to me from behind as I hear Rock and some of the other guys back in the kitchen laughing.

"I, I need to check on—" I start to say while he pushes me forward.

"Hey, Lindsey, are you okay? Andrew said some guy was giving you some trouble?" Kevin asks, coming up the staircase trailed by Andrew.

Ignoring him, Chris steps in front of me. "Let's get outside before this gets worse." As we cross the threshold, I take a deep breath, which I assume can be felt by Chris, who still has his hand on my waist.

Standing between Chris and Kevin, I visibly take another deep breath.

Chris looks intently at me and again asks, "You okay?"

"Yeah," I say as I'm flooded with emotions. I realize I'm still filled with fear, fueled by adrenaline from that little scene with the Neanderthal. I feel guilty for leaving the party without Melissa and Elena, when I would have been completely upset and alone if they had left without me. I'm frustrated that Chris had to "save me," but also excited that he is interested enough to get involved. I'm also very relieved to know that Andrew had not abandoned me as I had originally thought.

Speaking to no one in particular, I say, looking down, "I need to check on my friends …"

"Call them. You're coming with me." Kevin says it like he is my dad and I should just accept whatever he says.

Chris runs his hand back through his hair and looks at Mike. I realize that the group of guys I'm walking out with is starting to slow down, and soon we are standing in a circle in the street.

"Andrew, can you get a ride with ..." Kevin starts to say, but Andrew cuts him off, "Done. No problem. Talk to you tomorrow." Andrew and the other guys start to talk among themselves.

Standing now with a mix of Kevin's and Chris's friends, it feels a bit weird. Chris and the twins are talking among themselves.

"Chris," I start, and at first all three of them turn to me, but then the brothers turn away and start walking slowly down the street. Chris stands there looking right at me.

I take a step closer to him and realize that Kevin takes a step as well, to stay next to me. "I just, um ... I just ... wanted to say thanks."

"Anytime, Lindsey. You sure you're okay now?"

"Yeah, thanks." As he stands there smiling at me, I can't turn away from him.

Giving me a warm smile, he turns back to his friends.

"Hey, Andrew, I wanted to thank you too."

"No problem. I just feel bad I didn't walk in as soon as I saw you, but that room was filled with South guys and Kevin and the guys were already out back. I just figured you would be okay for two minutes ..." Then turning to Kevin, he says, "You saw it in there; the place was crawling with South guys."

"Thanks, Andrew," Kevin says, and with that Andrew nods and heads toward the cars. I can't help but think that Andrew cares more that Kevin appreciated his actions than that I do. Interesting. Guys have an interesting view of their friends' girls. Guy code.

We are only a few feet from the other guys, and Kevin turns to me and says, "Are you sure you're okay?"

"Yeah, I'm fine."

By now several North kids have come out of the party, and as I catch bits of the story in their chatter, they apparently have heard of the scene we just left. Terrific, just what I want to be—the center of attention.

Andrea walks up like she is the queen and stands right next to Kevin. *Could this get any worse?*

"Hey, Kevin."

"Andrea," Kevin says with clear frustration.

"Laura had to leave early, and since you live down the street, I told her you would take me home. Hope that's okay." *What?*

"What?" Kevin says, turning to Andrea. He glances at me and then at Chris. Clearly frustrated, he pulls Andrea by her arm a few steps away and starts talking to her.

While Kevin is momentarily distracted, Chris steps closer to me, but on my far left so I need to turn to talk to him. He asks, "You sure you're okay?"

As I try to eavesdrop on Kevin and Andrea, who clearly are sharing intense words, I say, "Yes, I'm fine. You really saved me in there. That was ... well, it was really nice of you." I look up at him again.

"Like I said, anytime you need anything, Lindsey." *Sigh.*

Then Elizabeth and the rest of the Fab Five come over. Elizabeth stands right next to Chris, visibly claiming her turf.

"Hey, Chris," she says with a big grin.

"Hey," he replies in her general direction.

What a night this has turned out to be. First I have no one to talk to, then I get saved by Chris Buckley and think maybe I have an amazing ride home, and now I'm back to being alone.

I see Melissa and Elena come out and head over to the growing crowd. I glance over to Chris, who is still standing next to me with Elizabeth chattering away at him. Melissa comes over and grabs my arm. "Are you okay? What happened?"

"I'm fine. Nothing happened. Just some guy being a jerk."

I notice Chris looking over at me. Kevin returns, looking very frustrated. "Melissa, do you mind if I take Lindsey home?" I'm flustered by my own reaction to this. On the one hand, I was hoping

Chris or Kevin would be *asking me* if they can take me home, and on the other hand, I love how guys take control of situations.

"Oh. Of course, that's fine. See ya, Lindsey," she says while giving me a knowing look.

"Bye, guys," I call back, with a private look to her that says I have no idea what is going on.

"Bye, Lindsey," Chris says in a deliberate attempt to get my attention.

"Bye, Chris," I say and realize that he just gave me a smile and a wink. What does that mean? Does he have any idea I notice everything he does? No time for that now.

By this point, the party is really breaking up and kids are pouring out of the house.

Andrea is walking away with some other guy but keeps looking back at Kevin. Interesting.

"Ready?" Kevin asks, looking at me.

"Sure."

As we walk toward where I assume his car is, Kevin takes my hand. Walking down the road, he pulls me close—so close our arms are touching from shoulder to hands. I'm still keyed up from the evening when he asks, "You okay?"

"Yeah."

"Sorry that guy gave you trouble."

"That's okay. I … um … I guess I thought you were giving Andrea a ride home," I say, surprising myself with my directness.

"That was *never my* plan," he says firmly.

"Oh, so what was your plan?" I ask, feeling a little victorious as I recognize that I actually sounded a bit coy.

"My plan?" he asks, looking down at me.

"Yeah, your plan?" I repeat.

"Well, my plan was to offer to take you home," he says, smiling and watching me for my reaction.

"I see," is all I can say, as I'm still so tense from the party. When we reach his car, he opens my door and closes it after I get in. I sit there completely self-conscious of my hands in my lap, wondering if he will take my hand again.

"Ready?" he asks.

"Yep," I say, noting his two hands on the steering wheel.

Then, placing one arm over the back of my seat to back out, he moves closer to me, and I am suddenly hypersensitive to everything happening around me. I force myself to keep looking forward and freeze my entire body. "I'm sorry you had a bad night," he says, and he leans in and lightly kisses my cheek.

I can't think. As soon as we start moving forward, he grabs my hand from my lap, pulls it into his, and moves them both so that our hands rest on the console between us. I'm reminded of Chris holding my hand. On the drive home, Kevin squeezes my hand a few times. I can't believe what a surge of excitement this one gesture gives me. As we pass the twins' place, I can't help but wonder where they are. Glancing down the empty road, I wonder where Chris is. Is he driving Elizabeth home? Nearing my house, I'm terrified that Kevin might want to kiss me. I don't know what to do. Oh, man. What if he finds out I have no idea what to do? Worse, what if he finds out I'm a bad kisser? Oh, man.

As we pull into my driveway, I'm wishing it was endless so that I didn't have to let go of his hand and deal with whatever is coming next.

"What time do you have to be home?" he asks.

"Midnight; why? Are we late?" I ask, feeling a bit frantic.

"No. You're twenty minutes early. Want to walk down to your dock?"

"Sure." *What does that mean?* Kevin parks his car and squeezes my hand one last time before letting go to get out of the car. I get out on my side, grabbing my purse on the way.

"The path is this way," I say as I gesture to the right of the house.

Kevin reaches his hand out to grab mine. "Okay. Let's go."

I smile back at him and move closer to him as he holds my hand,

and we start down the path. Hearing something in the woods, I turn to see what it is.

"What?" he asks, looking back for an instant.

"Nothing. I thought I saw … nothing. Sorry," I say as I am not sure what I saw. *A car moving? A person?*

At the back of the house, he squeezes my hand again, and that is all I can think about.

He says, "It's really nice back here."

"Yeah, it's pretty cool."

"So, are your parents home?"

"Yeah. They're probably asleep, or waiting to hear the alarm chime so they know I'm home."

"Oh, um, should you go in and turn it off so they don't worry?"

"No. It's fine."

"Let's go over here." I am so excited that he wants to hold my hand, but I feel like this must be it. He is going to kiss me, right?

We continue to walk off the path into the grass. Quickly it gets dark as we move away from the area near the house, which is brightened by the landscape lights. Then Kevin stops and turns me so that we are facing each other. He looks down at me and grabs both my hands in his. My stomach tightens and my heart starts pounding in my chest.

"Hey."

"Hey."

"Look, Lindsey, I'm sorry about Andrea and that guy," he starts. "I should have just taken you to the party myself, and none of that would have happened." Then he lets go of my left hand and takes his right hand to pull back a stray hair that blew across my face. "I wouldn't have let you out of my sight." He keeps his hand on my face. Pulling my face toward his, he leans down to kiss me. As his lips gently touch mine, I shut my eyes. He lets go of my hand, which has me pulling away from him for an instant as I assume he doesn't want to continue the kiss. In that same instant, his right hand gently holds my face against his, and his left hand wraps around me, pulling me a step closer to him. I feel so self-conscious as I tentatively put my hands on his arms. He presses his lips to mine. It is such a nice moment.

I become self-conscious again and start to pull away. He lets us part lips, but we still stand very close. I open my eyes to see him opening his as well. Then he smiles. I am so relieved.

"I better let you get inside." And with that, he gives me one more quick kiss. He drapes his arm on my shoulder, and we start walking back to the front of my house.

"Are you around tomorrow?" he asks.

Looking up at him, with a smile I reply, "Yeah."

At the door he grabs both my hands, squeezes them, and leans in to give me a quick kiss. While still close to me, he says in a hushed tone, "Sleep well. I'll call you tomorrow, okay?"

"Sounds good. Thanks for the ride."

"Sure. Good night, Lindsey."

"Good night," I say as I let go of his hands and go inside.

All's well that ends well.

A high school party. A run-in with a Neanderthal. A kiss with Kevin. But the reel I replay over and over in my mind is Chris stepping in to save me. One look from him seems to fuel endless energy. A look. A touch. A shared moment. Does he even notice these moments? Does he know they change me?

11 HOMECOMING DANCE: *I'M IN WAY OVER MY HEAD.*

AS I SLIP MY dress over my head, the nervous excitement is building. My dress is sapphire blue to match my eyes and has a touch of iridescence in it. The bodice is fitted, as I would get lost in any style that is too full. My shoes are fantastic; Mom let me get a pair of delicate heels, which have a fabric tie that crosses in front of my ankles and forms a small bow at the back. It is my purse that I am most psyched about. Mom let me splurge a bit, and we picked a small clutch with Swarovski crystals on it. I can't quite zip up the back of my dress so I head to the staircase. "Hey, Mom?"

I can hear her walking to the stairs. "Oh, Lindsey, you look terrific!"

"Thanks. Can you zip me up?"

"Sure," she says as she comes up the stairs.

"The dress really looks very nice on you. The color is perfect," she says as she pulls the zipper up the last few inches to my neck.

"Thanks, Mom."

"Excited?"

Looking down at my purse and fidgeting with its contents I reply, "Yes, completely!"

"Well, your first high school dance. Have a great time," she says as she gives me a hug from behind. "What time is Kevin coming?"

"I guess he should be here any minute."

"Okay. Well, we'll be downstairs. You know we're going to take pictures."

"Yeah, that's fine."

"Do you want me to get the door?"

"Um, I don't know. What do you think? Should I?" I ask, turning to face her as I'm weighing the pros and cons.

Ding-dong.

"Here we go," Mom says with a big smile. "Ready?"

"I guess so," I say, dashing to the mirror one more time.

"I'll get it. Come down when you're ready," Mom says as she heads for the door.

"Hello, Kevin. I'm David Brooks, Lindsey's father."

Mom and I look at each other as we hear Dad opening the door. I check my dress one more time and then grab my purse, double checking that I have my phone and wallet with me, while I overhear the exchange below.

"Hello, Mr. Brooks," Kevin responds in a rather formal manner.

"Come on in. Let me take your coat."

"Thank you, sir."

"Please have a seat. I'm sure Lindsey will be ready shortly. So, you're headed to the high school for the dance, I guess."

"Yes, sir. Well, we are planning to go to dinner first, sir."

"I see. Where are you planning to go?" I hear Dad say as I come around the bend in the stairs into the foyer. I see Kevin sitting in the living room, which is by far the most formal room in the house. Nice, Dad. As Kevin hears Mom and I come down the stairs and sees us enter the room, he stands up. No one really says anything for a minute as I finish descending the stairs, and I suddenly become completely self-conscious in the awkward silence.

"Hi, Lindsey, you look terrific," he says with a smile. Good start, but then again, standing with my parents, it probably would be impolite not to compliment me.

"Hi."

Mom jumps in as she heads down the hall. "I'll be right back with a camera; hold on for just a minute. David, can you come help me?"

"Help you do what?" my clueless father says.

"David," Mom says, with her tone that indicates she is not fooling around.

"Excuse me, Kevin," Dad says as he gets up. Winking at me, he heads to the back of the house.

Kevin takes a step closer to me and in a quiet voice says, "You really do look very pretty, Lindsey. Here, these are for you," and he hands me a nosegay with pink flowers. I smile and am happy to receive them and relieved that we do not have to navigate pinning on a corsage.

"Thank you very much," I say as I manage briefly to look him in the eyes. Mom and Dad walk back in, and I can see the smile in Mom's eyes so I throw her a glare so she won't say anything about the flowers and embarrass me.

"Okay. Can you two stand in front of the fireplace?" Mom asks.

As I turn to walk over to the fireplace, I notice that Mom has changed the candles on the mantle so that they're blue. How does she do it? She has found the time to buy candles to match my dress just for this shot. She is crazy. And amazing. I turn to face my parents and am happy to have the nosegay to hold. Kevin looks down at me with a smile and very respectfully takes a step closer so that his shoulder is just behind mine and puts his right arm behind me, just touching the small of my back.

"Oh, perfect," Mom glows. Firing off several shots, she starts to give directions as Dad rattles the ice in his cocktail. Poor Dad; he probably does need a drink tonight.

"Okay. Can you look at each other?" *Thanks, Mom.*

Taking a deep breath, we look at each other and laugh a little.

"Okay, Mom, that's enough," I say as I walk out of the portrait. Kevin follows me a few steps, and suddenly I can't wait to get out of there.

"So, Kevin, I think you were saying where you are taking Lindsey to dinner," Dad says in his best trial voice, taking command of the room. I roll my eyes.

"Yes, sir. If it's acceptable, I was planning to take her to Grand Rapids to a new restaurant, Pulse." Kevin responds like he is a witness trying to recall the details of the night in question.

"Oh, in town." Dad starts like Kevin has suggested that he take me to some unknown land. "Well, I've heard only good things about Pulse, and I trust," and with this he stops looking at his drink and puts the full force of his glare on Kevin, "you will take care of my daughter and have her home safely by midnight. Right, Kevin?"

Are you kidding? I better have fun tonight as this is likely the first and last dance I will ever get to go to.

Kevin keeps looking my dad in the eyes and doesn't miss a beat. "Yes, sir."

"Well, then, have a good evening," which is apparently Dad's way of dismissing the witness.

I take a deep breath and head to the front closet to get our coats.

"I'll get your coat, Kevin," Dad says like he is Mister Helpful.

Standing next to me, Dad whispers, "Just in case." And he hands me a wad of cash. "You know you can always call and I'll come get you, right?"

"Yeah, Dad. Thanks," I say in a heartfelt way, looking up at him with a smile I can't contain. I feel a little bad for him. Tonight must be as nerve-racking for him as it is exciting for me. Then there is this awkward moment where Dad doesn't know what to do. I can see the mental calculation in his face. Should he help put Kevin's coat on or just hand it to him? Men. They always choose the power play. He holds up Kevin's coat so that he can slip into it. I give Dad a knowing glare. Nice move.

"Bye," I say to them both, grabbing my purse off the table.

Kevin opens the door and holds the storm door open for me.

Looking back, I call bye one more time, but Dad is clearly not done making Kevin understand who is in charge.

"Kevin," he says to get his attention, "I expect you to respect the Brooks name and bring her home to me ... well, uh, safely this evening."

Are you kidding me? "Respect the Brooks name"? What are you doing?

"Yes, sir," is all Kevin says.

Rolling my eyes, I head to the car. Nightmare.

"Sorry about that," I say as we walk down the path next to each other.

"No problem, I figured as much," Kevin says, shrugging it off.

"You did?"

"Kind of. I mean, he is a big trial attorney, right?"

"Yeah. So?"

"So, I just figured. Anyway, you really do look fantastic, Lindsey," he says as we approach his car.

I force myself to look at him and say, "Thanks." As I catch his eyes for a moment, we both smile, and I finally take a real breath. He opens my door. I climb in and adjust my dress as best I can so I can cross my legs without showing too much leg. Kevin walks around the back of the car and turns the heat up for me as soon as he gets in.

"I told my folks that we would stop by my house for pictures. I hope that's okay."

"Um, you think your dad's going to make me promise to get you home safe?" I ask with exaggerated emphasis.

"Oh, he'll probably ask you to sign an agreement before we leave."

"Nice," I say with a smile, as I'm pleased we're off to a good start.

We are quiet driving to his house. I'm very conscious of holding my flowers as he has not taken my hand. Arriving at his house, I get a pang of anxiety that I won't know the right things to say and do inside.

"Ready?" he asks.

"Sure," I say as I start to get out of the car.

As we walk up the steps to the front door, his mom opens the door and with a huge smile says, "Hello, Lindsey, don't you just look lovely."

"Thank you, Mrs. Walker."

"I'm so glad you stopped by. Isabella and Rick are still here, and I would love to get a picture of all of you together," she continues as we enter the foyer.

"Hi, Lindsey," Mr. Walker says as he shakes my hand.

"Hello, Mr. Walker."

"Hi, Lindsey! Hey, Kevin," Isabella calls over from the living room.

"Hi, Isabella. Hi, Rick."

"Hey," says Rick. Man of few words.

"Here, let me take your coat, Lindsey," Kevin says from behind me.

We all pose for several pictures as couples and as a foursome. Then Mrs. Walker asks, "Do you girls mind if I get one of just the boys?"

"No problem," Isabella replies for us both, which is fine by me. Then we all say good night, and no one mentions what time anyone has to be home. It is so much better to be a guy. My dad has probably already set a timer so he'll know the second I'm late.

&ɔ☙

We finally pull up to a restaurant that has Christmas lights all around the awning and is filled with candles inside.

"Oh, is this it?" I ask; I can't help but gawk at the restaurant.

"Yeah, that's Pulse; you like it?" Kevin asks as he U-turns and finds a spot to park on the street down the block.

"Oh yeah, it looks so pretty," I reply and immediately think I should have thought of something clever to say.

"Let's go," he says as he starts to open his door, so I do the same on my side. Kevin comes around to my side of the car to join me. Walking with me, he puts his hand on the small of my back. I'm so excited to be here and to be going to the dance, I can't help but smile. He uses his hand to guide me between the cars as we cross the street and head to the restaurant.

"I wonder if Andrew and Lynn are here already," Kevin says as he opens the front door to the restaurant. "There they are," he adds.

"Good evening. May I take your coats?"

"Sure," I say as I slip out of mine. I'm so glad Mom had the foresight this fall to get me a nice full-length coat. How does she always know just what to do? Kevin gives them both to the hostess and tells her we see our friends. As we approach the table, I'm hoping that Lynn will be nice to me. I don't know her that well, so I really don't know what to expect. I smile nervously as we approach the candlelit table. Andrew and Lynn both stand up, which I find a promising start. The guys shake hands and say "hey" to each other, and I'm suddenly reminded of my dad greeting a business associate. Then Andrew comes around the table to give me a hug, which I'm both shocked by and grateful for.

"You look terrific, Lindsey," he says as gives me a warm and very close embrace. Why am I so conscious anytime I make physical contact with a guy? Does he know that he just smashed my chest against his?

"Hi, Lynn," I try.

"Hey, Lindsey," she says with a smile.

"Great dress," I continue, in hopes of warming the atmosphere.

"Thanks. I love your purse," she replies as we all sit down. I sit next to Kevin and across from Andrew.

The waitress comes over and takes our drink order. Dressed in suits and cocktail dresses, it feels a little weird that we all get sodas, but I guess restaurants have high school kids come in all the time and do the same thing.

ᏸᏟᏰ

The guys, who have been doing most of the talking, turn the conversation to who is the strongest in the class.

"I think Jason is. He's a linebacker and could take anyone," Kevin says of one of our football team's linemen.

"Yeah, but David, that sophomore wrestler, seems pretty tough to me."

I haven't said anything yet during dinner and we are almost done with our entrees, so I'm feeling very self-conscious that I am, as usual, going to be seen as the quiet one. Summoning up some courage, I decide to jump in.

"I bet I could give them a run for their money," I say, without looking up. Everyone stops. They stop talking; they stop eating; they stop everything. For a second, no one moves at the table except me.

"What?" Andrew asks and is smiling at me and then looks around. Kevin is staring at me, so I look over at him.

"I, um, I don't ... uh, what do you mean? Any of those guys could bench-press you," Kevin says, with a bit of a shocked face while he is clearly trying to be polite to me but cannot get over what I just said.

"They could bench-press her one-handed," Andrew adds with a smirk.

"Oh, of course, they could," I say as I look around and realize I have their complete attention. "No, I guess I mean on a pound-for-pound basis."

"Oh, okay, you win. You are probably the lightest girl in the entire high school," Andrew jabs through a bit of a laugh as he pokes Lynn with his elbow. I look at her and realize she thinks I'm claiming to be the thinnest girl at school, and she is momentarily not pleased.

"No, no, what I mean is … okay, I bet with certain things I could give them a run for their money."

"You mean like who can do the most flips? Yeah, you probably win that too," Kevin says. I can tell he is glad that at least I'm finally talking, so I decide to keep going.

"Okay, yeah, that may be true, but I mean, take abs strength. I bet I can do more sit-ups in a minute than any of those guys."

"Really? So you can take Jason and David," Kevin asks and is clearly captivated by the banter.

"Yep," I say with an unusual wash of confidence, which also has Andrew and Lynn intrigued.

"So, who else do you think you could take in a sit-up contest?"

"Hmmm, let me see," I say, wiping my mouth with my napkin, which adds to my deliberate pause. "I guess I could take just about everyone I know. Oh, well, there is one exception, of course," and as I deliver these last few words, I look up at Kevin with a grin so that they all assume I'm trying to play up to him. But as soon as he smiles, I turn to Andrew and say, "Jennifer. You know she really has very strong …" and I'm interrupted by Andrew's outburst of laughter as he looks at Kevin and says, "Oh, she got you good. Good for you, Lindsey!" He makes a fist and we bump knuckles.

"Nice," Kevin says as he puts his arm around the back of my chair. As I take a drink of soda, I find it interesting that both Kevin and Andrew seem to really enjoy my jabbing Kevin.

As the waitress clears the dishes, she asks if we want dessert. Although I love dessert, I decline as I don't want to cost Kevin any more money and want to be polite. So Kevin asks for the check, and we decide to head to the dance. I'm sure that Kevin and Andrew will pay the check, but just in case, I delay leaving the table until after the bill arrives so that I can at least offer to pay.

"Thank you all for coming in this evening," the waitress says. As she starts to place the bill on the table, Kevin grabs it out of the air.

"Thank you," he says and pulls a credit card from his wallet.

Reaching for my purse between us on the floor, I say softly to him, "Can I please ..."

"No, I got it," and with that he puts a credit card in the folio and hands it to Andrew, who already has his card out as well.

"Thank you," I add while looking him right in the eyes, which of course unnerves me and seems to make him happy. So I foolishly smile and turn away. As I'm fidgeting with my purse, I'm fairly certain he is still looking down at me smiling. Why do I have to always look away? The waitress quickly returns the folio to the table and thanks us again.

"Shall we?" Andrew says, and I'm reminded of Jon, as this is the first half of our daily greeting. I hope he's having fun tonight.

"Sure," Lynn says, "I can't wait to get to the dance."

As we head over to the coat check, I say to Kevin, "Hey, I'm gonna stop in the ladies' room."

"Okay, I'll meet you at the front."

As I head to the bathroom, I'm selfishly happy. I'm glad to have a few minutes to myself before the dance. I'm happy that Lynn did not come to the bathroom with me as girls are fabled to do with other girls. I wonder if this is a sign that Lynn was just being nice at dinner and doesn't really like me. For the moment, however, I don't care, as I'm delighted to let my guard down, even if it is just for two minutes. While there, I look in the mirror to check my teeth to be sure nothing is stuck in them all night. I touch up my makeup and put some fresh lip gloss on. Then I start a mental debate: if I put a mint in, does it look like I want to kiss him and is that too forward; versus if I don't put a mint in and he does kiss me, is that some kind of dating faux pas? I play it safe and pop in the mint. One more look up and down to be sure my dress isn't caught somewhere it shouldn't be, and I head back out. As I walk through the restaurant, I chew up the mint to get its benefit while destroying the evidence. I see Kevin smiling at me, with his overcoat already on.

"Ready?" he asks as he slips my coat on for me.

"Sure, did they already go?" I ask as I pull my hair out of the collar.

"Yeah. They just took off; come on." He puts his arm around me again as we cross the street. I notice he is nice enough to come over to open the passenger door even though he had already used the remote to unlock the car.

As I get in, I try to quickly fix my dress so that it covers as much of my legs as possible before he gets in and notices. Or is he watching from the back as I shift it?

He gets in, checks his cell phone, and says that some of the guys are already at the dance. As he backs out of the parking space, I notice two guys coming out of an alley.

Gasping, I involuntarily jump a little.

"What?" he asks as he looks first at me and then to where I'm looking.

"Sorry. I'm sorry; I thought that second guy had something— there!" I say as I freeze where I am. Kevin sees it too. *What is it? Something shiny—a knife?* Kevin immediately locks the doors.

"Do they have something ..." I ask as I'm stiffening by the second.

"I don't know and I don't plan to find out; hold on," Kevin says as he backs up in a spurt and then guns the car forward. We are only ten feet from the light, which just turned red. Kevin looks both ways and floors it through the intersection anyway. Dad's words are flashing in my mind as we pick up speed. I gasp again and slam one hand down on the armrest and bring the other up to my chest as I'm pressed back into the seat from the force of the burst of speed.

"Wasn't that light red?"

"I think it was."

I notice that Kevin is looking in the rearview mirror, so I look in the side mirror and ask, "Can you see them?"

"They just ran and jumped in a car that was behind us about half a block."

"Are they ..."

"Yes." And with that he pushed the gas pedal even farther. I put both arms on the dashboard to brace myself.

"They're coming?"

"I don't know …"

Taking a deep breath, I look out the back window and see headlights gaining on us.

"What should we do?"

"Hold on." As we race down the street, I wonder if we are heading in the right direction, as I really don't know this city at all.

"Do you know where you're going?"

"Yes," is all he says as he intently looks back and forth from the rearview mirror to the front window.

"They are catching up to us. I just need one more block."

"I can see them coming up on my side!" I say as I see the headlights approaching.

Suddenly Kevin hits the brakes and puts his turn signal on to turn left. The car coming after us slows for a second, and then as we turn left into a police station, they race past us so fast I can't even make out faces through their heavily tinted windows. Kevin pulls into the lot and circles around the station to pull back out on the road.

"Do you think they were following us?"

"No idea. Doubt it; probably just a coincidence. Hey," he says in an affectionate tone as he takes my hand. Then he pulls my still-very-tense hand off the console between us and wraps it inside his. "Hey, we're gonna have a great time at the dance."

"Yeah," I say, looking over to him for an instant, smiling.

"You know, Lindsey, I'm really glad you came to homecoming with me."

As I lean my head back in the seat, I can't help but smile. My first dance. He turns to look at me, so, of course, I turn my head toward the front window and avoid his gaze.

&CB

As we pull up to the school, I realize that, for dances, all of the students park in the faculty lot, which is closer to the cafeteria, where the dance is being held. This minor factoid reminds me that I really don't know anything about dances. Suddenly I feel butterflies in my stomach.

Getting out of the car, I'm filled with anticipation, excitement, nerves, and questions. Will he ask me to dance? I can do a double back on floor exercise in gymnastics, but can I dance with a guy? Will Kevin ask Andrea to dance? Will he leave me to talk to the guys? Will I be left alone? Will I get a chance to talk to Melissa and Elena? Will I see Jon and his date here? Will anyone ask me to dance? Will this be the only high school dance I ever go to? Will Dad be waiting at the door when we get home? I'm in way over my head. Then I remember the nosegay of flowers that Kevin gave me—should I bring them into the dance or leave them in the car? Quickly I scan the parking lot and see two senior girls carrying similar bouquets. Okay, take the flowers inside.

I feel Kevin's hand in the small of my back again as we approach the school's side entrance. We enter the building and turn into the cafeteria. How nice it looks. Kids have hung streamers all over, and there are tables along the sides with tablecloths and flowers. There is a balloon arch for photos on one side and a DJ up front. I smile as I look around and see all the other kids and the cafeteria dressed up for the evening.

"Come on; there's Andrew," Kevin says as he nods in the direction of a group of couples standing near the tables. Kevin greets the guys, as several of the girls tell me how nice I look and I return their compliments.

Then I hear Kevin whispering to Andrew. I catch only a few words, but they make it clear he is asking Andrew if they saw anyone when they left the restaurant. I can't tell what Andrew is saying. They keep talking in hushed tones, so I turn to see who I can talk to as I don't want to be standing alone. I see Melissa and wonder if it would be rude to head over and talk to her. I want to do the right thing, so I stay put, in hopes that Kevin will come back over. There are only a few couples dancing right now. I'm not sure if it is just that no one dances at a dance or if it's just too early. Kevin walks by with Andrew, stopping to say he'll be right back. Great. On my own, and I have only been here five minutes. Looking back at Melissa, I see she is out on the dance floor. I give her a big smile as she looks my way.

I decide to get some punch to kill some time. As I reach for the ladle, Jon comes up and hands me a full cup.

"Here you go, Lindsey. You look fantastic."

Love the Crush.

"Thanks, Jon. You look very handsome yourself." Oh. I just realized I haven't told Kevin how nice he looks. Hmmm. Maybe I should. Maybe it's too late.

"Thanks. You been here long?"

"No. Just got here, but the cafeteria looks great, doesn't it?" I ask as I turn back to face the dance floor.

"Yeah. It really does. I better get back to my date. Maybe I'll see you later?" he says to me. Smile.

"Okay, Jon. Great to see you." And it really was, but now I'm on my own again. Wait a minute—is Kevin talking to Andrea again? Okay. Seriously, is she after him, or is he really still after her? I am determined not to watch, but just then Kevin looks at me, and so I start to walk away.

Seeing Elena, I head in her direction.

"Elena, you look terrific!" I say as we exchange a hug and a kiss on the cheek.

"You look adorable, Lindsey!"

"Thanks." As we stand there chatting, I try to be nonchalant about seeing what Kevin is up to with that witch, Andrea.

"Looking for someone?" I hear from behind and turn around to see Kevin smirking at me.

"Want to dance?" he asks, and I say, "Sure." We head over to the dance floor, where a slow song is playing. Suddenly I'm terrified as I realize I haven't danced with anyone since eighth grade when I danced with Chris Buckley.

As Kevin picks a spot for us to dance, I notice that the entire soccer team is slowly walking onto the dance floor with their dates. At least we won't be alone. Quickly I check to see how the senior girls stand so I can try to mimic what they are doing. No time to worry. In a flash, Kevin has one of his arms around my waist and is guiding my right arm up to his shoulder. Thank goodness he is taking the lead. I put both my arms on his shoulders and feel him pull me in toward him with his two arms behind my back.

Somehow I can feel where he is looking even though I'm looking past him to watch the other couples sway to the slow beat. He has me close to him, but not so much so that I feel pressed; just close enough that I'm nervous I'm going to step on him. Why is he watching Andrea?

Thankfully, the next several songs are fast, so I don't have to worry about that. I actually love to dance, and it feels great to dance with a room full of students all acting a bit crazy.

After a few songs, I see some other people leave the dance floor, so I suggest the same to Kevin. "How about we take a break?"

"Good idea. It's getting hot in here. You want some punch?"

"Sure."

As we head over to the punch table, I take a quick look at my watch and realize it is already nine forty-five. The dance only goes till eleven.

"I'm gonna go to the ladies' room; I'll be right back, okay?"

"Yeah, sure. I'm gonna go too—I'll meet you back here, okay?"

"Okay."

After checking my hair, I head back to the punch table. No sign of Kevin. Where does he go? Everyone else seems to stay near their date. I grab another cup of punch so I look like I have some reason to be here. Then I see Kevin dancing with Andrea. *Slow dancing. Are you kidding me?* They're a couple inches apart, but she is looking right at him and talking with a big grin on her face. Where is her date?

I have no idea what to do. A very popular song is playing, and everyone seems to be on the dance floor. I turn to grab something. Cookies. Okay. I'll eat a cookie. I didn't have dessert at dinner.

I would have ordered dessert if I knew I'd be left alone half the night.

Then one of the teacher chaperones comes up to me to chat. Great. The entire time I'm trying to be polite to him, I'm wondering what my date is doing. Then I feel someone touch my arm.

"Hey, Lindsey," Chris says to me while looking out on the dance floor. Sigh.

"Hi, Chris." Wow, he looks even better in a suit.

"Having fun?" he asks, with his eyes still roaming the dance floor. I wonder if he has lost his date as well.

"Oh yeah. Great dance."

"Would you like to dance, Lindsey?" he says, and now he looks at me and puts his hand on my arm as he starts to lead me out to the floor before I can even respond.

"Um, well," I stammer, as I'm not sure if I should be dancing with someone else while I'm on a date. *What am I thinking?* My date is dancing with his supposed ex, so, yes, I should dance. Without waiting for my reply, Chris pulls me into him so that we are close but not touching except where he is holding my right hand and has his left around my waist. Is this Chris being respectful of the fact that I'm here on a date with someone else, or is it how friends dance? Or does Chris actually want to dance with me? I am seriously enjoying this dance way too much. Does Chris know?

"Having fun?" Chris asks again. *Read my mind much?*

"Yes." I wonder if he knows I mean I am enjoying this dance more than any other of the night. Trying hard not to move my fingers at all, I am acutely aware of each spot our hands touch.

"Do you remember our first dance?"

My breath catches as I stop dancing for a moment. Chris pulls me in closer. He shifts our hands so that our fingers are interlaced, and my heart quickens as I shut my eyes in delight. It feels too good.

Like a blissful dream interrupted, I feel another arm on my waist so I immediately pull back to see who it is. As I do, I hear Kevin say in an agitated tone, "May I cut in?"

And with that, he takes me in his arms and pulls me tight up against his chest, looking at Chris during the exchange.

As we turn, I look for Chris, who is watching me intently. Our eyes lock for an instant before he winks at me and turns around to leave the dance floor. Okay—that was intense.

"Sorry," I say to Kevin, although I'm not sure I really am.

"Don't be sorry," he replies.

"I … um … I saw you dancing with Andrea … and then Chris asked me to dance, so …" I start looking around the room.

"I'm the one who should be sorry. I should never have danced with Andrea. You were in the bathroom and the song *was* a fast one, so I figured one dance was no big deal. Of course, it didn't take Mister Charming over there long to find you, did it?" he says as he pushes me away just enough to look at me. I force a smile. Why couldn't you have just let me finish one dance with Chris? As I look around, my smile turns genuine, looking at all the kids at my first dance. Relishing my thoughts, I look at him, soaking up his attention. When I break the look and turn my head, he pulls me closer and rests his head on mine, gently pushing my head onto his chest. Fortunately the music continues with two more slow songs, so I get to enjoy the moment for a while longer.

Soon the DJ picks up the pace, and the floor is packed with kids dancing in small groups. We dance to several popular songs, and seeing all my friends dancing and laughing is fun.

The music ends and the DJ announces he'll be playing the last song of the night. It is a very upbeat one. Kevin starts to lead me off the dance floor. I notice Chris, who is standing with Elizabeth in a large group of couples, glancing over at us. I think Kevin noticed too because he grabs my hand and pulls me closer to him asking, "You ready to get out of here?"

"Sure."

We get our coats, and I head over to Melissa and Elena to say good night. Kevin says good night to a group of seniors, and then he and Andrew whisper to each other, bump knuckles, and smile.

We are quiet heading to the car, but I couldn't be much happier with how the evening has gone. Kevin is holding my hand. I danced with Chris! All in all, this has been a great night.

It isn't until after we get in the car that the internal panic button goes off. What do seniors do after a dance? What does he think we are doing? Oh man.

"I talked to Andrew earlier about the guys at the restaurant. He said that when he and Lynn left, two guys came out of the alley, saw them, and went back in the alley. They were parked right next to it, so when the two guys came out, they were literally right next to Lynn."

"Really?"

"Yeah, and one of them even said 'sorry' to Lynn for startling her."

"That's weird."

Why are we talking about this? "Do you think I did something wrong?" I ask, because I am totally confused.

"You? No, not at all," and with that he grabs my hand, which helps me to relax. As we continue to drive, I start to wonder where we're going. Then I realize we are headed to my house. I'm starting to wish that we had more time as this was such a good night, one I know I will remember for a very long time. Unconsciously I gently squeeze his hand with mine. I become aware of my action when I feel more of a response than I could ever have predicted. He looks at me and pulls my hand onto his leg. Okay—my hand is now on his leg. I am suddenly afraid to move a muscle—so I don't, until we pull into my driveway. I try to see where my parents are in the house. Will Dad be greeting us at the door?

As Kevin parks the car, he lets go of my hand and opens the driver's door. I take a deep breath, open my door, and step out. Walking around the front of the car, Kevin meets me with an open hand, which I gladly take.

"I hope you had fun, Lindsey," he says as he bumps me a bit with his shoulder in a playful gesture and turns to face me.

"Oh, I did," I say, looking up at him now. As I continue, he takes my hands and steps closer, and I say, "Thank you so much."

"I'm the one who should thank you. Sorry about those guys outside the restaurant."

"Oh, that was nothing. You got us out of there, and we didn't even get a ticket," I say, trying to move on.

Then he kisses me. Suddenly I think of Chris. I break the embrace and pull back. As we look at each other, I say, "I better go in; I think it must be around midnight."

"Actually you're a half hour early. I didn't want to cut it too close in case dear ol' dad is around." This makes us both smile.

"Well, thanks again," I say as I step away.

He pulls me in one more time for a quick kiss. "I'll call you, okay?"

"Okay," I say and turn to enter my house.

Creeping up the stairs in my still house, a smile emerges across my face. I can't believe Chris remembers our first dance.

12 AUDITIONS: *SHOULD YOU TRUST ME? ALWAYS.*

MONDAY AFTERNOON AFTER AUDITIONS, Chris and I leave the auditorium and head over to my locker to get my backpack. As we get close to my locker, he slows down and turns toward me so that my back is toward the wall. Standing directly in front of me, he says, "So, trust me to get you home safely?" and moves a half step closer to me. Instinctively I step back, brushing my hair against the wall behind me.

"Should I?"

"Should *you* ...?" he emphasizes as he leans his left arm against the wall above my right shoulder.

"Should I ... trust you?" I say teasingly, with half a smile. As I hear myself say it, something between us shifts ever so slightly. He holds my eyes. Is it me? Is it him?

In a slightly more serious tone and with a barely perceptible physical shift, so he appears a fraction taller, he declares, "Should you trust me? Always." I blink. Suddenly I'm not sure we are talking about a ride home. I'm not really sure what it is we are talking about. He looks at me and I feel frozen.

We look at each other for a moment too long.

Wow. My stomach drops. *Why would that happen?* I look down. Before I can fully process what is transpiring between us, he leans in and bumps my left arm with his right and jokingly asks, "So, how about that ride?"

"Sure, thanks. Let me text my mom so she knows she doesn't need to pick me up," I answer as I pull my phone out and send my mom a quick text.

"You totally got the part of Van Helsing," I say as we start to walk down the hall toward the student parking lot.

"I hope so. You're the perfect Mina."

"Doubt that. But I'll definitely come see the play!" I say, looking up at him with a grin.

"Nice," he says as he bumps my arm. *Nice.*

"I can't believe we'll know later tonight who's in and who's out. I'm nervous," I admit.

"Well, at least we'll know quickly. I wonder how long it'll take them to post the names on the website. Here, wait, let me check," Chris says as he pulls out his phone.

"You think Mrs. McKnight will have it posted already?"

"Well, she's probably already decided, so why not?"

"Hey, Chris," calls Mrs. McKnight from down the hall. We both look up from his phone and then glance at each other as she walks over to us.

"Hi, Mrs. McKnight."

"Hi, Lindsey."

"We were actually just checking the website," Chris says with a hopeful smile. Exchanging a quick glance with him, I know we are both hoping she has some good news for us.

"Well, that is exactly what I wanted to talk to you about. Chris, I was hoping to catch you before you left. Do you have a minute?"

"Uh," he says, giving me a quick look of indecision.

"Oh, no problem, my mom will pick me up," I say as I step away.

"Oh, Chris, are you taking Lindsey home?"

"Well, I was planning to."

"I only need about five minutes."

"Oh, okay. Lindsey, here, take my keys. I'll meet you at my car, okay?"

"Sure. Good night, Mrs. McKnight," I say as I take the keys and walk away. I am determined not to look back at them. As I open the door to go outside, the cold air sends a shiver down my spine while my mind tries to deal with the fact that I probably didn't get a part in the play. Wrapping my arms around myself and leaning into the wind, I realize that if I had gotten a part, Mrs. McKnight would probably have told me. I wonder why she wants to talk to Chris. Maybe he is not getting Van Helsing, after all. I knew it would be hard for us to bump the seniors when there are so few parts in this play, but I thought Chris would make it. I hurry over to his car. Sitting in his car out of the wind, I decide that it's probably better not to be in the play anyway. It would just cut into my gymnastics and studying time.

I see Chris open the door across the street as he leaves the school, but I can't see his expression because he's too far away. As he walks toward me, he has his collar up and his shoulders hunched against the wind. He seems to be trying to avoid looking at me, which I realize is very uncharacteristic. As he gets in the car, I'm both nervous and excited to hear his news.

"That wind is brutal," he says, sitting down and rubbing his hands together for warmth.

"Okay, so what did she say?"

"Who? Mrs. McKnight?"

"No, the Queen of England," and with that, he gives me a big smile. Then he tries to compose his face and be more serious.

"You sure you want to know?"

"Look, if you know I didn't make it, just tell me. It's fine. What did she want to talk about?" I ask, hoping that I did make it.

"Okay. First, you need to promise me something."

"What?" I say, giving him a cautious look as I'm suddenly suspicious.

"That either way, since one of the nights the play is on is Halloween, you will go out with the cast and crew after the show." Before I can even respond, he says, "That's my condition. Come on; there will be a huge Halloween party somewhere anyway, but you have to promise to go with us or you have to wait to find out."

"So you know?"

"Yes."

"To be clear, you know about both of us?"

"Yes. Now promise," and as he says this, he turns to me and gives me the biggest smile. What else can I do? I don't think I could deny him anything.

"Fine, I promise," I say, bracing for the inevitable disappointment. Biting my lip, I take a breath.

"Well, she wanted to talk to me about taking a different part."

"What did you get?"

"Dracula," he says in his best overly dramatic Transylvanian accent.

"I knew it! I knew you would be perfect as Dracula! That's so cool. Aren't you excited?"

"Yes. Very." Then he just looks down and away from me. Here we go. Nightmare. We might as well get it over with.

"Look, don't feel bad, it's fine. I knew I would get cut. I hardly have any time anyway. Just say it," and with that, I look away and realize I'm holding my breath.

"Well," he says, looking down at the steering wheel, "Mrs. McKnight said she felt really bad." I knew it. My shoulders seem to drop a bit as I press my lips together.

"Because she forgot to tell you when she saw you that you got Mina!" he bursts out. I snap my head up to look at him, and we both have huge smiles.

"Are you kidding?"

"No, I'm not. She said that she thought we would both be good in the play, and when she saw our chemistry together on stage, she thought that we would be the most convincing pair to play Dracula and the object of his intense interest, Miss Mina," he says with such emphasis I can tell he is mocking Mrs. McKnight. "Isn't this great!"

"Yes," I say, and I can't help closing my eyes briefly to soak it all in.

"Wait, so why did you make me promise about Halloween?" I ask. As I say this, he starts the car and turns away to back out of the parking spot. In that moment, I think he is trying to hide a smile and is deliberately avoiding both looking at me and the question.

"Chris?"

"Hmm?"

"Why?"

"Oh, I don't know. Just to take you off track, I guess."

"Oh. Do you know who else made it?"

"No. She said it would all be posted later tonight. Practice starts Wednesday morning. I can pick you up on the mornings of rehearsals."

"You sure?"

"Yeah, no big deal."

We sit quietly the rest of the ride home, and all I can think of is how much fun it will be to have a part in *Dracula* with Chris.

⁎℀℁

I walk in the house, and I'm hoping Mom and Dad are both home. I check the kitchen and see Mom getting dinner ready. Dad is out back grilling something.

"Hey, Mom, guess what?" I say, with a voice filled with excitement.

"What? Did you get it?" she asks, spinning around to look at me.

"Yes, I got Mina! Can you believe it? I'm so excited!"

"Oh, that's terrific! I knew you would do well. You'll be just wonderful as Mina."

"Thanks, Mom. Oh, and you know what else? Chris got Dracula! Which, of course, he didn't even try out for—it's gonna be awesome rehearsing with him."

"I'm sure it will."

I ignore her implicating tone and reply, "I'm going out to tell Dad."

ⅎℛ

Wednesday morning, we have an all-school assembly for first period. So the halls are filled with kids buzzing about with friends as we all head to the auditorium. Melissa and Elena both come by my locker so we can go to the assembly together. As we stand there chatting and watching all the kids start to flow toward the auditorium, Kevin walks up to us with Andrew.

I haven't heard from Kevin since the dance Saturday night.

"Hey, guys," Kevin says to our small group.

Turning toward him, I'm pleased that he stopped to talk to us.

We all sort of respond to the two of them with a collective "Hey." Kevin and Andrew step out of the way of all the kids moving through the crowded hallway so we are all standing in a small circle.

"Did you hear? Lindsey got the part! She's playing Mina in *Dracula!*" Melissa announces.

"You did? That's great!" Kevin says, looking a bit too surprised.

"Yeah," I say, glancing at Melissa, who is pleased with herself.

"Wow, you got the lead. That's really cool," Andrew adds.

"Thanks."

"I have practice tomorrow and most of this week, so I don't think I'll see you in study hall," Kevin says to me.

"Oh, okay." *Does that mean you want to see me and can't, or that you don't want to?*

"So, do you guys have plans for Friday night?" Kevin asks—but is he asking me or all of us?

Melissa reads the beat of silence between us and tries to be helpful. "No, we really haven't talked about this weekend. What about you guys?"

"Oh, well, I thought maybe we could do something Friday, Lindsey?" Before I can even process this, Melissa and Elena's excitement and impatience fill the moment.

"She'd love to!" Melissa answers for me.

Andrew smiles and turns away, clearly amused that Melissa is so excited for me. Kevin glances at Melissa and then at me.

"Yeah, that would be great." As the first bell rings, I shut my locker and we start down the hall. Kevin stays next to me and continues the conversation. "Do you have rehearsal after school Friday?"

"Yeah, but that would be right after school."

"Okay. Well, maybe I can drive you home from rehearsal and then we could go out later?"

As we head into the crowded auditorium, we agree to meet up after rehearsal Friday.

80 03

Lying in bed, my mind turns to Melissa accepting a date for me. What do seniors do on second dates? Staring up at the ceiling of my room, with a furrow in my brow, I keep seeing an image of couples on dates in movies I've seen. Fast guys with faster hands on girls. No-o-o-o, it can't be like that. That's just Hollywood. Right?

Oh, man.

13 AN EVENING AT HOME: *WHY IS EVERYTHING A CODE?*

FRIDAY AFTER SCHOOL, WE have rehearsal for the play. This is the last time that we'll rehearse around a table. The three rehearsals scheduled for this week were to ensure that we know our lines as well as the timing of each line so we don't start speaking too early and cut off another character. Tomorrow we'll begin to block the scenes, as the set designers are just finishing the backgrounds. As I enter the auditorium after school for our first reading on stage, I see all the chairs set in a circle for us and several actors are already on stage, chatting.

"Hey, Lindsey," I hear from behind me. Looking back, I see Chris just entering the darkened auditorium.

"Hey, Chris."

"Last time sitting down."

"Yeah. Do you know your lines for the whole play? I think we have to do it without the script today."

"I think so. I still have a couple of rough patches, but I should be okay. I think you knew yours a week ago, so you should have no problem."

"I don't know," I say, shaking my head, "I'm sure I'll be saying 'Line, please' a time or two."

"Have you thought about the staging yet?"

"A little; have you?"

"Yeah, I think the staging is gonna be important."

"Yeah, I wonder what our costumes look like."

"I can't wait to get my cape!" Chris says, pretending to whip a cape in front of his face.

೮೦೦೪

"Okay—great job everyone. Tomorrow we practice from four to six. Be sure to come in the main door and bring your student ID card so you can get in the building. We'll go through the staging, and as always, I want your ideas and input. This is a play about desire and the fight to save poor Lucy and Mina's soul. For some of you, this will challenge your ability to convey vulnerability, and for others dominance. See you tomorrow at four sharp," says Mrs. McKnight, ending our rehearsal.

As we break up into groups, Chris says, "Hey, I can drive you tomorrow if you want."

"Are you sure?"

"Yeah, no problem."

"I'm babysitting for the Greenburgs after rehearsal; do you mind dropping me there?"

"No problem."

As we step outside, I see Kevin in his car waiting at the curb.

"Guess your ride's here," Chris says, looking over at Kevin's car.

"Yeah, see you tomorrow."

"Yeah, see you tomorrow Mina," he says, looking over to me before he heads to the student lot.

Kevin has stepped out of his car and is waiting for me with the door open.

"Hi, Lindsey."

"Hi. Thanks for picking me up."

"No problem," he says, closing my door.

"You ready to go?" he says as he sits in the driver's seat.

"Sure."

"How was rehearsal?"

"Good. I only blew a few lines."

"After I drop you off at home now, Rick and I thought we would pick you and Isabella up at about seven tonight. Does that work?"

"Sounds good to me."

"I think we're going to get some pizza for dinner, okay?"

"Sure, whatever you want."

"Okay, and then we thought we could go hang out at our place."

"Okay."

"Our folks are going out to dinner and a movie, so we should have the place to ourselves," he says as he looks in my direction. I am convinced he is looking for my reaction.

"Oh, okay."

Buzz. He checks his phone, and I can see that it's Andrea. I look out the passenger-side window and hear him hit the ignore button. She really needs a new obsession. As we pull in my driveway, I thank Kevin for the ride and head in my house.

ಐ ೞ

As I get ready to go out, I can't help but wonder what Kevin and I are doing. Homecoming was fun, and when we hung out in study hall it was nice, but we haven't talked about our relationship or what "this" is. I'm not even sure what I want it to be. As I think about it, I've been so busy I haven't really taken the time to figure out what I want with Kevin. I've now gone to my first high school dance, have had my first date, and increased my status at school by dating one of the coolest seniors. It's just unbelievable. I'm still one of the quietest girls in my grade, but at least now I'm not invisible. As this occurs to me, I wonder how much I really like Kevin. Am I hanging out with him because he is so highly regarded by everyone? Or do I really like him? As this question runs through my mind, the doorbell rings. No time. I grab my purse and head downstairs.

"I got it," I call out, hoping Dad doesn't try to have another chat with Kevin. Apparently I'm just in time, as Mom gives me a smile and heads back to the family room.

"Do you know where you're going yet?"

"Pizza, and then I'm not sure." Not sure where in his house we will be hanging out.

"Home by midnight," Dad calls out.

"Okay."

"Have fun," Mom adds.

"Thanks," I call back as I grab the front doorknob and open the door.

"Hi, Kevin."

"Hi, Lindsey, you ready?"

"Yep." Walking down the path, I can see Isabella and Rick in the back of Kevin's car.

While we drive to town, Isabella talks almost nonstop. Although she's been vocally animated since I got in the car, I realize that I have no idea what she's saying. Refocusing on her monologue, I realize she is going on and on about some actor and all the drama in his life. I keep nodding politely and saying things like "really" or "wow," but I really couldn't care less about any of it.

At the pizza place, Kevin and Rick talk about sports and some action movie they saw recently. When the check arrives, I feel my usual wave of panic as I realize we are done with dinner and are about to go back to their house, where I'm afraid we'll be all too alone. What does Kevin think is going to happen there? He seems like such a nice guy, but all I hear about is how much guys expect. Does he expect something? He has been totally respectful so far, so why am I worried?

As we leave the pizza joint and walk over to the car, Kevin drops back a bit from Isabella and Rick, so I drop back with him.

"Hey, you were pretty quiet at dinner. You okay?"

"Oh. Sorry. Yeah, I just hadn't seen that movie and don't really follow Hollywood gossip—sorry."

"Right! She must be on the Internet all night getting all that stuff."

Arriving at his house, my stomach tightens up. I wonder what we are going to do now. I look at my watch; it's only 8:50 p.m. *Great.* We have three hours to kill. I wonder what Isabella and Rick have planned. I can only imagine what Rick has in mind.

"You guys want to watch a thriller? There's one on pay-per-view," Kevin suggests.

"Sure," chimes in Isabella as we enter their house.

"Sounds good," I say, thrilled that there is in fact a plan. Kevin is clearly surprised at my enthusiasm and seems pleased with himself. He shows us to their kitchen and asks, "Lindsey, you want a beer or soda?"

"Oh, um, how about a Diet Coke or water?" *So lame.*

"Sure. Isabella?"

"Sure, I'll take a Diet Coke as well." *What? Okay, so maybe I'm not so lame.* Kevin brings in four sodas, and I'm relieved. Before we start the movie, I ask to use the bathroom. When I come out, I hear them in the family room so I head there and suddenly feel self-conscious as I realize all the lights are out. I step slowly into the room and see that Isabella and Rick are sitting very close together on one couch and Kevin is on the other. He pats the seat next to him, which on the one hand gives me a sense of relief that I don't have to decide where to sit, and stress on the other, as this is looking a bit too cozy. Do these guys think we are all going to sit together and make out? Oh, man. Kevin starts the movie, and much to my relief, he moves next to me and takes my hand. Okay. This I can handle. The movie is suspenseful and I love a good thriller, so the time passes quickly. We all jump a few times during the critical scenes and laugh at ourselves for doing so. When I realize the movie is almost over, I start to get nervous again. What is next on the agenda?

As soon as it ends, Rick and Isabella stand up, so I start to get up as I figure we're all going somewhere. Kevin pulls my hand back to the couch and smiles at me. "Where are you going?"

"Oh, sorry." Right. I'll just stay here in the dark with you. As if he read my mind, he changes the channel to music, which fills the room. I have no idea where Isabella and Rick went, but I hear her giggle and then they are drowned out by the music. I swallow hard and sit up a bit to take a drink of my soda. As I set it down and sit back into the deep couch, Kevin leans into me. Oh, boy. I am both excited and scared to death. As he comes closer to lean across me, I press back farther into the couch. Sitting to my left, he moves his right arm behind me on the top of the couch and reaches his left hand across me onto the couch and leans on it. He closes his eyes as he presses his lips to mine. I'm still nervous, but I figure I can't be the worst kisser in the world if he is back for more. Trying to relax, I focus on how it feels. I'm suddenly self-conscious wondering what to do with my hands. I put my right hand so lightly on his side I'm not even sure he can feel it. Then I realize he must have, as his lips start to respond. His left hand slides across the couch and moves onto my waist. I move into hyperdrive, totally paranoid where his hand is going. He slides a bit closer to me on the couch, so I slide down more to keep some distance between us. Does he notice this? He must. Too much thinking going on. I pull my lips away. He lets me pull back a bit, but stays inches from my face.

"Hey," he whispers and then steals a quick kiss.

"Hey," I whisper back, daring to look him in the eyes.

He seems to be searching my eyes, then smiles and closes them again as he starts another gentle kiss. I'm again spinning in the fear of where that hand is going. Thankfully, he just squeezes my waist and continues to maintain its precarious position. His kiss gains in strength a bit. I pull away again, as I want to keep this all under control.

"It's probably getting late. Do you want me to take you home?" he asks in a hushed tone.

What does that mean? Suddenly I want to leave immediately.

"Oh, yeah," I say as I try to get up, although he doesn't move so I look directly at him.

"Lindsey, that's not what I meant, and you should know it."

"What?" *Why is everything a code?*

"Believe me," he says, shutting his eyes for a moment, "I would stay here with you, but I don't want you to get home too late, okay?"

"Okay," I say while I feel my face blushing quickly. His kisses me one more time, and stands up.

I get up and grab my jacket and purse. We start to walk toward the front door, and I ask, "Aren't we taking Isabella home?"

"Rick'll take her in my mom's car later."

As we leave the house, I think I hear them in the living room, which has the soft glow of flickering candlelight. I can't help but speculate as to what's going on in there.

∞ ∞

As I am taking off my makeup and washing my face, my mind returns to the same questions I had when I was getting ready for our date. Do I really like Kevin? If my friends hadn't said yes to this date, would I have said yes or no? Crawling into bed, I'm obsessed with trying to figure out whether I just like the attention Kevin is giving me or if I really like him. Except for the Crush, he is the first guy since elementary school who has given me the time of day and I'm enjoying the attention, but I'm not sure that I really have feelings for him. Of course I think he is a nice guy and I really do enjoy being with him, but do I feel this way simply because I like the attention from someone who is so popular? What am I doing with Kevin?

My mind naturally wanders to Chris. Just thinking of him makes my stomach drop. Wonder who makes his stomach drop.

14 PLAY REHEARSAL: *HE BARELY BRUSHES HIS LIPS TO MY NECK.*

SATURDAY MORNING. I'M A little nervous walking into the gym, which I have intentionally arrived at a bit early.

"Hey, Lindsey."

"Hi, Coach Dave."

"You're ready early."

"Yeah, I was hoping to catch you for a few minutes before practice."

"Sure, what's up?"

"Um, I wanted to let you know that I, uh, well, I um … I made the play."

"That's terrific! What part did you get?" he says with a big smile, placing his hand on my back as we walk over to the floor together.

"Mina—but you know what this means, right?"

"It means you maybe miss a few workouts. So what? You're gonna work that much harder when you're here, right?"

"Yes!" I say with such excitement and relief that he seems genuinely happy for me.

"Well, send me an e-mail with the dates and times so I can be sure to see you in the show—okay?"

"You don't have to go."

"Of course not. I want to."

"Thanks, Coach!" I feel so excited now that I run over to the floor ready for an extra-hard workout.

ℬℭ

After lunch at home, I suddenly feel exhausted and decide to take a nap before rehearsal. As usual, I fall easily into a deep sleep. I dream that I'm freezing, standing outside, in a terrible storm, without a coat. I'm all alone.

Not surprising, I wake up to find we are having a classic Midwestern torrential rainstorm with a fierce wind. As I get dressed, I can't shake off the chill from my dream. I find my confused thoughts wandering to Kevin. Do I like him or just as a friend? Slowly my mood shifts as I feel more and more excited about the play and spending time with Chris.

ℬℭ

When the doorbell rings at 3:35 p.m., I realize that I've been so preoccupied with thinking about Chris that I wasn't watching for him to arrive.

"I got it," I call to my folks, who are in the house, somewhere.

I grab my backpack, which has my homework and copy of the

script, as well as my duffel bag, for babysitting later, and hit the stairs.

Reaching for the doorknob, I wish Chris was really coming to pick me up. Not just as a friend giving me a ride, but *really* picking me up.

"Hi, Lindsey," he says, looking adorable with the hood of his coat pulled up over his head and rain running off his broad shoulders. Smiling despite the miserable weather, he is holding an umbrella for me.

"Hi, Chris. You could just have called me from your car; you didn't need to get out of it in this weather," I say as I step under the umbrella.

"I'm not going to call you when I can just ring the bell," he says, dismissing my idea.

"Well, thanks for picking me up."

"No problem."

&OCß

Arriving at school, we park in the main circle so there is not too far to run through the continuing downpour to reach the front door. I grab my backpack and pull my hood over my head, tucking my hair into the hood as best I can.

"Do you need this duffel bag?" Chris asks before we get out.

"No, that's for when I babysit."

"You need all this to babysit? What, they can't provide you dinner so you bring your own food? Hard to imagine you eat much," he asks, smiling as he zips up his jacket.

"Nice. No, they let me use their indoor pool and hot tub whenever I babysit."

"Really."

"Yep," I gloat as I start to open the door.

"Hold on; I'll come around with the umbrella," he says as he

132

turns, opens the car door, grabs the umbrella from the backseat, and slams the door—such a gentleman. How does he look so cute in this miserable weather?

⁂

Of course, Mrs. McKnight starts rehearsal right on time, and the first several scenes run fairly smoothly. We finally get to the scene in the play that I'm most nervous about. I have no idea how we're going to stage the scene where the script describes the action as:

> Mina's Bedroom
> Dracula prepares to drink of Mina's blood.
> Enter Van Helsing and Arthur.[1]

Mrs. McKnight starts, "Okay, in this scene, Mina," nodding in my direction as I stand up and enter the main stage area, "will be in a white nightgown." *What?* As she says this, I can't help but glance at Chris, who raises an eyebrow while I suspect he is only pretending to be engrossed in reading his script. Great. I get to wear a nightgown in front of the entire high school. Because wearing a leotard half my life isn't embarrassing enough, let's also put her in a nightgown under a spotlight.

"Mina," she continues as she walks over and takes my arm. "Okay, stagehands, we need the bed," she calls offstage as she leads me over to where she indicates she wants the stagehands to bring the bed.

"Adam, cue the music." Immediately the auditorium is filled with a heavy and imposing piece filled with strings.

"Okay, lights, please." The entire stage goes dark except for a small pool of white on the area encircling the bed.

"Dim the circle, please. Okay, that's it. Mark that setting, Adam."

"Got it," is all we hear from the intercom Adam has in the control room.

"Okay, Dracula, you're up." Chris joins us in the center of the stage. I am panicking with nerves. Who knows what Mrs. McKnight is planning for the scene?

"Okay," she says, turning to face Chris and me, as we stand in a tight triangle. I think I'm already starting to blush.

"This is it. Chris, this is *the* scene. You need to convince everyone that you are determined to have her." In response, several of the students on the fringe of the stage snicker. Mrs. McKnight glares at them, and they are instantly silenced.

"Mina, you are on the bed." I walk over and sit on the bed.

"Okay, let's see how you two do with the scene—let's give it a go. Make it believable. Forget everything else but the obsession between you." With this, Chris nods, turns toward me, and walks toward the bed.

"Ready?" he asks. I shrug and nod as I lie down on the bed. We had not talked at all about the staging of this scene, but I was certain we both had contemplated how it could play out. I'm dying to know what he's going to do. For a second he stands there, and then he goes to the side of the bed that is furthest from the audience. I assume he does this so as not to block the audience's view of me too much throughout the scene. The truth is, if Chris stands directly in front of me, the audience would probably not even see me. He moves in closer to the bed, putting one hand down on the mattress. I scoot over just a bit toward the audience to give him room. He kneels on the bed with one leg and half stands on the other.

"Okay. This scene should last for several minutes before Van Helsing and Arthur walk in," Mrs. McKnight says as she thinks we are close to being ready. Turning to Van Helsing and Arthur, "Don't enter at all this time. Let's first just see what they can do and how long they can hold the scene on their own. And … action!"

I look up at Dracula and he looks down at me for a moment. Then he reaches across me with his right hand. Instinctively, I prop myself up on my right elbow. He leans down to put his weight on his right hand, which is now across me at the waist, and puts his left hand behind my head. I realize that no one else is moving. Everyone is watching us. The music is powerful and intoxicating. He slowly wraps his fingers around my neck and through my hair. He is making it obvious that he is looking all over me: my eyes, face, and décolletage. I'm not sure how long we are supposed to stretch this moment. He looks me in the eyes, and while hardly moving his lips as he doesn't want anyone else to know he's talking yet, he whispers, "Lean back." I feel his arm pull me closer and slide down so that my shoulder is in the bend of his arm, while his hand moves up and strengthens his hold so that he is supporting my head. I stiffen with tension but lean into his arm. Still leaning on his right arm, he uses his left to lay me back on the pillow a bit more. As I'm trying to figure out what to do, again he whispers, "Hey," and as I look him in the eye he widens his eyes for a flash to let me know I should hold his gaze. Holding his gaze, I lie back on the pillow. He bends down, and I don't know how close he is going to get. Careful not to touch his torso to my chest, he bends all the way down to me. He barely brushes his lips to my neck. He is on my right side, away from the audience. I can't help the blush that fills my cheeks.

"Nobody move," commands Mrs. McKnight in a hushed tone. I stiffen immediately, as I'm afraid of what she might say. "Mina, you are captivated by Dracula in an eternal way. As he comes down to your neck, which, by the way, Dracula, that was just perfect." As she is saying this, I can feel his warm breath on my neck and ear, and it is all I can do to focus on her words. I can't understand how he is holding this position while she continues, "so when he comes down to your neck, why don't you try reaching up with your right hand and touching his head or the back of his neck?" At this, he pulls back a bit, and I realize he's rewinding the scene. He leans in again toward me and is looking right into my eyes, which completely unnerves me. Then he starts to come into my neck, so I reach up and barely touch the back of his head as he comes to my neck again and brushes his warm lips against my neck again.

"Enter Van Helsing and Arthur," Mrs. McKnight directs in a soft but firm tone.

> Van Helsing: Let her go.

Van Helsing is played by a senior, who holds up a large gold crucifix as he enters the scene. Chris whips his head around to see Van Helsing and Arthur enter. When he sees the crucifix, he delivers his line in a snarl.

> Dracula: Throw it away.

As per the script staging, Chris grabs me in both his arms. At this point, I know I am supposed to scream, but I'm so into the scene—and Chris—that when he grabs me, I let out a gasp. Van Helsing takes it as my scream and continues the scene.

> Van Helsing: All right.

I remember the scripted action after Dracula's next line, word for word.

> Dracula rips open his chest and
> makes Mina drink the blood.

If possible, my body tightens a fraction more in anticipation of action. Chris delivers his line with total command of the auditorium.

> Dracula: So, you play your wits
> against mine. Me, who command
> armies hundreds of years before you
> were born. There is no way in this
> life to stop me. And to that end
> this.

"Hold the scene. Okay. What I think we are going to do here

is have Chris wear a white shirt with a Velcro strip down the front. Chris, you will rip the shirt open, and then you need to lift Mina's head and bring her lips to your neck. While you hold her head close to you, deliver the next line. Okay?"

Chris nods.

"Okay. Action."

Chris turns back from Mrs. McKnight, takes a visible breath, and briefly closes his eyes. I watch every move he makes. As he opens his eyes, he fixes them on mine. He pulls me up a bit, so I lean on both my forearms, still looking up at him. He pretends to rip open his shirt, and then, so the audience can't see, he turns slightly away from the audience and wraps his right arm around me so my face is next to his neck. I stiffen so much I am sure he can feel the tension running through me. I try to keep my face close without touching him. Angling his head down and turning toward the audience, he says his line in a harsh and vicious tone.

```
Dracula: Now she will be blood of
my blood, kin of my kin; later, my
companion in the night. You are my
slave and helper.
```

"Terrific," Mrs. McKnight says as she starts to applaud. I cannot move away from Chris fast enough. My cheeks are burning from embarrassment, and I'm not even sure why. Everyone starts applauding and whistling. Chris smiles and glances my way, but I can't look directly at him yet.

"Okay, I think we pull the curtain two beats after Chris finishes his line. Chris, that was fantastic! You do that on opening night, and you'll bring the auditorium to a standstill." Mrs. McKnight continues with me, "Mina, well played. You just need to be completely enamored with Dracula, hanging on his every word and desperate to be with him." Then she turns to address the entire group in a louder voice, "Okay, it's almost six; let's call it a day. Great job everyone. Adam, can you come up here when you're done in there."

As she is talking, I look right at her. Realizing that in her last comments to me, she's referring to Chris's line "later, my companion in the night," I feel my face start to flush again, and I'm glad we're done for the night. Immediately I turn for the stairs to get out of the single pool of light on stage and hide a bit in the darkness offstage. Everyone heads for the doors, and I grab my coat and backpack.

Chris moves near me and grabs his backpack and coat. I'm not sure if my face is still flushed, so I turn quickly and start walking up the aisle. Is it just my imagination, or is everyone watching the two of us? Do they know I have a complete crush on him? Were my feelings obvious in the scene? Oh, man, I hope not.

"Hey, Lindsey," Chris calls so I slow down and turn toward him; I'm confident we are now far enough in the shadows.

"Hey, I think that went well, don't you?" he asks.

"Oh, yeah. You were amazing," I say as we walk out together.

"I hope what I did was okay. I mean, I hope it was okay with you."

"Oh yeah, I think you were very convincing, and I agree with Mrs. McKnight, the kids are going to love this show," I say with genuine enthusiasm, but I can't quite look at him yet. The silence between us feels a bit awkward, and I'm not sure why.

As we approach the doors, we notice that the rainstorm has not let up at all. Chris steps through the door first and holds it for me while he opens his umbrella. I dart under it, and we walk the short distance to the car. Once inside, he starts the car and puts the heat on, but then we don't move. Looking over to him, I confirm what I have thought was true since we left the stage. His gaze is fixed on me.

"What?" I ask through half a smile, and then quickly turn to look back out the front window.

"You know what I realized today?"

"No, what?"

"That the only time you look at me is when there is a stage direction."

Whipping my head around to face him in shock I stammer, "What?

That's not true." And I'm suddenly acutely aware of everything I am looking at now. I automatically turn my head down and catching myself, I smile and give him a sideways look.

"See, that's what I mean," he says, cocking his head at me.

"Sorry," I start, looking at him briefly, and then as a full-on blush burns my face, I look down and continue, "It's not you; it's me. I'm sorry." And now I'm totally embarrassed. *Can we please not have this conversation?* The rain is pounding the car.

"I'm sorry, Lindsey; I'm not trying to ..." he ends in frustration. As lightning cracks above us, my attention is momentarily drawn outside, and I notice that everyone else has left. "Lindsey."

I look over at him.

"I wasn't trying to embarrass you now, or in there. If I did, I'm sorry. I would never do that to you." I can sense that he is speaking from a place of real honesty, and I believe him. But I just want to get off the topic.

"It's not you. Anyway," I continue and notice that I'm looking away again, "so, ah, what are you doing tonight?" I ask in hopes of moving on.

He starts the car but doesn't answer. Okay. This is weird.

We drive most of the way hearing only the rain pounding on the roof of his car, interrupted occasionally by thunder and lightning. The more I think about his nonanswer, the more I realize we may not be such good friends as I thought and I'm probably asking questions that are none of my business.

"Look, I'm sorry I asked; I wasn't trying to pry. I was just trying to ..." *Ughh.* Thankfully, he cuts me off.

"Lindsey, you of all people can ask me anything." This gets me to look at him in total confusion. He needs to be watching the slick roads, but he sneaks a quick glance at me and looks frustrated. Why does it feel like there is tension between us when we aren't even ...

"I'm ... It's ..." he says as he runs his fingers through his wet shiny hair. He glances at me, and I look at him, and shaking his head, he says, "Well, the truth is, I'm going out with a group, including

Elizabeth. It's her birthday and she asked me last weekend when we were at the dance while standing in front of a lot of people. I just didn't want to be a jerk." Wham. TKO. I turn to look out the passenger window and bite the side of my lip.

"Well, that sounds great. I'm sure you'll have a great night," I say as cheerfully and lightly as I can muster, although acid is churning in my stomach.

"Jeez," is all he whispers. Chris has lived on the lake his whole life, so I know he knows how to get to the Greenburgs' house. Neither of us talks the rest of the way there.

As we pull into the Greenburgs' driveway, I feel sad and a touch jealous. I'm sad that Chris and I are just friends, and a bit jealous of the evening ahead for Elizabeth. As Chris pulls into the long driveway, he slows the car just off the road and stops, a long walk away from the actual house. I assume this is where he plans to drop me off, so deliberately not looking at him, I grab my backpack and duffel bag, ready to go. Suddenly the car moves again, and Chris pulls the rest of the way up to their house.

"Wait," he says, so of course I do.

The rain continues to pound all around us.

"Look, Lindsey. I don't know what to say. I'm really glad we're in the play together. I wouldn't want to work with anyone else." I can tell he feels badly; I just don't know why or what to say. "I know you need to go in. I just—jeez. I'm sorry, Lindsey." I have no idea what he's sorry for, but I feel like the sadness inside me is building.

"Thanks for the ride," I say as I step out into the rain. I pull out my umbrella, but I don't open it as I feel like getting wet. Walking up to the Greenburgs' porch, I can feel him watching me. I ring the bell and wonder how long he's going to sit there. I can't stop myself from turning toward his car. We make eye contact only for an instant before the Greenburgs' door starts to open. As I enter the house, I hear him backing out of the driveway.

৪০৫

Babysitting for the Greenburgs is easy. They have one six-month-old who loves to sleep, so I play with him for a while, change him, give him a bottle, and put him down for the night by eight o'clock. By this time, the rain is barreling down, and the wind is howling. Before leaving, Mrs. Greenburg said they would be going to dinner and a movie and then to the country club, so not to expect them until about midnight or so. After the tension of rehearsal and the personal drama later, which I still do not understand, I decide to use their indoor hot tub to relax. I change and check the baby one more time, then move the baby monitor to the pool room. I grab a Diet Coke, the Greenburgs' home phone, and my cell phone. I turn the stereo on low so I can soak and listen to music while the storm rages outside. In my head I hear Mom say I shouldn't swim in a storm, but I ignore the drilled-in advice and slip into the steaming water. Checking my cell phone, I am relieved not to have any messages and note that it is eight thirty. Switching from the hot tub, I get in the pool, which is refreshing in comparison. I know I should study, but I'm just not in the mood.

At nine thirty I am finally starting to feel relaxed as I return to the hot tub after checking on the baby. I'm getting tired already. I wonder what Chris and Elizabeth are doing. My mind flashes to last night with Kevin, and I cringe as I'm certain Elizabeth would want to go further with Chris. And why wouldn't he go further? Isn't that what every guy wants? I dunk under the cool water as if it'll wash away my misery.

৪০৫

"Did you have fun?" I ask the Greenburgs when they arrive at about eleven forty-five.

"Oh yes, Lindsey, thanks. How was the baby?" Mrs. Greenburg asks.

"Oh, he's never any trouble. I had the monitor with me in the pool room the entire time," I say apologetically.

"Lindsey, you are the most reliable young lady I know," Mrs. Greenburg cuts me off.

"Here you go, Lindsey," she says as she hands me a few folded-up bills, which I'm certain are once again more than I earned.

"Thank you," I say as I put my coat on and grab my backpack and bag.

"Oh, Lindsey, we have plans in the city next Friday night. Could you sit again?" *Why should I have a life? Even my neighbors know I can't get a date.*

"Sure. No problem; what time?"

"Could you be here around six-thirty again?"

"Um, yeah, that should be fine." I will probably be free on New Year's Eve too. Oh, and prom night—why don't we go ahead and book that too?

"I'll take you home, Lindsey," says Dr. Greenburg.

"Thank you."

When I get home, my house is quiet. It's even too late for Baron to get up; instead, he lifts his head, confirms it's me, and goes back to sleep. I head to the kitchen for a glass of milk. Walking in the dark kitchen, the world beyond our kitchen bay window is glistening from the day of soaking rain. Suddenly Baron is barking and running in the front of the house. Worried this will wake my dad, I rush over to hush him. He is running from window to window, barking like crazy.

"Shhhhhhhh! Baron! Would you stop it!" I whisper sternly at him. "What is the matter with you? Shh!"

Suddenly he stops at one of the side windows, gets down low, and starts growling. I stop as I have never heard him growl before.

"Baron?" my dad bellows from upstairs. Both Baron and I stop and turn toward the staircase where we hear my dad's voice. Baron barks up at my dad a few times.

"Dad?" I call, and Baron turns toward me for the first time.

"Lindsey? What's going on?"

"Nothing, Baron's just gone crazy."

"Baron, go to bed," my dad commands from his room, so Baron whines, gives the window one more bark, and heads to his bed. "Good night, Lindsey," Dad calls to me.

"Night, Dad," and I hear my dad shut their door.

"Sure, everyone listens to him," I say as I give Baron a scratch behind the ears and go up to bed myself.

As I lie in my bed welcoming the deep sleep I know will come, I think about my day and night. My body is heavy from the day. Thoughts mingle. Baron. The Greenburgs. Prom Night. I hope desperately that someone asks me to my senior prom. Not just anyone—but, Someone … Someone …

My eyes snap open as I recall where Someone is.

15 FLOWER DAY: *WONDER IF I WILL EVER KNOW.*

MONDAY WAS COLUMBUS DAY, so we didn't have school or rehearsal. Today is flower-order day—a day I'm sure many look forward to, but I dread. Complete nightmare. I'm not planning to send any flowers as Kevin hasn't called me since Friday night when I saw him for pizza, and I'm assuming the lack of contact means that whatever we had is over. I doubt he will send me any flowers, and I'm not going to be humiliated by sending one to him and not receive any in return. The thing I find most interesting is that I'm more bummed about knowing I'll go through seven periods without receiving a flower than I am about the change in things with Kevin.

I haven't seen Chris since our weird ride to the Greenburgs' after Saturday's rehearsal. I wish he would send me one—just one—carnation. Is that so much to hope for? And yet I'm confident of the outcome. I'm sure any flowers he orders will go to the fabulous Elizabeth. I avoid the flower-sales table in front of the cafeteria as much as possible throughout the day.

৪৩৪৩

As I enter English class, I'm hoping I have timed it so there will be no chance for Chris and I to chat before class begins. I see Amanda is chatting him up, which, for once, I'm grateful for. I approach my seat, deliberately diverting my eyes and trying to walk slowly, in hopes that the bell will ring by the time I sit down. I'm fairly sure Chris is watching me while he's busy nodding and generally facing Amanda.

Saved by the bell.

After class, I quickly gather my books and papers and head purposefully for the door.

"Lindsey."

I ignore this as if I can't possibly hear him over the noise of the departing students. I reach the doorframe; make it into the hallway. Excellent. Heading for the cafeteria, I'm stopped when I feel a familiar hand on my arm. Hello, Dracula.

"Lindsey, hey, wait up."

"Hey." I try to pull this off like it is the first time I've seen Chris today.

I see I have clearly failed when he tilts his head and smirks at me, knowing I have been trying to avoid this little chat. "You headed to lunch?" he asks.

Quickly calculating the probability that I will faint if I eat nothing until dinner at over 90 percent, I reply, "Uh, yeah, I guess so." Terrific. Now I will get to be with you as we reach the flower-ordering table and have to watch as you order a dozen for the lovely Elizabeth.

"Cool," he says as he matches my stride. "How was babysitting? Did you go swimming?"

"Oh, fine, yeah, the pool is a great bonus." *Wonder what great bonus you got Saturday night.*

"How was the birthday?" I say and deliberately look at him.

"Oh, fine, I guess. What did you do Sunday?" Moving to a new topic quickly, are we?

"Nothing much; studied mostly."

As we approach my locker, I encourage him to go ahead so he can dance on over to the table to order his flowers without me being around. "I'll see you in the cafeteria. I'm gonna drop off my books at my locker."

"No problem, I can wait," he says as he walks with me to my locker. Interesting. *Why are you waiting for me?* I put my books in my locker, and then we head back toward the cafeteria. I take a deep breath because I really do not want to witness this. As we approach the table he says, "Hey, guess it's that time again."

"Yeah, it's kind of silly."

"Oh. Well, yeah, I guess so." *Whew.* He's not stopping; guess he took care of that this morning.

Entering the cafeteria, I see Melissa eating with some kids we both know. "I'll see you at rehearsal," I say, while still looking around the room.

"Yeah, I'll pick you up in the morning." His reply grabs my attention.

"Oh, you really don't have to keep schlepping me around; my mom can take me."

"Lindsey," he says in a very slow manner like I am a child, "I keep telling you it's not a problem. I'll see you at six forty-five," and with that Chris heads over to sit with some guys and I head to the table where Melissa is sitting.

⁂⇛

Friday morning, and I am dreading school. Frick'n Flower Day. Hey, maybe that's what we should call it next year!

First period, and I'm in chemistry with Jon. Thank goodness for adorable, reliable, totally crushable Jon. In the midst of our first lab experiment, two senior girls drop in with flowers. All work stops, of course, except at my table, where I turn my back to the flower train and keep working.

"Here you go, Jon," coos one of the girls while she gives Jon three carnations. Lovely.

"Thanks," he says as he looks to see who they are from. I suppose I should feign interest.

"So, Jon, who sent them?"

"Oh, just a friend. I'm surprised you didn't get a bunch."

I can't contain a small sarcastic laugh before I bend down to look through the microscope one more time.

೫೦೮೩

As I head to English, I am dreading the next little flower moment. I sit down and notice that everyone, of course, is in a ridiculously exuberant mood, having all this affection poured on them. We make it through most of the class with no flower deliveries. I'm hoping there was a mix-up and maybe no flowers will arrive during this class.

Just my luck. They show up in the last ten minutes of class. The bucket is filled with flowers, and I immediately hope that some are for next period, or this is going to be totally humiliating. Amanda gets four in this class alone. Another ten or twelve kids get one or two flowers (but who's counting?). The senior girls keep Chris's for last so they can pretend he didn't get any.

"Okay. Well, I guess that's about it. Oh, I'm sorry. We almost forgot—Chris Buckley."

Right. I'm sure you almost forgot him. You all drooled over his older brother Jake for years and now, even though Chris is younger than any of you, you would jump at the chance to go out with him.

They walk over with six carnations in a variety of colors. I don't know what most of the colors mean, but I do know that an orange carnation means a secret admirer and pink means I like you. Chris gets four pinks and two oranges. How lovely for him. Flower Day puts everyone in a good mood, even Ms. Lowen, who dismisses us a few minutes early.

"Hey, Lindsey, headed to lunch?" Chris asks.

"Yeah," I say, trying to hide my sulking mood. As he walks with me, casually holding the stems of the carnations, I can't help but wonder who they are from.

"Looks like you got a nice arrangement there."

"Oh, I guess. Silly, right?" he says, reflecting my comments earlier in the week.

"Yeah," I say with a smile and actually meet his eyes. He looks back with a spark in his eyes and a broad smile. Delightful.

"Hey, don't forget we have another staging rehearsal Saturday afternoon. I'm taking you, right?" he asks as I put my books in my locker.

"Yeah, if you're sure that's okay."

"Would you stop! I'll be at your house about three-thirty again, okay?"

"Sure."

"Hey, what do you have going on tonight?" As he says this, I turn back to look at him and am again reminded of his multiple admirers.

So, a bit more tense, I reply, "I'm babysitting again at the Greenburgs."

"Really? That's cool. I think it's great they go out so much."

"Yeah, I think they like to go to the city for the theater. Cool, right?"

"Totally. Okay, Lindsey, see ya tomorrow."

ೞೞ

Seventh period, study hall. Still no frick'n flowers. I'm in such a funk I think I've lost an inch in height. I'm dreading every minute of this period. In walks Kevin, and for some stupid reason, I look up at him. As our eyes meet, I give him an awkward half smile; his smile comes easy as he waves, and then sits with the guys. Okay. So maybe he's just playing it ultracool. Maybe his plan is to tease me a bit, like he's not going to sit with me or send any flowers to me all day, but at the last possible hour, flowers will be delivered to me and then he'll join me. I'm struck again by the realization that I care more about not getting flowers from anyone than I do about this thing between Kevin and me being so short-lived.

No more time to ponder the world; I have to study French. Why do we even learn French? Do all of five million people speak the language? I mean, sure it's beautiful, but why can't our school offer something interesting, like Mandarin Chinese? Not likely I'm going to get high school to change its curriculum. Oh, well; back to studying.

Halfway through last period, a gaggle of seniors come bouncing in carrying two buckets of flowers. They start with Kevin, who gets three. I just want to leave. Another guy at his table gets four, and six other people in the library get one or two each. The entire time the senior girls are calling out names and delivering the flowers, I pretend to be studying, while in reality I'm eavesdropping on each of the deliveries. My worst fears are confirmed. I made it through another Flower Day without receiving a single one.

I'm determined not to make eye contact with Kevin. It's embarrassing enough not to get flowers, but I've also become aware that, to Kevin, I'm not even worth some kind of conversation. I mean, I get that we only hung out for a few weeks, but how long do you have to be together to be worth some kind of concluding conversation? Wonder if I will ever know.

ജ്ഞ

Lying alone in the darkness of my room, I mentally run through the day. What if Kevin didn't call because I'm the worst kisser in the world? What if he told all the guys this? Oh, man. What if he's not really a gentleman at all, like he pretends to be, and instead he told all the guys we went all the way? This is just a fleeting thought, as I'm confident in my ability to judge a person's character. I honestly don't think he'd do that. I can do a powerful giant swing on bars, can land a rock-solid front tuck on beam, and, yes, I do believe I can spot a gentleman.

16 MY BIRTHDAY: *YOURS, CHRIS.*

TODAY IS TUESDAY, OCTOBER 21. On rare occasions like today, I lie in bed for a few minutes before I start my day. Today I am sixteen years old. I think of the words to the old Johnny Burnette song, "You're sixteen, you're beautiful, and you're mine." Thinking about these words, I realize that I'm still kind of my parents', and somewhat my own. I'm certainly not anyone else's. Smiling a little to myself and with my eyes still closed, I wonder if I'll ever really be anyone else's. Or will anyone ever really be mine.

I get up and walk to my bathroom, where I look in the mirror to see what sixteen looks like. I wonder what twenty-six will look like. Thirty-six? Wonder what'll be my best decade. Wonder what I'm getting for my birthday.

I get dressed in a new outfit Mom and I got in the city before school started. I love leather jackets, and we found a completely cool one in blue, with a zipper in front and buckles at the waist and neck. The silver buckles play off my metal purse with Swarovski crystals on it. So cool. Too bad I don't actually have a boyfriend to go out with on my birthday. Or even to just call me.

&)(&

I'm not in any of the scenes being run through at rehearsal this morning, so I cut through my yard, heading for Isabella's house to catch a ride with her.

"Morning, Mrs. Castiglioni."

"Happy birthday, Lindsey! Sixteen—what a wonderful year! Wow, you look terrific—new jacket?"

"Yes. Thanks, Mrs. Castiglioni." It's so nice of her to remember. Maybe this will be a good birthday.

"Happy birthday, Lindsey," Isabella chimes in as she runs downstairs.

"Thanks, Isabella," I reply as we head to her car in the garage.

"What are you doing to celebrate?"

"Oh, I think we're just going to have dinner at home. No big deal."

"That should be fun. I wonder what your folks will get you?" she asks, shooting me a look.

"No idea. I keep hoping for a car, but I doubt my dad will do it. And even if he does, it will probably be some old beater."

"You never know."

"I guess."

&)(&

Walking up to my locker, I see that someone has decorated it, which of course ignites a flush in my cheeks.

"Happy birthday, Lindsey," Jon says as he slams his locker and comes over to give me a hug. He is so nice and respectful; he hugs me quickly and just around my neck and shoulders.

"Thanks, Jon. Wow! They did a great job. Do you know who did it?"

"Well, I think you need to figure that out on your own."

I can tell he knows, but I agree that it's really up to me to figure it out. Opening my locker, which is covered in wrapping paper, I see a card has been slipped through one of the slots in the top section. Ripping it open, I confirm my suspicion with a big grin, "Melissa and Elena. They're so nice." Jon waits as I switch my books and carefully shut the locker door so as not to tear the paper covering the front.

I walk away feeling a bit taller.

ഇOര

As I walk into English, I wonder if Chris knows it's my birthday. That might be too much to hope for. Turning the corner, I see that Amanda is sitting on Chris's desk. Nice. Passing his desk, I hear Amanda chatter on and on about how great Chris will be as Dracula. Oh, well, even if he does know it's my birthday, there's no way he can break away from her, as she is literally on his desk and in his face.

"Okay, everything under your desk," Ms. Lowen begins, and the class reacts with a collective moan. We know this request is the precursor to one of her notorious pop quizzes. Thankful I'm ahead in our reading, I put my books under my desk, ready for the test to begin.

ഇOര

As soon as the bell rings ending the period, Chris turns to grab his books out from under his chair and then looks up at me. He smiles and says, "Happy birthday, Lindsey." Foolishly I bite my lip, trying to hide the huge smile I'm feeling at the realization that he does know today is my birthday.

"Thanks, Chris," I say, looking right at him. My direct eye-to-eye contact is rewarded with the gift of a full smile in return. Of course, it is more than I can take and I look away as I grab my books. He steps to the side so we can walk out together.

"So, what are you doing to celebrate?"

"I have practice and then just dinner with my folks."

"Well, you must be doing something. Getting your license?"

"Well, yes, I am doing that. My mom is picking me up early from practice so I can get it tonight. I hope I pass," I add with a crooked grin.

"Oh, you'll pass. What do you think you're getting for your birthday?"

"No idea. I would love a car. That would be cool, wouldn't it? I could finally stop begging everyone for a ride."

"Yeah," he responds with some enthusiasm, and then adds, "but you know, for me, it's never a problem. I'm happy to do it, Lindsey."

"Thanks."

"Wow, who decorated your locker?" Chris asks as we step around the corner.

"Melissa and Elena; isn't it cool?"

"It looks great. Nice to have good friends."

As we walk into the cafeteria, I can't help but think that yeah, it is nice to have friends who take the time to do something like that for me. I know Melissa and Elena are closer to each other than I am to either of them, but it was very nice of them to come in early and decorate my locker. Chris and I have never sat together in the cafeteria, and since I don't want him to leave me standing with no one to talk to, I grab the first opportunity to be the one to have somewhere to go, and say, "Speaking of Melissa, there she is. I need to go thank her. See ya later, Chris."

"Yeah, see ya."

"Melissa—you didn't have to do that!" I say, approaching the table where she's sitting.

"Happy birthday, Lindsey," she announces louder than necessary in order to ensure everyone sitting nearby can hear as she gets up to greet me with a hug.

"Thanks," I say, rolling my eyes as everyone at our table wishes me well. I head to the lunch line to get my normal grilled cheese and milk. As I reach for my milk, I see Chris standing next to me.

"Hey."

"Hey," I say as I follow him to the cash register. *Man, guys eat a ton,* is all I can think looking at his tray. After he pays, he picks up the chocolate cupcake he bought and puts it on my tray.

"Happy birthday, Lindsey."

"Thanks, but you don't have to do that."

Shrugging he adds, "My pleasure. Hey, send me a text or give me a call and let me know what kind of car you get." What? Send you a … You want *me* to call *you*? What does that mean? Are we just friends—is that why I should text you? But you bought me a cupcake. Does that mean more? Stop it. If he wanted to date, he'd ask. He asks everyone else. Just friends. So sad.

It is a great lunch hour. Somehow everything seems to be going my way, at least so far. I'm more outgoing than normal, and I seem to be the center of attention. I don't normally like all that attention, but today, somehow, it all seems to work.

&⁊⁊⁊⁊

"Happy birthday, Miss Lindsey," Mom says as I get in her car after a shortened practice.

"Thanks, Mom."

"How was your day?"

"Terrific."

"Really? That's great. Are you ready for the test?"

"Yeah, I think so. I hope so," I say, flipping through the book one last time.

"I'm sure you'll do just fine. I thought I would drop you off for the test and go pick up crab legs for all of us at Cape May Crab Shack."

"Thanks, Mom. That sounds terrific." Mom knows that it's one of my favorite dinners. Even though I'm nervous about the driver's test, I can't help but smile at the fact that things just keep going my way today.

As Mom drops me off, I realize that this is a big deal. Mom has dropped me off so I can do this on my own. Signs of things to come: a driver's license now; college in two years; and, one day, my own place. Closing my eyes, I relish the joy the independence of a driver's license will bring. I no longer will have to ask friends for a ride, but I will need to ask my parents to borrow their car. I open my eyes as I consider that reality. Oh, well. One step at a time.

Stepping up to the service desk, I'm nervous that I won't pass.

ഇറ

Nearly an hour later, I walk out of the building toward Mom's car and proudly hold up my new driver's license. It's my ticket to freedom. Excellent. Sixteen's gonna be good.

ഇറ

Sitting down to dinner, life is good. Given the short week and my birthday, Dad is staying in town. He pops open a bottle of champagne. Much as my parents may appear to be the most conservative people you'll meet, in reality, they have a great view of life. There are always a couple bottles of champagne in the refrigerator just in case there's something to celebrate. It's a great tradition—which Mom acquired from her father. Al, my grandfather, is a great character. He would be so happy to see me toast my birthday with a glass of the bubbly. I have had alcohol only a few times in my life—on special occasions, like for a wedding toast, when Dad lets me have a sip—so I figure I might as well enjoy it.

"Well, a toast to our lovely Lindsey. You work so hard in school, at gymnastics, everything you do." And pulling something out of his suit coat, which he had on the back of his chair, he hands me two rectangular black velvet boxes. "Happy birthday."

Looking back and forth from Mom to Dad, I'm about to explode. "Two?"

"Mmmm," is all Dad says as he sips from his crystal stem.

"Jewelry boxes? But you always say it's not your job to buy me jewelry."

"It's not. I'm still leaving that to your boyfriends and husband."

"Open them," Mom says, and I can see her excitement as she raises her eyebrows.

"Which one first?"

"You pick," Dad says. Snatching one up, I'm hoping it's a watch or a bracelet, as the box is the right size. But Dad doesn't seem to have changed his view that buying jewelry is not his job when it comes to me. I pop it open and see there is a tiny piece of paper folded inside. *What's this?* I unfold the note they must have printed on the computer, which reads, "Go out front."

"What is this?" I ask as I push back from the table. I run to the front door and hear my parents follow me. I'm about to burst in hopes that it's a car. Flinging the front door open, I shove the storm door aside and step onto the front porch. In the driveway is a brand new shiny black Audi.

"*No!* It's beautiful!" I scream as I run outside to get a closer look. I look back at my parents standing in the doorway. Dad has the keys dangling in his hand. Dashing back, I snatch the keys from him as he asks, "Don't you want some shoes?"

"No! Oh, well, yes—can I take it for a drive? Please?"

"Well, we need to be sure the insurance has kicked in, and that won't happen until I go by our agent's office tomorrow night."

Hugging them both, I say thank you over and over about ten times before I dash to the driver's side and notice the doors automatically unlock as I get close. I sit inside. It smells so good.

After about ten minutes of checking every button and turning every knob, it suddenly hits me: there were two black velvet boxes. Heading back inside, I realize how cold my feet are.

"We were wondering how long you would be out there," Mom says, finishing her crab and wiping her hands.

"Sorry, but the car is amazing! Thank you so much. So is this for me as well?"

"Yep," Dad says, with a curious look on his face.

Picking up the box, I can't imagine what it could be. Snapping it open, I gasp. Tears form in my eyes as I look at Dad.

"Yes," is all he needs to say. It's a double strand of pearls with a flower diamond clasp. It's, or I guess, was, my grandmother's.

"She wants to be sure you get it, so she decided to give it to you now."

"Thanks, Dad," I say with a crack in my voice. "Can I go call her?"

"Sure, but why don't you finish eating first? I got your favorite cake."

"This is just the best day! I can't believe you guys got me a car!"

"Well, a car is a lot of responsibility, Lindsey. I expect you to take this responsibility seriously."

"Yes, I know, but it's also so cool!"

"I know, I know. Hey, before you head upstairs, I also wanted to tell you something."

"Okay," I say, worried he is going to say something like, I can only drive it when he is in the car with me.

"I have taken on a big case in Chicago, which is why I have been spending so much time there. But this one looks like it will last awhile, so I'm going to need to spend most weeknights there and just be home on the weekends."

"Yeah, okay. So can I drive to school once the insurance stuff is good?"

"Yes, you can drive the car to school, but, Lindsey, what I am trying to say is that I am going to be taking an apartment in Chicago so I can leave some stuff there and just be more comfortable than being in a hotel all the time."

"Sure, okay. That makes sense," I say, relieved I can drive myself soon.

"Okay," Dad says, looking at Mom. Something passes between them, but I don't know what it is and tonight I don't care.

೫೦ൾ

After finishing dinner, I go up to my room to call my grandmother. Glancing at my cell, I realize there is a text from Chris.

6:42 P.M. Hi Lindsey.

7:30 P.M. Hi Chris. Guess what?

7:31 P.M. ??

7:31 P.M. GOT A CAR!!!!!!

7:31 P.M. :-) Nice!

7:32 P.M. Thanks for all the rides, but will be driving myself soon – am so psyched!

7:32 P.M. Glad for you. Can I come over and see it tonight?

Geez … guys and cars. But why not; he can look at the car and I can look at him. Ha!

7:35 P.M.   U sure?

7:35 P.M.   Y. Can I come over now?

7:35 P.M.   Sure

ঙ෬

While I wait for Chris to arrive, I call my grandma and thank her profusely for the pearls. I can recall her wearing them on special occasions, and I can't wait to have a reason to wear them somewhere special myself. I just adore my dad's mom; she has always made me feel special. I think that is actually her gift; she makes everyone feel like they are the most important person to her. I need to figure out how she does it.

ঙ෬

Walking out to meet Chris, I can't help but be excited that he wanted to come over. I know he probably just wants to see the car, but there's no harm in hoping. One can always hope.

"Hey," I call as he gets out of his car. Then I see he's holding a card. Hmmm. This really is turning out to be a nice birthday.

"Hi, Lindsey, this must be it," he says, gesturing at the obviously shiny new car in the driveway.

"Yeah, I can't wait to drive it."

"Well, let's take it for a spin!"

"I would love to, but the insurance doesn't kick in till Thursday."

"Oh, well, maybe Thursday then. Happy birthday, Lindsey," he says, handing me the card.

160

"You didn't have to do that," I say, taking the card with a big stupid grin.

"Open it," he says with that amazing smile.

"Okay." As I slip my finger in the envelope, I notice he takes a step closer to me. The card is a simple picture of a lake nestled in forest full of the lovely colors of fall, and inside, the card is blank except for what he wrote:

Dear Lindsey,

Happy sweet sixteen to the sweetest girl I know.

Yours,
Chris.

I'm trying hard not to change my facial expression as I read it and thank him, but my mind is reeling. Is this a friend-to-friend card? Or is it more? What does "yours" mean?

"Thanks, Chris," I say, glancing at him and trying desperately to read his expression.

"Sure," he says, looking at me, and suddenly I get that weird feeling again. Awkwardly I look away from him and at my new car.

"Well, I guess I should let you go."

"Okay, well, thanks for coming over and thanks for the card."

"Sure, I also wanted to see if you're planning to go out with the cast and crew after our last full rehearsal Saturday."

"Oh … um …" *Will you be bringing the lovely Elizabeth with you?*

"Come on, it'll be fun," Chris continues and it does seem like he wants me to go, but I really don't want to go if he is bringing a date.

"Is anyone else going?"

"Oh yeah, I think a big group is going; most of the cast and crew, I think. Come on, you should come with us."

"Just the cast and crew?"

"Yeah, come on," he says, tilting his head with that killer smile.

"Okay. Sounds like fun. Thanks." And if it's just cast and crew, she won't be there.

"Great. My dad isn't pulling our boat out until Sunday, so I thought we'd use it one more time. I'll pick you up on it and bring you into town. I'm also picking up the twins." Okay; if he liked me, he would not be picking up the guys too. *Friends.*

"Sure, sounds good. See you tomorrow."

"Happy birthday, Lindsey."

ಐಐ

Wednesday morning, I'm so excited to get my last ride from Isabella. As I head out the front door, Baron bolts outside and runs for the forest. Exasperated, I call and call him. He is racing and I don't have time for this. I go to the kitchen and get a box of his treats, take them out front, and shake the box. He stops, looks back at me, barks a couple more times into the forest, and then runs to me and his treats.

"What are you doing? You can't make that much noise at this time in the morning! Get inside." Tossing two bones into the hallway, I close the box of treats and put them away while he pants and enjoys his bones.

Heading outside, I turn to lock the door and hear something in the distant forest. Maybe something was out there? A deer? I don't see anything as I head over to Isabella's. As I am a few minutes late, she already has the car out of the garage when I get to her house, and we have a relatively quiet ride to school.

It is a cloudy day as Isabella and I are walking across the campus to the main school entrance. I feel my phone buzz, so I pull it out to see what it is before I go into the building.

7:36 A.M. Nice car Lindsey.

Huh? It's from a number I don't have in my phone book. Someone must have gotten a new cell number and not told me yet. But who could it be? Oh well; nice to get the message. Nicer to have the car!

"Hi, Jon," I say with way too much enthusiasm as I come around the corner and spot him at his locker.

"Hey, Lindsey, what's up?" he asks, reading my exuberance.

"Oh, nothing."

"What?" he coaxes me.

"Okay, guess what?" To this, he slams his locker and steps over to mine with a huge grin to match my unusually broad smile.

"What?" he asks.

"Guess."

"Come on, what?" he asks, stepping even closer as he genuinely appreciates that I'm about to share some big news.

"I got a car for my birthday," I beam at him.

"Awesome—what is it?"

"An Audi A4," I reply, slamming my locker with a bit of flourish.

"Cool! Did you bring it today?" he asks as we head down burnout hallway.

"No. I need to wait for insurance—I'll have it tomorrow. It's black."

"I'm sure it's terrific; I can't wait to see it. Audis are incredible."

As class starts, I wonder who sent the text. I can't imagine who would have changed their cell number. I would think the last thing anyone would want to do is change their cell phone number. In today's world, it's like changing your name.

∞∝

Thursday morning I am walking on air as I get ready for school. Today I get to drive my new car to school. I love that it unlocks when I get near it and that I can start it with the push of a button. In my driveway, I take deep breaths of the new-car smell and can't stop smiling all the way to school. The power of the engine seams to fuel my self-confidence as I pull into the student parking lot.

After school and gymnastics practice, I head to the drama room to pick up my costumes. Mrs. McKnight said she would leave them in her office with my name on the garment bag. I can't help but sneak a peek inside. I look past the dresses from the time period of the play to the back of the bag, where I see the nightgown. As much as I want to hate it, I must admit it really is a pretty white cotton gown, with a lot of delicate lace on it.

I start down the hall leading to the main door out to the parking lot when I feel my phone buzz. I bet it's Mom checking on me for my first solo drive home. Wonder how long I'm going to get a check-in for every trip.

6:16 P.M.   Don't tell anyone about this text.

Huh? Who sent this? Another new number. Random. I walk outside to the student lot. There are only a few cars left, as most of the sports teams finished with practice at five thirty or so. As I get closer to my new car, I feel a rush of excitement. I just love having my own car.

Although it is already pretty dark, I think I see that my right front tire is flat. In the low light, at first, I'm not sure. But as I get closer, that awful possibility becomes a certainty.

Dad is going to kill me.

How could this happen? Great! I have a car one day, and now Dad is going to take it away. What should I do? Still holding my phone, I feel it buzz again. What now?

6:19 P.M.   Guess Who? Keep this a secret. Don't tell anyone.

I spin around to see if someone is watching me. I don't see anyone but a couple of guys leaving practice. What does that mean? I scan the student parking lot, the football stadium, the entire campus. As I'm trying to process all this, I hear someone nearby and jump.

"Hey, Lindsey." I turn around to see Kevin walking up. I breathe a big sigh of relief.

"Hi, Kevin." Great. My non-breakup buddy is here, and I'm stranded with a flat tire.

"Is this the new car?"

"Yeah," I say, gesturing to my shiny new prize.

"Awesome! Do you ... need help driving it?" he asks, half laughing in what I think is a flirty tone.

"I seem to have a flat," I say, pointing to the tire.

"Are you kidding?" he asks, walking around to the front of the car to see it. "How did that happen?" he asks.

"I have no idea; I just came out of practice and ... this." I want to throw up.

"Okay, well, I can change it for you."

"Oh, I don't want to put you out. And honestly my dad is weird about stuff like this and probably will want the dealership to change it. I can just call my parents," I stammer as I start to pull up my home number on my cell.

"Lindsey. Seriously ... if you don't want me to change it, I'll at least take you home. I'm not leaving you out here in the dark. Come on. It's no problem," and he gestures for me to walk toward his car.

"You sure?"

"Absolutely; come on. That's so weird."

"Right!"

∞∞

"Hi, Mom."

"Hi, Lindsey. Are you headed home?"

165

"Well, um," sigh, "I um … I had a little problem," I say, glancing at Kevin. He looks over at me with a sympathetic smile.

"I have no idea how it happened, but when I came out from practice, I had a flat tire. I'm so sorry, Mom."

"Are you kidding?"

"No. It's the craziest thing."

"Oh, okay. Well, I'll have your father call the dealer, and I'll pack up and come get you."

"Oh, well, Kevin Walker is giving me a ride home," I say, forcing a smile as I glance at him in appreciation.

"Oh. Isn't that nice? Okay. Well, we'll see you soon."

"Okay, um … do you think Dad will …," I start to ask.

"Oh, he'll be fine; things happen. We'll get it taken care of; no problem."

"Thanks, Mom. Bye."

"See you soon."

"So, how's gymnastics going?" Kevin asks in an effort to keep the conversation going.

"Great. I won two events and All-Around on Wednesday." Interesting—I have no problem bragging to Kevin; when Chris asked earlier, I was pretty vague.

"That's great. You must be a good gymnast." As he says this, I almost gasp as I look out the windshield and lock eyes with Chris in his car across the intersection from us. Terrific. Kevin and I aren't even dating anymore, and just my luck, we see Chris.

"Thanks," I say, humored by my own double meaning.

I am paranoid as I enter the house at the wrath I am about to incur.

"Hi," I call hesitantly as I enter the foyer.

"Hello, Lindsey," I hear Dad call from the kitchen. Here we go.

"Hi," I say as I enter the kitchen, a bit nervous.

"So, what happened?"

"I don't know, Dad. I'm so sorry. I have no idea. I drove to school. No problem. But when I came out from practice, I had a flat tire. It's the craziest thing."

"Okay, well, as long as you're okay. Here's the service number for your warranty. Be sure to program it into your phone."

"Okay, thanks."

"Tonight."

"Okay. I'll put it in tonight."

"I called them already, and they'll come by here for the key and then tow the car into town tonight and fix it in the morning. Your mother said she can pick you up at school tomorrow and take you over to pick it up. Okay?"

"Yeah, thanks," I say in shock, not believing Dad is so calm.

"Look, I'm sure you must have just driven over some nails or something. Just some bad luck. No harm done."

"Thanks, Dad." That's it? Are you kidding me?

"Lindsey, can you get a ride with Isabella in the morning?" asks Mom.

"Oh, I'm sure I can. I'll text her after dinner."

80CB

Not able to fall asleep, I turn on the small lamp next to my bed and creep barefoot to the bureau, open the top drawer, and pull out the card from under my clothes and carry it back to bed. I've already read its message so many times I have it memorized.

"Yours, Chris." If only.

17 NORTH VS. SOUTH: *GAME ON.*

IT'S SATURDAY, AND WE have a gymnastics meet at South High. Also, there are freshman, JV, and varsity football games at South today, so most of the North students will be at South High School at some point this afternoon. And best of all, since the meet is on a Saturday, Dad will come with Mom and watch me.

Our meet is at ten in the morning, so we'll be done well before the varsity football game. My car has been fixed, so at about eight thirty, I drive myself to South, where I'm supposed to meet the rest of our team in the gym at nine. My folks will drive over later, just before the competition. This is the first time I fully realize the freedom my license is giving them too.

Entering South, I'm not exactly sure where to go because I have never been inside this school before. I'm wandering around the hallways looking for a clue as to where the gymnastics gym is located when I see several football players and some other students. My phone buzzes.

8:47 A.M. Hey Lindsey.

It's Chris. Wonder what he wants this early. I step into a side hall to get out of the football player traffic.

8:47 A.M. Hey Chris.

8:47 A.M. U going to the football game at south?

8:47 A.M. Y. u?

8:48 A.M. Y. Don't you also have a gymnastics meet at south this morning?

8:48 A.M. Y

8:48 A.M. I think I am going to come by and watch the meet. Ok?

Nice of you to let me know you want to come watch Elizabeth compete. The good news—I can kick her little gymnast butt with one hand behind my back.

8:49 A.M. Sure.

8:49 A.M. 10 am right?

8:49 A.M. Y. C u then.

8:49 A.M. Gr8 cya

I continue down the hall trying to find the gym.

Buzz. I feel my phone indicate another text message.

"Well, well, well, my little friend, Lindsey." I hear a voice I recognize, but can't place. "Remember me?" he says as he steps closer.

I can't place the face shadowed by his worn baseball cap, but the voice. I know I've heard it before.

Scratching his full beard with one hand, he continues, "Guess I didn't have this at the party."

169

The Neanderthal. Great.

"Um … yeah … hi." Unfortunately I do remember him.

"So you're here to watch me play football?" Looking at my duffel bag marked "North Gymnastics" in huge letters, he continues, "Oooh, you must be a gymnast, huh?"

I just stand there looking at him. He steps closer, and his amusement seems to increase in direct correlation with my discomfort. I can't see anyone in the halls behind him. I feel anxious; he's getting too close, and I don't see an easy exit. Soon I'll be late for meeting my team.

"Um, yeah, I need to go," I say as I look down. Clenching my duffel bag, I attempt to move around him.

"Hey, Lindsey. Let's go, the gym is this way," I hear from Coach Parker. Whew.

Looking around the Neanderthal, I see Coach Parker. "Thanks, Coach."

"See ya later," Rock calls after me.

As I follow my coach, I check my cell phone.

8:52 A.M. Hello again. Keep this text a secret. Tell no one. Where are you?

Who is this? What does it mean? Crazy! I wonder if someone is playing a joke on me.

I enter the gym with Coach Parker. The team has started to stretch and will soon begin warm-up rotations.

I give my folks a nod when they enter, each carrying a cup of coffee. Glancing up at them, I see Dad reading his e-mail and Mom getting the video camera ready. As I put on my grips to warm up on bars, I can feel someone watching me. For some reason, I am sure it's not my folks. Looking at the stands, I see Mom digging in her purse. Then I see Rock and three other goons watching the warm-ups like they are at a Vegas show. Terrific. I hope he's dating someone on South's team. Suddenly I am totally conscious of being in a leotard. As I chalk up for bars, I overhear some of my teammates.

"Hey, Elizabeth. Guess who just came in to watch you?" Peggy chirps.

"Oh, I better hit now!" Elizabeth responds. I turn toward the bars and catch a glimpse of Chris climbing the bleachers to find a seat. I assume the two guys with him are Joel and Mike since the three of them are always together. Why do all the best-looking guys hang out together? And given that guys are actually loyal to each other, it seems to mean that if you date one guy, you are off-limits to his wingmen. Guy code.

Well, Elizabeth, I don't know if you will hit your routines, but watch out, because I do believe I will be throwing a few tricks of my own. I had agreed with Coach Dave, who I will always think of as my head coach, that I would not put all my tricks in the high school meets, at least until the state competition. But some rules are meant to be broken. I wonder if Jennifer will tell Coach Dave if I throw my *real* routines. Where are her biggest loyalties—the Fab Five or a teammate? No idea, but completely worth the risk. You want to see some gymnastics today, Chris? *Game on.*

As I mount the uneven parallel bars for my warm–up, I start with my regular high school moves. As I enter my second giant swing, I throw a release move, which my high school teammates have never seen me do, catching the bar rock-solid. Following my standard routine, I do a long hang kip-up, cast to a handstand, giant swing, pirouette, giant swing, and then decide I'm going to throw a real dismount. I also throw one more release move before my double flyaway dismount. Sticking the landing with only about a two-inch step forward on my right foot, I finish. As I step away from the bars, I notice that the girls have stopped talking and Elizabeth is glaring at me, but much to my delight, appears speechless for the first time.

"Lindsey."

"Yeah, Coach?" Hmm, wonder what he's going to say. I follow him to the side of the gym where we can chat privately while I take my grips off.

"Are you planning to do that in the meet?"

"Is that okay?"

171

"Fine by me, but if Coach Dave asks, you'd better be sure he knows it was your idea."

"Done. Anything else?"

"Any other surprises for me?"

"Um, you mind if I change my second pass on beam?"

"You gonna break anything?"

"Not planning to."

"Well, then, they're your routines."

"Thanks."

"Can I ask why?"

"Oh … um … my dad is here, and he doesn't get to see many of my meets." While this is a true statement, it is not the real reason.

"Oh, where is he?"

"He's in the red buffalo plaid shirt, on the right."

"Oh, okay."

We finish warm-ups and sit as a team, waiting for the meet to begin. I sneak a glance up at Chris, and much to my shock, Rock waves. Nightmare. Chris sees him waving at me. I fumble around in my duffel bag pretending to be busy. Jennifer scoots over and whispers to me, "You throwing the good stuff today?"

"Thinking about it." *Please don't ask me why.*

"I'll make you a deal."

"What?"

"I'll throw in some of mine too, and we don't tell Coach Dave."

"Done." *Awesome.*

North is on bars first, and South is on vault. I am last on the uneven parallel bars, which is the position reserved for the gymnast the coach expects to get the highest score. Jennifer doesn't do a release move but does throw a back, with a full twist, as a dismount. As she leaves the bars and walks toward me, we give each other our traditional double high five.

"Kill 'em," is all she says as our hands slap and chalk puffs all around us.

As I'm waiting for the judges, I hear someone yell, "Come on,

Lindsey!" It's Chris. I feel like I just got a jolt of power. The judges signal, and I salute them with a huge smile. Gymnastics smiles are easy. You learn at a young age that every tenth counts and a smile can endear a gymnast to the judges. Turning to mount the bars, my smile vanishes as I enter my bubble. I always think of myself as competing in a bubble because I don't hear or see much of anything else once I begin to focus. I am completely, single-mindedly, focused on each element. During each trick, my body moves on its own, as if every muscle is programmed to react in a particular manner in order to complete one element in position, ready to execute the next. I throw a release move that is huge for a high school meet. I get great amplitude and catch the bar solidly at the end of the trick. I am vaguely aware of applause as I set up for the dismount. My dismount is a two-footed solid landing, which I hold in a bent-knee position for a second to prove I stuck it and do not need to take a step. Then I stand up and stretch as tall as I can; then I step to the side and signal the judges. I hear Dad whistling for me and more applause.

As I leave the floor, I feel Coach Parker's arm around me. "Nice. South hasn't gone yet, but I guarantee, you just won bars."

"We'll see."

Score: 9.75. I didn't see what Jennifer got, as I was competing when her score was displayed. But seeing my score, I catch Coach Parker's eye and he winks. *Yes.* One down; three to go.

I look up at Mom, who gives me a confused look. She knows my routines by heart and knows the tricks I'm supposed to do in the high school meets. I just shrug at her in response. Happily she knows I can't come over until the meet is completely over.

Vault is next. Coach Parker catches Jennifer and me. "I don't know what you two are doing or who is throwing what at this point, but I have already turned in Jennifer as last on vault."

"Sounds good," Jennifer says, and we give each other a knowing smile. Elizabeth would have been our team's best vaulter if Jennifer and I were not competing, so I can't help but think she is annoyed that we are on the high school team.

Elizabeth vaults and gets a very respectable 9.05, which I plan to destroy. I glance at the stands and see Chris, Joel, and Mike applauding for her. Wait till you see this, boys. I notice the Neanderthal leaning back on his elbows, not applauding. Great. I walk to my starting spot on the measuring tape, which runs next to the vault runway. Each gymnast knows exactly what distance she needs to start her run at so she will be set up perfectly, on every run, to mount the horse. I get two vaults, but today, I am so charged, I feel like I only need one. Just in case, I decide to throw the big one first. I do a roundoff off the springboard and flip over, landing on the horse in a handstand. Pushing off with all my might, I do a flip off the horse with a full twist in a layout position. In order not to risk an injury too much, I don't go for the complete stick on the landing, but take a small step forward with my right foot. Pulling my foot back so that it is next to my left, I turn and signal the judges.

Coach Parker walks with me back to where I will start my second vault as he does with all the gymnasts. "You took a step," he says with a sarcastic tone and a smile.

I smile triumphantly and keep walking. I feel like I could conquer the world right now. My next vault will be a traditional mount and is not worth as much, but I know the crowd usually loves to see a Tsukahara. I land and again take a small step. I signal the judge and head back to sit with my team, completely satisfied.

Score: 9.45. This will be close, as Jennifer is a good vaulter. Jennifer chooses the first vault I did, but doesn't get the push through her shoulders that I had, costing her amplitude points. As a result, she has to pike down and take a big step to the side. I may actually win this. Jennifer's score: 9.30. Two down; floor is next.

I'm not even considering South as competition. At this point I have seen them on two events, and their gymnasts aren't even close to Jennifer and me. Their highest score so far is a 9.25, and that was a gift. Jennifer is a more powerful tumbler than I am but I have better dance, so this could go either way. Elizabeth competes right before me, and I must admit, hits her routine well—for her. I walk over to the edge of the floor, where I will start my routine. Now I am facing the audience, so I glance up and Chris waves. I don't react; I'm entering my bubble. The judges signal me; I plant a giant smile on my face and salute back.

First pass, I throw a double back in a pike position and land standing up, staying in the pose a moment to demonstrate the landing. Second pass, I throw a double twist, landing with only a small step, which I cover with a dance step. Only one tumbling pass to go: punch front to a step out, landing into a roundoff, whip back, full. Holding my last pose, my smile is now huge and genuine. Not bad at all. Finishing my last dance move, I signal the judges.

I am dying to tug my leotard back down given who is in the crowd, but resist the urge till I'm off the floor. That is a ridiculous deduction, and I know from experience, leotards always feel like they are higher than they really are.

As I head back to the team, I pass Jennifer, who quietly says, "Nice job. I haven't even decided how much to put in." I smile, and secretly hope she doesn't put in much. I glance up at the fans again— Mom gives me a big smile and Dad gives me the thumbs-up.

Score: 9.55—take that, Elizabeth.

I hear Coach Parker whisper, "Yes." Then yell, "Let's go, Jennifer," and we all start to cheer her on.

She throws two big passes and takes it easy on her last tumbling pass. Jennifer's score: 9.35.

Beam is next. This is gonna be all me. I have won beam in every meet I have been in for two years. *Bring it on.* I may be a bit shaky at times on the ground, in life, but four feet off the ground on a four-inch-wide beam, I'm rock-solid. Elizabeth barely escapes falling off on her second flip-flop. I feel bad for her because a big bobble like that is hard on your concentration for the rest of the routine. She does pull it together and hits the rest of her routine fairly well, so we all cheer her landing. I notice that Chris has clapped for everyone from North, not just Elizabeth. Jennifer is next; she throws everything in and hits. Nicely done. We all cheer her landing. Jennifer's score: 9.55.

I'm more than ready. I chalk my hands and feet and mentally run through the routine while I wait. I salute the judge and step on the board Coach Parker has set beside the beam. I take a deep breath, place my hands over the beam, and enter the bubble. I press slowly into a handstand, hold that for two seconds, and then, arching my back, I lower my legs into a reverse plange. I hold this a moment and then step down onto the beam. Vaguely I hear my team and the audience whistling and applauding. I set up my first big tumbling pass with a few poses. I step to my chalk mark, take a breath, and then do a flip-flop, layout back, layout back, and land dead center on the end of the beam. Another deep breath; only two big moves left. Two jumps; more poses. One more deep breath, and a punch front. Almost there. I set up for my dismount: roundoff flip-flop, back off the beam, with a full twist in a layout position. One step to the side on the landing. I salute the judges, radiating confidence.

As I walk back, Jennifer greets me with our double high five. "Awesome!"

"Lindsey, what a great meet!" Coach Parker says.

"Thanks," I say as I grab my bag and wait for my score. I had a few balance checks, but I think it was enough. As I start to shed my competitive focus, I realize the gym is freezing, so I put on my warm-up jacket and pants. My score is taking forever. The two judges keep discussing it. Mom has the camera ready to record the score, as she always does. Chris, Joel, and Mike are chatting, and the Neanderthal is noticeably relaxed.

Score: 9.70. Four for four. Now this is a good day! Sixteen is turning out to be a great year.

I'm packing my stuff away in my gym bag when Jennifer comes over. "Great job, Lindsey! You deserve the sweep!"

"You had a great meet too."

"Thanks."

The public-address system announces that North won the meet and that I won All-Around. I don't know when a win ever felt so good. As the announcement ends, I look over and Chris whistles. My parents are beaming.

As we're packing our gear, I hear Peggy say to Elizabeth, "Aren't you going to talk to Chris before he leaves?"

I busy myself tying my shoes, but I watch Elizabeth grab her duffel and head to the stands. A bit reluctantly, I walk over to the stands too, to chat with my parents. I know they will want to talk before they leave. I walk over slowly because Elizabeth is heading up for the section where Chris, Joel, and Mike are sitting just beyond my parents. Approaching my parents, I see the guys stand up as Elizabeth reaches their row. She puts her duffel bag down and clearly plans to talk to them for a while. Suddenly my win is not so fantastic.

"Well, you had a pretty good meet there, kiddo," Dad says as he stands up.

"Lindsey, what were you ..." Mom starts, but I cut her off.

"Yeah, Mom, we can talk about that at home, okay?" I give her a look that I know she can read as "not now." Eavesdropping, I catch bits of what Elizabeth and the guys are discussing. They seem to be talking about what they are doing later, although it sounds like Elizabeth is doing most of the talking.

"Well, you hit everything beautifully," Mom finishes.

"Thanks. I'm gonna head home, but I don't have a lot of time because I want to come back and see the football game. If there's time after the game, I may stop at home again, but ... I may just go straight to rehearsal from there. Oh, and I have plans tonight—okay?" At least I hope I still do.

"Busy, busy, it all sounds like fun. Hopefully we'll see you, but your father and I are going in town for dinner and a movie, and then your dad will probably want to swing by the club."

"Okay, have fun," I say, and then force myself not to look up at Chris and Elizabeth. Turning around I start down the bleachers, but the Neanderthal steps in front of me. My parents assume I want to talk to him, so they excuse themselves and pass us to leave. Thanks a lot.

"Wow, you can really flip," he says, while standing one bleacher level below me so we are closer to eye-to-eye. "That was amazing," he continues, putting his foot on the next bleacher up, like we're settling in for a chat.

"Thanks," I say as I sidestep around him.

He counters by moving in front of me. He looks even rougher than I recall.

"You're coming to the varsity football game later, right?"

"Um … yeah … I guess."

"Well, hey, I'm a linebacker, '56'. Look for me in the game." Then leaning down into my face, "I'm sure *I* will see *you*."

Backing away, I step by him quickly. I feel him watching me. Deep breath. Does this guy really get any dates like this?

"Hey, Lindsey!" I hear from above. Turning around, I see Chris wave at me. Elizabeth shoots daggers at me with her eyes.

"Wait up. I'll be right back, guys," Chris says as he steps past Elizabeth. She puts her hand on his arm, and Mike and I make eye contact. I don't want any part of this little scene, so I turn and head back to the team. Walking away, I hear Chris say, "What?" in an exasperated tone. Then I hear Coach Parker's shrill whistle that means the whole team needs to have a meeting.

As the team gathers, Elizabeth enters the circle with a very angry look. Terrific.

"Great job, ladies. Everyone contributed to this win. Lindsey, congratulations on winning All-Around—great meet. Okay, who's driving themselves, or going home with their parents?" A few of us raise our hands, and Coach Parker takes note. "Okay, the rest of you—let's head out to the bus. It's out the front main entrance, where we arrived."

I pull my coat out of my bag, put it on, and put my gym bag over my shoulder before heading to the stairs. I walk very slowly, as I don't want to catch up with any of the other girls. As I turn the corner and go down the stairs, I interrupt Elizabeth and Chris talking on the landing. He looks very stressed. Turning toward me and running his fingers through his hair, he softens his features into a smile and says, "Hey, Lindsey." As much as I would love to talk to him, Elizabeth turns with her hand on her hip and looks like she wants to spit at me.

"Hey," I answer and practically run down the stairs.

"Lindsey, wait," Chris calls.

I slow down and look back tentatively.

As he walks down to me, Elizabeth follows. He stops on the step where I'm standing, turns to Elizabeth, and says, "Bye," in a firm tone. It's clear something is not right between them.

"I'm sorry; I didn't mean to interrupt," I say as I turn to continue down the stairs.

"You didn't interrupt anything," he says, catching up to me. "Great meet, Lindsey." And with this, Hurricane Elizabeth passes us heading down the stairs.

"Thanks, but I feel bad. If you want to go talk to her, it's fine."

"No. Forget that. You were fantastic; I had no idea how good you are. You won every event," he says, clearly surprised, and stepping closer to me.

"Oh, I guess. Thanks." I start to head down the rest of the way, and happily Chris walks with me.

"Hey, who was that guy you were talking to?"

"Oh … um … nobody," I reply a bit uncomfortably.

"What do you mean 'nobody'? Does he go to South?" And for some reason, Chris stops at the next landing and turns to look at me. I think he can sense I don't want to talk about this. I stop too.

"Yeah, I guess."

"Lindsey, he obviously knows you. He knew your name. Are you seeing that guy or something?"

"What? No! No, I'm not. Why would you think that?" *What gave you that impression?* I don't even want to ever see the Neanderthal again. Hmm. Maybe you were as interested in my conversation with the Neanderthal as I was in your conversation with the Hurricane.

"Okay, then what?"

Sigh. "Well," I start and look down the hall to make sure we're alone. Biting my lip, I look at Chris and am momentarily taken with his piercing eyes. They seem to be looking straight into my heart.

"He was the guy that kind of gave me a bit of a hard time about a month ago at that South party."

"What? Are you kidding me? Jeez, Lindsey."

"What? I ... I ..." *Why are you mad at me?*

"Why didn't you tell me?"

"Tell you what?" I stammer, looking up at him.

"Why were you talking to him?"

"I wasn't, I ... I was trying to get away from him."

"He was watching you the entire meet. Jeez. I couldn't tell it was him; I wish I knew," Chris says as he looks away, shaking his head and hooking his thumbs in his back pockets in a clearly agitated way. Then he looks back at me and must see the hurt in my heart.

"I'm sorry," is all I can stammer. Man. I win the meet, but this couldn't be going any worse.

"Hey. No. I'm sorry, Lindsey. I just ... I mean, if I knew it was *that* guy, I would happily have had a little chat with him," he says in his charming way.

"Oh. You don't have to do that."

"Someone should, and believe me, I'd be happy to. I can't believe he sat there the whole time."

"It's fine."

"No, it's not fine," he says in his Dad tone. Then with a shake of his head and a slight shift in mood, he continues, "Well, anyway, you were fantastic. I really enjoyed watching you. You looked terrific."

"Thanks," I say, and looking up at him, everything else disappears for an instant. Catching myself, I look away and reluctantly say, "Well, I guess I better get going."

"Come on; the parking lot's this way," Chris says, pointing down the hall. As we turn another corner, I see Joel and Mike waiting. As soon as they see us, they start walking in our direction. Then I see Hurricane Elizabeth waiting farther down the hall.

"Oh, well, I think I actually parked in the wrong place. I'm down this way."

"Oh, okay. Shall I walk you to your *brand-new car*?" he says with emphasis.

Meanwhile, Elizabeth pretends to be looking for something in her bag when I know she's waiting for Chris. I don't want to be in the middle of this.

"Hey, Lindsey. Wow, that was terrific! How do you do that stuff?" Mike asks.

"Oh … you know …"

"I'll catch up, guys. I'm gonna …" Chris starts.

"I'm fine, Chris, really. Thanks. I'll see you guys."

"You're going to the football game, right?" Chris asks as I head down the hallway.

"Oh, yeah, I'll be back, and I'll see you at rehearsal."

"Okay. Great meet, Lindsey. See you later," Chris calls after me.

Yeah, great. I throw every trick in the book and still don't get the guy.

I must have parked in a faculty lot because there are only two other cars besides mine. As I approach my car, I begin to pull a bit out of my funk. I did win All-Around, our team won the meet, and I still have my awesome new car. Reaching the car, I stop in shock. My left front tire is completely flat. Again? How's that possible? Dad is going to kill me for sure. I circle around and check the back of the car. Thankfully it seems fine. Alarmed, I spin around to see if anyone is watching me. No one's nearby. Across the student lot there are some people, but they are so far away, I can't even tell if they are kids or adults, guys or girls. Stepping forward, I see that *both* front tires are flat. This is too weird.

⁊〃

I grab my cell phone and call the roadside assistance service number Dad gave me. They say they will pick it up within ninety minutes. I need to call my parents. I may never be allowed to drive again.

"Hello?"

"Hi, Dad. Um ... I don't even know what to say."

"What is it? Are you okay, Lindsey?"

"Yeah, I am. But, man, you aren't going to believe this. I have two more flat tires. I'm so sorry, Dad. I have no idea what's happening."

"Wow, where are you?"

"I'm still at South. I came outside, and Dad, I can't believe it."

"Okay, well, we'll figure it out. We'll turn around and pick you up, okay?"

"Okay, Dad. I just called to have it towed. I am ... I'm ... Who would do this, Dad?"

"Lindsey, it's fine. We'll be right there, okay?"

"Okay, thanks, Dad." Hanging up, I turn back to look at the tires. Suddenly I'm getting mad. Really mad. Who *is* doing this? I wonder if it's the same jerk who's sending the text messages. I grab my phone and find the last message. I hit reply. "Who are you and what do you want?" I hit send. I immediately get a message back that my text is undeliverable. I try this with each of the random messages I haven't deleted. All undeliverable. Okay. Think, Lindz. Maybe it's not related. Looking at my car, my spine tightens.

80 CB

"Hi, Dad," I say as I see my dad getting out of his car.

"What happened, Lindsey?" he asks, walking around the car.

"I told you I don't know."

"Well, did you drive off the road somewhere?"

What? "No, I just drove here from home."

"You must have done something."

"No, Dad. When I drove here this morning, it was fine." Looking at Mom in his passenger seat, I can see she is sympathetic. "And when I came out here ... This."

"And you called the roadside assistance?"

"Yes, they said they would be here in about ninety minutes to pick it up. They said to just leave the key on a tire. Is that okay?"

"Yeah, here," he takes the key from me and starts to walk around the car looking at all the tires. I just stand there, watching in the uncomfortable silence. Finally he balances the electronic key on one of the good tires and heads to his car. Terrific.

The ride home is quiet. Quiet is better than getting a lecture, I guess. Mom tries to chat a bit and Dad does respond, but in short, abrupt sentences.

At home, Dad goes into the office and turns on an opera. Too bummed out to go to the game, I text Melissa and Elena that I'm skipping the game and that they should go have fun. I spend much of the afternoon studying. On one of my several trips downstairs to get snacks and as a study break, I see Dad finally come out of his office to get something to eat too. I recognize one of his favorites, *La Bohème*, pouring out of his office. Confirmation he's working on a case.

"What case are you working on?"

"Oh, just getting started on a file. How's the homework going?"

"Fine."

"Lindsey, who was that guy you were talking to after the meet?"

"What guy?"

"That big guy on the bleachers."

"Oh, no one." I turn to go.

"The body shop called and said the tires were slashed. You really have to be careful where you park your car."

"I thought that was where I was supposed to be and I was just early."

"Well, next time be sure you are in the main lot, okay? I'm sure it was just some boys acting up."

"You think?"

"I'm sure it was kids—they think it was a knife, they probably saw your car, and, well, we were unlucky. They probably didn't even know whose car it was. Anyone giving you trouble at school?"

"No."

"Okay. You know, Lindsey, if you want things like a new car, you need to take care of them. It's your responsibility."

"I know. Okay."

As I walk upstairs, I can't help but wonder who would do this.

18 A NIGHT OUT: *SWEET DREAMS.*

IT'S LATE SATURDAY AFTERNOON, and Mom drives me to our dress rehearsal. I tell her I can probably get a ride home, but if not, I'll call her. Either way, I agree to call her at six so my parents will know my plans before they leave for dinner.

I enter the auditorium a bit early and sit about twenty rows from the stage, in the dark. I curl my legs up against my chest and wrap my arms around them. Stewing a bit, I contemplate who would do this to me.

Quietly Chris walks into the aisle where I'm sitting. With my chin on my knees, I tilt my head and look at him.

"Is this seat taken?" he asks softly.

"Nope," I reply with a slight smile.

"I didn't see your car out front."

"Yeah, that," I say and look away from him toward the movement on stage.

"Did you crash it already?" he asks with a smile and a small laugh as he playfully shoves my arm with his elbow and slides down low in the seat next to me.

"Well. Not an accident, but I have two flats."

"What? I was just kidding. What happened?"

"Well, after I saw you and Elizabeth ..." I intentionally refer to them together in hopes I can read his reaction. He takes a breath, creases his brow a bit, and pinches his lips. Is that frustration? "I went out to my car, and there it was with two flat tires. And I already had a flat the other day."

"You did? Jeez, Lindsey, I'm sorry. How could you get two flats—again?"

I just shrug, and then, looking down, ask, "Do you think someone would ..."

"What?"

"Well ... I don't know ... do it to me on purpose?"

"No. You think someone did it to *you*?" I shrug again, and he continues, "Probably just some guys acting dumb, but no one that knows you."

"You sure?" I say, looking up at him, clearly sad and frustrated.

"No way. Hey, how did you get home?"

"I called my folks. They were still on their way, driving home from the meet."

"Oh. You know you could have called me."

"Oh, thanks, but I didn't want to interrupt." And with that Adam's voice comes over the intercom, calling the cast and crew to the stage. I grab my garment bag as I get up, and Chris places his hand on my arm.

"Hey, are you okay?"

"I guess."

"Look, no one would do that to you on purpose. That's crazy, Lindsey."

"Yeah, I guess. I mean, I don't know who would be so cruel. Anyway, we need to get up there."

"Yeah, okay. One thing." He takes a firmer hold on my arm. I look at him.

"Are we still on for tonight? I can take you home after rehearsal too, if you need a ride."

"Honestly, I don't want to be in the middle of anything or cause any trouble."

"In the middle of what?" he asks innocently.

I give him a look.

"What?"

Seriously—are you playing dumb, or do you really have no clue? "You and Elizabeth," I clarify.

"Mina, Dracula," Mrs. McKnight calls as a greeting from the aisle as she walks into the auditorium.

Continuing intently, he says, "First, *you* are never in the way, and second, come with me tonight so I can explain. Okay, Lindsey?"

"Is Elizabeth coming?" I ask while looking down at the ground.

"No, Lindsey, she's not coming, at least not with me. I have no idea what she's doing," he says, looking right at me and gently pulling my arm to get me to look at him, and for some reason I believe him. I know I want to believe him.

Before I can process a response, we hear from the intercom, "All cast members, please get your costumes on for the first scene."

"If you're sure," I say, looking back at him.

"Definitely. Don't leave here without me. Promise," he says and puts his hand on the small of my back, guiding me down the aisle. I close my eyes for a second, enjoying this brief touch.

"Lindsey, promise you won't leave without me," he whispers as we climb the stairs leading to the stage.

"Only if you promise I'm not in the way," I whisper back.

"Deal," he says firmly.

With that we both hurry backstage to get ready.

೮೦೧೪

Most of the rehearsal goes smoothly. This is the last full rehearsal before opening night on Halloween, Friday, October 31. It's also the first rehearsal where no one but the actors are allowed on stage during any of the scenes, and only the stagehands are allowed between scenes.

Backstage I change into a white tank top and bikers' shorts to wear under the nightgown. I leave the top tie undone so the nightgown is open a bit. I think it will look right for the scene. The time for the critical scene arrives, the one that I think of as *our* scene. While the curtain is down and the stage is dark, I lie down on the bed. Chris moves to the back side of the bed and puts one hand on the mattress as we have practiced. He kneels on the bed with one leg, and standing on the other, he is ready to begin. He moves slightly as the curtain rises so his right hand is against my torso. I look up at him because this is not how we have been rehearsing our scene. He is looking at me intently. He doesn't move away an inch.

The curtain is up. We start the scene as planned, and in the dim light of the stage, it is as if we are alone in the room. Still fixing his eyes on me, he leans down, putting his weight on his right hand, which is now pressed against my waist, and places his left hand behind my head. The music intensifies and draws me into the scene even more. He slowly wraps his hand around my neck and his fingers through my hair. He looks up and down my body, which makes me blush as I become more and more self-conscious. He pulls me closer, so that I slide down until my shoulder is in the crook of his arm while his hand moves up to support my head. He gently places my stiff torso back on the pillow a bit more. I keep my eyes fixed on his. Carefully he bends down and barely brushes his lips to my neck. Before he sits up, he whispers, "A promise is a promise." I can't help but smile. Although I know it is part of the staging, it feels so natural to reach up and touch the back of his head. He pauses for a second and then brushes his lips on my neck a second time, which is not the staging we practiced. I hope it wasn't just an accident, as it sends a thrill through me, which I'm trying desperately to contain. As my pulse quickens, I am terrified that he will know I am no longer acting.

```
Van Helsing: Let her go.

Dracula: Throw it away.
```

Chris encircles me in both his arms. I force myself to gasp so I don't blow the scene.

଀଀

Rehearsal ends, and I go to the girls' bathroom backstage and change back into my jeans and a sweater. I pick up my garment bag containing my costumes and head back out on stage, where I assume Chris is waiting. There are only a few kids left, but even in the darkness of the auditorium, I can see him sitting about ten rows back. So nice. There isn't a better chauffeur in the world. As I approach, he gets up and moves to the aisle.

"Ready?"

"Yeah."

"Here, I'll take that," he says and reaches around me to grab my garment bag.

"Thanks," I say and then remember I need to call my parents. "Oh, I almost forgot; I need to call my folks," I tell him, pulling out my cell phone. There's another text:

> **3:57 P.M.** What are you doing right now? What is your dad doing? This is not a joke. Your dad should mind his own business. Tell anyone about this text and you will regret it.

"What?" Chris asks.

"Huh? Oh, nothing." I must have reacted at least a little for him to ask. I need to control my reactions when reading these crazy texts. Delete.

I hit the button to call my mom. "Hi, Mom."

189

"Hi, Lindsey, do you need me to come pick you up?"

"No, Chris Buckley is giving me a ride home. I won't be home long as I have plans tonight." Should I have said "we" instead? Could we be a "we"?

"Okay. What are you doing?" Mom asks.

"The cast and crew are heading into town for pizza. Chris is picking me up and taking a group of us into town on his boat."

"Okay. Well, your dad and I are leaving shortly. We should be home around twelve thirty or so—but you still need to be home at midnight, okay?"

"Yeah, no problem. Have fun."

"You too."

"Oh, your dad said that they can't fix your car till Monday."

"Are you kidding? Why not?"

"I don't know. You want to talk to your father?"

"No, okay, bye."

"Bye, Lindsey."

As we step outside, we are reminded by the chill that it is late in the fall and snow will be arriving soon. Chris does not automatically unlock his car until his hand is inches from the handle so that I don't even have the option of opening my door myself.

"Thanks," I say as I get in.

"Sure," and with that he walks to the trunk and puts both our garment bags inside.

He starts the car and says, "Too bad we have to pull the boat out tomorrow—feels like the season is over."

"Yeah, it might get pretty cold out there tonight."

"No worries. I'll keep you warm," he says with a smirk. Okay. Overload. No response at all. He saves me by continuing, "We'll have the snowmobiles out soon. You'll have to go snowmobiling with us this winter. You didn't come out much last year. You should see Mike. He's out of control on a snowmobile."

"Yeah, Joel said he got some award in Colorado last year."

"Yeah, he's insane. He jumps those things so high I don't know how he keeps control. So it's five forty now. I think everyone is

190

meeting at seven o'clock in town. Do you want to go home first? Or we could hang out?"

"Um … I think I should go home first if that's okay." *Hang out, like buddies?*

"Sounds good. I'd like to get a shower in anyway."

As we pull into my driveway, I have the feeling he wants to say something. When we stop, he silently gets out of the car, so I pick up my purse and get out too. He goes to the back of his car and removes my garment bag from the trunk. As I reach for it, he says, "I got it," and gestures to my front door. It feels weird—like there is electricity between us. Does he feel it too?

"So, how about I pick you up at six thirty—does that give you enough time?"

"Yeah, that's fine—I'll be out on my dock."

"You don't have to do that; I can come up to the house."

"No, that's silly. I know you're picking up other kids. I'll be down there."

"It will take two minutes to walk up to your house; it's no problem."

"Why don't you just text me when you are leaving your dock? That way I can meet you out there, and you don't need to dock your boat."

"Okay, see you later. Hey," he continues as he hands me my garment bag. After I grab the bag, I realize he is waiting for me to look at him, so I do. "Lindsey, I really enjoyed seeing you compete today. You're an incredible gymnast, and I hope you'll *invite* me to another meet sometime. I don't want to hold you up now because we don't have much time, but tonight I hope we do have some time to talk. I hope you know that *you* are the one I want to spend time with." *Blink. Swallow.* I am completely overloaded. He holds my gaze with his eyes. Again he lets me off the hook.

"Okay, see ya in a few." And with that, he turns back toward his car, and I turn to unlock my door.

The alarm is on so I know my folks have already left. As I enter my bedroom, I see forty dollars on my desk. Thanks, Dad. He never wants me to be caught short.

I change into a fresh pair of jeans and put on a beaded belt with a turquoise and pink-beaded flower buckle and a colorful top with a foil print. I change my purse to an Elvis-themed metal one that was an awesome find at a boutique near Twistars gymnastics club, where I competed last year.

Even though we are going to be on a boat, I grab a pair of heels as I don't want to be too much shorter than Chris. This is when I realize how much I'm hoping he kisses me tonight. I hope that he tells me he does not like Elizabeth and that he wants us to be together. I know that is too much to hope for all in one night, but hopefully at least he'll show some clear interest. He said he wants to talk, I hope he wants to talk about *us*. He must know I'm not one of these ridiculous girls who wants to be "friends with benefits." I hear that some girls even do things with guys they are not in a relationship with. So crazy.

I decide to take some mints in my purse, just in case. I also brush my teeth and fix my hair and makeup.

My phone buzzes, and I feel my back tense up. I realize that it could either be *them* again, or maybe it's Chris.

6:40 P.M. Ding Dong

I grab a leather jacket as I know it will be cold on the lake tonight. I give myself one more check in the mirror and head downstairs to meet Chris. As I walk around the corner from the back staircase and enter the kitchen, I see a shadow move on the back deck and scream. Quickly I realize that it might be Chris. He must have heard me as he is already knocking on the French doors and looking inside. He sees me with my hand on my chest, closing my eyes and breathing in relief. I can hear him say, "Sorry," through a smirk.

I greet him, "Hi."

"Hi. Sorry. I didn't mean to scare you," and he obviously still thinks this is a little funny.

"I thought we were meeting on the dock," I say, leaning on the door a bit.

"Yeah, well—I didn't mean to startle you. You ready?"

"Yeah, let me just put the alarm on. I'll be right out."

Pulling the door shut, I step onto the back porch.

"So, who else is coming with us?" I hold my breath; I'm nervous about his answer.

"We're picking up Joel and Mike."

"Of course, who else? Is anyone already on the boat?"

"Well, no. It's just the four of us." With this, I stop walking.

"What? I thought the whole cast and crew were coming?"

"Yeah, they are, and I think some other kids too; we'll meet them there. Come on," he says as he starts to walk again.

"Wait," I say, and so he comes back to where I'm standing. "I can't interrupt guys' night out. I can't ..."

Chris steps closer and interrupts me, "Lindsey. The only reason they're coming is because I didn't want you to feel uncomfortable. I figured you'd feel better if we went in a group, but then of course you saw Elizabeth talking to me so I thought maybe it would be better if I didn't pick up too many people. Like I said, I want to spend time with you." Tilting my head, I really don't know what to say. Once again he saves me from having to say anything. "Come on, it'll be fun. Besides, you promised," and with that he puts his arm around me and makes a bit of a show of turning me back toward the boat.

"It's really cold," I say to fill the void.

"Yeah, weather said snow tonight."

"Really?" He helps me into the boat first, then goes back on the dock to untie it. The water is black, and the sky is dark with clouds as we leave the dock. I see Chris send a text to somebody. As we pass the forest between our houses, we can see lights ahead at the Kirkwoods' place. I sit in the back of the boat, as it is hard to stand in the wind, both from the weather and the speed of the boat. Guiding the boat up to the dock, Chris waves to Joel and Mike, who are walking toward us.

"Do you want help tying it up?" I ask.

"No. They can jump in; I should be able to get close enough. Hey, Joel; hey, Mike," Chris yells over the motor.

"Hey, Lindsey," Mike says.

"Hi, guys," I say. Joel gets in first, and as soon as Mike steps on the boat, Chris guns the motor in an effort to catch them off balance. He succeeds a bit as Mike grabs the side rail and Joel pretends he's surfing. The motor and rush of water behind it are so loud that it's hard to hear anyone, but I see Chris say something to Joel and then Joel takes the wheel. Chris turns back and sits next to me.

"You okay?"

"Yeah, aren't you cold standing up out here?"

"Yeah, a little, but it's okay. I wonder if we'll be coming home in snow."

"You think? I love the first snow." My head is flung back suddenly as Joel presses the motor for more power. In seconds, we are flying across the lake. I grab the seat and can't help but smile at the thrill of the speed.

"I'll be back after I check on Speed Racer over there," Chris yells as he gets up to take back control.

Soon we are approaching town, and Chris brings us into the dock so quickly I'm afraid we'll hit it. I start to get up to help moor the boat, but Mike waves me back down. The guys get us tied up to the Emit town dock in no time. Joel comes over, and I grab my purse. Mike is already on the dock, so he gives me his hand as I step off the boat and onto the dock. We both seem conscious not to hold hands any longer than absolutely necessary, as it somehow seems weird in front of Chris. Odd to think that, since Chris has never asked me out, but somehow Mike, Joel, and I all know if I am with anyone here, it's Chris. I wonder what Joel and Mike know? More than I do at this point, I'm sure. We all start to walk over to the main street in town, where the pizza place is located. Wonder who'll be there.

Entering the restaurant, I see our group sitting in the back. Most of the cast and a lot of the crew are already here. Adam must have invited Jon to come along, as he's sitting next to Adam. Adam enjoys the theater more than Jon, but occasionally Jon will help Adam try something new as a special effect. Joel and Mike pull another table over and add it to the two already pushed together.

"Hey, Jon," I say as I take the seat Chris offers me next to his.

"Hey, Lindsey—or should I say, 'Welcome, Miss Mina!'" Jon says in his best Transylvanian accent.

"Nice. I saw your boat at the dock; have you been here long?"

"No, 'bout fifteen minutes, I guess."

"Lindsey, you want something to drink?" Chris asks.

"Sure, Diet Coke?"

"Okay."

"Anyone else need anything?" Some of the guys ask for Cokes. Chris calls the waitress over and orders a few pitchers of Coke and Diet Coke. Everyone is chatting away about the show and the scenes, hoping it all goes well. After a while, we order several pizzas. I listen to Adam and Jon for a while as they talk about the latest video game that's out.

Turning toward Chris, but to no one in particular, I say, "I'll be right back."

"Okay," Chris says and turns back to talk to Mike about how they hope we get a lot of snow this year.

It's a small ladies' room with only a single stall, which is currently occupied, so I touch up my lip gloss while I wait.

As I leave the bathroom, I double-check my zipper to be sure it's up. Does everyone do that?

Walking back to our table, I am shocked to see that three of the Fab Five have arrived, and Elizabeth has taken my seat next to Chris. I don't even know what to do, so I slow to almost a stop. Joel and Chris have their backs to me, but I catch Mike's eye for an instant. Quickly I turn around to go to the bar. The restaurant is so small I can't hide anywhere.

"Can I help you?" the bartender asks. *Yeah, can I have a whiskey?*

"Yes. May I please have a glass of water?"

"Sure thing." As he fills a glass, I look in my purse to find a dollar to tip him, but seeing my cell phone I'm wondering if I should call Melissa to pick me up. I cannot sit through dinner with the Hurricane and Chris.

"Hey," says Jon as he comes over, pretending he's watching the hockey game on TV. Thank goodness for the Crush.

"Hey." *Thank you for coming over* is all I can think while I force myself to look at the TV rather than our table.

"Looks like our pizza just arrived; want to go eat?" he asks and seems to know I don't.

"Sure," I say without much enthusiasm. Walking over, I catch Joel's eye, and then he whispers to Chris.

Turning to Jon, I quickly ask, "Who do you think will win the Cup this year?"

"I don't know. I like the Senators; how about you?"

"Hey, Lindsey," Chris says, standing in front of us.

"Hey," I say a bit nervously.

"Hey, guys, we can pull up another table for you," Joel says as he raises his eyebrows to Mike. Mike gets up and they add another table at the end.

Elizabeth makes it clear she has no intention of moving, so I head over to the new seats. Chris and Joel exchange looks. Chris grabs my jacket off the back of my old chair, and Elizabeth asks, as if she doesn't know exactly what she has done, "Oh, I'm sorry, did I take someone's seat?" *Why are you even here?* While Chris is turned away, I ask Jon, "Hey, if I need a ride home, could I get one with you?"

"No problem. Anytime, Lindsey. Just let me know."

"Lindsey, let's move over here," Chris says, putting his arm around me and bringing me over to the new table.

Glaring, I whisper, "This is exactly what I didn't want."

"Please come here," he says, pulling me over to the bar area and away from our table.

"I really don't want to do this."

"Lindsey, I'm so sorry."

"Look, if you want me to go, I would rather that you just ..."

"What are you talking about?"

"What am I talking about? Look, I can get a ride home with Jon. No problem." And with that, I start to step back to the table.

"Lindsey, is that what you want?" Chris asks, holding my arm, and I can feel the whole table watching us.

"I told you I don't want to be in the middle of anything, and I definitely do not want a scene."

"Do you want to know what I want?" Chris asks, still holding my arm and eyes firmly with his. "I already told you, I want to be with you. I had no idea she would be here. I couldn't believe it when she sat in your seat. Truth is, I'm furious, but I don't want it to ruin our night. Do you want to go somewhere else to eat? Let's go. I'll do whatever you want. Just please don't leave with … well, with anyone else."

"Is that the truth?"

"I told you once before, you can always trust me. I won't lie to you, Lindsey. Do you want to stay here, or would you rather go somewhere else?"

"Let's stay," I say, looking down, as I know this will be a nightmare.

"You sure?" and I start to walk back to the table. I'm holding my purse with both my hands, as I don't know what else to do with them. Mike is the first to acknowledge us coming back. "Here you go, Lindsey," he says, pulling out a chair for me.

"Thanks." Chris puts my coat on the chair to my right and then puts his on top of mine, and then he sits down. Interesting, he knows I can't leave without my coat, which he has cleverly put on his chair under his coat. In a weird way, I'm very pleased by this little development.

"What kind of pizza do you want, Lindsey?" Chris asks in an attempt to bring this all back to a normal night out.

"I don't care, anything's fine."

Trying to be helpful, Mike hands over a pepperoni pizza. "Thanks, Mike," I say as I take the slice. Chris takes several for himself. I am acutely aware of Elizabeth whispering to her friends. I eat my pizza rather quietly.

"Hey, Dracula," Elizabeth calls. I force my eyes to stay focused on my food and force myself to take a bite of pizza, although I've lost my appetite. Ignoring her, Chris says, "You want to get some ice cream after?"

"Whatever you want," I reply shortly, looking at him quickly.

"Dracula—so, what happens at midnight? Should all the fair maidens be nervous?" Elizabeth calls over the chatter at the table.

I look at Jon, who catches my glance while he and Adam are quietly talking. He gives me a sympathetic smile. I smile back and roll my eyes. I can tell he appreciates the inside joke. Glancing the other way, I can tell Chris, Joel, and Mike are silently exchanging a lot of information as well. I keep sipping my Diet Coke, mostly to have something to do without talking. Chris fills up my glass with his right hand and suddenly puts his left hand on my leg and gives my knee a squeeze. Are you kidding? I deliberately cross my legs. Not to be put off so easily, he puts his arm across the back of my chair. Now I think I'm mad at him, so I turn and give him a look of disapproval. He is not so easily discouraged. I thought this would get him to drop his arm, but instead he scoots his chair closer to me and puts his hand on my back. Holding my gaze he whispers, "I'm right where I want to be, next to you. You want me to leave, just say the word. But know that I came here to be with you." There is just too much going on, so I look back at my drink and take another sip. Deep breath. Truth is, I want to be with him too, just not with Elizabeth at the same table. Thankfully the waitress comes over and asks if we want anything else.

"Chris, you want to split a dessert?" Elizabeth asks from down the table. I can't help but close my eyes in frustration.

"No, thanks," Chris says, squeezing my shoulder. A few of the kids order dessert. Soon several of the actors from the other end of the table move to our end to talk about the show and laugh about funny moments in rehearsal. As I get wrapped up in the cast chatter, I start to relax a bit. Soon Mike asks for the check, and everyone digs out their wallets and throws money at him. I grab my purse to contribute, but Chris puts his hand on my wrist and says, "I got it."

I'm somehow certain that Elizabeth will take note that Chris paid for me. I'm sure this will cost me much more later.

"I'll be right back," Chris says, and for some reason, I'm shocked he's leaving me and look up at him with more concern in my face than I intended.

"What? I'll be right back. I'm sure Jon will watch out for you while I'm gone," he says with a wink. I can't help but smile as I realize he's noticed Jon's interest in me and acknowledge to myself how much I want to be with Chris. Focusing again on the conversations around me, I hear Joel and Mike talking about camping and rock climbing. Not wanting to interrupt, I take a sip.

Jon comes over and leans on the back of Chris's chair. Without missing a beat in his conversation, I see that Joel has noticed this as well. Interesting how Chris and I have no real status, but I'm confident Joel is watching me like I'm his best friend's girlfriend. Maybe this means Chris wants to be my boyfriend? Stop it, Lindz. Back to reality; you are having dinner with Hurricane Elizabeth.

"Hey, you want a ride, or are you okay?" Jon asks. I know Joel and Mike are listening even though they appear to be engrossed in their own conversation.

"Um ... I'm not sure yet. Is that okay? Are you leaving now?"

"Hi," Chris declares like he is marking territory.

"Hey, Chris, can't wait to see you as Dracula in the show."

"Yeah, I'm sure you'll be at the show."

"Wouldn't miss it," Jon replies with a broad smile to Chris and then me. I can't help but smile, as I'm impressed with Jon's confidence as he stands up to Chris, knowing full well our friendship runs deep.

"You guys ready?" Chris asks Mike and Joel. They both nod and get up, grabbing their jackets. I decide to be a bit coy and wait for Chris to overtly ask me to go with him. Glancing at Mike, I get the distinct impression he's surprised and a bit impressed that I don't jump at the chance to leave with Chris. I'm sure most girls fall at their collective gorgeous feet. These three are never without a date unless it's by choice.

"We'll uh … meet you at the boat—okay?" Joel says as they head out.

"Sure," Chris says as he leans down and whispers, "Hey. Can I please take you home?"

Without looking at him I ask, "Are you taking her home?"

"I don't know who 'her' is," and I can hear the smile in his voice, "as you are the only female I've noticed all evening." Turning toward him, I can't help but smile. With that, he knows he's won. He puts his coat on and holds mine so I can slip into it.

"Thanks," I say, looking up at him.

"Anytime," he says, looking right at me, and then he puts his hand on my waist as he walks me out. Yikes. I can't believe the attention Chris is giving me. But I don't want to be just another girl in his world of dating—I want desperately to be the one he wants as his girlfriend. Given his track record, I know this isn't likely.

Stepping outside, I zip my jacket and pull my collar up around me against the cold air.

"Well, that was terrific," he says, looking over at me.

"Oh yeah, best night ever," I say with as much sarcasm as possible.

"Lindsey," he says, slowing down, "I didn't know she was going to be there."

"Mmmm."

"Lindsey, look, we're taking the guys home, but it's still early. Can you stay out so we can talk for a while?" he says, stepping closer to me.

"If you want," I say with a shrug, but am actually thrilled with the offer.

"Good. It is what I want. By the way, what did our friend Jon want?"

I don't reply, as I'm sure Joel or Mike will let him know anyway.

"I knew it wouldn't take him long to check in on you."

Joel and Mike are already at the boat when we get there. Now the guys are talking about going snowmobiling. They have more plans for cold-weather activities than any ten people I know. I know nothing about snowmobiling, so I just listen and nod. Meanwhile, my hands are deep in my pockets, as I'm already freezing.

"I'm going to sit down," I yell over the motor, and Chris nods. Once I do, Chris guns the motor, and we fly skipping across the lake. He looks back at me with a smile. I can't help but smile back.

We reach the Kirkwoods' place first. In the dark cold night, their dock is, as my grandmother would say, lit up like a Christmas tree. Chris quickly docks the boat, and I'm again impressed with his nautical skills. I guess if you spend your life on a lake, these things come naturally. Joel steps onto his dock, and says over his shoulder with a smirk, "Have fun, you two." Mike just glances back at me and then turns to walk to his house. And I just want to die. Chris looks back at me for a second and then pulls away from the dock. I know it's probably the last time we'll be on the lake this year, so I try to enjoy the crisp snap of the wind on my face and the view of the lights on the houses and docks along the lakefront.

Having turned away from Joel and his comment, I have my knees pulled up in an effort to stay warm while I look at the far side of the lake. From this distance, the dock lights almost look like large stars twinkling in the night sky. I'm lost in my own thoughts. Does Chris really want to be with me? Will we talk tonight? Or anytime? Will I ever get a kiss from Chris? Will I ever feel like I'm with Chris? Does he just want a date tonight, or does he want a girlfriend?

"Hey, Lindsey," Chris calls over the wind to me.

"Yeah," I yell back as I start to get up and walk over to where he's steering.

"Didn't you leave your dock lights on?"

"I'm sure I did. Why?"

"I think we've gone far enough past the Kirkwoods' place and the forest, but I don't see your dock yet."

"Really? Are you sure?"

"Yeah, I mean we've gone pretty far. I'll turn on the spotlight so we can see." With that, he cuts the engine so that we are moving very slowly. At first, I'm not even sure what we're looking at, as the water and beach are all so dark.

"Yeah, there's Isabella's dock up there," Chris says as he points to some lights ahead, which I also recognize as the Castiglionis' dock. "Hold on, and I'll turn around so we can find your dock."

I'm sure that when Chris picked me up, it was already dark enough that I had turned on the dock lights. It seems very odd, too, that my folks hadn't triple-checked to be sure the dock lights were on before they left. Given that we have never before lived on a lake, they are much more cautious than a lot of our neighbors, who have spent years raising their families here. I know they left before me, but even if they had run back home for some reason, I'm sure they would have left the lights on, knowing I would be out on the lake tonight.

Chris adjusts the spotlight so we can continue searching for the dock.

"There it is," Chris says as the dock comes into view. We're barely moving when he slides his boat next to my dock. I start to climb out, and he says, "Wait, let me go first and tie it up. It's really dark tonight." And with that, he turns the spotlight to where the boat meets the dock and jumps off the boat, holding the rope. He ties the boat to the pier and then pulls the boat closer so that it rests against the pier. I step out easily, as now there is no gap between the dock and the boat.

"There's a light switch right over here," I say as I head over to the beach side of the dock and open the light cover. I flip the switch up and down a few times, but nothing happens. "That's really weird. They don't work."

Chris walks over and tries the same thing. Then he turns to the house and asks, "Where are your folks tonight, Lindsey?"

As he says this, I follow his gaze and realize the entire house is dark.

"They were going for dinner in town, but I'm surprised the house is completely dark. If nothing else, I think the landscape lights should be on."

"No problem. I have a flashlight on the boat. Let me get it, and then we can walk up. Hold on one sec."

Why would all the lights be out? Didn't I leave a light on in the house? I usually leave one on for Baron.

"Okay," Chris says, turning the light on as he steps off the boat. I'm still so cold, I have my hands in my jacket pockets and my purse hooked on my wrist. As Chris lights the path with his left hand, he puts his right arm very lightly around me. As we walk together, I am very conscious of trying not to step away from him nor step so that I am closer. Much as I'm getting a thrill having him next to me, I don't want to send any signals. Given that I've no idea what Chris and I are really doing, how can I possibly send the right signals anyway?

We are about five steps from the patio when I slow down. Chris matches my pace and stops when I do. "Let me find my key," I say, starting to look in my purse. Chris aims the flashlight to illuminate my purse.

Snap. Both of us whip around to scan the tree line next to my property as we both heard a twig break.

"Let's go," Chris states in an authoritative tone as he grabs my arm and forces me back in the direction of the boat.

"What was that?" I whisper as he is rushing—almost pushing—me back to the boat.

"I don't know. Come on, let's go," he says. He quickly helps me get back to the dock and then on the boat. "Sit down," is all he says and jumps in the boat and starts the engines again. The roar of the motor is deafening as we speed away in the dark.

I shiver as much from the air as from my thoughts. Why are the lights off in my house and on the dock? Was someone in the woods? Was it just a deer?

In a few minutes, we're in the middle of the lake and heading back toward the Kirkwoods' pier. I grab onto the rail and pull myself forward to where Chris is standing. "Where are you going?"

"Probably just a breaker out or something, but it didn't feel right back there. My folks are out tonight too, so I'm taking you back to the Kirkwoods."

"Why don't I just call my dad?" I yell over the engine.

"Yeah, you can do that when we get there."

The Kirkwoods' pier and house is still lit up when we pull in. Chris calls Joel on his cell, and while they're talking, I call Dad.

After a few rings, I turn to Chris, who is off his phone. "No answer. Since they went out to dinner, Mom probably told Dad to ignore the office for a while."

"Joel and Mike are coming out here. I'm sure everything's fine, but it sounded to me like someone was in the forest."

"I thought it was just me, but I thought so too. Maybe it was just a deer."

We both can see Joel, Mike, and Mr. Kirkwood walking from the house, so Chris ties up the boat and climbs onto the deck. He gives me his hand, and I climb out after him. I think he gave my hand a squeeze before he let go.

"Hi, Lindsey, Chris," Mr. Kirkwood calls.

"Hi, Mr. Kirkwood; I'm so sorry to bother you," I reply.

"No bother. The boys tell me that your house is black as night and that you thought you might have heard something in the forest. Is that right?"

Chris responds, "Yes, sir—I'm sure I must be wrong, but I didn't want to leave Lindsey there alone and I know my folks are still out."

"No, certainly not. You did the right thing."

"I'm sure this is all just a misunderstanding. I'm sure I can just go home. I'm so sorry."

"Don't be sorry. Let's head back over and have a look, shall we?"

"Sure, we can take my boat," Chris says as he starts to get back in.

"Joel, why don't you go grab some flashlights? And get my toolbox from the pool house," Mr. Kirkwood calls to Joel as he climbs in and sits next to me. "And get a blanket for Lindsey," he adds.

"You okay, Lindsey?" Mr. Kirkwood asks.

"Fine, I'm so sorry about all this."

"Now stop saying that. It'll probably just take a minute and we'll have your lights back on."

Joel climbs in with three flashlights and a toolbox, and gives me a wool plaid blanket. I'm so embarrassed by all this, but am glad to wrap myself up from the wind.

Chris looks back at me a few times, which I think is sweet. Within minutes, we have reached my dock, and the three guys have us tied up. Mr. Kirkwood looks at the dock light switch and agrees that it looks fine, but it's clearly not working. They share three flashlights, and we all start to walk toward the house.

"Lindsey, do you know where your electrical box is located in the house?"

"Um … yeah, it's in the basement behind a closet door. It's in the corner on that side, closest to the lake."

Mr. Kirkwood says to Chris, "Why don't you wait here on the dock with Lindsey while Joel, Mike, and I take a quick walk around the house? Once we check it out, we'll call you two to come let us in the house—okay?"

"Sure," Chris says, and I'm relieved the guys are taking care of this. I'm also pleased to learn I don't have to wait out here alone.

As they head for the house, Mr. Kirkwood is panning his flashlight across each window and door they pass. He slowly walks around the back of the house and eventually gets to the corner where I told him the electrical box is located in our basement. They disappear into the trees and plantings around the corner of the house.

"You okay, Mina?" Chris asks with a wink.

"Well, it is a dark night. One never knows when Dracula might appear," I reply with a smile. He starts to move closer to me and is looking into my eyes, when we both smile, realizing that we are not alone. Looking down in embarrassment, I wonder what the guys are doing. They have been around the corner now for a few minutes, and I wonder if they are circling the house. Chris keeps looking back at me, but I know he is anxious to see what's going on. Then we hear the guys coming back at a jog.

"Let's get you back to our place, Lindsey; you must be freezing," Mr. Kirkwood says as he puts his arm around me and pulls me into a quick walk back to the boat. As I look over to Chris, I see him, Joel, and Mike exchanging meaningful looks. So now I really am curious. "What did you see?"

"No worries. I'll take care of everything with your father. Let's just get back to our place." We can all feel the urgency of the moment, but I'm terribly confused. What could they have seen? Why can't I just go inside and turn the lights on? Did they see someone in the forest?

We quickly get back in the boat, and Mr. Kirkwood gets on his cell phone. I can't hear him even though he must be yelling given the noise from the motor. Who can he be calling? Joel and Chris are whispering, and they look back at me a time or two. Mike seems very distracted and lost in thought.

We pull up to the Kirkwoods' dock, and Chris once again maneuvers the boat right up against the dock in a flash. As soon as we are close, Joel and Mike jump off and tie us up, so clearly we are staying here for a while.

"Lindsey, I can't reach your dad yet, but I left him a message that the power is out, and as a result you'll be at our place. I've asked that he call when they get the message. Chris, of course, you're welcome to come in as well."

"Thank you." And with that, Mike offers me his hand again, and I step onto the dock. Chris walks with me to the house. The landscape lights allow me to see the time on my watch: nine forty-five. I hope we are not interrupting the Kirkwoods' night. As we approach the house, my concern is abated as I see Mrs. Kirkwood fussing about in the bright large kitchen. Even so, I hope Dad checks his cell phone soon so that we can get home and let the Kirkwoods have their evening—and, perhaps, Chris and I can still have ours. Mr. Kirkwood opens one of the rear French doors and, holding it open, says, "Come on in, Lindsey."

"Thank you, sir," I say, smiling at him.

"Well, hello, Lindsey, it's so nice to see you. Hi, Chris, come on in everyone," Mrs. Kirkwood says, welcoming us.

"Hello, Mrs. Kirkwood, I'm so sorry to bother you all like this."

"Oh, what bother? We weren't doing anything anyway."

"You guys want to play some pool?" Joel asks us as he opens the refrigerator.

"Sure," Chris replies. "Okay, Lindsey?"

"Yeah, sounds good."

"Mom, we're gonna go play."

"Sure, you guys want some popcorn?"

"Perfect. Thanks, Mom."

Mike leads us to a room on the side of the house that is covered in paneling and has several seating areas, an oversize fireplace, and a pool table. I step over to the window and sit in one of the red velvet window seats. I look out the window into the forest and wonder if anyone is out there. Kids? Burglars? What if Chris had just dropped me off and someone was there? My thoughts are interrupted.

"You want a soda, Lindsey?" Mike asks. I look over and see he has pulled out a drawer built into the wall that must contain a mini fridge.

"Sure, Diet Coke?"

"Yep. Chris?"

"Coke."

"Joel—Coke, right?"

"Yeah. Better get glasses with Mom home."

"Yeah." Mike goes to the bar at the far end of the room and gets us each a glass with ice.

"No ice for me, thanks, Mike," I say, heading over to get my glass.

"You got it," Mike says as he hands me a soda with no ice. Chris comes over to the bar as well and gets his and Joel's glasses.

Joel is busy setting up the pool game.

"How about Lindsey and me against the brothers?" Chris says to the room in general.

"Oh, you guys play. I'll just watch," I reply.

"No. Come on; it'll be fun," Chris encourages.

"Okay, if you want to lose," I say with a smile.

"You can break, Chris," Joel says, trying to give Chris some hope with me as a teammate.

While Chris is chalking up and setting up his shot, I step over to Mike, as I think he is my best shot at getting some information.

"So what did you guys see at my house?" I ask. And Chris looks up at us, but then continues to set up his shot.

Mike looks at the doors behind him. He walks over and pulls the two pocket doors closed. *Crack.* Chris hits the cue ball and breaks. Then he walks over so that we are all standing in a small group.

"Hey, Joel. Why don't you put some tunes on?" he says.

"Check." And seconds later, the room is filled with music.

"I don't think my dad wants me to tell you, but I figure it's your house," Mike says as he leans on the pool table playing with the cube of chalk in front of him. I come up next to him and sit on the edge of the table.

"So?" I ask.

"Well, first it was very dark and hard to see, so it will be easier to see in the morning." We all jump as the doors Mike just closed begin to open. We glance at the door and stand up as we see Mr. Kirkwood coming in. Turning back to the table, I glance at Mike, who raises his eyebrows for a second and then sets up his shot. Clearly he does not want his dad to know what we were talking about.

"Well, Lindsey, I just spoke to your dad and gave him a brief view of things, but I wanted to let you know that they should be here in a few minutes. I also called one of my offices over in Grand Rapids, and two of my security guards are going to come over to check things out. I'm sure we will have this all wrapped up and you back home shortly."

"Here you go," Mrs. Kirkwood says as she walks past her husband with a tray filled with bowls of popcorn and what I think are chocolate-covered peanuts.

"Thanks, Mrs. Kirkwood," Chris says as he takes one of the individual bowls of popcorn and offers it to me.

"Thank you, Mrs. Kirkwood," I add.

"Well, you kids have fun. Lindsey, we'll let you know when your folks are here."

"Thanks."

Mr. and Mrs. Kirkwood leave again.

"Lindsey, you're up," Chris says as he indicates it's my turn at pool.

"Great," I say as I try to find a shot.

"Joel, get the doors," Mike says to his brother, who is closer to them. As I take a shot and miss, I hear the doors shut.

Chris steps over to me.

"Anyway, I don't think my dad wants you to know, but it looked to us like someone deliberately dug out the main power cable and sliced it," Mike says, looking right at me. Continuing, he looks at Chris and adds, "But it's a really dark night and kind of hard to see."

"Could you see the cable?" I press.

"Cut clean through," Mike says. I can tell this bothers him.

"Why would anyone do that?" I ask, turning to look back out the window into the thick shadowy forest.

Chris steps over to me and says, "Maybe your dad had someone doing some work and they cut it by accident."

"I guess; sometimes he has people around doing stuff. But why would anyone still be working this late? The lights were on when you picked me up."

"Come on, are we playing or what?" Joel asks after his shot.

"Yeah. Come on, let's play," Chris says as he encourages me back to the game.

"Yeah, okay," I say, but I'm still distracted.

I actually start to have fun as we all laugh at our bad shots and give high fives to the guys when they knock one in. After a while, I almost forget why I'm here.

During the course of the game, I really get the sense that Chris is flirting with me, and I'm completely enjoying the attention. But now and then, I catch a glimpse of Chris and Joel talking quietly. As the game ends, I think I know why.

"Mike, you want to go play on the Wii?" Joel asks, as he puts his stick in the rack on the wall.

"Oh. Sure," Mike says, glancing back at me.

"We'll be back." And with that, Joel slides another pocket door open, and they step out of the pool room, leaving Chris and me on our own. I'm pretty sure Chris set this up.

"Hey," Chris says as he playfully bumps my shoulder with his arm.

"Hey."

"Come here," he says as he gestures over to one of the plush window seats along the wall. Sitting down, I'm hoping he is aware that Joel's parents are probably in the next room and mine are arriving soon.

"Look, I had wanted to talk to you about some stuff tonight. Well, about us," and with that, I look up at him as I like the sound of an "us." "But this is all a bit intense, and your folks are going to be here soon. So I'm hoping we can get together tomorrow? Is that okay?"

"Sure," is all I say. Brilliant response, Lindsey.

"Okay. Look, Lindsey, do you want me to stay tonight until your folks get here, or would you rather I go?"

A bit hurt by this, I look away and say, "If you want to go, then you should. I'm sorry," and now I'm back to looking at the ground. "I don't want you to feel like you have to stay."

Incredibly he takes my hand in his and says, "Lindsey, I want to be here. I want to be with you. I also want to be sure you are okay before I leave. But I know your folks are on the way over, and the last thing I want to do is to make you uncomfortable. But *I want* to be here."

"Are you sure?" I ask as we both turn when we hear the main double doors open and hear Joel talking loudly, like he wants to be sure we know they are coming in. Chris starts to stand up, so I follow suit. Giving my hand one more squeeze before he lets go, he looks right at me and whispers, "I am sure, and I'm not leaving until you kick me out." I can't help but smile at him until I hear the group entering the pool room and I remember we are far from alone.

I find it fascinating how supportive guys are of their friends. Clearly Joel thought there was at least some chance that Chris and I might be in some kind of private moment and he didn't want us caught off guard. I admire the amount of support guys give so freely. Truth is, I'm jealous. If only girls could be as truly supportive of each other. I hope one day to find one friend I feel I can truly rely on.

"Hi, Lindsey," Dad says as he comes through the door. "What are we playing here?" Seeing how relaxed he is, I take a deep breath and smile. His calm presence makes me feel more relaxed already.

"Hi, Chris, good to see you," Dad continues as he reaches out to shake Chris's hand.

Chris approaches him with his hand outstretched.

"Good to see you too, Mr. Brooks, Mrs. Brooks," Chris says, acknowledging both my parents as they enter the room.

"I want to thank you for having sense enough not to leave my Lindsey at the dock and to make sure she is safe," Dad says while shaking Chris's hand.

"Of course, sir, I would never just leave her at the dock, and certainly not anywhere I thought there might be trouble."

"Well, I appreciate that," Dad continues, looking over at me. "I can't thank you enough for bringing her here when there was the possibility of some kind of mischief."

"No problem," Chris continues in a serious tone.

"So, what are we playing?" Dad continues, like we are all here for cocktails.

"Eight ball," Joel interjects to get Chris off the hook.

"Excellent."

"Guys, let's give the Brookses some privacy," Mr. Kirkwood says as he gestures for everyone else to clear the room. "I have the game on in the other room." Chris looks at me as he picks up his drink and heads out. I hope he doesn't leave yet. After the guys walk out,

Mr. Kirkwood says as he pulls the doors shut, "David, take as long as you need."

As soon as the doors close, I ask, "Dad, what's going on? Why didn't you call me back?"

"First of all, nothing you should be worried about. I think that Mr. Kirkwood and I are going to go over to our place with his security guards and just check things out. I'm sure that the power was just cut by mistake. But to be safe, I agree with Mr. Kirkwood, we will just take a look around first. Then we can call over here and have you and your mother brought over. Regardless, we aren't going to get the power fixed tonight, so we'll just head to my apartment in the city and stay there overnight."

"Okay. If that's what you think is best."

"I do," and with that, Mom and Dad start to head out to the group.

As my folks open the doors and head back to the main room with the group, I sit back down on the window seat, with my legs curled up on the bench. Looking out the window, I rest my chin on my arm as I stare out into the night. I can hear the group talking and the game in the background. I hear the guys come back in the pool room, and I glance over to them. Joel shuts the doors behind him, so we are again separate from our folks. Walking through, Joel turns the music back up a bit, and I realize that someone must have turned it down when Mr. Kirkwood came in. Without saying anything, Joel and Mike continue through the room and go off through the hidden pocket door again as they continue to rib each other about who is better at some video game.

"Thanks, guys," Chris says as the guys step out. I stay on the bench as I look over at Chris. Please be interested in me as a girlfriend. Not just for a weekend.

"What are my folks doing?"

"Mr. Kirkwood and your dad went into his office, and your mom and Mrs. Kirkwood are in the kitchen chatting away, having a glass of wine." As Chris comes around the table to me, I realize how tiring the evening has been, and I put my head back down on my arm and look out the window.

"Can I sit?"

"Sure." I cock my head so I can look over at him. Chris sits down next to me.

"You okay?" he asks.

"Yeah, just tired."

"You may feel tired, but you look terrific." And with this, he turns in the seat and rests his chin on his left arm, inches from my face. I feel the heat start in my cheeks as he smiles inches from me. "Lindsey, can I ask you something?"

"Sure," and I sit up a bit.

"What's going on with you and Kevin Walker?" Snapping my eyes back up to him, I'm confused.

"What do you mean?" I ask.

"What do you mean, 'what do I mean'? Are you still seeing him?"

"No," I stammer, shaking my head. Why does he think I'm seeing Kevin?

"You're not?"

"No, we're ... well, I guess we're friends."

"You guess?" he says, almost laughing.

"No, I mean I know. We're not seeing each other."

"You're sure?"

"Of course, I'm sure. Why?"

"Well, I didn't think you were dating, but then I saw him take you home the other night."

"Oh," I say with relief, "he walked out to the student lot right when I saw the first flat tire and was nice enough to give me a ride home."

"Oh, I guess that was nice of him. But moving forward, how about you call me if you get any more flats?"

"Okay." I want desperately to ask about Elizabeth, but I'm too taken with him in the moment.

"I'm guessing that the guys will be back soon—too bad for me,"

213

he says while he winks at me and I smile in return. "So I want to lock you up, Ms. Brooks. You already said we would go out after the show on Halloween—right?"

"Yeah, I mean if you still want to."

"Definitely. Okay, well, I also want to take you to the after-parties next Saturday after the second show—can we do that?"

"Yeah," I say as I feel a thrill sitting so close to him.

"Great, but neither of those will be a real date, as we'll be with the entire cast and crew, so can I take you to dinner the following Friday night?"

"That sounds great," I say and can hardly believe what I'm hearing.

"If it is up to me, I'll be monopolizing all your time. Is that a yes?"

"Yes, I'd really like that." It feels like he knows this took a bit for me to say, so he takes my hand and holds it in his.

"Okay then. Should we find the guys?"

"Sure," I say as I start to stand up with him.

"Can I have a hug?" Chris asks as he lets go of my hand and opens his arms up wide. Smiling, he pulls me into a bear hug. Conscious that any number of people could walk in, I make it a quick hug and hope he understands.

"Come on," Chris says, leading me through the hidden pocket door.

"I love that door."

"Yeah, the Kirkwoods' house has some cool stuff. Sometime I'll have to show you my place."

"Okay. Hey, do you know where the bathroom is?" I can't even believe he is talking about us doing things together.

"Sure, right over here."

"Thanks."

"I'll get the guys and meet you in the kitchen."

"Which is?"

"Sorry, take this hallway and then take a right, and you'll walk right into it."

"Thanks. And thanks for talking to me."

"Anytime, Lindsey. Anytime. You ever want to talk, just let me know," he says and gives my hand one more squeeze before he walks away.

I notice the intricate floor tile pattern as I head down the wide hallway.

"Hey, Lindsey," Mom says as I walk in the kitchen.

"Where's Dad?"

"Oh, he and Mr. Kirkwood went a few minutes ago to meet the security guys at our place."

"Any word yet?"

"Not yet. I'm sure he'll call soon."

"Okay."

"Are you hungry, Lindsey?" Mrs. Kirkwood asks.

"No, I'm fine. Thank you." Looking around, I see the guys on the couches in the family room area off the kitchen, watching a hockey game. Chris catches my eye and subtly nods for me to join him. So I walk over and sit on the couch with him. Mrs. Kirkwood and Mom chat about some charity event that apparently the Kirkwoods, Buckleys, and my mom and dad are attending in a few weeks in the city. The phone rings, and Mrs. Kirkwood gets it. I try not to eavesdrop but can't help it. Clearly Mr. Kirkwood is driving the conversation, so I don't get much.

"Okay, Joel, Mike, and Chris, can you please take Mrs. Brooks and Lindsey over to their place?" We all get up, and Chris and I share a glance. I bite my lip, as I am thrilled that he really does seem interested in me, but I'm stressed with how the evening is evolving and disappointed Chris and I are not getting any time alone.

Mike says he'll pull a car around to the front door and pick us up. We all thank Mrs. Kirkwood again before we head out front. Mom, Joel, Chris, and I head out the front door, and as we get into the car, I hear Mrs. Kirkwood set the alarm. I can't help but wonder if she would normally put it on when she knows Mr. Kirkwood should be home in about ten minutes or if he gave her some reason to be concerned about things tonight and told her to put it on.

Mike has brought a Cadillac Escalade out. Mom sits in front next to Mike, Joel climbs into the last row, and I sit in the middle row next to Chris. I'm again impressed with the Guy code. No one has to say anything, and they all just understand who goes where. Somehow if it were three girls and one guy, I know this would not have gone nearly as smoothly.

Mom tells me, "Dad says that we can go in to get what we need for the night and then we'll head to his place in Chicago, so we should be there before one in the morning and then you can sleep in—you can just skip optional practice for once."

Thanks, Mom, but what about getting together with Chris? I wonder if we will get any time together tomorrow. Looking out the window, I can't believe what a crazy day this has been.

As we pull up to the house, I see my dad, Mr. Kirkwood, and two other guys, who must be the security guys, standing out front with flashlights. As I climb out of the car, I turn to thank the guys and realize Chris and Joel are already out of the car. I look at Mike as he smiles and says, "Seriously, you didn't think we were leaving until we see what's going on."

"Yeah, I guess not," I say, realizing that like a car accident, this is all too intriguing to look away.

"Mrs. Brooks, this is Johnny and Michael," Mr. Kirkwood says as he introduces Mom and me to the two security guys, "and this is their lovely daughter, Lindsey."

"Hi," I say, as I think this is all a bit of overkill for the lights being out.

"Okay," Dad says as we all start to go into the house. The security guys both have extremely bright flashlights, and Michael leads us all in. Suddenly I become paranoid that everyone is going to follow me in my room and watch me pack my bag. Do I really want Chris, Mike, and Joel watching me pick my clothes out for tomorrow? As we enter the house, Mr. Kirkwood once again takes control, and much to my relief, has the guys stay downstairs. "Okay, I'll wait here with the boys while you get what you need."

Mr. Kirkwood has one of the bright flashlights, so they all stand around his pool of light while one of the security guards starts up the stairs, followed by Mom.

"Go ahead, Lindsey," Dad directs, so I follow, trailed by Dad and then the other security guard. At my parents' bedroom, Mom pauses, and so my dad directs Michael to go with me and he and Johnny stay with Mom.

"Sure, Mr. Brooks, right this way, Miss Brooks."

"Thanks."

It's weird going through my own house in the pitch-black. I start in my room and pack some clothes, my laptop, and cell phone charger, grab my backpack, and then head to the bathroom for all my stuff in there. Soon we head back downstairs and meet up with the guys. No one really says much, and for some reason, I feel really awkward in my own house. Chris walks over to me, and he looks so handsome in the low light, I can't even believe he's in my house. Thankfully my parents packed quickly, and my dad comes down carrying Mom's bag. I keep thinking that I wish I could grab a few minutes alone with Chris, but I just don't see it happening.

"Ready?" Mr. Kirkwood asks.

"Lindsey, you ready?" my dad asks.

"Sure." And with that, I reach down to pick up my backpack and see Chris pick up my overnight bag. I'm thankful it's so dark, because I can't contain my huge smile at this show of chivalry.

Walking toward my dad's car, Chris steps very close and whispers, "Hey, do you have your cell?"

"Yeah."

"Okay, will you text me when you get to your dad's place in Chicago?"

"I can if you want, but it'll be late by then," I whisper back.

"I just want to know you're okay—text me."

"You sure?"

"Yes, and I'll call you tomorrow to see when you'll be coming back."

"Okay, good night." And then as we step up to the rest of the group, my dad surprises me.

"Chris, can we drop you at your house?"

"Oh, I can take him," Mike says in an effort to be helpful.

"Thank you, Mr. Brooks, but the guys can take me."

"Okay, then, well, thanks for everything," my dad says and shakes Chris's hand again.

We all climb into our respective cars, and I watch Chris get back into the Escalade, wishing I was with him.

I don't even remember driving around the lake; I fell asleep too quickly.

⊗⊗

"Lindsey. Lindsey, wake up," I hear my dad saying.

"I'm up. I'm up," I lie as I start to look around and realize we are in a parking garage. In a few minutes, my fog lifts. I grab my bags as my parents climb out of the car and head up to my dad's apartment.

It's on a high floor, with a view of the city. The decorations are modern and sparse. As I get into the pullout couch bed, I am exhausted. Stretching out on the lumpy bed, I remember that I'm supposed to text Chris. I don't really want to text him first—I would much rather be the one responding to one of his messages—but I did tell him that I would let him know I got here. My cell is in my purse, which I left on the end table right next to me, so I pull it out.

12:36 A.M. Hey Lindsey. Did you get there yet? Chris.

I am so happy that he sent me a text. I feel so lucky to be getting Chris's attention; I can't even believe it.

1:22 A.M. Thanks for the text. Just got here. Thanks again for tonight, was very nice of you to stay with me.

In hopes of getting a response, I keep the phone out next to me and am rewarded immediately. As I hear the buzz, I squeal privately in delight.

> 1:23 A.M. Glad to hear it. Sweet Dreams. I will call you tomorrow. Yours, Chris.

Mine. I will sleep well tonight, lumpy bed or not.
Sweet dreams. Indeed.

19 RESEARCH: *A HUGE WEIGHT HAS BEEN LIFTED.*

BUZZ. RUBBING MY EYES and looking around, it takes me a minute to realize where I am. What time is it? Oh yeah, my phone. I hope it's Chris.

> **5:36 A.M.** Morning. Forget the Chicago case, for good. Tell no one.

My stomach tightens as I toss the phone across the bed. The Chicago case? What does that mean? Okay, I can't go back to sleep now anyway; might as well find out what case my dad is on. Why would kids at school care about his case? Pulling the pillows up behind me, I grab my laptop and connect to the Internet. How did anyone get anything done before Google?

This is not the first time I have googled my dad, so I'm not surprised by the number of hits his name retrieves. Surfing through the first page of hits, I see the usual stuff about my dad, but it all seems to be articles about past cases. Typically I try not to read all the stuff on the Internet about his cases, as I find it a bit disturbing—all these people doing unthinkable things to other people. After fishing around for a while, I finally decide to just try to pump Dad when he gets up. Fortunately my dad is an early riser, and as I'm packing up my PC, he walks out of the bedroom, carefully shutting the door behind him.

"Morning, Lindsey," he says, heading over to look out at the city.

"Morning, Dad," I reply. Thankfully Mom usually sleeps in on weekend mornings, so that often is when Dad and I get our time together.

"You want to walk with me to get some breakfast?" Dad asks.

"Sure, give me five minutes to change."

ೞಀೲ

After jotting down our order in a small notebook, the bored waitress tucks the pen in her hair and takes our menus in a manner that makes it clear she has been in this diner far too many years.

"So, Dad, what case has you back in Chicago?"

"It's still in the investigative state—not really a case yet. We're still putting it together really," he says while refolding his paper to read a new set of columns.

"Well, what kind of case is it?"

"It's a bit complicated."

"How about just the general idea? Murder? Theft? Can you tell me the general category of villain?"

Lowering his paper so he can see me, he assesses my interest. As the waitress puts our juice down and silently refills my dad's coffee, he folds the paper into a smaller rectangle and places it on the chipped table. Assuring himself that the only guy near us can't overhear him, as he's wearing earphones, he continues, "Okay, well, like I said, we're still pulling everything together, and we have a lot more work to do with the investigators. But we're pretty sure that a group of guys, well, maybe some are not guys," he says, trying to be politically correct.

Rolling my eyes, I prompt him to continue, "Yeah, whatever, a group of guys ..."

"Yeah, so this group of clever guys working together across several different divisions of an investment house, set up a complicated set of transactions that, skipping a lot of intermediate steps, caused hundreds of millions of dollars to be taken out of pension funds and placed into their well-lined pockets."

"Whose pension funds?"

"Well, lots of very hardworking folks—teachers, union workers, guys working very hard to support their families. The kind of guys I grew up with in Brooklyn. Dads who want to provide for their families and who put in years and years of hard, backbreaking work, who can barely make ends meet. For most people it's not easy, Lindsey. Remember, Lindsey, you should always respect a man who puts in a hard day's work. You know what your grandmother would say?"

And we both say in unison, "A hard day's work would kill you!" I smile and am enjoying the moment. Anytime I think about my grandmother brings a warm feeling.

As Dad adds cream to his coffee, which already has some, I get the sense he is ready to move to a new topic. So I jump in before he starts talking and changes the subject. "Dad, do you ever worry with any of the cases you take now that one of the 'bad guys' will, you know, come after you?"

His eyes narrow, and we both know he is thinking about the Case. I'm on thin ice, wondering which way he will go. After a deep breath, he eyes me carefully and continues, "There are lots of protections in place to prevent anything like that from happening. And I firmly believe that you have to just stand up and do the right thing. That's why I stayed with the government for such a long time. I like the idea of putting the bad guys away. They should all be put away for a good long time."

"Yeah, I agree—it's so cool that you do that, Dad. But have you ever—"

"So …" he interrupts me before taking a sip of coffee. And I know I am nearing the end of his patience on this, but want to try one more time. The waitress wordlessly puts our plates of bagels and lox in front of each of us.

"Yeah, but do you ever worry …"

"Look, Short Stack, part of being a member of society is one's ability to make a difference. This, these cases, putting these …" he hesitates as his eyes move in frustration while his hands reach for something that isn't there, "these criminals away. This … this is how *I* make a difference."

He waves his hand like he is dismissing the rest of his new practice when he adds, "Sure, I help Robert Kirkwood and Chris Sr. protect their companies, and in that way I help them through the law." Then really looking me in the eye with that command I know he brings to the courtroom, he whispers through his teeth, "But I think the real difference I make is prosecuting hard criminals. It's what I *need* to do. For society and for me." The emphasis he put on "me" indicates that clearly this is personal for him. Picking up his coffee and talking more to himself than me he adds, "And if that means I have to ignore a few crazy people, so be it."

Pushing the limits I ask, "Crazy people?"

"Oh, Lindsey, I'm convinced there are more crazy than sane people in this world. But crazy just likes to talk; they're all bark and no bite. You'll find that most people are."

"Who do you mean, the criminals?"

"No, the guys I have prosecuted may plead that they are insane, but they are smart, evil people. When I say crazy, I mean all the looney tunes who follow cases, have way too much time on their hands, and generally act crazy."

"Act crazy how?"

"Writing crazy letters, calling the courtroom clerks with their crazy ranting and ravings, now they're on the Internet spewing their conspiracy theories—all bark and no bite, believe me. The sad truth is that the real evil people don't talk about doing things—they do them. Nothing gets in their way. I try to get the evil people put away once they are caught. But the crazies—that is something you just have to put up with in order to do the good work." Grabbing his paper, he slides out of the booth and starts to put his coat on.

And with that, I know we are done with this conversation.

Walking back to the apartment, I decide to find out what my dad thinks about last night. "So, Dad, do we have power at the house yet?"

"We should by this afternoon. Mr. Kirkwood was kind enough to ask one of his contractors to come over and do the work even though it's Sunday."

"So what happened anyway?"

"Well, I'm not sure yet—but the electricians are supposed to be there at eleven or so. So once they take a look around, we'll know more. I'm sure it'll all be fixed before dark, so we shouldn't have an issue."

"Do you think someone cut the line on purpose? I mean, why would anyone do that?"

"I don't know. Kids today can find out how to do anything on the Internet. Probably just some local kids on a dare or ..." Dad steps to the side as a group of three joggers come at us down the sidewalk.

"Look, Lindsey, whatever it is, don't worry about it. I'll take care of it. We live in a great area, and everyone has a security system. You have nothing to worry about, okay?"

"Okay, Dad."

"And always remember, ignore all the crazy people. If you pay too much attention to them, you'll become one yourself!" he says as he puts his arm around my shoulder and gives me a squeeze.

He has never led me astray before, and he kept me safe even after the Case. I'm sure he's right—just someone with too much time on their hands. I take a deep breath. A huge weight has been lifted. As the morning progresses and we walk back to his apartment, my tension starts to dissipate. I feel my back loosen.

Dad spent much of the rest of the morning on the phone, while Mom and I showered and got ready to head back home. Our home in Michigan is several hours from Chicago, so I knew we would be in the car for a while and decide to use part of the time to catch up on some studying.

ॐ∞

I must have fallen asleep, because the trip seemed to go very quickly. The next thing I remember is pulling up to our house. Looking around, I'm not sure I'm awake.

"Dad, what's going on? Who are all these people?"

"Well, while you were asleep, we got an update from Mr. Kirkwood," Dad says, looking at Mom. Not a good sign.

"And?" I ask, as I see not only an electrician's truck in the driveway, but three other pickup trucks as well. Then I see a guy I don't recognize walking around the house.

"Well, it seems that the power was deliberately cut, so Robert Kirkwood thought it might be wise to have his security guys take a look around in the light of day. It was likely a burglary attempt, and fortunately they didn't even get in. With the Internet, everybody thinks they can do anything. I'm surprised they didn't electrocute themselves in the process."

"Really?" I ask as I climb out of the car.

Dad goes up to the security guy who is closest and introduces himself. I decide to check my cell phone and am delighted to see that Chris called. He didn't leave a voice mail, but he did send a text to see how I am doing.

When Dad is done talking, I ask, "So, what's the plan, Dad?"

"Well, you can go inside. I need to go around and talk to the other electrician and see what they need. They'll probably be in and out of the house for a while."

"Okay, I guess I'll go study." I do have homework to do and I can tell Dad doesn't want me around, but I don't know how much I can concentrate with all these guys outside. Heading inside, I just can't resist replying to Chris.

> 11:32 A.M. Hey. Just got home. Sorry slept most of the trip back.

Buzz. Yes! I am so psyched that Chris is calling.

"Hi."

"Hi, Lindsey. How are you?"

"Good, you?"

"Good. Hey, Joel told me that there are some security guys at your house. What's going on?"

"Oh, I don't know. I guess they think the power line got cut like Mike said last night, and I think they're just checking things out."

"Do they think someone was in the forest when we were there?"

"I'm not sure. My dad's just talking to them now, so maybe I'll know more later. What does Joel know?"

"He said that his dad suggested to your dad to have some security experts look around. He also had some of his electricians come over to fix stuff. Do you have power yet?"

"No, not yet, but my dad thinks it shouldn't take long."

"So, what are you up to today?" *Yes!*

"I have to write a paper, and then I have some other homework I should do."

"Okay, well, I'm headed to hockey practice. I'll give you a call later—do you think I could stop by later?"

"Well, only because we have so many guys here working, let me see what's going on."

"Okay. Hey, Lindsey?"

"Yeah?"

"Hey, ya know what? It's really simple. Do you want to get together today?"

"Well, um, do you want to?"

"Yes, I do. That's why I'm asking. So, do you want to get together?"

"Yes, I'd like to," I admit, and I'm certain he can hear my smile, just as I can hear his. Closing my eyes, I enjoy the thrill.

"Okay, then. Let's just figure out how to make that happen, okay?"

"Okay."

"Great—I'll call you later. Bye, Lindsey."

"Bye."

Sigh.

Rolling over onto my back on my bed, I close my eyes and lay my arm over my eyes, daydreaming about his gorgeous smile and blue eyes.

I spend the next few hours trying to work on my paper and my homework in hopes of getting Monday's assignments done and a jump start on the week. With rehearsals in the morning and practice each afternoon, the only way I can keep up is to use the weekends to get ahead. In the past, I've never had to work "guy" time into my schedule, so now I'm even more motivated to crank through as much as possible before Chris calls.

After finishing my paper and draining my laptop of power, I head downstairs to see what's going on. I notice that the lights are now on, and laughing to myself, realize I hadn't even tried my light switch since getting home.

"Hey, Mom, what's going on? Where's Dad?"

"Well, as you can see, the electricians have the power back on. Your dad is in his office with the two security guys, so you probably shouldn't bother him right now."

"Do they know what happened?"

"I don't think we'll ever know for sure, but it seems the line was cut. They think it was just a petty theft—someone maybe trying to break in or something. I heard one of them say it didn't look like a very professional job. I really don't know much yet. Your father will let us know once he gets things squared away."

"Okay."

Flopping on the couch, I turn on the giant TV Dad had installed when we moved here and search for a movie to kill some time till Dad emerges. I'm delighted as his office doors open in just a few minutes, so I pop up hoping to get some information. But I'm frustrated as only one guy, talking on a cell phone, walks out, and the doors are closed directly behind him.

About fifteen minutes later, the other security guy comes out of Dad's office, so I knock on his door while it is still open.

"Hey, Dad."

"Hi, Lindsey, listen, I'll be with you shortly. I just need to make one more call, okay?"

So I figure maybe I can get some clue from the security guys Dad has brought into our home.

"Hey."

"Hey."

"So, um ... what's going on?"

"Nothing really, just talking things over with your dad. We're going to head out to the backyard if your Dad needs us."

"Sure." Dead end.

Only a few more minutes of my movie, and Dad comes out, so I can finally find something out. "Dad, what's going on?"

"Lindsey, don't worry. I've taken care of everything. It's really no big deal. They think that maybe someone, who clearly was not a professional, tried to cut the power in hopes of breaking in. Believe me, if it were a professional, they would have done a much better job. There is nothing for you to worry about."

"Okay," I say cautiously.

"Look, they are checking everything today, and we are having a cellular security system installed that will call the security company if ever the power is cut again. It's all taken care of."

"You think they'll come back?" I say, surprised at what he is implying.

"No, no—they know everyone in the area is aware of them now, and they will simply move on to some other area rather than come back to the same house."

"But, you don't think they got in the house, right?" A completely creepy thought.

"No, they didn't get in—thankfully. We think that they heard you and Chris approach in the boat and took off in the forest. Nothing for you to worry about."

"Okay."

A few minutes later, when I hear Dad telling Mom he is leaving the next morning to go back to Chicago for work, I really relax, because I am certain he wouldn't leave if he was worried about us. I'm also pleased to hear that his plans include being back in town in time for the play.

ℴℴ

As I wait for Chris to pull in the driveway, I'm hoping he's on time, as Dad wants me home by eight thirty given that it's Sunday and therefore a school night. Chris suggested that we get some hot chocolate together, and I am excited to get together with him to do anything. As I see his headlights, I grab my coat and purse and head downstairs. I'm surprised to see Dad coming from the back of the house.

"Bye, Dad."

"Could you ask Chris to come in for a minute? I want to chat with him before you two leave."

Great. "For what, Dad?"

"Part of the job," he says, smiling triumphantly because he knows there is nothing I can do about it. *Ding-dong.*

Grabbing the doorknob, I'm afraid of what is coming, and also somewhat curious.

"Hey, Chris," I say, gesturing for him to come in.

"Hi, Lindsey," and seeing my dad in the foyer, he extends his hand and says, "Hello, Mr. Brooks."

"Chris. Good to see you again. Listen, Lindsey's car is still in the shop and I need to go to Chicago for the week and Diane has to go in early tomorrow, so I was wondering if you would mind taking Lindsey to rehearsal again tomorrow?"

"Sure, I was planning to," Chris says, glancing at me.

"Would it be too much to ask that you drive her to practice after school and then swing her by the dealership to pick up her car after practice? I understand that you have hockey practice near her gymnastics club, and I know Lindsey would like to get her car back."

"Of course—it would be my pleasure." I can't believe what I'm hearing. Why is Dad doing this?

"I appreciate that. Also, Chris, you are, of course, welcome to come over to study lines together or do homework—whatever—but I would ask that you two come right in from the car and not walk around the property, as it gets dark so early now."

"Got it, Dad, thanks. Ready?" I ask Chris, as I'm hoping Dad doesn't have any more kernels of knowledge for us.

"Sure, good night, Mr. Brooks."

"See you at eight thirty," Dad replies as he heads back to his office.

"I like your dad," Chris starts as we sit in his car headed to town.

"Yeah, nice that he wants you to drive me around town."

"I think it's kind of cute—he just wants to be sure you have a ride before he heads out of town."

"I guess," and all I can think about is how much I wish Chris would hold my hand. Keeping both my hands in my lap, I'm hoping this outing will clarify if we are friends … or more.

"So, you never told me about your time in London," I say, as I am genuinely interested.

"Oh, it was great. Very different from the good ol' Midwest."

"How so? What did you do?"

"Oh, the usual stuff—lots of museums and pubs. The classes I took in the spring had us going to many of the classic tourist sites and museums, which were great."

"What did you like the best?"

"I don't know—it was just a great experience."

"Did you make a lot of friends? Did the exchange students get together?"

"Yeah," Chris says, and I hear his mind working with this, so I turn to him.

"Yeah?"

"It's just a lot different over there, Lindsey. So, you ready for the show Friday?"

"Yeah, I guess. What do you mean, 'different'? Did you party a lot?"

"Have you talked to your friend Jon?"

"What? About what?"

"London?" Chris asks, and with this, he looks over at me.

"No, why? Did you see him over there?" I ask as I recall that Jon spent part of his trip to Europe in London.

"Yeah, I did. There was this big party one of the American exchange students threw that I guess Jon knows through his cousins," Chris says as we pull into a parking spot in town. "Look, Lindsey, I did go out a lot there. To be honest, I went a little crazy over there for a while, but then during the summer, I realized that's not what I want to be doing."

"Okay," I say, a bit confused.

"Look, sometime I'll tell you whatever you want to know, but for now, can we leave it at that?"

"Did you do something bad?"

"No. No, no, nothing like that. Just probably partied, and, well, let's say indulged a bit too much. Truth is, I've probably been doing that since starting high school—but now I see it for what it is. But none of that has to do with now. Okay?"

"Okay." *What does that mean? Were you with a bunch of girls? Did you do drugs? Did you drink at every pub? Do I care? I'm with Chris Buckley. OMG!*

"Lindsey, I like spending time with you. Can we just go with that for now?"

"Sure," I say, smiling while the questions continue to brew.

We chatted through our cocoa and drive home, talking mostly about the play and how excited we both are to be in it. As we circle the lake back toward my house, I can't help but wonder if we really are just becoming better friends and nothing more. Certainly nothing more is happening. As we pull into the driveway, I scan the windows for dear old dad. Chris gets out and walks me to the door.

"Good to see you, Lindsey," he says, and I see that he has stopped walking.

"You too. Thanks again for the cocoa," I say as I stop on the front step and turn to face him. He stopped one step below me, so that he is only a few inches taller than me.

"No problem. I'll pick you up in the morning—usual time—okay?"

Looking directly at him, I can't help but wish he would kiss me, but no luck. Turning to go, I say, "Okay, see you then."

Smiling, he says, "See ya." *Does he know I want a kiss? What if he just wants to be friends and he knows I have a complete crush on him? What if I am to Chris what Jon is to me? Please let that not be the case.*

20 PICKUP TRUCK: *WHO'S THAT GUY?*

AS I TURN IN the driveway, I look in my rearview mirror and am thrilled to see Chris has followed me into my driveway. As per Dad's request, he took me to rehearsal this morning, took me to practice at the club after school, and then shuttled me over to the dealership to get my car. Dad didn't ask that he follow me home, but I was hoping he would. Looking toward the house, I see a pickup truck and wonder if a worker is still here finishing the electrical work or working on the alarm system. As I round the curve in the driveway, I see some guy with Baron. *Who are you and why do you have my dog?* As I shift into park, my phone rings throughout the car, and I see on the panel that it's Chris.

"Hey, Lindsey. Who's that guy?"

"No idea. And why does he have my dog?"

"Stay in your car, okay?" Watching through my rearview mirror, I notice that Chris has parked to the side of me. *Is that so I could back out of the driveway past him if I needed to?*

"Why?"

"Let me go talk to him to see who he is, okay? And stay in the driveway; don't pull into the garage yet."

"Okay—you sure you should? Maybe I should call my dad first?"

"No, I got it. Just stay there for a second. Bye."

Hanging up, I keep my focus on Chris, who is walking past my car toward the guy. The guy meets him halfway, extends his hand, and shakes Chris's. I watch them talk for a few minutes. Chris looks back at me a few times, but doesn't indicate that I should come over so I decide to wait. It's already dark out so I can't really see much of the other guy's facial expressions. Just as I start to get restless, Chris starts to walk back, so I open my door to step out.

"Wait a second; I'll get in," Chris says as he comes around to the passenger side of my car. Pulling my door shut again, I wait for him to get in.

"Hey, did your dad call you today?"

"Why?" I ask as I reach into my glove box in front of Chris to pull my phone out to check who called earlier.

"He says your dad hired him to walk Baron."

"Are you serious?"

"That's what he says."

"Well, there is a message from my dad's office—let me check it." Just in case, I tap my phone so the message won't play through my car's sound system, but rather just to me.

"It's my dad's secretary; she says that he did hire a dog walker and that the guy has a key to get in and out to walk Baron. How weird is that? A few years ago, my dad would never have spent money on something like that," I say, looking at Chris.

"Well, I guess he did now. Did she give you a name?"

"Joe Mitchell."

"Yep, that's him," Chris says, eyeing him. "Listen, why don't I stay and hang out till your mom gets home, just to be sure."

"You don't have to babysit me. She should be home in about twenty minutes. I think I'll be okay for twenty minutes."

"Just the same, I'd feel better."

"Okay," and with that, I pull up the driveway and into the garage.

Entering the kitchen, I get us both a drink and call my dad's cell.

"Hi, Dad," I say, glancing at Chris, who is sitting at the island, watching me.

"Hey, kiddo, how's the car?"

"Oh fine—so you hired a guy to walk the dog?"

"Yes, did he show up?"

"Yeah, he's here. Why do we have a dog walker? I can walk Baron when you're in Chicago."

"Well, I don't want you or your mother walking around in the dark alone, just to be safe. I thought you'd be happy not to have to bundle up at night."

"I guess."

"I actually have a lot to get done so I can be back in town Friday, so is there anything else?"

"No—oh, does he come in the house?"

"Yes, he has a key and his own security code, so he shouldn't bother you."

"Okay, well, have a good night, Dad."

Turning back to Chris, I say, "Well, we apparently now have a dog walker. Dad says he doesn't want me or my mom walking Baron alone at night anymore."

Shrugging, Chris says, "I gotta say I think he's right, Lindsey."

"Is he still out there?"

"Yeah, I just saw him bring Baron around back."

Turning my head, I hear the garage door open. "That must be my mom."

"Okay." Chris walks to the front door, and even though I'm still sweaty from practice, I can't help but hope I might get that kiss tonight.

Opening the door, he turns and simply says, "Have a good night."

"You too. Hey, thanks for the rides today."

"No problem. You driving to school tomorrow?"

"Yeah."

"Okay, well, can I take you to the show Friday night? We're still on to go out for Halloween afterward, right?"

"Yeah, sounds great."

"Good, I know a lot of kids are going out, and there's at least one party so the whole cast should have fun."

"Sounds good. Thanks again."

"Bye."

Shutting the door, I head to the family room and flop down on the couch in complete frustration. Why does he have to refer to the entire cast? I think I read too much into my birthday card and the night out for pizza. Chris doesn't have a bad reputation, but I certainly think with as much dating as he has done, if he liked me, he would have kissed me by now. *Arrrggg.*

Mom confirms that the guy with Baron is our new dog walker, so I decide to head out and introduce myself.

"Hi, you're Joe, right?"

"Yeah, you must be Lindsey," he says, offering me his hand.

"So, you're a dog walker?" I ask skeptically.

"Yeah, among other things. Your dad tells me you're quite the gymnast."

"He did?"

"Yep. He says that's why you get home from school so late."

"Yeah, I guess. So are you coming to walk Baron every day?"

"Most days, yeah. I guess your dad travels a lot, so whenever he's out of town."

"Oh. Okay, well, do you want anything—a drink or something?"

"No, thanks, I'm fine. I'll bring him in soon, and then I'll be back around eleven."

"You have to come back and walk him at eleven?"

"Yep. I'll walk him each afternoon, early evening, and again at night."

"Okay, well, if you need anything, just let me know."

"Sure, actually I do want to give you my cell phone number."

"Oh, okay." Confused, I pull my phone out. "Joe Mitchell, right?"

"Yeah. Here, I'll call your cell so you have the number," and with that, he pulls out his phone, and seconds later mine vibrates.

"You have my number?" I say, noticing that he is pretty young, maybe twenty-five or so.

"Your dad gave me everyone's numbers."

Accepting his call, I add him to my contacts.

"I'm getting cold; I'm gonna head back inside."

"Yep, see ya tomorrow."

"Bye."

80C3

"Hey, Chris," I say, too excited that he called me.

"Hi, Lindsey. Is it too late to call?"

"No, it's fine."

"How did the rest of your night go?"

"Good. Talked to the dog walker."

"Yeah, and?"

"If you ask me, I think my dad hired him to watch me as much as walk the dog."

"Can't blame him, given all the trouble you get in. Seriously, is that so bad? If I had a wife and kids, I would want them to be safe if I was out of town on business a lot." So nice.

"I guess—just seems kind of weird. He's coming back at eleven to walk Baron again. If nothing else, Baron is going to love all this attention."

"Yeah, well, I'll let you get some sleep. See you tomorrow."

"Okay. Bye."

"Good night, Lindsey."

A good night indeed. Never too late for you to call.

21 HALLOWEEN: *WILL WE EVER HAVE OUR FIRST KISS?*

"THANKS FOR COMING HOME early, Mom."

"Well, I can't have Mina fainting on stage now, can I?" Mom says as she finishes packing her camera in a tote to bring tonight.

Ding-dong.

"I'll get it; it's probably Chris. He should be here soon."

Turning the corner, I see Joe answer the door.

"Hi, Chris."

"Joe. Hey, Lindsey. Are you ready?"

"Yeah, my costumes are right here in the closet," I say, walking over to get the bag.

"Here, I'll get it," Chris offers. I notice Joe has stepped into the kitchen to give us some privacy.

"Okay. Mom, I'll see you there."

"Have fun, Lindsey. You too, Chris."

"Thanks, Mrs. Brooks," Chris calls as we step outside.

238

"So why is Joe in the house? I thought you said he stayed outside most of the time."

"Yeah, he does, but Dad asked him to stay in the house tonight to take care of the trick-or-treaters. I guess he doesn't want to get TP'd tonight if no one's home to hand out candy."

"Yeah, that would be a mess. So, you excited?"

"Yeah, just afraid I'll blow my lines."

"You aren't going to blow your lines. You'll be terrific."

"I hope so."

"Did you bring a costume for later?" Chris asks as he opens the car door for me.

Cringing a bit, I reply, "I guess so. Thanks."

"So, what is it? You wouldn't tell me all week, but now it's Halloween," he asks leaning down toward me between the car door and the side of the car.

"You'll see tonight," I say, smiling at him.

"Okay, fair enough," he says just before shutting the car door.

“”

It's about five minutes before curtain, and I'm so nervous. Chris finds me backstage, where we are both in full makeup and costume. He looks amazing. He steps toward me in the darkness offstage, where I'm waiting to start.

"Hey," he whispers as the auditorium is filling with our friends and family.

"Hey."

"This is perfect—you as Mina and me as Dracula—on Halloween."

"Yeah, it's pretty cool."

"After the show will be great too. The party should be a lot of fun."

"Yeah, I'm sure it will."

"You know who I'm hoping you're dressing as?"

"No, who?"

"Mina."

What does that mean? You want me to go out in a nightgown? Or do you want us to go as a couple? Then we see the lights flash, which is our signal for the show to start in two minutes and to take our places.

"Really, why?" I say, confused a bit.

"Gotta go. Break a leg."

"You too," I say with a grin.

Chris just shakes his head and walks off. What does *that* mean? No time. Showtime.

₮₱

Just like a gymnastics meet, as soon as my first scene begins, I start to ignore the audience and focus on my role. The action goes by quickly compared to rehearsals—no starting and stopping to discuss the scenes. No rewinds and redos; we just plow forward.

It feels like we just started, and I'm already changing into my nightgown for *our* scene. I'm so excited to do the scene, but also terrified to go on stage in a nightgown and wonder if I can pull off this particular scene with everyone I know in the audience. I wonder if Dad will like Chris as much as he does after he sees this. I wonder if Elizabeth, aka the Hurricane, is here—this is really going to put her over the edge.

The curtain goes down, and I see Chris backstage. Walking shoulder to shoulder, he whispers, "Here we go," as he gently puts his arm around my shoulder and squeezes me. I creep across the dark stage chilled in my bare feet and lie down on the bed. Chris positions himself behind the bed. He moves in closer, leaning over me, and puts his right hand against me so I can't inch away. Then he places a knee against my right side. He is so close. I can feel my heart race. Chris is ready for the scene.

The curtain begins to rise, and I hear the momentary rustling of the audience. Then the entire room is still. I know there are several hundred people past the pool of light we are in, but they are silent. Chris puts his hand on my right arm. I look up at him, wondering if anything is wrong, as this is not how we staged the scene. He widens his eyes for a moment, which I take to mean everything is okay. Blushing, I wait for him to start. He is so composed, he pauses, intuitively building the tension of the moment.

He is looking at me so intently I let out a breath, as I am completely captivated by him. My waist is pressed between his knee on one side and his hand on the other. My stomach drops. I hope he has no idea the effect he has on me. I close my eyes briefly and try to pull my mind back to the scene.

The curtain is fully up. Still looking at me, he leans down to put his weight on his right hand, which he slides to the mattress so as not to put his weight on me. The audience is silent. The entire room is still, except for Chris. He purposefully places his left hand behind my head. The music starts and is as intoxicating to me now as it was the first time I heard it. He slowly wraps his fingers around my neck and gently grabs my hair. He makes a bit of a show of looking me up and down, and as predicted, I blush, but for some reason I can't take my eyes off him. As he did in rehearsal, he pulls me closer. I slide down so that my shoulder is resting in the crook of his arm, which feels incredibly natural. Gracefully, he adjusts his hand so that he is supporting my head. Slowly he lays my torso back on the pillow, just as we had rehearsed. He has a sparkle in his eye as, ever so slowly, he bends down and kisses my neck while his hand squeezes mine. I know I'm not wrong. He didn't just brush his lips on me; he *kissed* my neck.

I can't help but close my eyes and let out a breath. Suddenly I realize he must have heard my reaction, so I bite my lip in embarrassment. Snapping my attention back to my role, I reach up and lay my hand lightly on the back of his head. I notice again how still the entire auditorium feels.

As the scene continues, Chris grabs me in both his arms, and I realize how strong they feel around me and how carefully he is trying to hold me. I gasp audibly, ending my part in the scene. Van Helsing and Dracula exchange their lines.

Turning from the audience, Chris locks his eyes on mine. He pulls me up a bit so I am resting on both my forearms. Still looking at him, I see Chris rip open his shirt and turn his back slightly so he is facing away from the audience. Then, wrapping his right arm around me, he touches my face, gently pulling it near his neck. I stiffen as I did in all the rehearsals as I try to keep my face close to him without actually making contact. Moving his head down and slightly toward the audience, he says Dracula's line in a vicious and harsh tone.

```
Dracula: Now she will be blood of
my blood, kin of my kin, later my
companion in the night. You are my
slave and helper.

Curtain.
```

As I start to get up from the bed, Chris's hand lingers on my neck for a few more seconds. Then we are both rushing offstage for the change in scene.

༄ ༅

I'm not on stage in the final scene, so as I watch the three guys, including Chris. I am feeling relieved I didn't miss any of my lines. Since the cast is so small, Mrs. McKnight said we should all line up together to take a group bow. As the curtain comes down, the audience seems to respond really well—it sounds like everyone is applauding, and lots of guys are whistling loud enough to hail a cab in Manhattan. As I walk onstage, Chris comes over and takes my hand to be sure we will line up next to each other. It feels too good to hold his hand. The curtain stays down for a few seconds while we all get in a straight line. As it rises, Chris squeezes my hand, and I react with a huge and genuine smile. The audience continues to applaud loudly as we take two bows. Then we all applaud Chris as he steps forward for his individual bow as the lead.

A stagehand walks onstage to bring each of the girls a small bouquet of three roses. As he offers mine to me, I gratefully accept with a smile I can't contain. The curtain comes down a final time, and we all cheer for each other.

"You were terrific, Lindsey!" Chris beams.

"Me? You brought the house down!" I reply. Everyone is congratulating everyone else while we hear the audience end their applause and begin to leave the auditorium.

"Great job, everyone! It was terrific! Be sure to leave your costumes in the dressing rooms for tomorrow. Remember, tomorrow's show starts at six, so please be here at five. Have a happy Halloween!" I think Mrs. McKnight is genuinely pleased with the performance.

"Okay, I'm gonna change and then shower in the locker room," Chris says, looking at me.

"Oh, okay."

"I'll meet you in the lobby in a few, okay?"

"Okay."

"Finally, I'll get to see your costume," Chris teases.

"It's really not very good; it's kinda silly."

"I'm sure it's gonna be great. And we're gonna have a great time, okay?"

"Okay, I'll see you in a few."

                                                                  ȣ C3

After I talk to a few of the stagehands and put my costume away, I exit the stage by the side door and walk through the hallway leading to the lobby. My parents see me right away, and we work our way through the crowd to meet up. I give Mom a big hug and say thanks as she hands me a dozen pink roses.

"You were terrific, Lindsey. Everyone was. It really was a wonderful show."

"Thanks. I felt kind of stupid in a nightgown," I say, testing whether they are going to comment on that scene.

"Oh, it looked perfect for the scene. *Dracula* is a classic, and I loved that you kept the integrity of the original story. Kiddo, you really did a great job," Dad adds, pulling me into a bear hug.

"Thanks, Dad, and thanks for making the show."

"I wouldn't miss it."

"*Lindsey!*" I hear Melissa from across the room. I turn to see Melissa and Elena rushing over to us. In a far corner, I see Chris with wet hair leaning against the wall with Joel and Mike. Of course, the Hurricane has planted herself in front of him. Our eyes lock for an instant, and as I turn away, I think I see him push away from the wall.

"Mr. and Mrs. Brooks, wasn't Lindsey the star of the show?" Melissa says triumphantly.

"Well, we certainly think so," Mom agrees.

"You were terrific," adds Elena.

"Thanks, guys."

"Hello, Mr. Brooks," Chris says from behind my dad.

"Well done, Chris—you were excellent as Dracula. Very convincing."

"Thanks."

"Yes, I just told your mother that we both thought you did an excellent job," Mom chimes in. "Well, Lindsey, you have fun. Do you want me to take the flowers home for you?" Mom asks.

"That would be great. Can you put them in water tonight? They are so beautiful and smell wonderful."

"Absolutely. We're headed to the club with a few of the other parents, but I'll wrap them in a damp towel, no problem."

"Okay, well, you kids have a great night," Dad chimes in, but I knew it wouldn't be quite that easy. After he steps away, he turns back, like he just remembered that I have a curfew. "Home at midnight," he calls, leaving our circle. I catch Chris smiling as he looks down. *Subtle, Dad—very subtle.*

"What are you guys doing now?" I ask Melissa and Elena.

"Oh, we're headed over to Delaney's party—aren't you going?" Melissa asks, looking at me and Chris.

"Yeah, we're headed there as well," Chris confirms.

"Okay, well, great job, Lindsey. See you at the party!" Melissa and Elena turn away, giggling and whispering to each other, mischievously. I look around as they walk away and realize that a lot of people have left the lobby already.

"You ready?" Chris asks.

"Um, I just want to go talk to my coach before I go—okay?"

"Sure."

I see Coach Dave's face light up as he sees me walking toward him.

"Lindsey, you were terrific—what a great show! Completely worth missing a few practices for this."

"Thanks. Coach, this is Chris Buckley. He plays hockey in the rink near your club."

"How are you, Chris?"

"Nice to meet you, sir."

"You really didn't have to give up your night for this, Coach."

"I told you I wouldn't miss it, and I'm so glad I didn't. Chris, you were terrific as Dracula—you both really did a great job—I'd give it a perfect ten."

"Thanks, Coach."

"Well, I'm sure you have somewhere to go before you get home early to get some rest."

Rolling my eyes a bit I say, "Yeah, yeah, I won't be out too late. See ya."

As we walk away, Chris asks if I'm ready to go.

"Yep, but where's your costume?" I reply, looking into his gorgeous blue eyes.

"In the car. Pretty easy really—I have a cape and fangs. The real question is, where's your costume? Hmmm," Chris asks, smiling at me.

"In here," I say, raising a small duffel bag.

"Excellent. Let's go," and with that, we turn to cross the lobby toward the exit.

I look around and see that among the few people lingering are the Hurricane and two of her cohorts—I force myself not to look at them as we leave.

Chris opens the passenger-side door for me again. I hope he never stops doing that.

"Thanks," I say, looking at him and sliding into the deep bucket seat. Beyond Chris, I see that Elizabeth is just steps behind us. Terrific. As he shuts the door, I hear her call, "Hey, Dracula."

Straining to hear but not wanting to appear curious, I begin digging through my bag, hoping they will not notice how interested I am in every word they utter.

"Chris?" Elizabeth says as she approaches.

"What's up?"

"Are you headed to the party?"

"I'm headed out with Lindsey."

"Well, I'm sure she'll bore you by ten, so if Dracula wants to come out and play at the bewitching hour, text me." *Whore!* I am furious and don't know what to do.

Chris doesn't react. He just opens the driver's-side door and slides in. Before I can breathe, he has the car in reverse and we are pulling out, but I can hear Elizabeth and her evil friends laughing.

I don't even know what to say and hope that he does.

"So, you like roses?"

I'm still so distracted by the Hurricane I answer without even thinking, "Sure, they were gorgeous. Who wouldn't love 'em?"

"Well, that's interesting, because I seem to recall you telling me that they were ... what was it again? 'Silly.'"

"What?"

"Right before Flower Day. You said they were silly."

Are you kidding me? We both look at each other, and I can't believe this is what we are discussing. *Did you just hear Elizabeth offer herself to you after you dump me at home?*

"So, you do like flowers?"

"Well, I … um … well, yes."

"Then why did you say that?"

Are you trying to embarrass me? I look at him incredulously and have no words.

"I'm asking honestly."

"Okay," I start, and I can't believe I have to actually say this out loud. "The truth is that, yes, I do like flowers, but unlike you and everyone else," I say, looking out the window so we can't make eye contact, "I knew I wouldn't get any. And we were walking into the lunchroom, and I didn't want to stand there and watch you order a bunch for her. Okay. That's the truth." *And now you can dump me at home.*

"Hey," he says softly. "Lindsey. Can you please look at me?"

Deep breath. Then I look over at him. He glances at me as often as he can, given that he is still driving.

"Well, if you want to know the truth, I had ordered flowers for you, and only you. But you said that it was silly, so I went back and canceled them."

"Right. Don't do that."

"Do what? That's the truth."

"Really?" *Do you have any idea how I would have felt to get just one carnation from you?*

"Really. How many times do I have to tell you? I'll always tell you the truth." So I decide to try to take advantage of the opportunity.

"Okay, so tell me about London," I say, forcing my face not to change expressions.

Smiling, because he again knows he has me, he says, "London, huh? Not now."

"Why not?"

"That will have to wait, because here we are and now I get to see your costume—so what is it?"

"It's silly," I say, smiling at him.

"Well, you seem to be in all black from what I can see, which is a great start!"

"Really? Okay, well ..." *Need to remember he likes black.* Pulling out the ears and tail I continue, "I'm a black cat. Dumb, right?"

"No, I think it's cute. You ready to go in?"

"One second." I put the ears on and grab my purse. "Okay." Reaching for the door handle, I feel Chris grab my arm.

"I need you to promise me something," he asks in a more serious tone, leaning very close to me. So close I can smell his cologne.

"What?" I guess I should just say yes now, because I can't say no to Chris.

"Promise me you'll let me take you home?"

I look down for an instant and then back into his eyes. "Do you want to take me home?"

"Yes."

I want desperately to ask if he plans to drop me off early and meet up with the Hurricane, but I am such a wimp.

"Okay. If you're sure."

"Great, let's go, kitty," he says, smirking as he climbs out of the car.

As I walk in the house, I immediately see my buddy Mark down the hall.

"Hey, Lindsey, you were amazing!" Mark yells and waves me over.

Turning to Chris, I say, "I'll be right back, okay?"

"Sure, I see Joel over there."

"Okay," and I squeeze through the crowd to the group where Mark is standing. He reaches over and gives me a big hug. Given the conversation I overheard with the Hurricane, I eagerly embrace him.

"Thanks."

"It was a great show," Mark continues.

"Thanks, we had a lot of fun."

"Hey, you need a drink. What do you want?"

"Oh, is there soda or something?"

"Come on, you lightweight! I'm just kidding. Here, let's go in the kitchen."

I happily spend the next twenty minutes or so with Mark and his friends chatting about the show and their next rock-climbing trip. Finally, I excuse myself to find Chris. Walking into a large sitting room, which is packed with kids, I see Mike across the way by the fireplace talking to a group of guys. He catches my eye and nods for me to come over. As I'm trying to squeeze through the crowd, Isabella and Rick grab my arm and congratulate me, so I spend a few minutes talking with them. They are dressed as Tarzan and Jane. *I can't believe she wore that! No way her dad saw that costume.* Turning away, I continue to work my way over to the fireplace, when I see Jon. No sign of Chris. I give Jon a big hug, and he, too, is lavish in his praise. I tell Adam I think he did a great job, especially in picking the background music for the show. Happily, he said he will burn a CD of the music for me. I finally break away from them and turn to look again for Chris when Joel steps right in front of me.

"Hey, Lindsey! You were terrific tonight. Oh, hey, you look low; let's go get you another drink," and with that he grabs me by the arm and yanks me back toward the kitchen.

"Oh, okay. Hey, do you know where Chris is?"

"Oh, yeah, he's around. We'll find him in a minute." Given what good friends they are, I'm immediately suspicious, so I slow down against his grip and try to look around him.

"Lindsey, come on."

"Why? What's going on?"

"Nothing."

"Nothing?"

"Let's just get you a drink, okay?"

"Where's Chris?"

"He'll be back in five minutes, okay? Can I just get you a drink or something?"

And I know.

"He's with her, isn't he?" No response.

"Man," I say under my breath, looking down and shaking my head in disbelief.

"He's just trying to straighten some things out. But he asked me to ..."

"To what? Watch me while he is off with that ... that ..."

"No, no, Lindsey. It's not like that at all."

"Oh, really? Thanks, Joel," I say and push my way past him.

"Hey, hey, Lindsey, wait up," but I keep shoving my way through the kids, who react as I pass through as if they want to chat about the show. Suddenly, I'm in no mood. I see Mark. Bingo.

"Hey, hey, Mark."

"Hey, Lindsey."

"Did you drive here?"

"Yeah, why, you need a ride?"

"I think I might. I know I'm completely out of your way," I start, but he waves me off.

"Would you stop? Anytime. Just nod and I got you covered—okay? Hey, I thought you came with Buckley."

"Yeah, I did."

"Well, then, I'm definitely driving you home."

"Why?" and I see Joel over my shoulder trying to move into our circle. The one advantage to being small is that I can squeeze through the crowd faster than the guys. Mark notices Joel. Knowing Chris and Joel are such good friends, he leans in to whisper to me, "Sorry, Lindsey, but I saw that French maid go upstairs with Buckley." Pow. I want to hurl. Or scream. But mainly I want to cry.

"Thanks," I whisper back as I find myself holding his arm for strength. My head is spinning.

I look over at Joel, and he starts, "It's not what you think, Lindsey." And he pushes his way over and grabs my arm. Mark takes a swig of beer, but I know he's watching. Then we are all bumped a bit by the swell of the crowd, and now I can see directly up the stairs and down the upstairs hall. I see Chris come out of a room upstairs. He's looking down at the floor and running his hand over his face in frustration as he walks toward the stairs in my general direction.

When he looks up, our eyes lock. He stops. Then I see her—the Hurricane, dressed as a French maid—walking out of the same room Chris was in. He sees that I'm looking past him, so he turns back, sees her, and then whips his head back to me as our eyes lock again. I can't keep the hurt out of my face. He starts shaking his head no, and his eyebrows and palms rise like he is Mr. Innocent. I am flooded with emotion. He slows and almost stops walking. Guilty bastard. For once, I hold my eyes right on his. Could her top be cut any lower? I feel mortified. I turn away, but Joel grabs me.

"Whoa, Lindsey, listen to me."

"Let go of me," I say in a fierce whisper, trying not to cry.

"No, you need to understand."

"Believe me, I understand. I heard her pathetic offer."

"Do you really think he's interested in *that?*"

"You know about it? Of course, you do. Let me go." And I pull away, but he just holds me tighter.

"No, Lindsey, you need to talk to Chris. Look, all I can tell you is that he's never been like this."

"Seems to me he has been like this all through high school."

"No, what I mean is," and then I feel another hand around my waist. Lurching forward, I grab at the hands coming around me in a feeble attempt to pull them off me.

"Hey," Chris says, pulling me completely against him from behind. Since the party is so jammed with people and so dark, I doubt anyone can see this, but I feel like everyone is watching. Now my entire body is against his, and I can feel his strong arms wrapped around me.

"Hey, Lindsey. Hold on."

Turning my head and looking up a bit so that my face is closer to his, I snap, "Please, let me go."

"No," he says as firmly as he's holding me. Then bending down so he can talk into my ear, "Just wait a minute, okay?"

"Are you kidding me?" And I try to pull away, again with no success.

"Please, don't jump to conclusions. I keep telling you I want to be with you. *She* is doing this … oh man. Lindsey, don't listen to her. Okay? *Nothing* happened." I struggle to break free one more time. "Lindsey, please, I really like you, and *nothing* happened. Jeez." His arms become like a vise grip around me, and I know he can feel me breathing heavily. I turn and see her coming right at us with her two friends. As she walks over, I can feel Chris moving his head while still holding me firmly against him. Then Joel steps to my right and slightly in front of me. I see Mike working his way over as well. Wingmen. Guy code. Mark hasn't missed any of this, and I catch his eye as he mouths, "You okay?" to me.

"Hi, Chris, Joel, Mike," Elizabeth slurs in what I take to be her best drunken attempt at a sultry voice.

"Thanks for meeting me in the *bedroom,* Chris," she slurs and looks right at me. This makes me stiffen, which Chris must have anticipated because he somehow strengthens his grip, and I can feel his body tense up against me too.

"Let's go," Joel says, trying to get us out of this. Joel takes my arm, and Chris pulls me back toward the door. Mark moves through his friends toward us, and I catch his eye.

"Please, Lindsey, please come with me," Chris says to me as he pulls me over. Reluctantly I walk with Chris, who keeps me in front of him with one hand on my belt and one on my shoulder, while Mike weaves a path for us through the crowd. As most people are in the main part of the house, we find an opening at the front door. Mike turns and says, "Go on to your car. I'll get your coats." And with that, he heads upstairs, where the guys must have put the coats earlier. As he turns, we see the Hurricane has followed us and is getting closer. Chris slips his arms around me again and says, "Ignore her. I'm here with you, Lindsey."

As she steps closer, Mike steps in front of me again. The protection I feel from Mike and Joel is fascinating to me. Guys. They still move in packs, protecting each other's turf. She moves within inches from Mike's and my faces, and I can see how thick she has applied her makeup as she says, "Hey, Chris, just let me know when you want to *party* again." I go rigid and can feel my heart slamming in my chest.

Then she looks right at me and slurs, "Some of us aren't in elementary school anymore. If you can't …"

"That's it! Not another word!" Chris rages at her. "Lindsey, let's go," and I'm sure Chris feels me go limp in his arms in defeat. There it is. If you are shameless enough to offer yourself overtly to a guy, and in public no less, what wouldn't you do with that guy? I know I can't compete with that. Chris must know this too.

Stunned, I allow myself to be pulled outside as I hear her babble on and swear up a storm. The fall air already has undertones of winter in it and hits me through my thin velour turtleneck and black skirt. I wrap my arms around myself, and Chris puts his arm around me and pulls me forward.

"Hey, Lindsey!" I hear Mark, so I turn. But I have no words. I'm too shell-shocked. He steps close to me and says, "You want a ride home?"

"Thanks, but I'll take her home," Chris says to Mark. Mark stares him down for a deliberate moment, saying nothing, and then turns back to me, "You want me to take you home? It's no problem."

"Lindsey, please," Chris pleads to me. I look up at Chris and don't know what to do, but I know I at least need to find out what's going on. Plus, the truth is, I want to go home with Chris. I just want to be with him.

"I'm okay. Thanks, Mark."

"Fine." Then turning to Chris, he says, "She sure as hell better text me when she's home, or I'll be at her house at midnight."

"Okay, okay. She'll text you—okay?"

"Fine."

Chris turns me away, and we head for his car. Moments later, Mike runs up with our coats.

"Here you go, Lindsey," and he holds it so I can slip into it, which I do. Chris is smart enough not to say anything as we get into his car. I practically collapse into the seats and buckle up while he walks around the car. He gets in and I can feel him looking at me, but I continue to look out the passenger window at the train wreck of a party we just left.

"Hey," Chris starts.

"Don't," is all I can say. So we sit silently while he takes me home. It's all I can do to keep myself together as the images of the evening replay through my mind.

Driving home, I can't believe the clock says it is only ten forty-five. How did all this happen so quickly? As we turn into my driveway, I feel so disappointed.

"Can we please talk?" Chris asks as he pulls up to the house.

"Good night, Chris," I say as I grab my purse and reach for the door handle.

"No. Lindsey, please," I hear him say, but I climb out anyway. I see him get out as well, and part of me wants him to. I want him to make all this better, but he has a lot of work to do, that's for sure.

"No, you're not going in like this." But I keep walking around him and head for the front steps.

"Lindsey, please talk to me. This is not how I wanted tonight to go." *Snap.* Something in my mind changes.

"Really?" I say, spinning around to face him. "How did you see tonight going exactly? Because if you didn't see this coming, then why did you make me promise to go home with you? Huh?"

"Hey. Slow down," he says, putting his hands on my arms. I'm breathing so hard right now even I notice it. "Look, I'm not even sure where to start, because I'm afraid I'll say the wrong thing and you'll go inside. Can we please just sit and talk? I've been trying to talk to you for weeks. Please, Lindsey." Then we both turn to see headlights pulling in my driveway.

"What the … oh. It must be the dog walker. I thought he only worked when your dad's in Chicago?"

"Must be 'cause they went out tonight. How do I know?"

"Lindsey, can we just go somewhere and talk?"

"Do you really want to? If you're just going to tell me that you want to go be with Elizabeth, let's just cut to the chase."

"You know I don't want that."

"Do I?" But the crack in my voice gives away my feelings.

"No, Lindsey, no, I don't," he says softly and pulls me into him. Then we're covered momentarily in the white beams of the headlights, but they go off quickly. Held in his arms, I just can't resist him.

"I want nothing to do with her."

Pulling slightly away and looking up at him, I ask, "Promise?"

"I promise, Lindsey." And for the first time, I very cautiously pull him into me, which causes him to hug me even tighter. I just want him to hold me. I hear the door shut on Joe's truck and instinctively pull away from Chris.

"Jeez," I hear Chris say under his breath.

"Hi, Lindsey, Chris," Joe says as he walks a long way around the car so he doesn't have to come right next to us. "Why don't you go inside? I don't think your dad wants you hanging outside here for very long."

"Lindsey, please trust me," Chris whispers to me. I nod. Chris continues, but to Joe, "Actually, I agree, and since it's still early, we're gonna run over to my place for a while. Have a good walk," he says loud enough for Joe to hear, and then more quietly to me, "Come on."

Riding in silence again, I realize we actually are heading to Chris's house. I've been to his dock before, and in his living room for parties, but I've never really been in his house. We park, and he takes me around back, which I'm not sure would thrill my dad, given that like my house, Chris's is sheltered on both sides by the forest.

"Come on, we can go in the pool house." When we reach the pool house, Chris unlocks the door with a code and turns on the recessed lights. It's not quite as big as Joel's, but it's perfect. There's a big couch and several oversize chairs in the main room, and there appears to be a small bar and kitchen on the side.

"Come on in," Chris says as I step through the doorway. "You want a Diet Coke?"

"Sure." I sit in one of the individual chairs, as I'm not really sure what we're doing here and we do need to talk. In seconds, he fills the room with music and gets us both a soda.

"Will your folks care that I'm here?"

"No, they're probably already asleep, and I come out here all the time. Hey, come over here; you can see the lake." So I stand up and walk over to the large sliding glass doors.

"Here, this should help," and with that, he turns the lights in the pool house down, and sure enough, the lights around the lake appear to get brighter. I feel Chris step up behind me and put his hand on my waist.

"Hey, can you listen to me for a minute?" he says from close behind me.

"Sure," I say, anxious to hear what he has to say.

"Look, I just want to apologize for all the drama with her. If I could go back in time and do things different I would, but I can't. I just want you to know that I want to be with you. Just you, Lindsey." And as he whispers this in my ear, it's like I have no strength or willpower against him. I close my eyes and relax a bit. I know he feels this, as he pulls me in so that I am standing firmly against him. And it feels good.

"I don't want to keep asking you this, but it seems like everywhere I turn, there she is. Are you still interested in her?"

"No, not at all. I never was, not in that way."

"So, are you doing anything that would make her think you're interested? I don't want to be in the middle of anything. If there is any part of you that ..."

"No, Lindsey, you don't even have to finish. I do not want to be with her. I'm doing nothing to encourage her. The only reason I went to talk to her tonight was to try to convince her to just leave you and me alone. But clearly that's not going to happen."

"So what do you want?" I ask in the simplest terms I can think of.

"I want to be with you. Lindsey, I just want to be with you." Sigh. Without even thinking, I rest my head back on his chest and close my eyes. He responds by resting his head on top of mine. We both just stand there for a moment. I can feel him breathing against me.

Then he moves his hands off my waist and onto my arms. Bringing his hands down to mine, he interlocks his fingers into mine, and I eagerly hold his hands. Then he gently pulls away, and letting go of my hands, he turns me to face him. With his hands on my shoulders, he looks down at me, and I am struck by how handsome he is in the soft light.

"Lindsey, what do *you* want?" Without a word, I turn my face and rest my head on his chest. It feels so good as he wraps his arms around me and holds me. I pull my arms out of his and put them up around his neck. He seems to bend down a little so I can put my face in the nook of his neck. As he rubs my back with his hands, I feel drawn to him.

"Tell me why she ..."

"Shh ... we can talk about all that later. Can we just be here? Please, Lindsey?"

Nodding my head yes against his chest, I feel him reach down and grab hold of me very tightly and lift me up off the ground a bit.

"Hey!" I whisper.

"Shhhh," is all he says as he gives me a giant bear hug. I don't know what this will be long-term for us, but for right now, this is enough.

"Lindsey, it feels so right to hold you," he whispers to me over the music.

"Please, don't let go."

"I won't. I won't," he says as he pulls me in even tighter. "Thank you so much for staying with me tonight; you have no idea how much that means to me. I know it must be hard, given all that's happened. But I'm glad that you're here." And for some reason, I'm compelled to wrap my right hand around his neck and pull him closer to me too. He rubs his hands from the base of my back up my sides to my neck and back down. He repeats this movement, caressing my back, and each time he is moving his hands, I am more and more concerned where they are going as they move farther and farther from the center of my back to my sides. I can feel my back tense up. He must too.

"Relax, I'm not going to do anything, okay? I just want to be with you. Shhhh. Just relax, Lindsey." And it's like a command to my soul. I do. Burying my face deeper into the warm skin of his neck, I feel pulled in by him.

"Lindsey ..." he says in a whisper. We stand there for a long time, just holding each other. It feels warm and wonderful and somehow very intimate.

Buzz. Buzz. I hear my phone, but just want to ignore it. But he pulls me away from him.

"You'd better get that. I bet it's Mark, and after what he saw, he's a good friend to check on you."

"Oh, you're right," and I go to grab my purse and answer my phone.

"Hello?"

"Lindsey—it's Mark. Are you okay?"

"I'm sorry, Mark. I forgot to text you. Yes, I'm fine."

"You sure?"

"Yes."

"Are you home?"

"Not yet." And as I say this, I look at Chris, who is a bit annoyed at this level of honesty.

"Okay, well, can you indulge me and text me when you are home?"

"I'm really fine."

"Please, Lindsey?"

"Sure. Thanks, Mark."

"Bye."

"Sorry."

"Don't be. But I guess I better get you home. You probably have practice in the morning, and I don't want you to miss curfew."

"Yeah. Okay." And so we head out into the dark night.

I notice that he keeps his hand on the small of my back as we walk to the car, but he does not hold my hand. Why can't all the signals point in one direction? Sitting in his car, I wonder if he'll hold my hand. I hold my purse in my hands and sit and wait during the short ride to my house. As we pull in the driveway, I'm sure we both notice that Joe's truck is still there. How nice for Baron. I wonder if Dad has asked him to stay until I'm home.

"You'd better text Mark before he shows up," Chris says, with a bit of humor in his tone.

"Oh, yeah, let me do that now." As we climb out, I send Mark a quick text.

We are both quiet walking to the front step, and I think Chris is looking around trying to find Joe.

"Look, Lindsey, I know there's a lot more to say, but it's been a long day. We'll talk about it another time—okay?"

"Okay."

"You were terrific as Mina."

"Thanks, but you really stole the show as Dracula."

"Thanks. We're still on for tomorrow right?"

"If you want."

"Yes, that is what I want. I'll pick you up at four-thirty. Okay?"

"Okay. Hey, Chris?" I ask as we get to my front door.

"Yeah?"

"You swear nothing happened with her tonight?"

"Nothing. Absolutely nothing. I just told her to stop," he says looking down at me.

"Okay."

"Happy Halloween, Lindsey."

"Good night," and I turn to unlock the door. As I close the door, I can't contain my smile. Will we ever have our first kiss?

∞∞∞

Lying in bed, I am overcome by the images of the night: the Hurricane offering to meet him at the bewitching hour, Chris walking out of a bedroom with her, her disgusting offer in front of all of us. My imagination starts to run away with me as to what could have gone on in that bedroom. What if he did hook up with her in there? Of course, he would lie to me. What if he's trying to be friends with me, all the while he's hooking up with her? Maybe he's just playing some kind of sick joke with me. I mean, if he really did like me, wouldn't he kiss me already? He completely had the opportunity tonight in the pool house. Maybe Joel and Mike are in on it. They must be—he and I haven't even gone out on a date yet. Why are they so interested in me? Bastard. I bet he's sleeping with her—or doing who knows what.

I sleep restlessly as constant images of Chris with the Hurricane swirl in my dreams.

22 DRACULA: *REMEMBER YOU'RE MINE.*

SATURDAY MORNING I WAKE up and am furious. I am convinced that Chris is just playing with me for some sick kind of pleasure while he hooks up with that bitch. I am ready to spit nails.

Taking my cell phone, I head downstairs to grab a granola bar and drive to practice. I have several messages.

> **11:30 P.M.** Lindsey you Ok? Heard Elizabeth went after Chris. Nightmare. How did you get home? See you tomorrow at the show. Melissa

Great. Word is out that I'm the idiot Chris is playing for a fool.

> **11:59 P.M.** Glad you are Ok. Call me tomorrow. We should talk. You were great in show. Looking forward to second act tomorrow. Bye. Mark

I *will* call you later—I bet you can confirm my thoughts. But I doubt you will be up for hours.

1:36 A.M. Tsk tsk. You don't listen. Get dad to drop it. Or else.

Bring it on. I'm in no mood. Delete.

The sight of my new car in the garage momentarily eases my fury.

I am still steaming as I walk inside to the locker room when I feel my phone.

Buzz.

7:45 A.M. Morning. Can't wait for tonight. Dracula strikes again!

You probably just got home from spending the evening in the eye of the Hurricane. No time now; I need to work out. I will deal with you later.

I'm thankful that I'm in the club today, as I don't really want to deal with the high school scene. I hardly say a word at practice, which of course, no one notices, as they just assume I'm focused. Fine by me.

After practice, when I arrive home, I decide to start with Mark. I need a male opinion.

11:35 A.M. Hey Mark. You there?

11:36 A.M. Y.

I am not doing this in text. I dial his number.

"Hey, Lindsey."

"Hi, Mark. Hey, thanks again for being so cool last night."

"No problem."

"So, did you tell anyone?"

"Not me, but a few people saw, and then she freaked when Buckley left with you. It was obvious something was up."

"Yeah. So, did you see them go into that room?"

"Kind of."

"Come on, what did you see?"

"I just saw her go up the stairs downing something, and he was behind her. They went upstairs and then disappeared."

"Did you hear anything?"

"No. I saw them from across the room, but when I saw them, it didn't look like they were talking."

"Were they holding hands or anything?"

"Not that I could see—but, Lindsey, what are you doing?"

"What do you mean?"

"I mean, he went into a bedroom with her. What do you think happened?"

"I don't know. He says they just talked. That she keeps coming after him, and he says he keeps telling her no and to stop. What do you think?"

"Come on, Lindsey, I have no idea what really happened. Buckley seems okay to me, but there aren't many high school guys walking into bedrooms with girls throwing themselves at them and the guys say, 'Sorry, no thanks.' I mean, I guess it's possible, but it looks pretty bad. Why did you leave with him?"

"I don't know. I'm starting to think I'm an idiot."

"No, you're not. Just be careful. Look, maybe he hooked up with her, but it's kind of weird that he obviously wanted to be with you after, so maybe he is telling the truth and nothing happened."

"Would you ever turn a girl down?"

"For real?"

"Yeah."

"I have to say, I really would have to be into somebody else to turn down a girl who was that willing. Now you think I'm the jerk."

"No, I don't."

"Ya know, Lindsey, by holding you when she came over and went off, and going home with you after that scene, he did let everyone know, including Elizabeth, that he wanted to be with you."

"I guess. I just feel so foolish."

"Why do you care? Are you seeing him?"

"No, that's the worst part of it. I don't even know what we're doing. He says … but … well … It's all so ridiculous."

"Well, see how things go. If he's with her, you'll hear about it. Emit is too small, and her mouth is too big. Maybe he's messing around with her, but, Lindsey, maybe this guy really is into you."

"No, believe me, that is not the case."

"Why do you say that?" *Because most high school guys at least try to kiss the girl they like.*

"Forget it. Hey, let me know if you hear anything, okay?"

"You got it. Good luck tonight—you were awesome last night."

"Thanks, see ya."

"Bye."

I'm not sure what to think, so might as well hit the books.

Buzz.

    1:05 P.M. Hi Mina. You done with Practice?

    1:05 P.M. Y. Change in Plans my folks will take me to school will see you there.

Buzz. My phone rings, and I see that it's Chris calling. I hit the ignore button. *Buzz.* Chris calling again. Sorry, I'm studying.

    1:08 P.M. Hey. U there??

Wonder how you would feel if I told you I was in a bedroom with some guy and we were just talking. You can stew. I'll see you at the show.

⟆⟅

Mom is happy to drop me off at school for the show. Worst case, I can go home after the show with my parents, but hopefully I can still do something tonight. Even if things are bad with Chris, maybe I can get together with Melissa and Elena after the show.

"Thanks, Mom, I'll look for you and Dad after the show."

"Okay. Have fun, Lindsey!"

"Thanks, and I think I have plans tonight, okay?"

"Sure. Who are you going out with, Melissa? Chris?"

"TBD. Bye." I shut the car door and dash through the cold into the main school door. I can see Chris leaning against the far wall of the school lobby. He called me four more times through the afternoon, all of which I ignored. Okay, here we go.

"Hi, Lindsey."

"Hi," I say briskly.

"Hey, why didn't you call me back?"

"Sorry," I say without pausing as I head down the hallway.

"Hey, Lindsey, wait, what's going on?"

"Exactly."

"Come on. Can you clue me in?"

Like you don't know. Snap. I turn to face him. "Look, I don't know what kind of a game this is, but I'm not interested. I told you already I don't want to be in the middle of anything."

"Did something happen?"

"Oh, you mean like watching you walk out of a bedroom with a whore on your heels? Something like that?" I say, and having momentarily stunned him, I push the auditorium doors and storm in.

"Lindsey!" he yells, too loudly, in the almost-empty auditorium. I keep marching down the aisle as a few stagehands look over to see what the commotion is about.

"Wait!" he manages to yell in a whisper. And I know that what I really want is to be with him. I just want to be sure that he's not pulling anything with the Hurricane, or anyone else for that matter.

Catching my arm he pulls me, "Hey, wait." So I stop and face him.

"Lindsey, I thought you understood. Last night it all seemed … Well, I know not great, but … well, at least okay."

"Well, I got home and started thinking. I mean, and I don't mean to presume too much, but how would you feel?"

"About what?"

"Well, let's say that tonight—we're going to a party, right?"

"I would like to, yes," he acknowledges cautiously.

"Okay, so tonight let's say you can't find me for a while at the party. You look around, you try to, but I'm just missing. Then you see me come out of a bedroom in the middle of the party," and hearing this, he stands up straighter and pinches his lips and lets go of my arm, "and I'm followed out of that bedroom by, oh, I don't know, some random guy, and I tell you 'Oh, don't listen to him; we were just talking.' Meanwhile, he's going on and on about how he had a great time in the bedroom with me in front of the whole school. Are you telling me that's just fine by you?"

"No. No, I'm not. Don't even say that, Lindsey."

"Why?"

"Why? I'll tell you why. Come here." Taking my arm, he leads me up the stairs, across the stage, and all the way backstage, pulling me into a dark corner. He's almost angry, but I don't think it's directed at me. "Lindsey, I'm so sorry about last night. I know we have a lot to talk about, but know this. Nothing happened with me and Elizabeth. Nothing. And why don't I want to hear you talk about you in a bedroom with some guy? Because I can't stand the thought of you with anyone else. That's why." Taking a pause, he rubs both my arms in his hands, and taking a deep breath, he begins to move from frustration or whatever that was to warm and caring as he starts to talk to me again. Listening to his words, being this close to him, seeing him in the shadows of the theater, he's too perfect. My mood totally changes. "Look, Lindsey, I really like you. More than I want to admit, especially given all this other stuff and the fact that we have yet to have a real date, but I do. I know this is weird, and please don't take this the wrong way and get mad, but clearly, if I wanted Elizabeth, I could have her—but," and he steps forward so that he's now inches from me and looking right into my eyes, "I don't. I want to be with you. I know last night was a nightmare for you, but give us a chance. I'll do anything you want. I just want to be with you." When we stand this close and he says things like this, it's like I'm a puppet and he is the puppeteer. All I want is to be in his arms again. "Can we please enjoy being in the show together and go out tonight and have fun?"

"Yes."

"Yes? Really? That's great, thank you. Lindsey I don't know what got into your head, but I've never told you anything but the truth. Last night, being with you at the pool house, was the best. Just being with you is the best." And with this, he slides his hands down my arms and takes my hands in his. "We okay?"

"Yes."

"Okay. Listen, can I ask you something?"

"Sure."

"I want you to be my girlfriend, Lindsey, and I do not," and closing his eyes and shaking his head like he is shaking out a bad image, "want you to see anyone else." Looking back at me and rubbing my hands with his thumbs, he continues, "Is that okay? Can we make this exclusive?"

Closing my eyes, I can't believe what I'm hearing. My stomach drops and I look down, but I can't suppress how happy this makes me. My eyes are moist with relief. He sounds so sincere, and it's so much more than I had hoped for earlier in the day.

"Lindsey, can we do that?" he asks in a whisper, pulling my chin up to face him. Looking up at him, I smile even more, which causes a single tear to fall from my eye. Letting go of my left hand with his right, he brushes the tear away and holds my cheek in his palm.

"What's wrong?" he asks with concern in his expression and surrounding his voice.

"Nothing. Nothing. Are you sure that's really what you want?"

"Yes."

"Me too. Yes."

He responds by smiling and pulling me into a big hug.

We can hear the stage starting to fill with people, so I pull back. "We better get ready."

"Yeah, you okay now?"

"Yes. Chris, I'm sorry for all this and for not talking to you earlier. I just ..."

"Forget it; I'm the one who's sorry. Let's go, beautiful."

Blushing, I tilt my head, but keep looking into his deep blue eyes.

"Come on; let's go, Mina. This is gonna be even better than last night—right?"

"Right!"

And with that we walk across the stage to the dressing rooms, holding hands. As we approach them, he guides me around in front of him.

"So, we'll talk, but you're okay, right?"

"Yeah."

"And it's just us now, right?"

"Yes," I say with a huge smile. Thankfully, he smiles just as enthusiastically back to me.

"That's all that matters. I'll meet you in the lobby after the show again, okay?"

"Yes," I say, nodding. I love that even though kids are walking all around us, he is still holding my hand and caressing it with his thumb.

"Okay, and no matter who I'm talking to tonight," he says with his eyebrows raised, "I hope that you'll walk right up to me, knowing that's where I want you."

"Thanks, Chris."

And with a wink and one final squeeze, he heads toward the guys' dressing room and I go into the girls'. If holding his hand feels this good, I think I just might faint if he ever does kiss me.

80CB

The show is going as smoothly as last night, and I'm the happiest I can ever remember. Slipping into my nightgown costume, all I can think about is that I can't wait to see what Chris does in our scene tonight. He wants to be my boyfriend. I smile uncontrollably every time I think about it. Dad didn't say anything negative about *our* scene last night, and everyone seemed to like the show yesterday, so I feel a bit more relaxed going into it tonight.

The curtain goes down at the end of the previous scene, and I see Chris backstage. "Hey, cutie," he whispers to me as he gently bumps my shoulder. I get ready for the scene by walking as quietly as I can over to the bed and lie down. Just like last night, Chris moves into position. I'm still self-conscious about being in this position, but it is also exciting to be so close to him. My heart is racing. I wonder if his is too. The curtain begins to rise. As most of the audience is probably comprised of the same people as last night, they become quiet even more quickly when they see the curtain move. Chris puts his hand on my right arm and squeezes it, and I take a deep breath, soaking in his touch. Like last night, his composure overwhelms me as he pauses momentarily, heightening the suspense.

We stare into each other's eyes, and I wish we were alone in his pool house again. I wish he would bend down and kiss me. My breath quickens as I'm lost in my thoughts.

Now the curtain is fully up, and the audience is completely still. Repeating last night's action, Chris removes his hand from my arm so as not to lean on me, and gently takes my head in his hand. The music starts, but tonight I am lost in his eyes and hardly hear it. As I feel him wrap his fingers in my hair, it feels like neither of us is acting. I can't help but close my eyes and let out a breath as his touch has a staggering effect on me. He continues the scene as planned, looking me over, and then, effortlessly, sliding me into the crook of his arm. He gently supports my head, and I'm so taken by him, I actually give him the weight of my torso. Letting go this little bit, I can feel his muscles tense to absorb my weight. As he bends down, I anticipate the kiss he gave me on the neck last night, but instead, he brushes his tongue along my neck, sending a shiver down my spine. I let out an audible breath, which I'm sure he knows he pulled from me. I can't help but close my eyes and let out another soft breath. I reach up and lay my hand on the back of his head and wrap my fingers around his neck, which I have never done in rehearsal.

```
Van Helsing: Let her go.

Dracula: Throw it away.
```

Chris grabs me in both his arms. Momentarily, I am reminded of him holding me from behind last night while the Hurricane blew. I gasp as directed in the scene.

The guys deliver the last few lines, and I think it is sweet Chris is careful not to pull me so close to him that I'm forced to press my lips to his neck. He always holds me close enough for the scene, without forcing anything between us. Then the curtain comes down.

As I get up from the bed, Chris gently squeezes my neck, and then he takes my hand as we walk offstage, shoulder to shoulder.

߷

We stand next to each other for the group bow. The audience is as appreciative as last night, and I'm sure this is one of the best nights I've ever had. A stagehand carrying flowers walks onstage and starts to give the flowers to the girls. While the audience is still applauding, Chris squeezes my hand, and then releasing it and looking at me, he walks offstage. *Where are you going?* He hasn't even had his individual bow yet. Before I know what's happening, he comes back with a bouquet of long-stem lavender and pink roses. He walks toward me, and in front of the entire audience, offers them to me. I'm stunned.

He then steps up to the line of actors, pauses a moment, and then takes his individual bow. The curtain comes down, and we all yell in delight that the show is over. Chris picks me up in a celebratory hug.

"Are these from you?"

"Yes. It was the least I could do," he says, putting me down and looking at me.

"You didn't have to do that."

"I wanted to. And I wanted everyone to know you're mine now."

Closing my eyes because I'm overwhelmed with happiness, all I can say is, "Thank you. I'm so sorry about earlier."

"You have nothing to be sorry about. Let's go have fun. Okay? You and me."

After a quick cast and crew meeting, I go to the dressing room and change. Then I head for the lobby. I see my parents first, and they congratulate me and both give me a hug. I tell them that I'm going out with Chris, and Mom looks like she is genuinely happy for me.

"Have a great time. Do you want me to take those home for you?"

"Um, sure, thanks."

"I'll put them in a vase in your room—okay?"

"Thanks, Mom." I can tell she knows this bouquet is important to me.

Jon comes up to me next, and I'm happy to see him.

"Hi, Lindsey—great job! I knew you would be even better tonight!" he says and gives me a hug.

"Thanks, Jon."

"Hey, Lindsey, can I talk to you for a sec?"

"Sure. What's going on?"

"What's up with you and Buckley?"

"What do you mean?"

"Are you seeing him?"

"Yeah, I guess," I say with genuine enthusiasm.

"Really? You could have your pick of guys—why him?"

"First of all, I do not have my pick of anything, and I don't know, I guess I like him."

"Why? He's just … I mean, I heard about last night. You know he hooked up with Elizabeth, right? And the guy has dated most of South and North."

"What are you saying?"

"Hi, Jon," Chris says, taking my hand.

"Chris," Jon says tersely. And to me, "Lindsey, are you going to Adam's cast party after?"

"Um, yeah," I say, checking with Chris, who nods that we are.

"Okay. Well, I'll see you there, and maybe we can chat. Feel free to ping me if you need anything." And then giving Chris a look, he adds, "Like a ride home or something."

As he walks away, I wonder what else he heard.

"What was that about?" Chris asks.

"Oh, nothing. You ready?"

"It's about last night."

"Yeah," and I desperately don't want to spend another evening focused on the Hurricane.

"You okay?"

"Yes!" I take this as a sign that we are moving on. Chris squeezes my hand, and we head across the lobby toward the doors when I see Mike approach us.

"Hey, Lindsey. Great job!"

"Thanks, Mike."

"Where's Joel?"

"He'll be right out; you guys go ahead. We'll see you at Adam's."

"Okay, let's go," Chris says, and we head to the door.

The winter air is biting as we cross the grounds to his car. I'm so happy Chris is with me and holding my hand. He lets me in the car first, and then goes around to the driver's side and gets in.

"Let's get the heat on. Hey, now I hope nothing will happen tonight, but if it does, if she says anything, please just walk away with me, okay?"

"You promise I won't find you in a bedroom with her?" I say half teasing.

"Lindsey, it wasn't like that. But, no, you won't."

☯

The party is a lot of fun. Chris stays by my side the entire evening, and we hang out with members of the cast and crew, laughing at all the mistakes we made during rehearsals and the two shows. I also get a chance to chat with Melissa and Elena, as well as Isabella and Rick. While we are talking to Mike and Joel about snowmobiling, Chris says he'll be right back. I assume he chooses to use the bathroom now because I'm with his friends and he figures they'll take care of things if the Hurricane comes up to me. I know she must be at the party by now, but I haven't seen her.

"Hey, Lindsey."

"Hi, Jon."

"Hey," he says to Mike and Joel.

"Lindsey, got a minute?"

"Sure, what's up?"

"Here," and Jon takes a few steps to the side so I follow him. I'm sure that Joel and Mike are watching and probably wish the music was lower so they could hear us.

"So, seriously, why are you with Buckley?"

"Why shouldn't I be?"

"Look, Lindsey, I don't mean to be weird, but you are such a nice girl, ya know? Buckley is a bit of a player, don't ya think?"

"How do you know?"

"What do you mean, 'how do I know?' Everyone knows. I told you, he's dated like everyone."

"So? Sorry, but look at him. Of course, he gets a ton of dates."

"Well, what about him going off with Elizabeth last night?"

"They just talked."

"Really? That's not what she's saying."

"He can't do anything about that, Jon. What is she saying? No, don't tell me. Man."

"Here he comes," Jon says, taking a swig of beer.

"Hey, Jon."

"Chris."

"I'll see ya," Jon says, catching my eye as he steps away.

"You ready to go?"

As we weave through the crowd, I see her. Damn. I was almost free. He must see her too, because he tightens his grip on my hand. As we approach her, my pulse quickens. Chris steps forward so that his back is to her and guides me in front of him so that he is between us.

"Hey, Dracula," blows the Hurricane. Chris says nothing, but I feel my body tighten.

"Hey," I hear Chris declare emphatically as we pass. Turning to see why, I see the Hurricane has planted her arm around his neck and is saying something in his ear. He holds my hand so tight it hurts.

"No. Would you get off?" Chris says, pulling her arm off him. I turn away because I don't want to watch this. Looking ahead, I see Mark watching us. Again, I feel embarrassed. Then I feel his arm around my waist, and I can feel him pressing against me. Still watching, Mark raises an eyebrow and shakes his head. Man.

"Ignore it. She's just being stupid," Chris says as he pushes me forward.

"My coat?" I say, looking back at Chris.

"Oh, yeah. Wait here, okay?"

"Okay." And he heads over to the stairs to get our coats. I don't want to look around, but I know she will follow him. Sure enough, I look up the stairs, and there she is. I want to scream. She disappears from view, and I don't know what to do.

"Hey, what the hell, Lindsey?"

"Hi, Mark." Depressing.

"Why the hell are you putting up with this?"

"He can't help it if she follows him, can he?"

"Did you come here with him?"

"Yes."

"Well, if I find out this guy *is* fooling around behind your back, I'm gonna kill him."

"Thanks, Mark. Hey, you promised to take me camping sometime," I say, trying to change the topic.

"Absolutely, a couple of us were talking about a group trip in the spring."

"Count me in!"

"We'll be doing some climbing too—you up for it?"

"Can you assure me that I'll live to see another day in the gym?" I tease.

"Absolutely, just stick with me. Hey, here they come."

Looking up, I see Chris looking right at me, and she is right behind him. I swear, as soon as she sees me, she grabs his arm. I can't take my eyes off them. He pulls away from her and bounds quickly down the stairs, trying to put distance between them. Shoving his way through the crowd, he stands next to me. I catch Melissa's eye from across the room, and she mouths to me, "Bitch!"

"Ready?" Chris asks as he takes my hand.

"Bye, Mark." As we step outside, Chris holds my coat, and I step into it. While I zip it up, Chris puts on his.

"I know, I know," is all he says as we head down the front steps. He puts his arm around me and pulls me in toward him, and while I want to be mad at him, I just can't help but be happy that we are together. Arriving at his car, he again opens my door, but before I can get in, he steps in front of the open door and asks, "You okay? Please don't be mad. I know you have a right to be, but please don't be."

"No, I'm not," I say, resigned more than anything.

"Thank you," and with that, he steps away and I slide in.

As he gets in the car, he turns on the music and the heat, and then grabs my hand.

"Hey, wait a minute. You need to take those gloves off. Well, at least this one," he says with a smile as he squeezes my left hand in his right. Letting go of my hand, he pulls my glove off and tosses it in my lap. Then he grabs my bare hand. I watch as he brings my hand up to his mouth, and I catch his glance as he kisses the back of my hand. Smiling, I lean my head back to rest against the heated seats. We don't say anything on the way home, and somehow the silence is comforting. Then I remember that this has got to be it. He has to kiss me tonight, doesn't he? Is he thinking about it? Are we going to my house or his pool house? Where do I want to go?

It's eleven twenty, so we have plenty of time before my curfew.

Chris asks, "How come you're so quiet? Please don't tell me it's …"

And I cut him off, "No. Not tonight, please?"

"Done. Thank you." I love that he knows exactly what I'm talking about and doesn't want to talk about her either.

"Is the dog walker working tonight?"

"Since my dad is home, I don't think so, but I guess I don't know for sure. Remember, no one even told me we were getting a dog walker."

"Yeah. So we're still on for a real date next Friday night, right?"

"Absolutely," I say and am already looking forward to it.

"Great. I'm planning a little surprise for you," and this tidbit has me looking at him as he smirks back at me. "You'll have to wait to find out about that, but I can guarantee we will have no uninvited guests."

"Thank goodness. I can't wait," I admit.

"Me too." It seems we are going to my place as he turns into my driveway. Butterflies start in my stomach, but I'm enjoying the excitement and electricity between us. He pulls into a spot and turns the car off.

"Okay?"

"Yeah," and I pull my door open and step into the cold air. I realize how cozy his car had been as the frigid winter air surrounds me. He takes my hand and leads me up the path. He pulls my arm as I step nervously onto the front porch, and I realize he has stopped on the landing step below. As he pulls me toward him, we are again closer in height with my step advantage. He grabs my other hand in his and turns me so that we are standing face-to-face. This has got to be it.

"So, Miss Lindsey. Are you ever going to kiss me?"

I step back involuntarily and look down in shock.

"Hey, hey, Lindsey, come here."

"I … I'm sorry, I just …" And I am completely off-balance. Why does he think *I'm* going to kiss *him?* In one instant, I went from excited and happy to completely lost. "I'm not like that. I know other girls …" I stammer while I step back away from him.

"No, no, no, stop, I'm sorry. I didn't mean it like that. Lindsey, I'm sorry. Come here," he says, shaking his head and stepping toward me.

"No, I … Maybe you're used …"

"Shhh," he whispers, and putting his right hand gently on my neck and the back of my head and his left around my waist, he pulls me a step forward so that my chest is against his. He looks right in my eyes, and somehow he knows I'm about to say something, but before I do, he whispers again, "Shh. It's just me and you." Then his right hand pulls me into him, and as our faces are only inches apart, I close my eyes and he presses his lips to mine. It is at once warm and soft, and also sends a shock wave through me. As we continue the embrace, I become self-conscious of my hands, which are still at my sides, so I bring them up and touch him lightly on his coat. As he embraces me even more firmly, I gently squeeze his arm in my hand. He responds immediately by parting his lips. Incredibly, it's so natural to reciprocate. It all feels so warm and exciting. I feel my breathing getting faster. Soon something changes, and his left arm drops to my waist and he pulls my hips to press against him. Since his jacket is unzipped, as he moves his arm, mine drops so that it is just touching at his waist. I enjoy the fact that I can feel the muscles in his torso tense with my touch, even through his sweater. I wonder if I'm doing anything wrong. In an instant, I become completely self-conscious. I realize I'm still touching his waist, so I lift my hands off him and pull my lips away, but he holds my neck close so that our faces remain a few inches apart in the dark night.

"Lindsey," he whispers to me, and I'm sure my name has never sounded so sweet. I hear us both breathing as he caresses my face with his thumb. I smile in response, and he pulls me into another kiss. As he pulls me more firmly against him, I can feel my chest moving in and out against him with each breath and wonder if he notices as well. Our heads tilt in opposing directions in unison as his tongue moves cautiously into my mouth. Something lets go inside of me, and I stop thinking about what is going on and just exist in my own desire. I put my hand on his back and move my lips so I can let out air and gasp more in. Somehow his kiss becomes more demanding, and he pulls my head more forcefully against his. My stomach drops. As I pull my lips from him, he lets our mouths part while still keeping our foreheads touching. It's so cold that we can both see our breath turn white with each release of air between us.

"Lindsey, you're gonna drive me crazy." I have no idea how to process this, so I let go of him and pull away.

"No, don't. Please," he says, and then covers my mouth in his. Again I release myself and get lost in him. I can feel my back loosen as I lean on him. He pulls me into him hard, and I can feel desire throughout his body. His arms surround me. I move my right arm up and touch the back of his neck, and he drops both his hands to my waist. Suddenly I'm all too aware that my parents might be watching this, and I pull completely away.

"What? What did I do?" he asks in a whisper.

"Nothing, nothing, I just ..." and looking at my house, he nods with understanding.

"Yeah," he says, looking at me, and I can't take my eyes off his. Then, with his right arm, he pulls me against him and moves my face to his with his left.

"I really like you, Lindsey." I look down and smile.

"Is that okay?" he asks as he lifts my chin and pulls my face up so that he can look at me again.

"Yes." Taking a deep breath, I close my eyes and again just say, "Yes."

He picks me up completely off the ground and gives me a big

hug. Letting me slide back down his body, he again kisses me as my toes meet the ground.

"Lindsey," he says in a slow, husky whisper. His voice pulls at me. As he leans his forehead against mine, we are frozen in the moment, enjoying the warmth of our closeness.

"Hey, when I say you are driving me crazy ..." he continues in a whisper. I immediately tense up, but he holds me firmly and continues, "No, no, Lindsey, believe me, it's a good thing. I'm just trying to keep control of things here. I *really* like you, Lindsey. Okay?"

"Okay."

"You have to know how much I do. I've wanted to kiss you for so long I'm about to burst."

"Really?"

"Yes. Are you kidding me? I've been trying to be a gentleman. I don't want to blow this with you, Lindsey. I don't know if I should tell you this, but I have wanted to kiss you for a very long time. Well, for now, let's say since I was in London, but I wanted to wait until I was pretty sure you were ready. I didn't want to rush you. I was planning to wait till next Saturday, but I just couldn't take it anymore. Are we still okay?"

"Yes, but can I ask you something and you promise not to get mad?"

"Sure."

"Did you really want *me* to kiss *you*?"

"No. Lindsey, I'm so glad you are the way you are. I love that you wait till I hold your hand, and that you want me to call you, or text you, before you'll reply. I adore that about you. You're so innocent, and I think it's cool," and as he says this, he runs his hand down my head, and pressing my hair to the nape of my neck, he pulls me in for another kiss. He immediately opens our mouths as he takes control and seems to demand me with his tongue. I'm lost in him again as I feel my heart pound, and my hands grab his arm and waist. We both release our joined mouths for air when he loosens his grip on my neck.

"This is going to be hard with you," he whispers, more to himself than me as he moves his body a few inches away from mine.

"I'm sorry, I didn't mean to ..." I say, embarrassed that I don't even know what I'm doing wrong. I let go of him completely.

"Please, don't ever apologize to me, especially when we're close, okay?" he says quickly and pulls me back up against him and looks straight into my eyes. "You can do anything you want. Believe me, nothing you do will bother me. Okay?"

"Okay."

"And if you ever do just want to talk, I hope you'll call me or text me—okay?"

"Okay."

And playfully he adds, "Or if you happen to get another flat tire and need a ride. Well, I better get you inside before your dad shows up," he says, smiling at me. "You look so pretty, Lindsey." And with this, I feel the blush build, and I look at him sideways. "Well, you do. I just want to be sure that after everything this weekend, you know you're still mine, just mine, right? No sharing."

"Yeah. But that goes for you too, right?"

"Lindsey, as far as I'm concerned, there are no other girls."

"Come on," I say, rolling my eyes and enjoying this playful moment between us as we embrace.

"Okay. Seriously, I will not be dating anyone else. Just you," and he kisses me on the forehead for emphasis. "Now what you need to do is to be sure all your so-called "buddies" understand that you're off-limits to them."

"What are you talking about?"

"Oh, believe me. I know they are your friends, but I see how Jon and Mark watch you. Anyway, let's get you inside before you freeze or I give up what little control I have and attack you," and with that, he pulls me into a deep dip as if we are dancing. I give a playful scream through a laugh as he bites my neck, playing into his character from the play. Then he tilts me so I'm standing upright again and takes my hand. We step to the front door, and both seem to be enjoying the closeness.

Once more, he encircles me with both arms, and we share one more soft, slow, warm kiss.

"Thanks again for the roses—they're beautiful. And thanks for a great night."

Smiling at me, he gives a kind of a playful grunt and leans down for one more kiss.

"Good night, Chris."

Leaning in, he whispers, "Good night, Lindsey. Remember you're mine."

ὼᾃ

Biting my lip, I cover my face with my hands as I lie in bed. My body is surging with energy. I can't believe I'm with Chris Buckley. Glancing over at the roses, I can't believe this is all really happening. And he gave me the roses in front of the entire audience. I hug my pillow and squeal with pure delight.

23 OUR FIRST REAL DATE: *ALL OF YOU.*

"SO, YOU MENTIONED THAT you knew you wanted us to go out when you were in London?" I say to Chris.

"I was wondering when you were going to bring that up. But what I actually said was that I have wanted to kiss you for a very long time—at least since London."

"Okay, but I don't get it. Why would you know then?" My cheeks are filling with color, but I am intensely curious.

"Well, actually I knew I wanted to date you the first time I saw you," Chris says, taking another bite of his steak.

"Yeah, right."

"I did. I know exactly when I first saw you."

"Okay, when?"

"It was the day you were moving in. The moving company truck was still at your house, moving your stuff in, and Jake and I were at the Kirkwoods' place. It was the August before eighth grade, and it was pretty hot out. We were all hanging out, playing some video games, and I decided to go to the lake to cool off. When I got down by the dock, I saw some movement over on your property and decided to take a closer look. You know, check out the new neighbors."

Chris and I have both stopped eating, and I am completely engrossed in his story. I had been watching Chris's every move since I moved in, but the thought that he noticed me is arresting.

He continues, "At first you were in the backyard playing ball with Baron."

"And where were you?"

Smiling, Chris cuts another piece of steak and replies casually, "In the forest."

"Watching me?"

"Being neighborly," he replies with a broad smile.

"Right."

"Then you walked over to the dock. You were wearing cutoff jeans and a tank top. I thought you looked good in that." Chris pauses here for effect before continuing. Raising an eyebrow, he goes on, "and then you pulled off the tank and tossed it, and your shorts, on the dock."

"Oh—I did have a bikini on!" I say, putting my hand on my face in embarrassment.

"Yes, you did." Then smiling he adds, "Pity."

"Nice. So how long did you watch me?"

"Not long. Well, long enough, I guess," he adds with a wink.

"Oh, man."

"After a while, I went back to their pool house, walked in, and called dibs."

"You what?"

"I called dibs."

"Dibs on what?"

"You," he states simply, and I can tell he's completely pleased with himself.

"What does that mean?"

"It means that they couldn't ask you out. Still can't."

"Just like that."

"Just like that."

"Maybe none of them wanted to ask me out."

"Maybe."

"Do you guys call dibs on all the girls at school?"

"No."

"So why me?"

"Because, Lindz, you're mine," and with this, he takes my hand and squeezes it. My mind reels. Chris just called me Lindz, which is how I refer to myself in my own mind. And although I know I should be offended at some level by his story, the truth is that my heart is melting.

"So then what happened?"

"They were interested."

"In what?"

"What I called dibs on."

"And?"

"So we all took a walk."

"A walk?"

"Uh-huh. It was a nice day for a walk in the forest as I recall."

"So what did you see in the forest?" I ask, playing along.

"Not much in the forest. But the lake was a bit interesting."

"Oh man, what did you see?"

"You were flipping off the deck into the lake."

"Oh great."

"It was pretty great. We thought you were a diver. I'll let you in on a secret."

"I'm afraid to ask."

"Okay."

"Fine, what?"

"Gymnast is better than diver."

"Better for what?"

"No, for whom."

"What?"

"The question you want to ask is better for whom."

"Okay, for whom?"

"Any guy."

"Great. Do I want to know why?"

"No, don't think so."

"How long did you all watch me? No. I don't think I want to know."

"Not long. You only flipped in, oh, I don't know, five more times, and then you headed back to the house. Show over—so we left."

"Terrific."

"Actually, as I recall, Mike was a bit pissed. He didn't think it was fair I called dibs when I hadn't even met you. Alex straightened him out. I mean, dibs are dibs."

"So what does all that have to do with London?"

"Okay. Well, I knew as soon as I saw you that I wanted to date you. So, as you may recall, I spent the first few weeks of eighth grade talking to you as much as possible."

"Go on."

Smiling he continues, "Well, after getting to know you a bit, I figured you weren't really into guys yet."

"And in eighth grade, you were Mr. Experienced?"

"Compared to you?" he asks with a smirk, so I roll my eyes.

"Point taken."

"So I decided I should be your first kiss, and I do believe I was—wasn't I?"

"Privileged information."

"I just told you all that, and I get nothing?" he teases.

"Go on."

"Okay, so at the eighth-grade dance, I asked you to dance, and do you remember what I asked you during our dance?"

"Maybe."

As we smile at each other, he continues, "I asked if you wanted to take a walk the next evening along the lake."

"Sounds vaguely familiar." Although the truth was I had visualized that dance and our walk a thousand times since it happened.

"Well, I enjoyed the dance—and the walk was even better—because

I finally got some time with you alone. Do you remember where we first kissed?" he asks, while caressing my hand in his.

"Yes," I confessed, staring into his eyes, feeling just as drawn to him now as I did then.

"Me too," and with that he squeezes my hand. "So since we were only in eighth grade, I thought it best to leave it at that until we were both … Oh, I don't know, 'ready,' I guess."

"So you knew we were ready in London?" I ask, as I'm completely confused how all this connects.

We are momentarily interrupted as the waiter clears our dinner plates and leaves the dessert menu.

"So, back to London, you were saying?" I pursue.

Buzz.

"Are you going to get that?" I ask.

"No, I'll check it later. Anyway, I'll tell you this. I had a lot of fun in London, and one night I was at a party where there were a lot of Americans and in comes Jon."

"Really? Did you know he was in London?"

"I had no idea, but when he came in, I made my way over to talk to him." *Buzz.*

"It's fine, just get it."

"No, it's fine. So I'm at … what?"

"Nothing. You were saying."

"What is it?" Chris asks, and as he looks at me, I can tell he cares.

"It's nothing. I'm sorry."

"No, what is it?"

"I was just wondering if you don't answer your phone when you're with me because you're being polite, or because …"

"Lindsey, I'm here with you." Hearing this, my worst fears are confirmed. Pulling my hands, I try to cover my face with my left hand, but he holds my right hand firmly in his.

"Look, I don't know who it is, but could it be someone that will bother you? Yes. That's why I don't want to get it." *I simply can't hide my disappointment.* "Okay, look," he says, pulling his phone out.

Sighing, he admits, "It was Elizabeth, okay. I won't lie to you. I'm not calling her. I'm here with you."

"Okay."

"Hey, Lindsey. Come on."

"I'm sorry, it's just ..."

"What?"

"How often does she call?"

"Please don't do this, Lindsey."

"Oh man."

"Hey. You want to go?"

"Can I ask you one thing?"

"Anything."

"Does anyone else call?" I ask, and as I look at him, he just blinks. I feel deflated.

"Lindsey, look at me."

"Yes."

"Yes, what?"

"I'm ready to go. Thank you for dinner," I say as I start to get up. Chris gets up too.

"No, Lindsey, just look at me."

"I'm fine, it's fine," I say, pulling away from him to get my purse.

"Lindsey," he says firmly, so I look at him. "Sit down, please."

"It's fine."

"Lindsey, please sit down." As usual, I find his request irresistible.

"Okay," I say and sit down. Chris pushes my chair back in, and as he sits down, the waitress walks over to see what we need.

"Lindsey, would you like a coffee or hot chocolate or something?" Chris asks.

"Sure, um ... how about a hot chocolate?"

"Make that two, and what can you recommend for dessert?"

"The chocolate lava cake is wonderful," the waitress replies politely.

"Excellent. We'll share that, and I'll give you this, just in case."

And with that, Chris once again takes control of the situation, making me feel taken care of. He gives the waitress his credit card. Then he pulls his chair right next to mine and puts his left arm on the back of my chair. He puts his left hand on my shoulder and takes my hand in his right hand. We sit silently for a few minutes.

"Hey."

"Sorry, I just …"

The waitress brings our coffee and dessert, and leaves the bill. Dessert looks fantastic.

"How many times do I have to tell you not to apologize to me? Look, I don't want to spend the evening on this, but I won't lie to you—she does call. I don't pick it up, and I don't call her. You're the only girl I call. I told you, this is exclusive, okay?"

Softening, I agree, "Okay. You sure that's still what you want?"

"I just spent the last fifteen minutes telling you that you were mine from the first moment I saw you." And with this, he offers me a spoonful of dessert from his spoon. I look him in the eyes and I open my mouth to take the dessert, and suddenly the moment feels very intimate. He pulls me in closer, and I shut my eyes.

Whispering in my ear he says, "Trust me, Lindsey, I won't let you down." This is like music to my ears.

Looking up at him I ask, "Promise?"

"Promise. You ready?"

"Are you?"

"Whenever you are," he says, smiling at the double meaning.

Buzz. It's mine.

"You gonna check that?" Chris asks a bit teasingly.

"Nope." And I pull off coy, which other girls seem to do so naturally but I think I only achieve in these rare moments.

⁎⁐

"Thank you so much for dinner—I loved that place."

"You're welcome, Lindz." I'm thrilled he's called me Lindz again. I hope the nickname sticks.

As we drive past my place, I notice that it's only nine o'clock, so we have plenty of time before curfew.

"Where are we headed?"

"When you are with me," Chris starts, and taking my hand to his lips, he kisses it and then continues, "you don't need to worry about a thing, my Lindz."

It's freezing outside as we get out of his car and head to his pool house.

"Are you sure your parents are okay with us being back here? I feel kind of ..."

"I told you that when you are with me, you don't need to worry about anything."

"I know, but how does it look to your parents if we go back here alone?"

"You're so cute. First of all, they wouldn't think anything, but second, they're out tonight, so no worries—okay, Lindz?" He pulls me into him as we walk behind his house, and I smile uncontrollably.

"Okay, now wait out here till I come get you."

"What?"

"Just wait here for a minute, okay? I'll be right out."

"Alone?"

"What? You'll be fine. I'll be two minutes."

"Okay."

"Close your eyes."

"What? Okay—but hurry."

With that, he enters the pool house and leaves me outside in the freezing night. It seems like I am outside alone for at least five minutes.

I finally hear the door open, and he says, "Keep your eyes closed."

"Okay."

Pulling me against him, he whispers, "Shhhh—okay, now keep

them closed." My stomach drops as he presses his lips to mine, and I am thrilled that he is kissing me. Pulling his lips away from mine, he continues, "Okay, keep your eyes closed and step in here." He guides me in with his hands on my waist, and I'm thrilled at the prospect of what he's doing. I feel the warmth of the pool house around me and know I'm inside when I hear the door close behind me. He positions me so that my back is against him and wraps his arms carefully over my shoulders so that they are around me without touching my chest. Whispering he says, "Okay, Lindz, open your eyes." Hearing him call me Lindz brings another thrill to the moment.

"Ohhh, Chris," is all I can say as I look around the pool house. Chris has started a fire and lit at least twenty small candles around the room. On the coffee table, there is a small white box wrapped with a red ribbon.

"It's just beautiful," I say, turning to face him.

"No, you, my Lindz, you are beautiful." He pulls me into a kiss. It feels so tender. As he pulls away, I realize how much I want to continue kissing him.

"Did you notice the present on the table? I got you something."

"Actually, I did notice that."

Taking my hand, he leads me to the couch, where we sit shoulder to shoulder and hand in hand.

"Lindz, I told you at dinner, I have wanted to be with you since the first day I saw you." He puts the gift in my hands as he leans into me, putting one arm behind me and against my back. "I really like you, Lindsey. I hope this shows you in a small way how much. I got this for you when I was in London."

"You did?"

"Yes. I wanted to be sure you knew that I have been thinking about you for a long time. I also want you to know that you are the only one for me." Taking my face in his hands, he gently caresses my cheek with his thumb. "If you ever need anything, I hope you'll call me. I'm with you—just you and me. I want this to remind you of that."

"Chris." He's killing me with his smile and melting me with his words. I am blushing as I stare into his incredible blue eyes.

"Go on, open it."

"Okay." As I pull the ribbon off the box, I can't even imagine what it might be. It is a small square box. Popping it open, I see a black metal mesh bracelet with a pink sparkly heart on it.

"Oh, Chris, it's so ... I can't ..."

"Don't say that. I want everyone to know you're with me. Do you know what they are?" he asks, pointing to the small pink stones. I'm surprised to learn as he continues, "They're pink sapphires—your favorite color."

"How do you know it's my favorite color?"

"Let's see, pink purse, pink belt, pink top, pink backpack ... Not that hard, Lindz."

Smiling at him I persist, "Chris, it's beautiful, but I can't ..."

"Don't say that. I got it for you. Here." Taking it out of the box, he slips it on my wrist.

"It's too much."

"No, stop. Lindz ..." Leaning into me, he kisses me while still holding my wrist and playing with the bracelet in between his fingers. As his lips part, I'm surprised to find how easy it is for me to mirror his movements. Gently pushing me down, he is quickly above me, and I'm almost lying on the couch.

"Chris," I protest.

"Shhhh," he whispers as he pulls me into another kiss. His mouth seductively covers mine. His tongue gently probes my mouth, and my stomach falls hard.

I seem to let go for just a second and respond to the kiss by touching his face with my hand. His response to me is always stronger than I anticipate. He pulls me near him, and suddenly we are both lying on the couch. Reaching for my head, he runs his hand over my hair, along my face, down my neck, and over my shoulder. I pull away from him, but his left hand wraps around the back of my neck, keeping me against him. His right hand finds my waist, and rubbing my stomach and side with his thumb, he continues, "I'm in no hurry. Okay? I just want to be with you. But please, don't pull away from me. Okay?" His carved features are highlighted by the candlelight, and I'm so taken by him, I simply smile.

"Lindz …" he whispers as he slowly lowers himself against me and teases my lips with his tongue. My hunger for him grows; I just want to feel his lips on mine. I put my hand on the back of his neck and am thrilled that his response is to press his lips to mine and pull our mouths open again. With his right hand, he pulls my left arm around his waist, and the kiss becomes quickened and more demanding. I'm lost in him for the moment. Nothing else seems to exist. Then I feel him run his finger along my wrist under my new bracelet.

Gently pulling away from his lips in an effort to maintain some control, I whisper, "Hey, can I tell you something?"

"Absolutely, what?"

"Thank you for telling me that story you told me tonight."

"It's all true," he replies, and with that kisses my neck. Thankfully it is too dark for him to see my reaction, I close my eyes and bite my lip in delight. Trailing his tongue up my throat, he kisses me again. I touch my hand to his face and enjoy the lingering kiss. Quickly, though, I feel nervous because his hands are in constant motion. They are on my back and my sides. As our long kiss continues, he moves away a few inches and starts to pull my shirttail out of my jeans.

"Hey," I manage to whisper during a kiss.

"Shhhh …"

"Chris, I just …"

"Hey. I'm not in any hurry—relax." And he continues to pull my shirttail out.

"Chris, I …"

"Shhhh, trust me, Lindz."

"I … I …"

"Shhh … here, that's all, okay?" he says as he starts to run his hand across the bare skin of my back. I can feel my stomach tense up in response to his light touch. His hands are so big that his thumb at times comes perilously close to my bra, but much to my relief, never moves up to it.

"Chris?"

"Yeah?"

"I'm sorry, I'm sure you're used to …"

"Hey. This is perfect. Just you and me, okay?"

"You sure this is okay?"

"Yes." And with that, he pulls me into another amazing kiss.

Lying together in the candlelight, we kiss for a bit, and then while he plays with my hair he asks, "Lindz, can I ask you something?"

"Sure."

"When you were with Kevin Walker, did he … Ya know."

"What?"

"Get 'handsy'?" Looking at him, confused at first, then it hits me.

Sitting up a bit, my mood shifts. "What did you hear?"

"Is there something to hear?"

"What? No, what did he say?"

"No, I didn't hear anything."

"What is he saying about me?"

"No, Lindsey, I didn't hear anything. I just want to know if he made you … uncomfortable at all."

"No, no. Why?"

"You sure?"

"Yes, I'm sure. We weren't even dating. We just went to the dance and hung out a little."

"He didn't try anything?"

"No. He was fine—why are you asking?"

"No reason. Just forget it, as long as you're sure."

"Yes, I'm sure. But why are you asking?"

"Forget that," he says, pulling me into a kiss, and as hard as it is to think clearly when I'm with him, I realize the imbalance here.

"Wait," I say, pulling out of the kiss. "Wait a minute. If we are going to discuss my date, let's talk about your many dates."

"No, let's not," he says, putting his hand behind my neck and pulling me into another kiss.

Smiling, I pull away. "No, no—wait a second here. Fair is fair, Mister Buckley."

"We're not going there."

"Why not?"

"It's not the same."

"What does that mean?"

"It's just different."

"Why is it any different?"

"It's different, my Lindz, because if he had gotten 'handsy' with you, I would be forced to protect your honor," he says with a devastating smile. And although I'm still curious about his past relationships, he is being so sweet I give in to him and his addictive kisses. Still nervous about his hands, I pull back again as he moves his hand to my side.

"I told you, relax. I'm in no hurry."

"You sure?"

"Yes, my sweet Lindz. Just relax, okay? We'll take our time, okay? I've been waiting since eighth grade to kiss you again, right? Okay, then, trust me." As he teases my lips again with his tongue, I feel exhilarated and think I'm so lucky to be with Chris Buckley I can hardly believe it.

Then I hear a husky voice in my ear, "But I guess you should know how much I want you. All of you."

80CB

It's almost midnight. As I lie in my bed reliving our first real date, I can hardly contain my excitement. I reach over in the darkness to touch my new bracelet and can't help but smile to myself, recalling how well the evening went. I'm with Chris Buckley. Sigh.

Buzz.

Sitting up in bed, I look at my cell phone. I hope it's Chris.

> **11:56 P.M.** Hi Lindz. Thanks for the best first date. Many more to come. Yours Chris.

> **11:57 P.M.** Thank you for tonight and 4 the beautiful bracelet.

Then I open the text I got during dinner; it's from Melissa.

> **8:22 P.M.** Hey – hope you are having fun!

Buzz. Yes! That must be Chris responding.

> **12:00 A.M.** Midnight and home. You need to get dad off the case. Time is ticking. Safe and sound????????

I lie back down and wonder what that means. Who is this? Do they know I'm home?

24 HOCKEY NIGHT: *FRIENDS OF YOURS?*

"HEY, LINDZ, I HAVE a hockey game Thursday night at our rink. Do you want to come and watch?" Chris asks as we leave English class together.

"Sure, I could come after practice—what time does it start?"

"Seven."

"How late will it go?"

"It should be over about eight o'clock. You could be home by about eight forty-five. Nine at the latest."

"I'll need to check with my folks, but I think they'll go for it."

"Great. Now, I can pick you up, but I need to be there early, so I should be at your place by six—okay?"

"I can just drive myself. It would be tight for me to get home and changed by then."

"You sure?"

"Yeah, no problem."

"Okay, so I hear there is a gymnastics meet on Saturday," Chris mentions with a glint in his eye.

"Yeah, it's an invitational."

"Interesting."

"What?"

"Nothing. I was just thinking it would be nice to be *invited* to a meet," he says, smirking at me.

"Chris?"

"Yes?" he asks, leaning on one shoulder as we stop at my locker.

"I was wondering if you are free Saturday to come to my gymnastics meet?"

"I am, and yes I would be delighted. Now, Lindz, wasn't that easy?"

"Yes," I say, smiling back at him.

Rolling my eyes and shaking my head, I switch my books, and we head down the hall.

⁊⁋

My evenings used to be filled with homework and longing. Now when I do my homework, I look forward to my nightly call from Chris. When my cell rings and I see it is Chris calling, I drop my book and sit up on my bed, filled with excitement.

"Hi."

"Hey, Lindz."

"Hey, Chris. How was practice?"

"Oh, fine. Did you ask your folks about my game Thursday?"

"Yeah. Mom said I can go, but I can't stay out after since it's a school night."

"Cool. Do you have a lot of homework tonight?"

Buzz.

"Um, I have a paper to finish and a French test, so I better not talk too long tonight."

"Okay. Well, I'll see you tomorrow—okay?"

"Okay. Good night, Chris."

"Night, Lindz."

Checking my phone, I see I got a text message.

8:23 P.M. What are you waiting for? End Chicago.

Damn. Who are you?

⋙⋘

Next morning as I pull into the student parking lot, I'm so excited because today, after practice, I get to go to Chris's hockey game.

Buzz. Great. Wonder if it is Chris or *them.*

7:23 A.M. Morning. Call your dad.

Do they know Dad stays in Chicago most nights? What else do they know? *Buzz.* Dad says there are crazy people everywhere. And I'm not bothering him just to hear a lecture on … crazy people or guys teasing me or whatever. Wonder if it's someone at school? I turn my phone off and pack it away. I'm not checking you again until school is out.

As I gather my books for the first few periods, someone grabs me from behind. I jump so far I hit my arm on the metal edge of my locker.

"Oh, sorry, Lindz, I was just … You okay?" Chris says.

My heart is racing as I nod my head. "Yes, sorry. I was just lost in my own thoughts."

"I guess. Is your arm okay?" Chris asks.

"Oh, yeah. Sorry. How are you?"

"Good. We're still on for tonight, right?"

"Yes, I'm excited to see you guys play."

"Yeah, I'm glad you're coming. We're playing South, but it's

298

at our rink. You should dress warm; it's cold in there, even in the stands."

"Okay. Thanks."

"Hey, Lindsey. Hi, Chris," Jon says as he approaches his locker.

"Hi, Jon."

"Hey, Jon. Lindz, I better get to class. See ya in English."

"Okay, bye. How are you, Jon?"

"Good. So you and Buckley are together, huh?"

"Yeah, I guess."

"Huh, shall we?"

"Surely." And with our ritualistic greeting, we head to chemistry.

⁎ ⁐

After school and practice, I head for my car as quickly as I can so I can get home and change before heading to Chris's game. Remembering that my cell phone was vibrating this morning, I dig it out and turn it on to see who called or sent a message.

7:24 A.M. Flip flop. We won't stop. Stop your dad.

I stop.

Who are you? Looking around the school's grounds, I wonder who is doing this. I can see Kevin on his phone. Is it you? Have I ever gotten a message when I'm with ... stop it. *Stop it.* Dad's words come back to me that if I spend too much time thinking about the crazy people, I will become one myself. Delete.

As I drive home, the phone buzzes again. Wonder if it's Chris. I shouldn't check while I'm driving, although I am totally tempted. But I should wait.

As soon as I pull in my driveway, I check my phone.

6:17 P.M. Hey Lindz. Looking forward to seeing you tonight.

> Don't leave after the game, will change quick and
> follow you home.

So nice. Not only is Chris handsome and athletic, he's such a gentleman.

> **6:23 P.M.** Sounds great. Just got home. C u soon. Good
> Luck!!

ഇൗൽ

As I enter the ice arena, I see a couple of the South players filling their oversize water bottles at a nearby fountain. I pass them as I walk over to the concession stand to get a drink.

"Well, well, well," I hear behind me, but I assume it's directed to someone else so I ignore it.

"Hello, Lindsey," and now I turn. At first I don't know who it is.

"It's me, Rock," he says, taking his helmet off. I can't believe it. The Neanderthal.

"So you came to see me play?" he asks me, and turning to his teammates, "I'll meet you guys in there." In his skates and gear, he looks huge. I feel dwarfed standing next to him.

"Hockey fan, are you?" he says, stepping too close.

"Um, yeah, I guess," I say, backing into the cement wall.

"Here alone?" he asks, leaning on the end of his hockey stick.

"Uhhhh ..."

"Here you go," the concession guy says as he hands me my Diet Coke.

"Thank you," I say, happy to have a reason to turn away. I quickly head to the rink and hear Rock follow me.

Pushing the double doors into the rink, a group of young, sweaty hockey players are coming the other way, so I step to the side of them

300

and their oversize hockey bags and sticks. I see that both teams are just getting onto the ice.

The Neanderthal steps in front of me. I can't believe he is here and plays for South.

"I got to go, but I'll find you after the game for some off-ice fun."

"What?" I reply, confused by his statement and still in shock he's here. I try to look for Chris, but the Neanderthal steps between me and the rink, blocking my view.

He says something else. Turning away, but with him still leaning down into me, I say, "No, I'm fine, thanks. I actually came here to see ..." but before I can finish, he cuts me off.

"You *are* fine," he replies with an eager grin. Shocked at his boldness, I see a North player skid to a quick stop at the boards across from the Neanderthal. Then two more of our players race over, stopping abruptly, right next to the first, in a way only hockey players can. Now I see that the three are Chris, Joel, and Mike. Chris glances at me, and seeing my look of desperation, he stares the Neanderthal down. Rock just smiles at the three of them and then slowly turns to me. "Friends of yours?"

Do I say Chris is my boyfriend? He has never called me his girlfriend in front of anyone else, so I decide I can't. "Yes."

"Should be an interesting game. I need to go. See you later, Lindsey."

"Uh-huh," I mumble, searching Chris's face. Chris winks at me and skates away. The twins follow. I climb into the stands and watch the rest of the warm-up. Each team is apparently supposed to stay on their half of the rink during the warm-up, but I think the guys and the Neanderthal are intentionally skating a bit over the centerline.

First Period.

Somehow, I'm not surprised when the guys and the Neanderthal all take the first shift. Chris takes the face-off as the center. Thirty seconds into the game, Mike and Chris both slam into the Neanderthal,

301

who had the puck. No whistles are blown, and play continues. Soon there is a shift change for South, and the guys skate to the bench.

The next two shifts are fairly uneventful.

Back on the ice, Chris and Mike make a nice passing play, when the Neanderthal slams Chris into the boards just as he was about to take a shot. Mike moves in and hits the Neanderthal from behind. A whistle is blown, and Mike gets sent to the penalty box. The players change, and I'm glad they're all momentarily off the ice.

I'm now wondering if it's just a coincidence that every time Chris and the twins are on the ice, the Neanderthal is too.

Next shift, the Neanderthal and one of his teammates both seem to be going after Joel. He gets hit from the side twice with no whistle.

Mike gets out of the penalty box, and the first period ends.

By now, there are a couple dozen spectators in the stands. I realize that since most of these guys can drive themselves, their parents no longer need to come to every game, but I wonder if anyone else thinks this game is a bit rough.

Second Period.

First shift, and Mike again goes after the Neanderthal from behind. Seeing the Neanderthal throw down his gloves, Chris and Joel race over and drop theirs. Two other South guys and the referees instantly skate over. Before the referees can intervene, the Neanderthal, Chris, and Mike are throwing punches. One referee grabs Joel and a South guy, and breaks up the fight. I can't be sure, but I think the Neanderthal and the guys are shouting at each other, and I'm paranoid it has something to do with me. Chris, Joel, the Neanderthal, and one other South guy go in the penalty box.

I watch the clock waiting for the penalties to expire. Three, two, one. They all come out and are now skating. Racing down the ice, the Neanderthal and Mike hit each other so hard, I can hear the crash. Meanwhile, Joel and Chris pass the puck back and forth, ending in a scramble in front of the net. I see their sticks go in the air and jump up as I realize one of them has just scored. I feel sort of out of place standing as I'm here alone, so I quickly sit back down. I wonder if Chris scored. I feel bad that I don't even know. The last few minutes of the period pass uneventfully as the guys are on the bench.

Third Period.

Once again, I notice that Chris and the twins always seem to take the same shift, and whenever they're on the ice, the Neanderthal is too. The Neanderthal nails Chris from the side, hard into the boards. So hard that Chris goes down. Mike immediately cross checks the Neanderthal into the boards, and the two of them have to be broken up again by the referees. Back in the penalty box. I hate to think that any of this is because of me, but I can't help but have that feeling. Maybe I shouldn't have come to the game. I think the guys are all taking a beating for no reason. Or are all their games this rough?

During the penalty, the skaters spend a lot of time in front of the North goalie, who is doing a great job blocking the shots flying at him. I can't help but admire the flexibility and athleticism of the goalies.

When their penalty is over, the guys race out of the box toward the puck, and again the game appears unnecessarily rough. In the final six minutes, there is a frenzy of hitting and skating to gain possession of the puck. Clearly South wants to tie it up, and North is pulling out all the stops to prevent a goal.

The guys go to the bench for a shift change. I can see how hard they are breathing as they gulp down water and squeeze it onto their faces. The final minute and a half of the game, and they all jump on the ice and race to the puck. I can't even tell what is happening as there are so many guys slashing at the puck and slamming each other into the boards. *Buzz*—game over. Yes! We won. Everyone heads to their bench and then to the locker rooms. I see Chris looking for me, and then, with his glove, he indicates that I should meet him in the lobby.

I intentionally wait until both teams cross the walkway and are in their respective locker rooms so there is no chance of running into the Neanderthal again. Even after the teams disappear, I stay in the rink, watching the Zamboni awhile, killing some more time. Finally, I get up from my seat and feel a bit lightheaded. I shake my head, trying to clear the stars away. Taking a last sip of Diet Coke, I step down to ice level. I try to push open the doors to the lobby, but the lightheadedness starts to take over. No, please don't faint. I take two steps forward into the lobby as voices in the lobby grow distant. I am losing it, but still conscious enough to know I don't want my head to hit the floor; it's cement. No! I lose my hearing. *Do not …!* Black.

I can hear someone ask me if I am okay. *Open your eyes.*

"Should we call an ambulance?"

"No, I think she just passed out. Can you hear me?"

Yes, I just can't open my eyes.

"Hey, what happened? Rock, over here."

"Lindsey?" Of course, the Neanderthal is here first.

"I'm … I'm …" I stammer, but still can't open my eyes.

"Lindsey!" I hear from far away, but I know it's Chris. I hear a loud noise.

"What the …" I think that's Mike, and I hear another loud noise. *Are they dropping their hockey equipment?*

"Lindsey?" the Neanderthal asks again. *Open your eyes!* The only thing worse than fainting is the few minutes when I'm lying there completely conscious but I can't yet open my eyes or sit up.

"What did you do?" Chris demands of the Neanderthal.

"What do you care? Just talking to your *friend*," the Neanderthal says with deliberate emphasis.

"Lindsey? Can you hear me?" Chris asks and takes my hand.

"I'm … I'm okay," I say as I'm finally able to open my eyes and speak.

"Why don't you move on?" Mike says, and I'm sure he's talking to the Neanderthal.

"Lindsey, are you okay?" Chris asks. "What happened?"

I push myself up, and tears fill my eyes; a few escape down my cheek. Terrific. As I wipe away the tears, I'm surprised to see how many people are standing around me. Still unsteady, I try to stand up.

"I'm sorry, I'm really fine," I insist as Chris helps me up and hands me my purse.

"Do you mind? She's with me," Chris says in his dad tone while putting his arm around me. Still feeling weak, I lean into him.

"Interesting. She told me you were just a friend," Rock says.

"Back off, okay?" Mike says, stepping in front of the Neanderthal.

"So you both with her?" the Neanderthal mutters as he picks up his bag and steps toward his teammates.

"Hey!" Chris yells in his direction. The Neanderthal and his friends just laugh in response.

"I'm so sorry, I'm really fine," I say to Chris, still fighting the tears, which automatically well in my eyes every time I faint.

"Okay. Let's go, guys," Chris says. Joel hands Mike his sticks and picks up Chris's hockey bag so I can continue to lean on Chris.

"Lindsey, what happened?" Chris asks as we head to the door.

"I don't know. It just happens sometimes. I don't know. I'm so sorry."

"Do you feel okay now?"

"Yeah, I'm fine."

"Did you hit your head, Lindsey?" Mike asks from my right.

"Um ..." Reaching up, I do feel a small lump on the back of my head. "I think maybe I did."

"Let me see," Chris adds while he reaches over and puts his hand where mine was. "Ouch, that's gonna hurt. Mike, can you drive her car home?"

"Yeah, no problem."

"What? Why is Mike ..."

"You just fainted, Lindz. You're not getting behind the wheel. Did you eat any dinner?"

"Um, I uh … Not yet."

"Jeez, Lindsey."

"I didn't have any time," I say, dropping my key into Mike's outstretched hand.

"You guys want to go for a bite at the diner?" Chris asks.

"Sounds good," Joel says.

"Sure, we'll meet you there," says Mike.

"Okay," Chris says as we reach his car.

"Chris, I better call home and check that I can be late."

"You can call, but I'm getting you some food before taking you home."

"See you guys there," Chris calls to the guys as he lets me in the passenger side of his car.

Grabbing my cell phone, I call home while Chris walks around the back of the car.

"So, we okay?" Chris asks as I put my phone away.

"Yeah, you sure you want to go to the diner? I could just eat at home."

"I'm sure. I thought you loved the diner," Chris says as he takes my hand in his.

"I do. Sorry about all this, Chris."

"Do you feel okay?"

"Yeah, it just happens sometimes."

"You have to eat, Lindsey."

"I do." He gives me a look of disapproval, and I have to admit, "Okay, yes, I didn't get a chance to eat yet. But now I get to eat with you."

"Much as I like to spend time with you, Lindz, I'd rather you were conscious," Chris says, teasing me. "Now, how's your head?"

"Oh, fine."

"That was the same guy that bothered you at the party and your meet, wasn't it?"

"Yeah."

"I knew it. He really needs to back off. Why did he say we were friends? What did you tell him?"

"I don't know. I guess before the game, when you skated over and then the twins came over, he asked if you guys were my friends, and so I said you were," I say, trying to be nonchalant.

"Why didn't you just tell him I'm your boyfriend?"

"What?" *Really?*

"Why didn't you just let him know I'm your boyfriend, Lindsey?"

"Um ... well ... I don't know."

Pulling into the pink neon light from the diner, Chris turns to me and asks, "I am your boyfriend, aren't I?"

"I don't know. You never ... I mean ... I didn't want to ..."

"Lindsey, when are you going to realize I like you? You can refer to me as your boyfriend, okay? Do you want to?"

"Sure, does that mean ..."

"What?"

"Come on ..."

"You're so cute. Yes, Lindz, I consider you my girlfriend. So can we agree that if that guy or anyone else is hanging around hitting on you, that you'll let them know the truth? That I am your boyfriend?"

"He wasn't hitting on me."

"Right. But not the point—can we agree?"

"Yes."

"That was easy, wasn't it?"

"Yes." I look at him in the soft neon light and am so happy to be with him. I want him to kiss me.

"No, no, don't do that," Chris says.

"Do what?" I ask, surprised.

"Don't give me that look. Let's go get you some food."

"Okay," I say, opening the door. *Can he see in my face that I want him to kiss me?* How embarrassing. I see stars again as I stand, so I grab the car door frame and bend my head down to try to stabilize myself.

307

"Lindsey!" Chris says and is at my side in an instant. "What is it? You okay?" His concern is comforting. Putting his arm around me, he bends down to look at my face.

"Just a little dizzy, I guess."

"Okay, come on." Chris pulls me against his side and we walk in together. I see the guys already have a booth. Mike looks concerned and stands up when he sees us.

"Lindsey, are you okay? She looks pale, Chris," Mike says, stepping toward us.

"Yeah, I know. I think we need to get some food in her."

"I'm fine. I'm so sorry."

"Fine? She almost went down again getting out of the car."

"I'll get the waitress," Mike says, raising his hand and trying to get her attention.

Walking over in her crisp white outfit, the waitress greets us warmly, "Good evening. What can I get you kids to start with? Oh, I'm sorry, do you need menus?"

"No, we're fine. Lindsey, what do you want?"

"Diet coke and the BLT sandwich, but not the triple-decker."

"Lindsey," Chris cuts me off and turning to the waitress asks, "could you please bring her a chocolate shake with the triple-decker BLT and some fries?"

"Really?" the waitress asks, as she doesn't know which order to bring.

"She just fainted, and she hasn't eaten since," and turning to me, "what, this morning?" Then back to our waitress, "What do you think she should have?" Chris says, giving her his killer smile.

"That true, dear? You do look pale."

"I guess."

"BLT and a chocolate shake; got it," she says, winking at Chris. Terrific.

"I'll have a Coke and a cheeseburger."

"Make that two," Joel chimes in.

"Three, but make mine a bacon cheeseburger."

"Oh, can I have a glass of water too?" I ask.

"You got it, sweetie. I'll have the drinks right out."

℘℘

"Anything else?" our waitress warmly asks after we've all eaten.

"Lindsey, you want some pie or something?" Chris asks me.

"No, it's late. I'm fine, thanks."

"Guys? Okay, then here," Chris says, handing our waitress his credit card.

"I'll follow you guys to Lindsey's house to drop her car off," Mike says, as if to confirm I still can't drive.

"I'm fine. I can drive myself home."

"Not a chance," Chris says, dismissing me. Instead of feeling insulted, I am endeared to see how protective he is toward me.

"I'll follow too, and bring Mike home," Joel says.

"Thanks. Hope you feel better, sweetie," the waitress says, placing the receipt in front of Chris. I realize that Joel is coming to get Mike so that Chris and I can say good night without an audience. Guy code. Got to love it.

℘℘

"Thanks, Mike," I say as he hands me my keys while Chris checks his phone.

"Anytime, Lindsey. See ya, Chris. Thanks again for dinner."

Looking up, Chris says good night to Mike as he heads down my driveway to join Joel in their car.

Buzz.

"How are you feeling, Lindsey?"

"Fine, really, just kind of a headache."

"Yeah, I bet," he says, rubbing the knot on the back of my head. "Well, get some sleep, okay?"

Buzz.

"Was that your phone?" he asks.

"Probably my mom; it's late. I better go in." We both turn to see a pickup pulling in.

"Right on cue—the dog walker."

Smiling as we both realize that we just lost our private good-bye, he pulls me in for a quick kiss before Joe walks up.

"Thanks again for tonight. I loved watching you in the game."

"I loved having you there and hope you'll come again."

"Anytime."

"Okay, go get some rest."

"Good night, Chris."

80CB

As I leap up the stairs and enter my room, I check my cell to see who just called or texted me.

> 9:11 P.M. Three chaperones home. But who's watching now?

I guess you are. Creepy. I step over to my windows and shut the drapes, shuddering at the thought that someone may be watching me. My head is pounding as I lie in bed with my thoughts racing.

80CB

I must have been sleeping lightly because I hear my phone buzz. Maybe it's Chris?

11:08 P.M. Dog walker is gone. Who's home now? Get dad
back from Chicago.

I decide to check to see if Joe has left. Stepping barefoot into the
hallway, I walk on the carpet as quietly as I can, but Baron hears me.
He runs up the stairs, and rubbing behind his ears, I can feel how
cold his fur is. Shivering, I realize that Baron just came inside, and
so *they* might be watching the house. I head downstairs to double-
check that the alarm is on. While walking through the dark halls, I
remind myself that Dad said there are all kinds of protections in place
with his cases; Dad's never led me astray. It's just someone with too
much time on his hands. Come on, Lindsey, grow up. This will all
blow over. It's got to be someone at school—but who? I go back to
my bed; my head is still throbbing.

Buzz.

12:00 A.M. Midnight. Forest is quiet.

Are you in the forest? How close to our house are you? They're
probably miles away and just playing with my fears. Turn your phone
off and go to sleep.

Buzz.

I must have fallen asleep and left my phone on. Hearing it buzz,
I wake up enough to check it.

1:00 A.M. Dock is quiet.

Are you on our dock? Tiptoeing to the back guest bedroom, I
open the curtains and lift the shade. I can't see anything on the dock,
as the dock lights are out and the landscaping lights go off around
eleven. I wonder if someone is out there. Stop it, Lindsey. Don't let
them get to you. I creep back to bed, and although my mom is home,
I wish my dad was too.

I get in bed and watch the clock tick the time away. I am predicting
I'll get another text at two o'clock.

1:58 a.m.

1:59 a.m.

Buzz. Nightmare. My head feels like it's splitting open. Between the knock I took earlier when I fainted, the fact that I haven't slept well tonight, and the stress of these texts, I decide I'll take some medicine after checking this text.

2:00 A.M. Asleep yet?

I sit up abruptly, concerned with what this text says. What's going on? Can they see me? Do they know they're getting in my head? I desperately want to sleep. Come on. They're just text messages. I bet there is some geeky app that makes it look like texts are coming from different phone numbers even though it's probably the same stupid guy. I need to put all this out of my mind and get some sleep. I turn my phone off in hopes that I'll get at least a few hours of rest.

⮑⮐

When my alarm goes off at five thirty, I'm exhausted after only a few hours of sleep—none of it peaceful. After my shower I finally build up enough nerve to check my cell phone. I am apprehensive as I see several new messages.

3:00 A.M. The Lake is still tonight. Are you?

4:00 A.M. Who's watching over you?

5:00 A.M. Birds are up. So are we. Alert as ever.

6:00 A.M. Freezing out here. Warm in there?

Are they really outside? Did they stay all night? Can you set up a computer program to automatically send text messages on the hour? I should google that and see if it's possible. Probably what they did. I'm so glad Dad comes home tonight.

312

༉༃

Friday. I drag through school, exhausted from the lack of sleep last night and wondering how I will make it through today's practice. Chris's practice tonight will be late, so I told him to go out with the guys because I need to get some sleep before my meet tomorrow. Happily, Dad is coming home tonight, and there are no texts from *them* through the evening. Even better, Chris sends several texts to me both before and after his practice.

༉༃

Saturday morning, we wake up to about a foot of snow and frigid temperatures.

"Hey, Dad."

"Well, hello there, Lindsey."

"You must have gotten in late last night, huh?"

"Yeah, I had to work late, so a few of us went to dinner in Chicago before I drove home."

"How's the case coming?"

"Oh, well, you know, it takes time to put together all the evidence."

"So, has the trial started?"

"No, no—not yet. We're still building our case."

"Seriously?" Should I ask him about the texts? I'm not really in the mood for a lecture, and I don't want anything to get in the way of my date with Chris. And let's face it, after the Case, there is not a chance he will drop whatever case he is on anyway.

"Yep. You know we have to be sure we have enough solid evidence to nail the accused. We don't want them walking away on a technicality."

"So, when do you think you will actually press charges?"

"Oh, probably not until early in the new year."

"Huh?" I wonder if I'll get texts till then. Maybe these are the guys who don't want to be charged.

"Your mother and I'll drive you to the meet, given the weather."

"Okay, but I need to be there at nine for warm-ups."

"No problem. We'll drop you at the school and then get breakfast before it starts."

"Okay. Oh, and I think Chris is going to come and watch too."

"Very good."

"I may go out with him again tonight."

"Well, if the weather is bad, I would just want you to stay in town—okay?"

"Sure. Thanks, Dad."

༺༻

As I sit in the car on the way to the meet, I feel it. *Buzz.*

7:45 A.M. Daddy's back. Who's watching yours?

Man. How do they know that?

༺༻

Warm-ups are about the same as every meet. Elizabeth is as cold as ever to me. When she sees Chris arrive, I think we will be in a deep freeze.

I notice Chris enter the gym just before all the teams are announced. He waves at me during the march in, and I just smile in response. My warm-up went well. Of course, knowing Chris is here,

I'm ready to pack my routines to ensure I do well. Five teams are here. Based on what I saw during warm-ups, Jennifer and I should do very well if we both hit our routines.

₧∓

The meet goes as expected, and the next ten days are a whirlwind of activity. It's the last week before the Thanksgiving break, so everyone has papers due and tests to prepare for. My days are filled with school, practice, and studying. Much to my delight, there are also plenty of calls and text messages from Chris. We even get to go on a date each Saturday. His nightly calls are the dessert at the end of my day.

But the text messages from *them* continue as well. Ignoring them as best I can, I still feel unnerved each time I receive one.

On the whole, though, the pattern of my days is busy and good. And those moments when I'm the recipient of Chris's smile or am holding his hand are the moments I crave. And every night, the movie in my mind replays each of our conversations, each touch, each moment.

25 THANKSGIVING WEEKEND: *A THIRD WHEEL.*

WE HAVE NO PRACTICE after school Wednesday since Thanksgiving is tomorrow, so I plan to spend the afternoon baking. Baking is peaceful. Mom took the day off to prepare for Thanksgiving even though it will just be the three of us. By the time I get home, she is done with her preparations, so I have the kitchen to myself. My favorite country music station is filling the kitchen as I begin to measure and mix. My plan is to make an apple pie, a batch of candied walnuts, and some homemade fudge. That should be plenty both for our family dessert tomorrow and to put together a sweet plate for Chris. Chris is going with the twins to pick their brothers up at the airport for the long holiday weekend.

With the walnuts and pie in the oven, I begin to pull out the ingredients to make the fudge. Realizing we are short semisweet cocoa powder, which I will need for the fudge, I walk to the wood-paneled locker room, grab my keys and coat off their hooks, and yell to Mom, who is watching TV, "I'm gonna run to the store for some chocolate."

"Oh, I can go for you."

"It's fine; it's not snowing. I'm just going to Donaldson's market in town. I won't be long."

"Just the same, I'll ride along."

Rolling my eyes, I reply with clear exasperation, "Mom, seriously?"

"You're right." *Yes!*

"I should be back, but just in case, can you pull the pies and nuts out when the timers go off?" Mom agrees, and I grab my stuff to go.

As I get in my car, I once again feel the thrill of this gift, which hasn't yet worn off. It's a clear, dark night as I head into town. No one is on the road. I assume everyone is home preparing for the holiday or already hosting visiting relatives. I don't see another car until I get close to town, where there are one or two parked on the street. As I pull into the parking lot, it looks like I'm the only customer. Donaldson's is a small market right in town that Mom uses for specialty items, but she goes into what we all refer to as College Town for the big shopping trips. I walk up to the door and see the clerk approaching the other side of the door with keys in his hand. Hurrying, he opens the door for me with a disapproving look and says, "We close at six for the holiday."

"Oh." I check my watch and see it's already a few minutes after six. "I just need some baking chocolate for a dessert."

"Go ahead; aisle four."

"Thank you!" I jog over to aisle four as I hear him lock the door behind me. I quickly return with the chocolate, pay the clerk, and thank him profusely. He lets me out the front door and promptly locks it behind me. As I cross the sidewalk in front of the store, I'm surprised how quickly the clerk turns off all but a few security lights in the store. The only light remaining is from a few high poles scattered around the parking lot.

As I step off the curb into the store's parking lot, I hear a car door and turn toward the sound. I hadn't noticed any other cars when I pulled in. I see the interior light of a car or maybe a small truck down the road at the edge of town just for an instant. Then I hear a deep bark, as if from a large dog. Continuing to walk toward my car, I hear more dogs barking, all as deep in pitch as the first. They sound excited. Or are they agitated? Turning back to where I saw the light, I think I see movement, but I can't be sure. Quickening my pace, I strain my eyes to see if something is actually moving, and I feel the key in my coat pocket. Then I see something galloping through a pool of dim light cast from a streetlamp. The barking is getting louder. Are they headed toward me? I stop momentarily to watch them. Sucking in air, I realize they are headed straight for me. I look behind me to see if something else is their target. Seeing nothing, I walk toward my car with a determined pace. The barking is getting louder, and they sound fierce. Should I run? Will that encourage them to chase me? Stealing one more glance back, I see they're in the parking lot and closing fast. No time. Bolting to my car, I know it always unlocks when I get close with the key still in my purse, but I'm taking no chances and click the electronic key to unlock my car and run with all the force I can muster, like I'm about to vault. I hear them barking more and more. Louder and louder. Closer and closer. Slamming to a stop, I grab the door handle as I see them in my peripheral vision about three car lengths away. I pull the door hard and hurl myself into the front seat, slamming the door behind me. Closing my eyes, I hear them hit the car. I force myself to open my eyes, and see one growling next to me and looking at me through the side window standing on its hind legs. Another is barking frantically and pacing by the side of the car. Were there three?

"Ahhhh!" I scream as it lands on the hood of my car. Its teeth are huge. They are all barking frantically and viciously growling. I lock the doors. Looking from one teeth-baring beast to another, I can't think. Where's the owner? Why are they here? Are they someone's pets? Doberman pinschers! *Hit the horn.* My brain tries to guide me, but I can't move. My arms are locked straight out on the steering wheel, and I'm pressing myself into the back of the seat. I force my hands off the rim and slam the horn. They stop barking and look around. I use the mental break from the incessant, pummeling barking to start the car. With the horn quiet, they return to their ferocious pursuit. Pursuit? Yes, they were after me. Still are. The large black and brown dog is still on the hood and barking in my face, so I use the rearview mirror and throw the car in reverse. As we move backward, the dog on the hood hunches down against the movement of the car. The two on the side continue to jump up on the window next to me. What if their paws get caught under the wheel? I don't want to hurt them. *Get off.*

"Get off!" I hear myself scream. Slowly, I continue to back up. They stay with me. Looking around, I see no one. The parking lot is empty, and I have plenty of room. I stay in reverse, and the two on the side back away as I give the engine a fraction more gas. Pressing the speed now, I turn to the one on my hood, still hunched down and growling. Drooling. Man. I slam to a stop, and its face hits the windshield. It yelps and then goes crazy barking at me. I start in reverse again. Faster. The other two are running around barking but staying a good two or three feet clear of the car. I blare the horn again. I get moving a bit more quickly in reverse. I glance at my uninvited passenger, but it seems undeterred. A quick look in the rearview mirror—I see a shopping cart carousel and swerve hard away from it and my two friends on my left. The quick move throws off the one on my hood. As it slides off, I hit the accelerator, and in a slight curve create some distance. I slam the brake and throw it in drive. With a sharp turn, I swerve wide of the three dogs, which are all on their feet now and running at the car. I swerve to the side again, determined not to hurt them.

I race to the entrance and look around for the dogs. Can't see them. Good! I floor it out of the parking lot and into the street. Driving at twice the speed limit, I fly down the street and spot the dogs in my rearview mirror, still chasing me. Thankful to be getting away, I continue driving too fast through town. After a few blocks, I can't see the dogs anymore. Then I feel my phone buzz. I hope that's Chris. Can't check while I'm driving. I'm breathing hard, like I just worked out. *What was that?*

Finally, turning onto my road and circling the lake, I take my first deep breath. I catch sight of my driveway, and I can't get there fast enough. I open my garage door and pull in. I close my eyes, put my head on the headrest, and breathe—finally. I can't let go yet of my vise grip on the steering wheel.

Bang! Bark! Bark! Bark!

"Ahhhh!" I scream as I cover my mouth with my hands and pull my knees into my chest. Oh, man. I look to my left and see Joe Mitchell with his hand near my window, where he must have just knocked. He looks more than a little shocked and concerned at my reaction. Baron is jumping all over and barking, as he is excited to see me. Great. Exhale. I close my eyes. Thankfully it's Joe. Opening my eyes, I look at him and mutter, "Sorry."

"I'm sorry, Lindsey. I thought you saw me."

Opening my door, I start to get out. I am really losing it. Get a grip, Lindsey.

"Where were you?"

"I ran to the store."

Looking past me into my car, he asks the obvious question, "Do you need any help? Did you get anything?"

"Oh … um … yeah." And I pull the small package out of my pocket. I show it to him. "Some chocolate. Do you like fudge?"

"Sure."

"I'll give you some. It should be ready in about an hour."

I enter the locker room, hang up my coat, and check my cell. It's Melissa.

6:27 P.M. Hey Lindsey. Headed to my grandparents. Have a Happy Thanksgiving!

"Lindsey, you okay?" Joe asks as he steps inside.

Ignoring the text, I reply, "Fine, yeah. Sorry about that. I … Uh … Sorry."

"You okay?"

"Yeah, yeah." I head to the kitchen and turn the music up louder and try to block out the questions in my mind. I can't deny that I'm shaken up, as evidenced by the tremor in my hand as I try to precisely measure the half-and-half. *Close enough.* As I continue to stir and combine the ingredients, more questions creep in. Were they just out for a walk? Did the owner think no one was around and so was letting them run without a leash? Do Doberman pinschers naturally chase? Does anyone in town own three Dobermans? No, not that I know of. Could it be someone driving through town to visit relatives for the weekend? Shake it off, Lindsey. Get a grip.

Buzz. Yikes! Who is that? Chris, yes!

> **6:47 P.M.** Hey Baby! On our way back. Going to college town want to come out?
>
> **6:47 P.M.** Thanks. U have fun with your brother.
>
> **6:48 P.M.** U sure?
>
> **6:48 P.M.** Y. Have fun.
>
> **6:48 P.M.** Ok. Will ping u later

୫୦ cଓ

Chris calls later in the evening, and it sounds like the guys had a great time hanging out together. I'm happy they did. I can't help but wonder how many girls they talked to. I finished all my baking and watched a psychological thriller with my folks, which was nice. As I lie in bed, I can't shake the image of that Doberman on the hood of my car.

୫୦ cଓ

Thanksgiving Day is filled with wonderful aromas of cloves, cinnamon, thyme, and of course, the turkey. My parents and I spend the day calling relatives, watching too much football, and eating too much food. It's so nice. Dad spends a lot of time editing papers and working on his computer, but at least he's home and hanging out with us. Chris calls several times throughout the day, and our plan is to get together in the evening to see a movie.

It's so nice to have a boyfriend. Someone who calls. Someone who wants to see me. Someone to make plans with. But not just anyone; it's *Chris Buckley*. I still can't believe he's interested in me. I love the entire process—talking to him to make our plans, picking an outfit, getting ready, the anticipation of him pulling in the driveway, and of course, the simple joy of seeing him at my door.

When he picks me up for the movie, I just love that he takes my hand, even for the short distance from my front door to his car. Pulling my hand into his, he also pulls me in closer to him as we walk. Smiling, I let my head rest momentarily against his shoulder. He doesn't say anything. It's so peaceful. I'm so happy. Hand in hand, shoulder to shoulder. The snow lightly falling. The silence between us makes me feel closer to him. I want the moment to linger. But as is always the case, it's all too fleeting. He opens the car door for me, and silently and happily, I get in. He puts the treats I made for him in the trunk and then climbs in the driver's seat. "Thanks again for the fudge," he says as he puts his arm on the back of my seat to back out my driveway.

"I hope you like it."

"I'm certain I will," he says as he leans over to kiss my forehead. *Can it get any better?*

"What?" he asks, and I realize I'm smiling like a fool from ear to ear.

Turning away and shaking my head a fraction, I mumble, "Nothing."

"What is it, Lindz?"

"No, nothing." Looking out the window, I can't imagine being any happier. Is he as happy? I look over at him driving. No idea. I hope so.

"I wonder if we'll see anyone else at the show?" I ask, enjoying our time together.

"Oh, I think maybe we will," he replies with a knowing smirk.

"Who?"

"Small town—bound to know someone," he says, and I know he's up to something.

"Come on. Who's going?"

"Promise you won't be mad?" *At you? Seriously, not possible.*

"Promise. Who?"

"The guys."

"Your brother, Jake; the guys?"

"Yeah ... and the twins ... and Alex." Alex is the twins' older brother. He and Jake are the same age and also best friends.

"With dates?" I ask cautiously.

"Not exactly," he starts and squeezes my hand, "but it'll be great."

"No, Chris, I can't go out with you and ... and ... that's guys' night out. No, I'm ..."

"No, no, no ..."

"You should have told me."

"I was afraid you wouldn't come."

"You were right! You could have told me if you wanted to go out with the guys."

"I do, but I also want to see you." As he squeezes my hand and flashes that irresistible dimpled smile, I'm helpless. I give him a sideways look. I've been looking forward to seeing him all day, but feel a bit awkward about the group date.

"A third wheel. No—I really don't want to ..." I start, but he lifts our hands up onto his leg and cuts me off.

"Lindz, would you stop? I want to see you tonight, okay? We're just going to the same theater. What's the big deal?"

"I just don't want to be in the way."

"You, my Lindz, are never in the way."

"Do the guys know I'm coming?"

"Sure."

"Did they care? Honestly."

"No. Why would they care? Come on. We'll have fun, okay?"

"If you're sure."

"I'm sure, and we're here—ready?" he asks, with another quick squeeze of my hand before he lets it go to get out of the car. We see the guys getting out of their cars a few spaces down.

Nervously, I get out, wondering how this will go. Will we all sit together?

"Hey, guys!" Chris calls over to his brother, Jake, and the Kirkwood boys.

"Hey. Hi, Lindsey," Alex calls over to me.

"Hi, Alex. Hi, Jake. Happy Thanksgiving, guys," I try. Jake just nods as he walks over to the movie theater. Terrific.

"Hey, Lindsey. Happy Thanksgiving," Joel says as he steps over and matches my stride with Chris.

I reply with a smile and stuff my hands in my coat pocket, as I'm not sure that this would be the best time for Chris and me to hold hands. Chris holds the door open for me, and I catch his eye for a moment as I pass through in front of the twins. Entering the theater, I see that Alex and Jake are already at the ticket booth. Chris bumps me a bit from behind in a playful way to encourage me to step in farther.

"You want some popcorn, Lindsey?"

"Sure, thanks." As we step farther into the lobby, I can't help but wonder if Chris already got tickets, or if Alex and Jake are getting them for all of us. My mental question is quickly answered as we step up to the guy taking tickets and Jake hands him a stack of movie tickets. Am I supposed to offer to pay Jake? I glance at Chris. He raises his eyebrow a fraction and gives me a quick wink as he gestures for me to enter first. Taking this as a signal, I turn to Jake and thank him as I enter. "Sure," he replies in a reserved manner he seems to use solely with me. We head to the concession stand to load up on popcorn and drinks.

Quickly the guys are all talking and laughing at one thing, then another, jumping from topic to topic, and leaping across the timeline of their lifelong friendship. It's fascinating to watch, although impossible to participate in. The rhythm of their friendship is played out in the fast-paced, clipped version in which each episode from their collective past is barely referenced and fully understood.

As we enter the theater, I'm near the middle of the group and completely self-conscious. I hope I'm sitting next to Chris. He better make sure we sit together! As we climb the stairs in the dark theater, I have a kind of wave of pressure pins run across my head—is that nerves? Now I'm annoyed with myself for being nervous. Alex asks if a row about three-quarters of the way up the mostly empty theater is okay. The guys confirm it's good. Alex walks down first, then Jake, and then Chris gestures for me to go next. Next to Jake? Terrific. Heading down the aisle, I wish I were next to Mike or Joel. Oh, well. As we all get settled, I put my coat behind me and sit down, careful not to bump Jake or Chris. I sit with my soda in my lap so I have something to do with my hands. Happily, Chris reaches over and takes my hand.

Buzz.

I can feel my phone, so I check it as the movie hasn't even started yet. I decide I can check it as the guys are all on their phones texting each other and laughing about it.

8:03 P.M. You need to listen up. Talk to your dad.

"Who is it?" Chris asks, leaning in for a look at my cell phone screen.

"No one," I whisper back and hit delete.

Moments later, I can feel my phone buzz again. Chris notices, too. But I ignore it and watch the preview. *Buzz.*

"Maybe you should check it, Lindz?" Chris asks, as he can feel my phone vibrate as well while he responds to a text on his.

"Oh, it's nothing." I wonder if it's *them*. Maybe it's Melissa or Elena.

Not two minutes later, it buzzes again.

"Lindsey, maybe it's your folks?"

"Okay, why do you guys text each other when you are all right here?" I say, opening my purse. He just shrugs with a smile, and I hear Jake snicker at whatever he is reading. Carefully, I look at my phone inside my purse. Sure enough, my screen is slowly filling with messages from *them*.

"Everything okay?" Chris asks, and I think he is curious why I'm not pulling the phone out.

"Oh, yeah. It's nothing," I say and turn the phone off so that I don't have to feel it buzz all night.

The rest of the movie is uneventful, except for the action on screen. Leaving the theater, we chat about the film as we slowly approach our cars.

"See you, guys," Chris calls generally to the group as he puts his arm lightly on my back to guide me to his car.

"Good night, Lindsey, Chris," Mike says as they stand in a small group.

"See ya, Chris. Happy Thanksgiving, Lindsey," Joel calls as he zips up his jacket against the dropping temperatures.

"Good night, guys," I say, happy with how the evening has gone so far.

Stepping up to me and patting my shoulder, Alex gives me a warm farewell. "Good to see you, Lindsey. We're probably gonna hang out and play some pool tomorrow; you should come over with Chris."

"Thanks, Alex. Happy Thanksgiving." *And thank you for trying to make me feel welcome.* Then there is a beat, and suddenly the group feels tight, uncomfortable. Alex is playing with his keys. Jake and I make eye contact in an awkward way.

"Night," he says, looking away, and then turning to the car, he waits for Alex to unlock it as I turn to go. He hates me. Or at least he hates me dating Chris. Chris says nothing as we walk to his car. This cannot be good. I search my mind for what I could have done that would turn Jake off from me so much. Chris opens my door. As I slide in, I try to read his face. Can't tell. As he shuts the door and walks around the car, I wonder if Jake was hoping for more of a real "guys' night out." Is it tonight he's upset about? Or does he just not like me?

"Ready?" Chris asks as he starts the engine.

"Sure." *Are you completely oblivious? Didn't you notice how your brother hardly talks to me?* I'm so glad that Chris and I drove separately from the guys so that Chris can take me home and we can have some time together at my house. Maybe Jake likes the fact that Chris never has a girlfriend so the guys can all just hang out. *Why isn't Chris talking to me?*

I feel him take my hand and look over to him in the soft green glow of the car's instrument panel.

"You okay, Lindz?"

"Oh, yeah. The movie was great." *And by the way, why does your brother hate me?*

"Yeah, the special effects were so cool." We are quiet the rest of the way home. I hope Chris will want to come into my house.

Pulling into my driveway, my excitement builds, thinking of being with him. As we walk up to the front door and Chris takes my hand, I hold onto it and enjoy the touch of his fingers interlaced with mine. Stepping onto my porch, I let go of his hand to get my key out. He opens the storm door for me.

Then Chris says, "Since it's Thanksgiving and your dad's home and my brother's in town, I should probably get home."

"Oh, yeah, of course," I say as cheerily as I can, although I'm enormously disappointed. I hope he will still kiss me good night, and maybe change his mind and come in. Did I do something wrong? Then he kisses me, and it seems like everything is okay. His kiss lingers, and it is sweet.

"Good night, Lindz," he says with one more quick kiss, and then he turns to go. I enter my house.

As I walk upstairs, I pull out my cell phone and turn it on to check my messages. I have one text from Melissa, two from Elena, and too many from *them.*

It is clear from the texts, which I delete as I read them, that they know what I did today.

8:04 P.M. Movie night?

8:06 P.M. Like a good thriller do you?

8:10 P.M. Need more action in your life?

8:40 P.M. Busy night.

8:45 P.M. 5 dates huh?

8:52 P.M. Better get busy talking to dad while he is home.
Stop him NOW! Or else...

Man. I hate this. Who knew I was at the movie? Only my family, a few friends, and ... well, the guys.

26 DATE NIGHT: *TIME TO GET READY.*

MY NERVES ARE SHOT. At this point, the general demands of being a high school junior are mere background noise. My life is like a movie I've already seen three times—it's all so familiar that I need to give it only halfhearted attention to keep up with the core themes.

High school gymnastics is a breeze, and club meets don't start until after winter break. *Dracula* is over. At school, I only have a week of exams to get through before winter break. It's my cell phone I fear.

But I can't ignore my cell, as it's my link to Chris, my friends, and even my parents. The irony of this is amusing. Inside my phone are the usual check-ins from Mom, and the "Are you studying enough" texts from Dad, and the texts that make my heart race. Those come, of course, from Chris. But my phone also holds messages from *them*. Each is another reminder that I'm on *their* minds. Every time the phone buzzes, I wonder who it is.

Fortunately, cell phones aren't allowed at school, although most kids will sneak text messages from the restrooms or when they think no one's looking. If you're caught using one, a member of the faculty or administration will take it until the end of the day. There's a part of me that would love to have my cell phone confiscated so that I can leave it at school for a few days and pretend I forgot it. But a stronger urge compels me to carry it all the time. As much as I don't want to get another text message from *them*, I can't ignore even one message.

At school I leave my cell phone in my locker in an effort to avoid feeling the vibration of any incoming messages throughout the day. I know that if I carry it and feel it buzz, I'll be completely distracted until I get a chance to check it. Only a few weeks ago, I was wishing for texts from Chris. Now when I feel its vibration, I wonder if it's a text from Chris, which will leave me feeling excited. Or will it be from *them*, leaving me anxious?

For the first time in my life, I'm glad people think of me as a quiet person, because even though I feel like I'm hardly talking at all now, no one seems to notice. Over the years, I think I've become very skilled at participating in conversations while hardly saying a word. This skill is serving me well.

Dad is working all the time now. Which isn't unusual. Even when he's home, opera music is constantly playing. Dad says the press will definitely cover his current case. He says they will be interested because some of the people involved are high-profile, which I'm sure is true. But I also know Dad has built a reputation of taking on cases no one else will and delivering a very high conviction rate. So I'm sure his name will add to the press's interest. Perhaps the press coverage will be good for me, as I can't imagine if the senders of the texts really are involved in the case, that they will have time to text me when they need to prepare to defend themselves. Chances are it's someone at school anyway. But who?

∞⃝

It's Saturday morning. I check my cell as soon as I get up, breathing a sigh of relief as there's nothing new.

Much to my surprise, Mom's up and dressed when I come down to the kitchen.

"Morning, Mom. Are you going somewhere?" Mom's never up this early on a weekend without a reason.

"Yeah. On the news last night, they said that a big snowstorm is coming. So Mrs. Kirkwood, Mrs. Buckley, and I are going to get an early start to Chicago so we don't have to drive through it. I'm picking them up at eight. I'll drop you off at practice. Your father spoke to Joe Mitchell last night, and he'll pick you up from gymnastics practice."

"I can just drive myself, Mom."

"You're not driving in this storm, Lindsey," she says, looking out at the snow, which is already coming down pretty hard. "I'll drop you off a bit early and then pick up the ladies and head to Chicago for the benefit. It will give all of us more time to help set up the auction items anyway."

"Does Joe have to spend the night here?"

"You know we're staying over in Chicago tonight."

"I know, but I'm sixteen. I don't need a babysitter."

"You're right. You don't need a babysitter. Joe's here for Baron," she says with a sympathetic smile. "Look. Your dad and I like Joe, and he could use the extra money. For your father and I to enjoy the evening, we need Joe to stay here. It's just one night."

"Great," I mumble, rolling my eyes.

Clearly my parents do not plan to let me drive in a snowstorm anytime soon. Given the amount of snow we get here in Michigan, I guess my fabulous new car will be spending much of the winter in our garage.

80C3

By the time Mom dropped me off, the snow was already several inches deep. Practice went well. When Joe picked me up after practice, close to a foot of snow had fallen, and the storm was still hammering down and gaining strength.

ꝏ

Saturday afternoon. Finally. Time to get ready for my date with Chris. I'm so looking forward to tonight. Chris and I are going to dinner and a movie. At least, that was the plan before this storm. He texted earlier confirming our plans and said he and the twins were going snowmobiling for the afternoon. We must have eighteen to twenty-four inches on the ground now. I'm hoping since Joe is pretty young, he'll be cool about things and give Chris and me some time alone. We never seem to get any time by ourselves, and I'm craving it. I just want to be close to Chris. I want to hold his hand. Anything. I can't wait for tonight. Chris is supposed to pick me up at seven o'clock. I hope he's early.

Buzz. Immediately I look at my cell phone. Maybe Chris is calling to see if he can come over early.

> 3:44 P.M. Monday is too late. Dad needs to drop the case now. You need to stop daddy NOW. Or we will stop you.

Who is this? Should I call my dad? If you really were tied to my dad's case, you wouldn't waste all this time sending text messages. The guys he puts away kill people. So who is it? Chris? No. The Neanderthal? The Fab Five?

Closing my eyes, I drop on my bed and force my thoughts to Chris. I enjoy the daydream of Chris. Sigh.

"Hey, Lindsey?" I hear Joe call from downstairs.

Getting up from my bed, I call down the hall, "Yeah, one sec."

"Hey, what's up?" I ask him as I near the top of the turned staircase; he's standing at the bottom, looking up at me.

"Hey, um ... I don't know what to do, but I just got a call from my neighbor that my dog was crying and whining, and then she heard him throw up."

"Oh, my gosh. Is he okay?"

"Well, Joanne, she's in the apartment next to mine, got the super to let her in my place, and she says he looks terrible. He's still throwing up and whimpering."

"You should go take care of him."

"I know. I think you should come with me. I don't live that far, and it shouldn't take too long."

Not a chance.

"No. I have a date with Chris; he'll be here by seven." Looking at my watch, I see that it is 5:05 p.m. and head down the stairs to convince Joe. "That's only a couple of hours. I'll be fine. I'm allowed to be home alone."

"I know. But with your folks in Chicago ... I don't know ..."

"Look, it's fine. I'll be with Chris till midnight, so if you go now, you can take care of your dog and be back way before I get home, right? No harm done. You can even bring him here." *Anything. Just go.*

"Yeah, I guess."

"So go. Tell you what, I'll ask Chris to stay until you get back." *Nice!*

"Okay, but if you're going to be late, by even five minutes, you call me—deal?"

"Deal. I hope your dog's okay," I say, following him into the kitchen.

"Okay," he says as he goes into the family room, picks up his backpack, turns off the TV and the lights, and is careful to put everything back the way he found it. "You're sure?"

"Yes, go."

"Okay, turn the alarm on as soon as I walk out. Thanks, Lindsey. I'll see you later," he says as he opens the front door to head out.

"Wow, what a storm. Drive safe!" I say, looking out at the dark, snowy storm.

Pulling the door shut, I lock it and go straight to the panel and turn the alarm on. With a jump in my step, I head back upstairs to enjoy a rare moment alone.

‘’

I'm getting very excited about seeing Chris tonight. There's nothing I would rather do than hang out with him.

I take my time getting ready and listen to music. Lost in my own thoughts and the music, I barely hear Baron barking. Realizing that he has been barking for a few minutes, I head downstairs to see what has him excited. As I enter the dark kitchen, I can see the storm has continued to worsen. Baron's looking out the back window and growling in a very uncharacteristic manner. I peek out the French doors into the darkness beyond and notice a dim light in the forest on the Castiglionis' side of our house. What is that? It's low to the ground, like a snowmobile. Who would be out in this weather? Are the guys still out riding? I move to the family room, keeping the lights off so I can see better outside, and shush Baron to be quiet as I take a closer look. I can barely see anything in the storm, but with all the blowing snow and the light from the landscaping, the moon is reflected on the snow, giving the night a kind of luminescence. Squinting, I think I see what look like two snowmobiles. But they aren't using their headlights. I can only see some dim lights, maybe on the sides of the snowmobiles or maybe a flashlight? That seems weird. Then I'm pretty sure I see a couple guys in black snowsuits standing by their snowmobiles. It must be the guys.

I've never called Chris before, but have often suspected he would like me to. I grab the phone in the kitchen to call his cell. Huh? Phones are out. Must be the storm; it happened a few times last year during big snowstorms too. I head to my room, grab my cell, and make my first phone call to Chris.

"Hi, Chris."

"Well, hello there, beautiful, and to what do I owe the pleasure of you calling me?"

"Wow, I can hear you so clearly. I wasn't sure you would even feel the phone with that suit on," I say, heading back downstairs to look out the window at him and the guys in the forest again. "I can see you guys."

"What?"

"On the snowmobiles. How come you don't use your headlights—isn't that kind of dangerous?"

"What are you talking about? I'm at home."

"Nice try. I can see you in the forest on the Castiglionis' side of my house."

"Not me. We got home hours ago."

The dim lights I initially saw go out. It's not Chris and the twins. Something feels wrong. Suddenly I go rigid. What if *they* are here for me?

Chris starts telling me about their ride, but I'm not really paying attention. I creep over to the panel and double-check that the alarm is still on.

"Chris," I say, interrupting him in a tone I know will get his attention and let him know I'm serious.

"What?"

"Maybe I'm just crazy, but ..." I feel uneasy.

"What?"

"It's nothing ... I just ..." Biting my lip, I'm torn as to how much to say. Is my imagination running away with me?

"Lindsey, what is it?"

"The snowmobilers I see."

"Yeah, somebody's taking a ride."

"They're just sitting in the forest with their lights off."

"So what? Maybe they're taking a break. The storm's pretty

bad …" Chris continues chatting. Should I ignore them? Dad wouldn't want me to cry wolf. But what if something is going on?

"Chris."

"What? Lindsey, are you okay?"

"Um, I, um … I'm sure it's nothing …" I try to start, but I don't know how to convince him that it could be more unless I tell him about the text messages. Are these guys the ones who have been sending the text messages? Will things be worse if I tell Chris about the text messages? They said to tell no one. But how will they know?

"Lindsey?" Chris asks, and I realize I haven't said a word. My mind is working on something. What is the connection I'm missing?

"I'm sorry. Chris. Um … there's uh … there's something I guess I should tell you. But you have to swear you won't tell anyone."

"What?"

"No. Swear."

"Lindsey, what are you talking about?"

"Swear," I press in a way I never do, particularly with Chris.

"Fine," he says, a bit confused.

"Well, I've been getting text messages."

"So?"

"It's probably nothing. I'm sure it is. But maybe … you may not like this." I delay as I watch the forest for any movement.

"From whom, Lindsey? And what does this have to do with the snowmobiles? Wait—from whom? Someone at school?"

"I don't know exactly. They're from different phone numbers."

"I don't understand."

"Okay, well, someone has been texting me, but when they send a message, each time it's from a different number."

"I'm lost, Lindsey."

"Yeah, well, the topic of the texts is always the same, so I'm sure it's actually from the same person, or at least the same group of people." My mind tries to work it all out. The texts. Is there something else?

"So, what's the topic?"

Something clicks in my head. It's like I can see events falling into place. Was it these guys that cut the power to our house before? The texts. Did they also let those Dobermans chase me? How far will these guys go? What if they came tonight to cut the power again? I don't want to be sitting alone in the dark. What if they came to *stop* me?

"Well, that I should get my dad off his case."

"Why would anyone text you about your dad's case?"

"I don't know, but lately they sort of end with the fact that I should get him off the case ... or else."

"What? What do you mean 'or else'?"

"I don't know, but the texts are always a bit ... I don't know, they're weird—kind of scary."

"Wait a minute—how many texts like this have you gotten?"

"Um, I guess I've lost count." *When did it start?*

"You've lost count? Lindsey, how long have you been getting these texts?"

"Oh, um ..." Okay, when did they start? As I think about it, I realize it's been months. Months? Yes. Oh man, gonna be mad now. "Well, for several weeks, maybe months, I guess."

"What! What did your dad say? Wait a minute, is that why he really got the so-called dog walker?"

"Well, no, um."

"What does that mean?"

I have no response as I consider how upset Dad's going to be when he finds out I told Chris first, even though it's probably nothing.

"Lindsey, does your dad know?"

"Well ..."

"Does your dad know?" he asks firmly.

"I haven't told anyone until now." And in an effort to defend myself, my pace quickens. "My dad says there are always crazy people around and it's nothing. So I did what he does and just ignored them. I thought it was ... well, I still think they're from someone at school. But now, I mean the messages did say that I couldn't tell anyone, but then I thought, well, maybe these guys outside are ..." and my voice trails off.

"Jeez, Lindsey. Where are they now? Can you still see them?" he asks and is audibly stressed.

"Yes. I think they're near their snowmobiles in the forest on the Castiglionis' side."

"Where are you?"

"Home. You know, I never thought about it before—but seeing these guys outside—what if the texts are from the same guys that cut the power off a few weeks ago? Maybe these are the same guys that gave me flat tires." Closing my eyes, I brace for his reaction as I feel my stomach churning.

"Did you tell the dog walker? And don't give me some bullshit about not telling him. *Tell* him about the texts and the snowmobilers, Lindsey."

"Well, um. Promise you won't be mad."

"*Lindsey*," he says like he is chastising a child.

"Okay, well, his dog got really sick and was throwing up and stuff, and I told him he could go home and take care of his dog, but that was before I saw these guys. There's one more thing I guess I should tell you. I got another text earlier this afternoon."

"Lindsey! Jeez. Okay. Let me think. Wait, when did you get the latest text and what did it say?"

"Um, it came at 3:44 p.m. and says, 'Monday is too late. Dad needs to drop the case now. You need to stop daddy now or we will stop you.' Chris, please don't be mad at me," I plead.

His pause makes me even more worried. Then he continues, "I'm not mad. Okay, what exactly did you see?"

"Well, by the time I saw them, only one was still moving on a snowmobile, at least I think it's a snowmobile, but he had only like side lights on, if it even was a snowmobile. Not his headlights—isn't that weird?"

I notice Chris does not respond immediately.

"Okay, is your alarm on?"

"Yes, I just checked. Do you think it's, I mean, do you think …"

"I don't know. Hold on, okay? Don't hang up." A few seconds later, he comes back on my line with, "and don't turn on or off any lights, okay?"

"Okay, what are you doing?"

"Just hold on." Then I hear him try the phone in the background. "The phones are dead," he says with tension pinching his voice.

"Yeah, mine too. Must be the storm," I say, and I quietly get a rawhide treat from the pantry and creep up the back stairs. Whispering to Baron, I coax him up the staircase with me by tempting him with the rawhide. I toss the treat into the bathroom, where Baron settles down chewing his treat. I walk into my parents' bedroom, where I can continue to watch the two figures outside. From the window, I see them move a bit and am now confident there are two guys out there.

"I'm gonna put you on hold," Chris says, and before I can respond, he's gone.

I realize I'm still in sweats. I walk over to my room and pull on a pair of jeans, a turtleneck, and a sweater while I wait for Chris to come back on my line. Walking back to the window, I'm immediately alarmed. Chris must still be on the other line. I don't want to wait anymore. I hang up and call him back.

"Sorry, I just talked to …" he starts.

"Chris!" I whisper forcefully. He's still talking. "*Chris!*" I try to yell while remaining quiet.

"What? What is it?"

"They're moving through the forest."

"Which way?"

"Um, I think toward my house. They're kind of moving from tree to tree." Suddenly my hands are trembling.

"Hold on."

My heart starts to race while I watch them move through the forest. Fortunately the snow is still reflecting the moonlight, so I can see them move.

"Okay, Lindsey. Here's what we're gonna do. Mike and Joel are already getting ready. They'll pick you up in a snowmobile in five minutes."

"What? Why can't *you* just come in a car?"

"Have you seen the weather? The roads aren't good; I can't drive to pick you up. Anyway, snowmobile is the way to go. And the guys are closer to you. Plus, Mike'll be there in a flash. Do you have ski pants?"

"Yeah, why?"

"It'll be really cold on the snowmobiles tonight, Lindsey. Put them and your Bluetooth on."

"You know I hate that thing," I start to whine as I forget the real issue at hand.

"Lindsey, please! Just for now, please, just …"

"Okay, hold on." Dashing back to my room, I grab my backpack and pull my Bluetooth earpiece out and put it in my ear. "Can you hear me?"

"Yeah, okay, now get dressed for the storm. You have a jacket with an inside pocket, right?"

"Um, yeah."

"Okay, put your phone in there. And lock up that crazy dog."

"Okay. Did you tell Mike and Joel?"

"What? That some freak related to one of your dad's cases has been texting you for—what? A few weeks now—and that you haven't told anyone? Yes, Lindsey, I did. Be upset if you want, but I think the twins should have some idea what they might be getting into," he snaps at me in a tone heavy with concern rather than anger. I feel so guilty.

"Chris?"

"What?"

"Are you coming?" I ask softly, as I'm concerned he's angry with me for not telling anyone sooner and all I want is to see him. I'm so tense.

In a resigned tone, he immediately replies, "Of course. I'm already in my garage, and I'll need to hang up soon to put my helmet on.

340

Look, you're probably right, it's probably nothing. But just in case, here's the plan: get dressed for the storm, do *not* pass in front of any windows, and stay low so they can't see you in the house—if they're even looking. Which they probably aren't because it's probably just a couple of guys out for a ride. Anyway, go out the front door and don't turn any lights on or off. Okay, Lindz?"

"Okay," I say, and my voice cracks.

"Lindz, listen to me," and since he's still calling me Lindz, I have hope that we'll be okay. "You're gonna be fine. As soon as you're ready, go to the Kirkwoods' side of your house. That'll keep you on the opposite side from where you saw the snowmobilers. Mike'll pick you up with a two-person snowmobile—he's incredible on a snowmobile, so you'll be fine. Just do what he says—and hold on, okay?"

"Okay."

"He'll give you a helmet with a walkie-talkie system so I can talk to you again once you get it on. Lindz, listen to Mike, okay?"

"Okay. What about you?" I pull the bathroom door shut, locking poor Baron inside.

"Are you getting ready?"

"Yes, almost done. I'm going down the front stairs right now," and I realize I'm whispering, as if those guys can hear me.

"Okay, I'm leaving now too. I'll go past the forest and see what these guys are up to. I'm sure it's just two jerks smoking or drinking or something and we'll all have a good laugh about this later. We're gonna ride to the club so we can grab dinner—I'm sure it will all be fine. Anyway, I'll meet up with you guys on the golf course, okay?"

"Promise?" I ask, as I'm feeling desperate to be with him.

"Promise, Lindz. Bye."

"Bye."

Click.

27 A COLD WINTER NIGHT: *I'VE LOST MY GRIP.*

I CHECK MY POCKETS one more time and pull my hat and gloves on. In the inside pockets are my keys to the house, my wallet, cell phone, and a small makeup bag just in case this whole thing is a big mix-up and I actually do get my evening with Chris. I just wish I could be cuddled up next to him watching a movie now.

As I turn the corner at the staircase, I crouch down, hoping not to be seen by my mystery visitors. Putting on my heavy boots, I think I'm ready. Okay, here goes. I set the alarm so I can leave without triggering it and peek out the front door. Only the porch columns and the blowing snow are visible. I creep outside and am immediately assaulted by the arctic air as snow slams into my face. It takes effort to fight the wind and close the door behind me. I run down the front steps as fast as I can in my boots and turn right to run around to the side of the house. *Wham.* I slip in the snow and slam down hard on my backside in the powder. Jumping to my feet, I brush off the wet, freezing snow, while frantically looking around to see who might be coming. Every shadow seems to move in the blowing snow. I can feel the adrenalin screaming through me. Seeing nothing alarming, I continue around the corner. I can't hear anything except the wind. I keep looking around for someone, something, to appear. Suddenly I am terrified that Mike won't get here before trouble does. Why are these guys on the snowmobiles here? What are they doing? I try to shut out the rush of terrifying images that fill my mind. I am out here in the night—cold and alone. My mind fills with every tortured scene from the mysteries I've read. What if the wrong snowmobile gets here first? What should I do?

Already, the snow is above my knees; walking takes tremendous effort as I struggle across my property. If I had to, could I run? I don't think so. And anyway, where would I run? I still see nothing. Where's Mike? Turning around, again I tell myself not to panic. Stay calm. Where are *they*?

In a few seconds I see a light begin to brighten at the front side of my house, and then I hear the roar of an engine. Instinctively, I put my arms over my head and crouch down as the snowmobile turns hard and stops, spraying snow everywhere. A figure, all in black, is already off the snowmobile. Much to my relief, he has a helmet in his hand and is offering it to me as I stand up. I unzip my jacket, pull my Bluetooth off my ear, and put it in my inside jacket pocket while he puts the helmet on my head and snaps the buckle.

"Lindsey, can you hear me?" and I recognize Mike's voice immediately.

"Yeah, it's too loud!" I say, reacting to the volume of the voice in my helmet.

"No, it's fine. When we're on the snowmobile, you'll need it loud. Let's go. Get on the back and grab these handholds."

"Okay. Chris?" I say as Mike starts to get back on the snowmobile.

"No," Mike commands as he turns his head closer to mine and gives me a look that says I should not argue. "He's on, but there's no time to chat; we need to go. Get on the back."

Frowning, I turn and swing one heavy boot over the giant snowmobile and sit down.

"Hold on," he says as he guns the snowmobile in one fluid motion. My arms can barely hold the grips against the force of the initial burst as we go from a standstill to who knows what in two seconds.

"Don't let go. If you fall off, try to roll, okay?"

"How about I just don't let go?" I hear several laughs, and am thrilled to hear Chris's in the mix. At the mere thought of him, my stomach drops. *Why does that happen?*

"Sounds good, but if you do fall, get up. I'll be back to pick you up as quickly as I can. Also, if you fall, talk to us as soon as you can so we know you're okay," Mike directs.

"Okay."

In no time, we are near the edge of my parents' property and a clearing that I assume is the road. As we cross the clearing I ask, "Is this the road?"

"Yes," Mike responds, but I wish Chris would.

"Okay, here is your first real turn," and with that we swing away from the house and onto the road heading toward the Castiglioni property. I'm surprised by the intensity of the pull this slight turn puts on my hands and almost lose my grip. I'm also scared that we are going to pass right in front of the two unknown snowmobilers.

"Where are we going?" I say, a bit too panicked.

"Lindsey, they probably have a headset on too. They could have the same frequency. You know where you are, right?" I hear Chris ask and am relieved that I can hear him.

"You don't want to say?"

"No. Not on the radio," Chris says, and I can hear the stress in his voice.

"First dip and slight climb; hold on," Mike says as we dip to the right and seem to be in a small valley. *Are we in the area between the road and the edge of the golf course?* Suddenly we pull to the right again and are tilting upward. I've lost my grip. I gasp into my microphone as my right hand flails in search of the grip.

"Lindsey?" Chris's concern is matching my level of anxiety.

"Sorry. I got it."

344

"Not good," comes over the headset as a whisper. I'm not certain, but I think Chris muttered it, although I have no idea why.

"We have movement," Chris says, and now I know it must have been Joel who spoke before. I'm guessing that the two mystery snowmobilers are following us. I can feel it.

"Lindsey, move closer, so you are right up against my back and crouch as low as you can."

I try to pull myself forward, but against the pressure of the wind at our speed, I can hardly move. And with my head tucked behind Mike, I can't see anything but a sliver of snow rushing past us as we ride faster than I care to think about. It is like an amusement ride gone wrong. I am breathing way too heavily. *Get control of yourself.*

"Chris, what do you have?" I hear Mike in my ear.

"They're on the move. I assume they saw the two of you and ran back to their snowmobiles. They're headed in your direction. I'm passing Isabella's place now." Chris gives the facts in a detached voice.

"Joel?" Mike asks.

"I'm on your right. I can see you ahead of me, but I can't see anyone else yet."

"Okay, let's get in a single line on the sixth fairway. Mike, since there are two of you, I should be able to catch up," Chris says with confidence.

"Got it," Mike says.

"Can you push it, Mike?" Joel asks.

"Hold on, Lindsey," Mike says to me.

"Aaahhhhhh," I scream. "Sorry." I start breathing like I have been tumbling hard. The rush of speed is frightening. Then I feel a rise building below us.

"What is that?" I yell.

"Hill," Mike replies calmly.

"Where are you, Chris?" Mike asks on the intercom.

"Huh," I gasp. "Sorry guys, I … I …"

"Chris?" Mike asks as if I hadn't spoken. They all seem so in control, and I feel like I'm going to faint. This would be a bad time for that. *Do not faint. Focus on holding on.*

"Thirty seconds from the ladies' tee," Chris replies.

"Okay, the order should be me, them, and then you," Joel says, and I assume that we are all going to line up on the next fairway. Then I remember the trees. Where are the trees?

"Mike, what about the trees?" I ask and can hear the fear in my own voice.

"Close your eyes and hold on. You'll be fine," Mike coolly says.

Oh my God. Oh my God. Oh my God, is all I can think.

"Lindsey, you can't talk, okay? We need the air," Mike says with authority. *Was that out loud?*

"Chris, where are they?" Mike asks.

"Behind me; I can just see their headlights. They don't know the terrain like us."

"We need to line up and pick up the pace," Mike says.

"Take it easy," Chris chastises.

"Sorry, Chris, but if you want to lose them, I need to take her over," Mike says.

I'm consumed with one thought—over what?

"That's crazy. She won't make it," Chris states, like it's a foregone conclusion. Maybe I would make it. What am I thinking? Make it over what?

I sense Mike twist to look back. "No choice; they're too close. We need to lose them. Chris, you bring up the back," Mike orders—and then yells, "And try to keep up!"

"Here I come," Joel says as I see lights brighten the back of Mike's coat.

"I'm in line too," Chris says, and even over the intercom, I can hear the frustration in his voice.

"Hold on, Lindsey," Mike says.

"Trees?" I ask, as I shut my eyes and grab on tighter.

"No, hold on," Mike replies, and I feel a shudder of new fear.

"*No!* They aren't that close!" Chris thunders.

"Take it easy. It's small. Let's see what happens." We hit a rise, and instinctively, I know we are going to be airborne.

"Oh, man," I whisper as I pull down on the snowmobile and squeeze Mike between my knees. I feel the machine start to fall, and then we land with a bone-jolting *thud*. I bounce down and then up and then lose the grip of my left hand. "Huuh!" I gasp as I lose a foothold too.

"Lindsey?" Chris yells.

"She's fine. Yeehaaa!" Mike says. "They may be talking to each other, but I don't think they can hear us."

Then I realize I already have my boot back on the platform and my left hand has found its handle again. My cold hands are throbbing in pain.

"I'm okay. It's okay. How far back are they?" I ask.

"I can still see their lights. I think they are gaining in the fairways," Chris says and is clearly concerned.

"Okay, Mike, you do what you need to. Chris, we need to run them all over," Joel instructs.

"No!" Chris says in his dad tone.

"The priority is Lindsey, right?" Joel asks, knowing what Chris's answer will be.

"No, you guys need to be safe," I chime in, as I feel guilty that we are all out here and they may be endangering themselves for me.

"Lindsey, stay out of this," Mike says in a soft tone. This makes me realize that none of this is up to me or Mike. Joel and Chris are making the decisions.

"Chris, there's no time. I can see them," Joel states.

There is a painful silence. We all wait for Chris.

"Mike, I swear—you be careful," Chris pleads. And with this, we all know that Mike is now calling the shots.

"Game on. I'll take the north side of the fairways, so worst case, I can go into the road. Joel, you go south, and Chris, you take the middle, staying a bit south," Mike says. He has clearly taken the lead, given his snowmobile talents.

My arms ache from holding on so long, and the muscles in my legs are shaking. I don't know if my legs are shaking because of the bouncing of the snowmobile, the fact that they are freezing in the bitter wind, or the sheer terror of what will happen if I fall off. Would one of my guys run me over by mistake? Would the other two run me over on purpose? I feel another swell under us. This one lasts a few seconds and feels endless.

"Oh man."

"No, no airtime. We ride this down; hold on," Mike says as I feel the snowmobile front drop down into what I assume is the downslope of a hill behind a green. The drop is fast, and I slam against Mike like I'm a rag doll.

"Whooh!" Mike says.

"What?" Chris demands.

"Nothing. Lindsey, you're doing great. Keep hold," Mike says.

"Okay, Chris, you and I need to confuse them. Crossing in front of you," Mike informs us all.

"Got it," Chris says. I'm fearful for all of us.

"Here we go!" Mike says as we hit the trees. We take a sharp right, then a sharp left. We slow down considerably. Sharp right, again; jet to the left.

"Please don't hit a tree."

"*I* will not hit a tree. *You* hold on."

"They're right behind us!" Chris says. "I'm going to the service road; maybe they'll follow."

"Got it," Mike says.

"I got one on me," Chris says so we can all hear, and then, in a whisper, the microphone picks up, "Come on, you fucker!"

"The other one is not taking me; he's going after Mike. Son of a bitch. Mike, you need to move!" Chris yells in his helmet.

"We're almost through; here we go. Hang on," Mike yells. And with that, we fly across the snow.

"Here it is, Lindsey, hold on," Mike says as we climb another incline. "They'll lose sight of us for a few seconds on the other side." Then my whole body goes rigid again as Mike turns off all our lights. *Bang.* My back is rattled, and my head bounces hard into Mike's back. He grunts but otherwise doesn't seem to notice. My right arm lets go of its hold, and my mind starts screaming, *Nooooooo!* My eyes are open, but without headlights, it is impossible to see anything.

"Lindsey?" I hear Chris say as my right arm grabs Mike's shoulder. I can't speak, so Mike replies for both of us, "We're good. We're dark."

"Lindsey?"

"I'm on."

"Jeez, Mike, take it easy," I hear Chris say under his breath.

"Lindsey, this'll be rough; hang on," Mike warns, with the first sign of strain in his voice. I feel the rise begin and crouch as low as I can manage. My fingers scream in pain as I grab the handle again. My shins are freezing in the wind. My breath has almost completely fogged over the glass pane in my helmet. The rise continues, and I've lost track of the hole we are on. When will the rise end? When will this ride end?

"Oh God, please," I hear myself say. I feel the ground disappear under us, and we start to fall. I think we are beginning to tilt.

"Shit," I hear Mike say and can feel his back and legs tense. I shut my eyes and brace for the impact. We drop for so long, I imagine we are falling into an endless black hole.

Crash. Swerving, we hit on the right side first, and I lose my grip with my left hand and start to fall off to the right. I'm off the seat when I feel Mike's right hand reach back to shove me back up. What if we both fall off? Has Mike ever fallen off?

"*Grab on!*" Mike yells. I grab his neck with my left hand and yank myself back onto my seat.

"Sorry," I say, more to myself than anyone else.

"Hold on," Mike commands again as I look up and see the navy sky disappear above me. We're going in the woods.

"Where are they?" I hear Mike yell to the others as I close my eyes, trying to put the trees and speed out of my mind.

"They stopped at the big trap you just went over, and they're swerving around it," Joel says in response, and then adds, "I can't even see you."

"Don't take her in the trees dark," Chris says.

"You do your part; I'll do mine. Take them around the trees between the second and third holes; that should give us the distance we need," Mike directs.

"*No*, not dark; you'll hit."

"Have faith, man. This isn't my first dark ride on this course," and we can all hear the smile in Mike's voice.

"Please," I plead.

"Oh my God," Chris says under his breath, broadcasting our collective sentiment.

We slow considerably. Then Mike maneuvers to the right, the left, farther to the left, back to the right again. We are going up an incline, then it falls and we are descending. I feel Mike work the brake and gas alternately as he turns the machine right and left and works the inclines and descents of the course.

"Almost there, Lindsey," Mike says, and I can't imagine how he can steer in the dark forest with no light to guide the path.

"Cutting in front," I hear Joel say.

"Got it," Chris replies.

"Hold on, Lindsey," and with that, we rocket forward and I'm thrown back. My arms resist the force against them out of utter fear of letting go and hitting the snow with a deadly impact.

"Can you guys see us?" Mike queries.

"No, I just see one of them," Joel says.

"I got the other one on me and can't see anyone else. Lindsey, you okay?" Chris says.

I can't speak, as I'm fighting a rush of tears building. I try to rest my head on Mike's back as we rocket forward, but it is instantly bounced off. We ride another swell and are airborne again. My stomach clenches hard, and reflexively I foolishly grab my belly with my right hand. Realizing I've released my grip, I try to grab it again but we are in the air. Wham. Small drop, but I'm thrown as I only have one hand holding on.

"*Grab me!*" Mike screams. And I grab his neck with my flailing hand.

"*Mike!*" Chris barrels into all of our helmets.

350

"She's fine. Lindsey, I can see the clubhouse; get the grip."

"Got it," I manage to spit out.

"Hold on. Last push. Where are they?"

"They must be talking too. Mine's headed back to the course. I just cut over to the fairway," Chris says.

"I'm about to cut this bastard off. Eat that!" Joel yells. "Oh yeah. Snowstorm!" I assume Joel just turned in front of the other guy and covered him with snow. Score one for us.

"Lindsey, I'm gonna drop you off at the door. Go inside the clubhouse, okay?" With this I open my eyes and can see a small but growing pool of light over his shoulder. I've never been so happy to see the clubhouse.

"Okay." I say shakily, both from the thought of being alone and from the bouncing snowmobile.

"*No*, you stay with her," Chris thunders.

"She'll be fine at the clubhouse. I'll swing around and chase these bastards with you two."

"No. Go with her, Mike—Joel, *tell* him," Chris bites.

"I can see the clubhouse lights in the distance," Joel says, evading the issue.

"We're pulling in the lot," Mike says as he turns our lights back on so that the driver plowing the parking lot can see us.

"Thank God," I say with a rush of relief.

"They're turning around. I have no room here. I'm going wide right to give them some space," Joel says.

"My guy just broke right. Wait, maybe he's turning around too."

"Are they leaving?" I ask, with the first sense of hope.

"Yeah, I think so," Chris says, and I hear the hope in his voice too.

I feel us slow to a stop, but I'm still shaking. Mike turns the engine off, and I'm amazed how agile he is as he gets off the snowmobile.

"Oh, yeah! That was great! Next time we'll do some real jumps, Lindsey! You were amazing!" Mike is yelling.

I can't move. I can't even let go of the handles.

28 THE CLUBHOUSE: *THANK YOU.*

"LINDSEY?" I SEE MIKE remove his helmet and wipe the sweat off his face, pushing his hair back as he pulls off his hat. I can't respond.

"What's wrong? Lindz, you okay?" I hear Chris ask in my helmet.

"Nothing," is all I can manage to get out. I struggle to open my hands, but there's a sharp pain in each. Mike sets his helmet on the snowmobile, and then I see someone open the double doors of the club. I feel Mike unhook my chin strap and pull off my helmet. My face feels frozen. I'm breathing heavily as I try to stand up.

"Here, Lindsey," Mike says as he offers a hand to help me get off the snowmobile.

"Thanks," I say, grateful for the assistance as I stiffly climb off and turn to the noise and lights approaching us. Chris. Please, let this be Chris. The two snowmobiles pull up next to the one we were on, which, now, I finally can see clearly in the bright lights of the club and see just how large it is. I watch the two machines park.

352

"Lindsey, it's Chris and Joel. It's okay," Mike says, grabbing my arm and putting one arm around me to stop me from backing up farther. I must have unconsciously been backing away from the approaching snowmobiles. I look over to him and see the concern and stress in his face. I nod in acquiescence.

"I feel ..." I say as I start to feel lightheaded.

"Mr. Kirkwood, is everything okay?" I hear from the doorway.

Then I see Chris, and I feel the sob building in my chest.

"Lindsey," Chris says, tossing his helmet over to Joel and hugging me. I just stand there and let him hold me, but I'm frozen—whether from fear or the cold, I've no idea. He pulls back to look at me.

"You okay, Lindsey?" he asks with clear concern coating his voice.

"Uh-huh." And he pulls me back in an embrace.

"It's fine now. Okay? You're fine. I'm here now; you're okay," I hear Chris say and want desperately to believe him. But I know *they* are still out there.

"Hi, Maria," Joel says to Maria, one of the regular employees at the club.

"Good evening, Mr. Kirkwood. Is everything okay?"

"Um, well, we had a bit of a problem. I'm sure my father would appreciate you overlooking the snowmobiles under the circumstances," Mike says as if he's on the club board, which, as I recall, his father is.

"Yes, sir. Please come in. On a night like this, I'm certain we can also wave the dress code, sir," she says with a smirk. The formality of the club suddenly seems surreal compared to the ride we just had.

"Would you please set up a private dining room for us with a fire?"

"Yes, sir, right away."

"I'm sorry, sir, but is Miss Brooks okay?"

"Oh, um ... Lindsey, come on inside." Chris guides me in.

"Hello," is all I manage to say.

As I feel the heat of the club, I begin to tremble.

"She's freezing," Maria observes, and with that, she becomes more mother than staff member. She pulls my gloves off and holds my bright red, wet hands. "Dios mio, we need to warm her up. Miss Brooks, please come with me."

"Um," Chris says, and I look back at him.

"You all must be so cold. Why don't I have one of the men's locker room attendants bring you some warm clothes from the shop, and I'll get some for Miss Lindsey. By the time you're changed, we'll have your room ready."

"I have to call my dad," I say quietly, looking down.

"The phones went out about an hour ago, and you can try, but none of the staff can get a cell signal anymore. Anyway, I'm sure your father doesn't want you catching your death, Miss Brooks," Maria responds, having no idea what I really mean.

"Maria, that's a good idea. Why don't you go get some warm clothes for Lindsey, and she can meet you in the locker room. Thank you," Chris says, and it's clear to all of us that he wants Maria to leave.

"Of course, Mr. Buckley, thank you," Maria says to Chris, and then turning to me, she continues, "I'll be in the locker room should you need anything, Miss Brooks." I try to smile and nod at her, but my face is so cold, I'm not sure my expression actually changed. I feel bad, as I know she's confused as to what's going on and is trying to be helpful to me in particular.

"I'll catch up, guys," Chris says, and Joel and Mike head for the men's locker room.

Chris takes my arm and pulls me around a corner, as he clearly wants to talk privately. Part of me wants to talk, but part of me is so cold and overflowing with emotion I can't think. I try to contain my emotions, but a few tears are still building in my eyes.

"Hey, what is it?" Chris asks, and his sincerity is almost painful.

"I … I don't know. Just everything. I'm so sorry."

"What are you sorry for? You haven't done anything. Look at

you—you're freezing. Maria's right; go take a hot shower and get warm, okay?"

"I have to call my dad," I say, still looking down.

Chris puts his cold right hand on my cheek and pulls my face up so I'm looking at him. "Hey, it's gonna be fine, okay?" My nerves are so raw all I can do is swallow hard to keep the sob inside and nod.

"Ah, Lindz, listen to me. Go take a shower and warm up. We'll get some food, and then we can call him together, okay?"

As I remember that Chris's and my parents are at the same function, I force my chin down and put my hands over my face, saying, "Your parents. The Kirkwoods too. What a mess."

"What about my parents?"

"I'm sure they'll be pleased to know that I pulled you into this mess."

"Hey, first of all, my dad was a Marine. He's seen worse than a snowmobile ride; and second, there's nowhere else I want to be than with you."

"Right, what a night," I say, and the shivers start to overcome my ability to control them.

"Okay, that's it. You need to get warm. We can talk later, okay? I'm not going anywhere. Oh, and give me your phone," he says as he digs his out of his inside coat pocket.

"What?" I say like I've been slapped into reality.

"I want your cell phone; give it. Yeah, Maria's right. No signal."

"Why?" I ask, as I can't imagine why I would give it to him.

"Why? Let's see ... so that you don't get any random messages while you're alone in the locker room for one; and two, so that you don't do something like call your dad alone. Give it."

I give him a look like this whole idea is ridiculous.

"Lindsey, you're really something. Can you please do me this one favor? I just don't want you getting any more texts tonight, okay? Just give it to me and go get warm in a hot shower, okay? Can you just do this, for me?" and again he pulls my chin up to look at him.

Totally unfair. I don't think I can ever really say no to him.

355

Resigned, I say, "Okay, but I get it back." I'm too cold and drained to argue. As I pull out the phone, all I can think is how much I want him to hold me again. I step forward and hand him the phone. I'm so relieved that he puts one arm on my waist. We are only inches apart, and he tilts my face up to look at him. I think maybe he's going to kiss me, but I'm just about to lose control of the sob that is still bubbling in my chest, so instead, I close my eyes and lean my head on his chest.

"Lindz," is all he says as he puts his head on mine and hugs me. I'm so glad that the gesture of resting my head on him is not rejected, and in fact, his response is to pull me in closer.

"I'm so sorry."

"Lindz, please stop saying that. I'm so glad you called me tonight. You have no idea," he says while stroking my hair.

We're both soaked and freezing, so I pull away and mumble, "I'll see you in a few minutes, okay?"

"Definitely."

And with that, I turn and walk to the ladies' locker room.

It is strangely quiet in here. With the storm, there must not be anyone in the club except the staff. When I reach my locker, I see that Maria has already placed a pile of towels and some clothes on the bench nearby. She's so thoughtful.

My jeans are stuck to my cold red skin. It's such a relief to peel them off, as they've been retaining the cold. I lay my wet jeans and sweater on the bench and hang my turtleneck and bra in my locker to dry. Since no one else is here, I leave the locker door open in hopes that everything will dry a bit faster.

The hot shower is heavenly. I have the water so hot that it's filling my shower stall with steam. I shiver as I remember I'm in the locker room alone, and my mind starts to wander. Are the snowmobilers gone, or are they waiting out there? What if they try to enter the club? Aren't the front doors usually unlocked? What if they're already in the club? Did I just hear someone? What was that?

I hurry to finish my shower and shut off the water, listening for any sounds of movement. Hearing none, I walk wrapped in towels to my locker. *Relax. Stay calm. You're fine. Don't let your imagination get the best of you.*

I start to look through the clothes that Maria has left on the bench for me to choose from. I know that there's not a large selection in my size in the pro shop, so I'm actually impressed with the number of items she found. I put on a pair of pink and white sweatpants that are a bit long, so I roll them at the waistband. The shirts she left are all huge, so I skip them and pick a coordinating pink and white club sweatshirt and zip it all the way up to my neck. The sweatshirt feels so warm that I finally feel the chill dissipating. She also left me a pair of thick cotton socks, which feel wonderful on my cold red feet.

As I don't want to be alone any longer than necessary, I go to the mirrors to begin drying my hair. Happily, I keep a locker with all my bathroom stuff at the club, so I'm able to pull myself together. When I return to my locker, again I see that my wet towels have been taken away. I shiver at the thought that people whom I have neither seen nor heard have been in the locker room with me. As I go through my locker to fold up my wet clothes, I see a perfect single red rose propped up in the back of my locker. Chris must have asked Maria to bring it to me. I put my wet gloves and hat in my coat pocket and grab my clothes, coat, boots, and ski pants and head for the door. Maria is waiting for me there.

"Maria, would you put this in water for me?"

"Of course, Miss Brooks. The gentlemen are in a small room off to the right of the formal dining room. I can put your clothes in a dryer while you eat."

I gratefully accept her kind offer and walk to the private room to join Chris and the twins for dinner.

As I enter the dining room, I see the guys also are outfitted head to toe in club wear. A huge fire is roaring in the fireplace, and candles are on the table. Hugging myself, I walk in quietly. Mike sees me first, and Chris must have seen him notice because he turns and walks toward me smiling.

357

"Hey, feel better?"

"Yeah, you?"

"Yeah, I'm fine. Nice outfit," Chris teases.

"Yeah," I say, and getting more serious I continue, "I really need to call my dad."

"Guys," is all Chris has to say, and I see Joel and Mike grab their sodas and leave.

"You guys don't have to go," I say.

"Oh, it's fine. We need to go order dinner anyway. What do you want, Lindsey?"

"Um, how about prime rib if they still have it?"

"You got it." I notice that Joel pulls both double doors shut, and I'm certain that no one will come back in until Chris or I open them. Typically the club is a flurry of activity, but tonight it's oddly still.

"So," Chris starts, "you want some privacy? Or do you want me to stay while you call him?"

I try not to show my disappointment that he's not holding my hand. Or me. "You can stay; it's fine. Can I have my phone?"

"Here you go."

"Any new messages?" I ask as I look at it.

"No, I don't think so."

"Here goes," I say as I check the phone. "I'm not even sure he will pick up at the party. Of course, no signal."

"We just checked the phone on the wall, and the landlines are still dead. Let me check my cell. Yeah, nothing."

"I bet I can still send a text. Let me try that."

> 7:51 P.M. Dad sorry to bother you. Please call me on my cell as soon as you get this.

"Let's hope he checks his messages," I say, hoping Dad will be able to assure me this is nothing serious. "Okay, it looks like that went through; but who knows?"

"Well, let's eat. I'm sure we'll hear from him. If you want, I can text my dad too. And I'm sure Mike and Joel would be happy to try to reach their folks. They're all sitting together for dinner."

"Okay, but let's give him a chance to read mine first." I really don't want to get all of our parents involved.

"I'll go get the guys so we can eat." And with that, he starts to leave.

"Chris."

"Yeah," he says as he pauses at the door.

"I … um, I don't … I guess I don't want to be alone," I say, a bit ashamed.

"Maybe I should hire someone to chase us every night if this is the result," he says, smiling as he walks back and pulls me into an embrace. As he kisses me, I almost forget why we're here. Playing with the zipper on my sweatshirt, he pulls back from the kiss, and keeping our foreheads still touching, whispers with an adorable smile, "So, what do you have on under this?"

"Hey!" I whisper back.

"Well?" he playfully lowers my zipper another inch.

"Not much, now stop."

"In that case, I think you definitely should wear this on all our dates."

"Maybe one day," I tease as we share another kiss.

"I can't wait," he replies with a big smile and takes my hand as we walk out to get the guys.

℘℘

When we arrive back in our private room, I see that Maria has put my rose in a small vase in the center of the table. Realizing I have not yet thanked Chris for the rose, I quickly whisper before the guys are close enough to overhear, "Hey, I almost forgot. Thank you."

"Hey, guys."

"This place is awesome when no one is here—we should all go

swimming!" Mike announces as they come back in the room. The twins can always be counted on to find the silver lining.

"It would be even cooler if all the staff left and we got to hang out here all night!" Joel chimes in.

"I doubt they'll leave us with the run of the place," I reply.

"Probably not, but I overheard some of the staff, and they're worried about the storm and wondering when they can go home."

I assume the guys are all thinking what I'm thinking. When are *we* going to be able to get home? Ignoring the obvious question, Mike continues, "This looks great. I'm starving."

"Here." I offer the bread to Mike. As we eat dinner, the guys exchange jokes about our varying snowmobiling skills. Laughing with the guys, I'm distracted and enjoy my dinner. Checking my cell periodically, I find my dad has yet to reply to my text.

Maria and one of the male staff enter the room with their arms filled with our dry clothes and set them down neatly on chairs by the windows. She proceeds to tell us that she and a few others are going home, but that a few employees will remain until we leave. This information stresses me more, as I'm sure all of the staff would like to go home given the storm.

"Maria, can you keep the flower for me? I can come by and pick it up tomorrow," I try to ask Maria in confidence.

"Of course, Miss Brooks," she replies too loudly, as she picks up the small vase and single rose, drawing the guys' attention.

"Aren't you getting enough flowers, Lindsey? You need to take them from the club?" Joel teases, and I think he's ribbing Chris more than me. I just roll my eyes.

"Thanks, Joel, but I didn't take it from the club—he did," I say, playfully gesturing to Chris.

"Me?" Chris asks.

"Okay. Okay. I shouldn't have asked to keep it. Sorry."

"Sorry to disappoint you, but it was just on the table. Why would you think I took it?" Chris asks.

"Sorry, okay. I know you and the guys think it's silly to want to keep it."

"Do you keep the flowers on the tables at every restaurant you eat at?" Joel teases.

"No, Chris sent it to me in the locker room. Anyway, let's eat," I say, embarrassed and hoping we can change topics. Looking at Chris for the first time during this exchange, I see the good humor drain from his expression and seriousness spread in its place.

"What do you mean you got it in the locker room?"

"Can we just drop it?"

"You said you got it in the locker room."

"Yeah, you told Maria to bring it in," I say, taking another bite of my steak.

"Did one of you two send a rose to Lindsey in the locker room?" Chris asks.

"What?" Mike asks.

Snap.

"Oh my God," I whisper as I cover my mouth with my hands.

"What is it?" Mike asks with intensity.

In his dad tone, Chris asks again, "No joking, guys. Did either of you ..." he repeats as he stands up.

"No," Joel answers firmly and knowingly stands as well.

"No," Mike says softly.

"It's them ... *They* were in the locker room with me ..." And my voice trails off.

The room is painfully still.

29 A PLAN: *THEY'RE WATCHING ME.*

"JOEL, GO ASK MARIA if she was just being nice and gave it to Lindsey," Chris orders Joel. "Mike, find George and have him ask if any of the guys sent it in for some reason and give him some story why he needs to check and lock every door and window," Chris says while I stand up and he puts his hands on my shoulders. My hands are still over my mouth.

"They're watching me," I whisper.

"Guys, go! Lindsey, come here," awith that, he shoves me away from the window and then circles the room, closing all the curtains. Mike and Joel run out to find Maria and George as I drop to my knees on the floor.

"Lindsey, tell me exactly what happened in the locker room."

"Chris, what if they were in there when I—"

"Put it out of your mind. Tell me what happened," Chris commands, grabbing me by the shoulders with one hand and checking his cell in the other.

"Okay, um … I went in. I left my clothes on a bench near my

362

locker spread out to dry. Then I took a shower, and it was weird—all of a sudden, it seemed so quiet, and I remember I kind of freaked out for a second. I thought I heard something, but figured my mind was just getting the best of me. I ..."

"Lindsey," Chris says to focus me back on my recounting.

"I hurried to finish my shower and went back to my locker. Maria had left some clothes for me to choose from, so I got ready and stuff, and when I turned to my locker—which I had left open because I thought no one else was here—I saw the rose and just assumed you told her to bring it to me. But she didn't. *They* were in there. Awww. Chris, what if they saw me in the shower?"

"Saw you? Jeez."

Joel and Mike walk back in.

"None of the guys sent it in, and George sent everyone but him, two other guys, and Maria home," Mike says as Chris and I stand up.

"Shut the doors," Mike tells Joel. "George has them checking all the windows and doors. The two guys are also doing a quick sweep through the club to see if anyone else is here before we all go."

"What about Maria? Did she?" I ask, already knowing the answer.

"No, she thought you must have brought it in from the lobby or something," Joel replies reluctantly.

For an instant, there's nothing to say.

I check my phone and tell the guys, "No reply from my dad. Still no good signal. I should send him another text," I say in a feeble attempt to make myself feel better.

"Okay, they know where we are. We need to get out of here without them knowing," Mike starts the plan.

"Yeah, but how?" Chris asks.

"No, they just want me, I should ..." I say, standing up.

"Lindsey, please," Chris says, cutting me off, and moving into a tighter circle, he takes my hand.

Stepping closer and looking at me, Mike says, "Lindsey, even if you weren't with Chris," and with this he and Chris exchange a look, "we would be in this for you. You're our friend too, but the fact is that you *are* with Chris, so even if he weren't here, Joel and I would be all in."

"Absolutely," Joel adds with conviction.

"Lindsey, where's your coat?" Chris asks, heading for a pile of clothes.

"I think Maria put my stuff over here."

"Send your dad another text to call as soon as he can. Guys, can either of you make calls yet?"

"Nothing."

"Me neither, but we all should send our folks texts to call one of us."

"What are we gonna do? Aren't we vulnerable just sitting here?" I ask, feeling like a trapped cat.

Mike continues his plan. "Okay, well, the club owns a couple of trucks equipped with snowplows. I think we should tell George and the others to use them to go home and leave their cars here. No way they can make it home otherwise in this storm, anyway. Chris, you and Joel should ride in one of the trucks too, and get them to drop you off at Lindsey's place. I'll take Lindsey on one of the snowmobiles with no headlights. Hopefully, they'll think we're all in the trucks."

"No, I take Lindsey," Chris says, squeezing my hand.

"Hear me out. Lindsey—put your ski pants and boots on and get ready, okay?" Mike says as he starts to put on his outerwear as well.

I look at Chris for direction. He nods at me and releases my hand. With this loss of contact, somehow I know I've also lost any input I may have had into the plan. But I'm so scared; I'm glad the guys are here, vehemently trying to figure out what we should do. I'm in no position to develop a plan, as my mind is consumed with images of two guys throwing me around in some dirty, dark room.

Mike continues, "I take Lindsey, dark, to our place. We have better security than she does, and we're closer than your house, Chris. You and Joel get out of the truck at Lindsey's place. Joel, you wear her coat so they'll think Chris took her home, in case they are, still, ya know." Listening intently, I force myself not to look at them while Mike's talking. I continue to keep busy getting dressed. This seems to encourage Mike to continue, "Joel, you and Lindsey need to switch coats. You guys go in her house and turn a bunch of lights on so they think she's there. Then sneak over to our place through the forest on foot. In this weather, your tracks will disappear in a couple of minutes." As I listen to his plan, I think Mike is on to something.

"Not bad, but I take Lindsey, and you and Joel go to her place."

"No. Sorry, Chris, but you won't be nearly as fast going dark on the snowmobile, and you know it."

"He's right, Chris. Lindsey, give me your coat," Joel says.

"Should we wait to hear from our folks?" I ask as I slip out of my coat.

"Hold on," Chris starts, but we can all tell the plan is already in motion.

"No time. They have the advantage of knowing where we are and probably have been watching us for the last … what—an hour? We need to move."

"We should have the club cut the lights so they don't see us getting ready," Chris suggests, and now we know he's on board. "They'll just assume the storm took 'em out. We get a few flashlights and cut the power. We'll use the trucks with the snowplows to make a point of going to the front door to pick up Joel, dressed as Lindsey, the rest of the staff, and me." Taking a frustrated breath, Chris continues, "And while they're watching the front of the club, you and Lindsey leave from the golf cart driveway in back, dark, and let's hope they don't notice."

"Done."

"What about our folks?" I ask again.

"I sent a text to my dad. Guys, you send one too, in case somebody checks, but there's no time, Lindsey. Who knows if any of them will even check their phones during the party? Jeez, they were in the locker room with you." The weight of this statement is piercing. "We move. Joel, go talk to George. Tell him just what you have to and have him talk to the staff. Then cut the power to the club. Also, ask him for the flashlights. I'll get the snowmobiles ready. We good?" Mike asks.

"I'll meet you at the entrance as soon as the staff is ready," Joel says, holding my coat and finishing lacing up his boots.

"Tell them they have two minutes," Mike commands. "Chris, you have two minutes too. Then bring Lindsey to the basement."

"Yep" is all Chris says to Mike as he turns to me. Mike and Joel leave as the plan moves into action. "Don't stop—finish getting ready, Lindsey," Chris says as he grabs his coat.

"Shouldn't I call my dad? Maybe he could ..."

"Lindz, there's no signal and no time. Mike's right; we need to move. You can try him as soon as you get to the Kirkwoods', okay? Besides, he's stuck in Chicago. What's he gonna do? No one can drive in this storm. Who's he going to send? Cops? How are they going to get here? First thing we need to do is get you out of here."

"They were in there when I took a shower ..." I whisper as I pull on my hat.

Closing his eyes, he says in a soft tone to himself, "I know." Continuing more to me, "Lindz, come here. Don't think about that, okay? They were in there, but they didn't do anything. Maybe they're just trying to scare you, right? They haven't touched you, and we won't let 'em. Mike'll get you to his house, and I'll meet you there."

Looking down as I finish tying my boots, I say, "I would rather stay with you."

"Oh, Lindz." Grabbing me and pulling me up so I'm standing, he says, "You have no idea how much I would rather stay with you too, but Mike's right. He'll be faster than me with no headlights on. And I think it's better if you guys travel dark. That's our only chance to get you out of here without them seeing you. You'll be fine with Mike, okay?"

"Okay."

"But if anything happens, I'll have my helmet with me. You really need me, I'll get to you, okay?"

"Promise?"

"Promise. Oh, Lindz," he says as he touches my face lightly with his hand. I put my hand on his arm as we step closer to each other.

"We're set … Oh, sorry," Joel says he rushes back into the room holding flashlights.

"It's okay," I say, a bit embarrassed.

Snap. Suddenly we're all standing in the dark.

"Game on," Joel says in an ominous way.

"What did you tell George to get him to turn the lights out?" Chris asks.

"I told him that some seniors from North heard your folks were out of town tonight and basically wanted to force you to have a party at your place. That they were following us on the snowmobiles and would be waiting for you to leave to show up at your place to trash it. Since they're from North, I told him they don't know this course, and if we could just go dark tonight, we could all go to our house instead and keep you out of trouble. I told him I was sure it was what my dad would want. I think he thinks you're in some kind of trouble, but who cares? He killed the lights, and I think he figured no one would know."

As we pass through the faint glow of the "Exit" sign above the door, Joel hands each of us a flashlight.

"Miss Brooks, are you …" a strange voice asks.

"*Chris!*" I whisper, grabbing for him.

"Oh, I'm sorry. It's just me, George O'Brien, club manager. I didn't mean to startle anyone."

"It's fine," Chris assures him, while reassuring me by putting a hand on mine, which is still clinging to his arm.

George continues, "We're all set. I thought I would bring Miss Brooks down to the basement to meet Mr. Mike Kirkwood. One of my guys already filled the three snowmobiles with gas. They're loading two onto the trailer beds out front, and we've got the two-person snowmobile ready in the underground garage. You can drive it straight out from there and get directly onto the course. The other two are on one of the trucks we'll use to take Mr. Buckley and Mr. Joel Kirkwood. Given that we're driving the two of you home, as I understand things, we're hoping they'll think we're storing the other snowmobile for you, and that's why we pulled it around the back. You sure you don't want to just leave the last snowmobile here and you could get it tomorrow?"

"No, no, my dad wouldn't want that. I'll drive it back," Joel says quickly.

"Perhaps Miss Brooks should ride in the trucks?"

"No, no, she loves to snowmobile. Thanks, George," Joel says, slapping George on the back and encouraging him down the hall.

"Great," Chris says to the group in general, and then turning to me, he takes both my hands. I give him my keys and the code to my alarm. "You'll be fine. Okay?" Nodding at him, I try not to think about them watching us. "Remember. I'll be on the headset, okay? I'll see you soon."

"Promise?" I mouth the word to him, grateful I can still see him in the dim emergency lighting.

"Promise," he mouths back to me, and with a final wink and pulling me the few feet down the hall to George, he squeezes my hand and turns to George. "Don't leave her alone until she's with Mike."

"Of course not, Mr. Buckley. Please follow me, Miss Brooks."

George guides me swiftly down a staff hallway that leads to a cement staircase. The club is strange in the darkness. As we descend the stairs, the only noise we hear is our own. I wonder if *they* are listening. George enters the basement first and looks around before taking my arm and leading me inside.

"Okay, this way." We weave our way around the rows and rows of golf carts and maintenance equipment. I'm jumpy and wondering if this is where they're hiding.

"Lindsey? George?"

"Hey, Mike!" I'm relieved to hear his voice. We move toward

it and are soon in an open area where Mike is standing next to the snowmobile.

"Chris?" Mike asks, putting his helmet on. I can hear Chris's response as the basement is so still and the snow outside is muffling any sounds around the building.

"Yeah?"

"Okay, George just brought Lindsey down here."

"Okay, you guys ready?" Chris asks.

"Lindsey, you ready?"

I pull my hat on and nod as Mike hands me my helmet.

"Yep, we're good. How about you?"

"Yeah, except that Joel can't zip Lindsey's coat," Chris says, and I am pleasantly distracted by the amusement in his voice.

"Okay, George, can you open the garage?"

"Whenever you're ready."

"Okay, wait for my cue."

"Got it. Tell Chris I'll be up in the second truck in two minutes."

"I heard him. I'm taking my helmet off to get in the truck, so I'll be off for a few."

With that, George grabs a ladder and unscrews the bulb in the garage door opener. "I can't remember if this is on general power or if we put a battery in, and I was a kid once too—so, just in case, let's take it out so it doesn't go on." *Clever man.*

"Okay. Lindsey, I'm gonna pull out fast, and we're gonna race for the forest in hopes of getting away before anyone notices. Hold on tight when we start."

"Okay."

"You did great last time. Now you're a pro," Mike says, and his attempt at levity helps. "Okay, here, let me help you with your helmet." He fixes my strap and tightens the helmet, then taps me on the top of my head, indicating I'm good.

"Can you hear me?"

"Yeah."

"Okay, get on. Let me know when you're ready."

I climb back on the snowmobile and hope that no one is going to grab me from behind.

"Okay, I'm ready."

"George, can you open the garage door?" Mike says while signaling George with a thumbs-up.

The snow finds the gap between the basement cement floor and the slowly rising garage door and swirls inside. As soon as the opening is about four feet, Mike roars the snowmobile to life and lurches through. I duck against his back and hope we make it, as I'm not sure the door is high enough for us to fit through. Mike's confidence is impressive, as he sits straight up and we sail under the door into the deep night. The world is covered with snow, which gives us a bit of visibility even though all the club lights are off. We rocket up and to the right as Mike follows the driveway around the back of the club. Turning to the left, he heads for the forest. I dare to look back and see the darkened clubhouse disappear behind us. I wish I could see whether anyone else is watching.

"Lindsey, you okay?"

"Yeah."

"Okay, hold on." With that, he guns the snowmobile and we race across the open course toward the forest. The wind is pounding me, and snow is blowing all around us. It continues to fall at a steady pace. We ride up and down across some gently rolling hills, and I hope the whole ride is like this. Then I see blackness ahead, and I know we're approaching the forest. I wonder if *they* are following us.

"I don't think anyone is following us, do you?" I ask.

"I haven't seen them. We're almost in the forest." Mike slows down and steers us into the forest.

"How far in are we going?" I mumble as we enter.

"Far enough that they won't want to follow us," Mike replies.

"I'm on. We just got in the truck," Chris says. At the sound of his voice, I close my eyes and force myself to maintain my grip. Opening my eyes again, I can only see the back of Mike's coat. In my peripheral vision is a blurred image of the night, interrupted by darker forms that I assume are the trees we are flying by.

"In the forest," Mike updates Chris and Joel, who I assume is also listening.

"Company?"

"Not yet."

"The roads are bad, even with the snowplow, so we're moving slowly. Lindsey, you okay?"

Thrilled I am invited to talk, I eagerly respond, "Yes, I'm good."

"Hold on," Mike says as we turn to the right.

"Oww ..." I whine.

"She's fine; just a bush. Sorry, Lindsey."

Pull to the right, the left, the right. Mike slows down to a crawl as we hit an extremely thick part of the forest.

"Let's get out of this," Mike says, turning to the left and steering us farther away from the golf course.

"You guys see anything?" Mike asks.

"Nothing so far. Nobody on the road but us. Just coming up to the Greenburgs' place. Okay, I see lights there, so if anyone is watching, they may think just the club lost power, or they may know something's up."

Pull hard to the right, slight left, swerve right, and then left. We continue to weave slowly through the forest.

"Okay, Lindsey, I can see your house," Joel says to the group.

"Everything looks fine, Lindsey," Chris says, and I know he is trying to calm my nerves.

"We're pulling up in front of your house now, Lindsey."

ⅎↃ

In my helmet I can hear Chris and Joel thanking George and saying good night after getting the snowmobiles off the trailer. I can hear them ride the short distance up to my house before they start to chatter again.

"Cut it out," Chris says and tells us that Joel is throwing snowballs at him.

"Doesn't Lindsey do this to you every night?" Joel says, laughing.

"Come on, Joel," Chris says, a touch annoyed. Then with clear frustration, I hear him say to Joel, "Geez Joel, come on! You're supposed to be Lindsey. What are the chances she could jump and hit the ceiling?"

"Sorry, sorry, let's get inside. I'm freezing."

"Lindsey, we're in your house. Where are you guys, Mike?"

"Deep in the forest. It'll take me some time."

The ride is exhausting as we weave through the trees.

After a while, Chris asks for an update.

"I think we have four more holes to go. Any sign of them?"

"Nothing here. Joel is turning the lights on downstairs, and I'm upstairs looking out at the property. I don't see anything—but the truth is, I can't see much with this snow."

"Okay, well, I'm gonna get out of the forest and see how far we've come."

My arms are aching in the cold wind created both from the storm and from being on the snowmobile, but I'm heartened to hear we are finally coming out of the forest. We start to pull more and more to the right.

"Shit," Mike says as we hit a bush on the right. My right hand rips off its grip, and I'm hit hard by branches. "Ahhhh ..."

"Lean left, Lindsey, and grab on!"

"Got it."

"You okay?" Chris asks, and I feel bad as I hear the concern in his voice.

"I'm good." Fatigue is heavy in my voice.

"Not much farther, Lindsey," Mike says to console me.

As we enter the clearing, Mike floors it and we bounce forward, the wind fierce around us.

"Hold tight, Lindsey."

As we jet forward, something catches my eye. "What was that?"

"What?" Mike asks, and I sense him scanning the area as we dip into a depression.

"I thought I saw a light."

"Where?"

"To my right, about two o'clock."

"What do you have, Mike?" Chris asks, and I think he's running.

"One sec, we're in a gully. Coming up. Oh, man. We got company. Guys, get out here!"

"Damn. Joel, let's go."

"Since they made us, I'm putting our lights on. Lindsey, hold on; I'm going full power."

"What? Where are they?"

"I got one up ahead, on the right. He's coming right at us."

"Oh my God," I hear myself say.

Mike demands more power from the snowmobile, and the thrust presses me back. I strain to pull myself forward against the wind.

"There's two of them. Get out here *now*!" Mike shouts.

"What do we do?"

"You hold on." My hands tensely grip the handles with renewed force. They ache under the pressure.

As our pursuers come closer, I can't help but worry that we'll collide. I feel a rise below us and know we are going to feel some air on this one. I close my eyes as we leave the ground. Bracing for the landing, I'm relieved we hit squarely and keep moving. Mike pushes the machine to get back up to full speed quickly.

"Guys, where are you? There's no time," Mike asks.

"We're leaving her house now."

"Mike ... I see light on your back," I say, terrified.

"I know. Where's the other one?"

I look around and tell Mike, "Coming up on our left."

"Damn," I hear Chris in my head.

"What happens if they hit us?"

No one answers. The lights get brighter around us, and the noise gets louder as their engines roar.

"No way I can outrun them with both of us on this," Mike says. "Lindsey, hold on." And with that, Mike kills our speed. Our sudden loss of momentum hurls me forward into Mike, who braces against me. Both our pursuers edge past us momentarily. Mike hits the gas again, pulls hard to the right, and I'm surprised I'm able to hold on.

One of them zips in front of us, and Mike avoids him to the left. The other cuts us off from the left. Mike pulls hard to the right, and we head down a swell. I slam into Mike's back, again losing my grip for an instant. Climbing to the crest of the current swell, we are again even with them. My arms are screaming for relief as they ride perilously close to us.

"Where are you guys?"

"Coming as fast as we can. Hold on, Lindz." Chris tries to sound hopeful.

Again one of *them* cuts us off. Mike swerves hard to the right. My left hand flies off the handhold, as in the same instant, the other guy arrives to our left, even closer than before. Mike pulls harder to the left, pounds the gas, and I can't hold on!

Bam. Hitting my right shoulder hard, I pound into the ground. Stunned for a second, I hear screaming in my head.

"*Lindsey!* She's off!" Mike says to the group.

"Lindsey, are you okay?" Chris is forcing his voice to stay calm.

"I can't turn around. I got a pond on my right, and the other asshole on my left. *Get out here!*" Mike screams in my head.

Gaining my bearings just a bit, I roll over and am grabbed by the shoulder and slammed onto my back. A black form is over me. *Slam.*

"Asshole won't let me turn back to her—*Where are you guys?*" Mike yells.

I hear Chris swearing as the weight of the figure above is forced on my midsection, momentarily knocking the wind out of me.

"Mike, is that you?" I scream.

"Lindse*y!*" Chris says through clenched teeth.

"Who are you?" I hear myself whisper as I try to move.

As the figure reaches down to me, I feel sheer terror. I can only see his black shape and the shine from his helmet. Shuddering uncontrollably, I want to yell, but my voice is frozen. I literally can't move. The figure reaches for my throat, and I struggle to hit him as hard as I can. He grabs both my arms and pulls them to the ground too easily, jamming them under his knees. Still struggling, I finally scream, *"Chris!"*

"Where, Mike?" Chris thunders in my head. Then my helmet is roughly pulled off and tossed aside.

The figure pulls off his helmet; a ski mask hides his face. Suddenly he's inches from my face. A voice, deep and gruff, says, "Listen to me, you little bitch. I could take you right now, but we don't want to have to do that now, do we? Tell your dad to drop this *one goddamn case,* and we'll leave you alone. You tell him I had your sweet little throat in my hands, okay? I watched you in the locker room, too, and did nothing. *Nothing.* That is what he needs to do—'nothing.' No one is going to jail. You *got that?*"

Stunned, I just look at him. Then light begins to reflect on his helmet.

"Fuck." Grabbing me with renewed force, he slams me back on the ground with incredible force. I realize he must have been holding me by my coat at the collar. I hear his snowmobile roar to life and listen as the sound disappears into the night.

I can't move. *Lindsey, get up.* Dazed a bit, I sit up. Scrambling to my feet, I try to find the guys, but all I can see is a glint from my helmet a few feet away. I scramble over to retrieve it.

As I brush the snow off my helmet, I hear the guys talking.

"What do you mean he's gone?" Joel is asking.

"I don't know; he just pulled away. Lindsey, are you okay? I'm doubling back," Mike says.

"Where are you?" I scream.

"Lindsey! Where are you? Are you okay?" Chris yells into my helmet.

"I'm okay. Chris, someone's lights were just on me for a second."

"Can anyone see her?" Mike is yelling.

"Wait. I think I see some lights. Oh, I see someone—over here! I'm over here!" Waving my arms, I see a snowmobile coming into view.

"She's on the third near the three traps," Mike says, and I can hear his snowmobile roar as he nears me.

"Get her on yours *now*!" Chris demands.

"I'm just pulling up to her. Lindsey, are you sure you're okay?"

"Where are they?" Joel asks, with stress evident in his voice.

"Yes, I … I …" and I start to lose my composure. Then I see another snowmobile, and in an instant, the third comes into view.

"Chris?" I ask into the night.

As one pulls up right next to me, I know it's Chris.

"Chris, we need to get out of here," Mike says as Chris gets off his snowmobile.

"Are you okay? What happened?" Chris asks.

"I'm fine. One of them …"

"Chris, we need to go. They could come back. Lindsey, get on," Mike says as he grabs my arm.

"Okay, okay. Mike's right—you're sure you're okay?" Chris asks.

"Yes, please …"

"I'm riding with Lindz. Mike, you get on the …"

"Done. Let's go," Mike says as I climb onto the back of the two-person snowmobile.

Clinging to the handrails, I'm happy Chris is getting on with me. Mike jets forward, with us just behind and Joel in the rear. I'm so happy to be riding with Chris and relieved that we're all riding together with our lights on. I know it's not far from the third hole to the Kirkwoods' place. I wrap one arm around Chris and hold onto him instead of the grip.

"Okay?" I ask.

"Yes," Chris says with conviction. Removing my left hand from the other handhold, I wrap both my arms around Chris and try to lean my head on his back and pull as close to him as I can.

"Anyone see anything?" Mike asks, and I'm sure he's scanning the entire area.

"Nothing," Joel says.

Except for these few words, we are all quiet crossing the golf course and the adjacent road.

As we slow to a stop at the Kirkwoods', I take a moment to gather myself, my head still resting on Chris. I can tell he's waiting for me to move before he gets up.

"Lindsey?" Chris asks cautiously.

I lift my head and am struck with fatigue. I shiver in the fierce cold. Chris gets off in one fluid motion and then helps me to my feet. He puts an arm around me and guides me as we follow Mike to the house.

Joel is at the front door and opens it. We all step inside and take off our helmets. Joel checks the alarm. "No breaches; we're good."

"Lindsey, did they hurt you?" Chris asks, pulling off his hat and using it to wipe the sweat from his face.

"No, not really."

"Lindsey, I'm so sorry you fell off," Mike says, pulling off his gloves and unzipping his coat.

"No, it wasn't your fault; it was me."

"What happened?"

"I fell off when they kept cutting us off. I just couldn't hold on any longer," I say, my voice trailing off and looking down, ashamed of my weakness.

"Then what? Did you say that one of them was on you?" Chris asks, taking me by the shoulders.

"Yeah. I hit the ground, and as I was trying to get up, one of them grabbed me and slammed me on my back."

"Are you okay?" Chris asks.

"Shit," Mike whispers.

"Yeah, he said …" and then I start to lose my control. Fighting for composure, I look at Chris.

"It's okay. We're here now. What happened? Did he touch you?"

"No, I mean—not like that. He pulled my helmet off, and then his …"

"You saw him?"

"No, he was wearing a ski mask."

"What did he say?"

"I … I … I …"

The phone ringing breaks in. Startled, we all realize the lines must be back up.

"Tell us what happened," Mike presses.

"My dad's going to freak."

"Let's get it in my dad's office; there's a speakerphone in there," Joel says, jogging down the hall.

We head down the hall and enter what must be Mr. Kirkwood's office. There's a beautiful large table on one side of the room with a speakerphone on it. I pull out my cell phone to look up dad's number and realize he has been calling me every few minutes for a while.

Joel picks up the line. "Hello?"

"Lindsey?"

"Dad?"

"Lindsey? Where have you been? We've been calling and calling. Are you okay?"

"We are now."

"Are all the guys with you?"

"Yes."

"Lindsey, what's going on? We all got texts from all of you, and then we couldn't reach any of you. We've been getting very worried here. Are you sure everyone's okay?"

"Yes, Dad, we're all fine. But, um, I'm sorry, Dad, but I think I do need to fill you in."

"I should say so. You said you're all there, right?"

"Yes, Mr. Brooks," Chris steps in.

"Hello, Chris. Lindsey, are we on speakerphone?"

"Yeah, the guys are right here."

"Pick up the phone."

Glancing at Chris, I pick up the handset as he nods in frustration. "Yeah, Dad?"

"Lindsey?"

"Yeah?"

"What happened? Maybe you should just fill me in."

"What? Why?"

"Well, maybe you can't talk freely? Is it something …"

"Dad, no. The guys saved me tonight."

"They what? You're sure?"

"Yes. Definitely."

"And you're all fine?"

"Yes, Dad."

"Okay, Lindsey; I just wanted to be sure. Everyone here is worried. We've been trying to reach any of you. Let me get everyone together on this end and let them know I reached you. Then we'll call you back—okay?"

"Okay. Dad?"

"Yeah, Lindsey?"

"I do think everything is okay now, so please don't get upset—okay? But I need to tell you …"

"Give me a minute to gather everyone and let them know you are all okay, and I'll call you right back." *Great.*

"Okay."

"He's getting all your folks together, and they'll call us back."

"Okay. Do you want anything, Lindsey?" Chris asks as the guys start to take off their coats and ski pants.

"No, I'm fine."

"Here, Lindsey, I'll take your coat," Mike offers. We all strip off our winter gear and sit down at the table, anxiously waiting.

Buzz. Chris takes my hand in his. This simple touch is comforting to me. Mike hits a button to answer the call.

"Hello?"

"Hi, Mr. Brooks, this is Chris."

"Hi, Dad."

"Hi, Mr. Brooks, this is Mike."

"And this is Joel."

"Thanks for calling back so fast, Dad."

"Sure. Okay. Lindsey, now what's going on? Are you all okay?"

"Yes, we're fine. But I think something did kind of happen. It's a bit of a long story."

"Okay. What do you mean it's a long story? Lindsey, what's going on?" he asks, a bit confused.

"Who's there, Dad?" I ask, knowing the guys are as curious as I am.

"Your mother, Chris Sr., and Robert Kirkwood—the other ladies will be up as soon as they are done with the benefit."

"Okay. Well, I don't really know where to start. Several weeks ago—well, I guess a few months ago actually, I started to get some weird text messages."

"What do you mean 'weird'?" Dad asks, while Chris mouths the words "months ago."

Furrowing my brow in frustration, I continue, "To be honest, they all sort of said that I shouldn't tell anyone about them, and Dad, I was going to tell you, but when we stayed at your place in the city that night and we talked about your cases, you said there are crazy people everywhere, and so I thought this was no big deal—but now, maybe they were … well … I guess, threats," and I could hear my pace quicken.

"Threats? What kind of threats? Who is sending you these messages?" Dad asks in a tight voice.

"They basically say I should get you off a case. And I don't know who is sending them, Dad, because they always send them from different phone numbers."

"How long has this been going on?"

"Um, I don't know exactly. Um …" Then something clicks. "Since my birthday."

"Lindsey," Dad whispers, and then he's silent.

"Dad?" I ask, letting go of Chris's hands and leaning on the table with both mine. Chris puts his arm around me and rubs my back while we all wait for my dad to respond.

"What happened that you decided to tell me now?" he asks in his cross-examination tone.

"Well, um … I thought I saw a couple of guys on snowmobiles in the forest near our house. I don't know exactly why, but I got a little nervous." I look up at Chris because I don't want him to feel bad either and say, "I called Chris." Happily he puts his hand on mine and squeezes it.

"Why didn't you call me?"

"The phones were out. You were in the city … and … with the storm … I don't know."

"Okay, okay. So what happened? Chris is with you now—right? And why are you at the Kirkwoods'? In one of Joel's texts, he said you were all at the club."

"Yes. We were at the club, but we're all at the Kirkwoods' now. Anyway, when I was on the phone with Chris, those guys started to approach the house."

"What happened?" he demands.

"Dad, please don't be mad."

"I'm not; go on."

"Okay, so Chris called Joel and Mike. They picked me up in their snowmobiles because they all thought it would be easier than driving cars in the storm."

"Wait a minute. What about Joe Mitchell? Wasn't he with you? Did he go out and see what was going on?"

"Well, actually, his dog got really sick—throwing up and stuff earlier today, so I told him since I was going out with Chris anyway—I told him to go take care of his dog."

"Lindsey, are you …" he says in a furious but contained tone.

"Dad! That was my fault, okay. Can we just …"

"Okay, okay. So, what happened?"

"Well, when we started down the road, the two guys followed us on their snowmobiles." Deep breath.

"Are you sure they were following you?"

"Well, I rode with Mike. I've told you how good he is on snowmobiles." Glancing at Mike, I get a half smile of modest pride.

"Yeah." I can hear the anxiety in his voice.

"Anyway. We started down the road and Chris joined us, and the guys kind of coordinated their movements and, well, skipping the details, Dad, it became clear they were chasing us. The guys did a great job getting us all to the clubhouse. As soon as we reached the clubhouse lights, those two other guys left."

"Lindsey, did they get close to you?"

"At that point, one got kind of close to Chris; but no, not me."

"What do you mean, 'at that point'?"

"Well, sir," Chris continues, giving me a break, "we thought that we were fine. There was no sign of those guys, so we tried to reach you and our folks just to fill you in. But the phones were still dead, and at that point, we thought it was over."

"Continue," Dad says deliberately.

"Yes, sir. A few members of the staff were there, and we were all pretty cold, especially Lindsey, so we all took showers and changed into dry clothes and then we had some dinner."

"Okay."

"Then we realized that one of the guys, well, sir, I'm sorry to say, it seems that one of the two guys got into the ladies' locker room."

"Lindsey? Did you see them?" he demands.

"No, no, Dad. They ... well ... geez. They left a rose in my locker, Dad."

"A rose?"

"Yes, sir," Chris answers, trying to deflect some of the intensity.

"Why would they—? Then what happened?"

"The guys were terrific, Dad."

Mike interjects, "We figured that we needed to get Lindsey out of the clubhouse as quickly as possible, without them knowing. So we came up with a plan to leave so that, if they were still watching, they would think Joel was Lindsey by having him wear her coat and having him and Chris drive to your house, Mr. Brooks, in one of the club's trucks with a snowplow. Chris had a great idea to cut the power in the club so they wouldn't see Lindsey and me leave from the back of the club on a snowmobile." Guy code. Even though Mike is relating the plan as he devised it, he is careful to give credit to Chris for a key component.

As we fill in our parents on the evening's adventures, the guys convey all the details up to the point when I fell off the snowmobile. I can feel both ends of the phone tense up as we approach this part of the story. The stillness in the Kirkwoods' house is eerie. Mike finishes describing the last few minutes when he and I were on the snowmobile. As he's completing his story, Joel gets up to look out the windows, reminding me that this may not be over—although for some reason, I think it is, at least for tonight.

"Lindsey, were you hurt when you fell?"

"No, no, I'm fine." I don't want to tell any of them how banged up I really feel.

"So, after you fell off, Lindsey, what happened?" Dad asks. I can hear the managed control in his voice. He is as much lawyer as father on this call.

"At first, I wasn't sure if maybe it was one of the guys, but then he kind of sat on me." At this, Chris briefly closes his eyes and looks down, and moves a bit forward in his seat, taking both my hands in his.

Locking my eyes on our interlocked hands, I continue, "Then I knew it wasn't any of these guys, so I just reacted. I tried to hit him, but he grabbed both my arms and put them under his knees. Then I guess I was so scared or shocked or something, I didn't even realize he must have grabbed me by the collar of my jacket. Then he ripped my helmet off, and he took his helmet off and he started to … well, kind of growl at me."

"Lindsey, do you remember what he said? Can you try to remember his exact words?" The interrogator continues to probe.

I close my eyes and hold Chris's hands, trying to recall. "I'll try—I'll ask everyone to please pardon the language I'm about to use." Drawing a deep breath, I begin, "Okay. So this is what I think *he* said. Um ... Okay." My foot must have been shaking because Chris puts one hand on my knee while he firmly holds both my hands in his other. "Listen to me, you little bitch. I could take you right now, but we don't want to have to do that now, do we?"

"David," Mom says softly while Chris whispers, "Jeez." He pulls himself forward to sit on the edge of his seat so that our knees are now touching. Protectively, he puts his left arm around me and starts rubbing my back, while he holds both my hands in his right hand. I am so comforted by his touch. The simple act of his thumb rubbing my back is so soothing.

"Mom, please, just let me get through this, okay?" and I can't keep my voice from cracking.

"Then he said that I need to get Dad to drop this, '*one goddamn case* and we will leave you alone.' Then he told me to tell Dad that he had my sweet little throat in his hands." Swallowing hard, I tried to continue, "He wanted you to know he watched me in the ... this is embarrassing." Looking at Mike and Joel, I can't believe I have to say this in front of all these people.

"Lindsey, it's okay," Chris says to me.

"Lindsey, nothing will leave this room," Mike says to reassure me, and I can see the compassion in his eyes.

"Okay, um ... so he wanted my dad to know that they watched me," and closing my eyes and shaking my head, I try to finish, "in the locker room, and they pointed out that they did *nothing*. He kind of hooked on that word; he said that you should do nothing too. He said, '*no one* is going to jail—you *got that*?' Then I guess he noticed the light and I guess the noise of one of the guys' snowmobiles, and he threw me back down on the ground." I glance at Chris. This last bit of information causes him to wince. "And then he was gone so fast, all I knew was that I was back on the ground, and I heard his snowmobile pull away. That's it; that's everything." As I finish, Chris pulls me to his chest and kisses me on the head. I rest my head on his shoulder and feel drained.

No one speaks, then Chris breaks the silence. "Mr. Brooks?"

"Yes, Chris."

"I don't mean to overstep anything here, sir, but I think Lindsey is pretty much exhausted."

"Oh, of course. Lindsey, are you okay? Are you hurt?"

"Yeah, I mean, no, I'm fine. I'm just tired—but what else do you need?"

"Lindsey, are you sure you're okay?" Mom asks.

"Yes, Mom. Please don't worry."

"Boys, you did a very fine job this evening." Mr. Buckley gives the guys a well-earned compliment.

"I couldn't agree more," Dad adds.

"Okay, let me think," Dad says in a thoughtful tone.

"Dad?"

"Yes?"

"I'm so sorry," I say with my voice cracking. Thankfully, Chris takes my hand in his.

"There's nothing to be sorry for. When did you say this started?"

"Basically, when I got my new car. It was right around my birthday, I guess."

"Okay, just sit tight. Stay with Chris and the guys, okay?"

"Okay."

"I'm going to talk to Chris Sr. and Robert, and then we'll call you back. Lindsey, if anything else happens, you call 911 first—then call me—you got that?"

"Why? I thought you said ..."

"Lindsey, I'm not taking any chances, okay?"

"Okay."

"Just stay put. We'll call you back soon."

"Is this serious, Dad?"

"I'm sure everything will be fine. I'll call you back soon."

Click.

"Lindsey, it's gonna be fine, okay?" Chris assures me.

"Yeah, okay."

I barely catch my breath before the phone rings. Mike hits the speakerphone button and says, "Hello."

"Hi, guys, Lindsey," my dad starts, and he is all business. "I'm here with your father, Chris, as well as your father, boys. The first thing I want to do is thank Chris for having the good sense to act quickly when Lindsey called you. Your first thought was obviously for her safety. And to all three of you young men, I can't thank you enough. When the evening started, you couldn't have known what was going to happen, but the fact that you all were willing to put yourselves in harm's way on her behalf means more than I can say."

"Chris," his dad starts, and I can see that upon hearing his dad's voice, he sits just a little straighter, "you did exactly the right thing. I'm sure you knew Mike could get to Lindsey faster. I know it could not have been an easy decision for you not to get her yourself, but you did the right thing by putting her first." I couldn't help but smile at Chris when we all heard this. Chris, who had been focused on the speakerphone as his dad spoke, moved his eyes sideways to look at me and gave me one of his killer smiles and a wink.

"Boys," Chris's dad continues, and we all could sense the shift in his tone, "we've talked about it and agree it is best for you to stay together tonight. Now, there is probably nothing to worry about, but just to be safe, keep an eye out for anything unusual. Okay?"

"Got it, Dad."

Clearly his marine training has given Chris's dad the lead in the tactics department, as he further instructs, "Given that these guys have had at least two opportunities where they had access to Lindsey, I think it is highly unlikely that they actually want to inflict any harm. We think they want to send a message, and I would say that they did that. I don't think they will be back this evening. That said, boys, we think it would be best for you to stay up tonight. Watch the property for anything unusual—just to be safe. You see anything you don't like, you call 911 on one phone and me on the other—okay?"

"Okay, Dad," Chris confirms.

"I'm going to call my security firm. As soon as they can drive the roads, I'll have a few guys out at the house," Mr. Kirkwood adds.

"Thanks, Robert. I'll contact the lead agent on this case and be sure he is aware of all this as well," Dad adds.

"Okay. Guys, keep the alarm on. We'll see you as soon as we can get out of Chicago in the morning," Mr. Kirkwood says. I'm happy to think about having them all back with us soon.

"Boys, I want a text every hour on the hour—okay?" Mr. Buckley requests. Mr. Buckley continued to give the guys a few more instructions, but I stopped listening and shut my eyes.

I open my eyes when I hear my dad's voice and try to focus. "Given the severity of the storm, which is still barreling down on us, we aren't going to be able to get home tonight. There are just too many roads closed right now. We'll leave as soon as the plows catch up in the morning, but we'll have to stay here at the Drake tonight."

"If anything unusual happens, call the police right away; don't wait. Okay? David is going to talk to the local police so they'll be on alert." Chris's dad gives the final direction.

"Dad?" I ask, breaking the brief silence as the plan for the evening seems to have been set.

"Yeah, Short Stack?" At which all the guys look at me and smirk.

Rolling my eyes I continue, "Dad, is all this necessary?"

"I'm sure it's all nothing—but I don't like the fact that *you* are getting threats. I'm sure it will all be fine."

"Then why do you need to call the police?"

"Lindsey, we aren't sure what we're dealing with here. It's just a precaution so that if you do have to call the police, they will take you seriously. I do think you all should know that we think there's a chance these are the same guys who cut our power earlier this fall.

So while they haven't yet done anyone any real harm, we all need to be alert."

"I'm so sorry; you are all ..." I start, while Chris squeezes my hand and Mr. Kirkwood jumps in.

"Don't give it a thought. None of this is your fault. We're all happy to help out. Boys, no games tonight, okay? Stay alert."

"Yeah, we got it," Chris says for all of them.

"Okay, bye, Dad," I say, hoping Mom is there too.

"Bye," they all sort of say at the same time.

30 THE FINAL PLEA: *WHY ME?*

"YOU OKAY?" CHRIS ASKS as we walk hand in hand into one of the sitting rooms on the Kirkwoods' second floor. Apparently Mr. Buckley Sr. doesn't want me on the first floor tonight, just as a precaution. The twins are downstairs and are giving Chris and me a few minutes alone.

"Yeah. I'm so sorry about all of this. What a nightmare. Thank you so much for coming tonight."

Embracing me tightly, Chris whispers, "I just wish those guys never got near you. I should have ..."

Pulling back and looking him right in the eyes, I rush to say, "No, you did everything you could. Can you imagine what would have happened if you never came to get me out of the house?"

Moving closer for another comforting embrace, Chris says, "I know, but don't think about that. You're safe now, and I'm not leaving your side."

"Listen, can I ask you something, Chris?"

"Sure."

"If my dad keeps the case these guys are interested in, I'm guessing I may be under even tighter lock and key for a while."

"You don't think he'll drop it? I'm sure if you want him to, he will, Lindsey."

"He has to keep it. He can't drop a case. I'm going to tell him not to." *He can never drop a case again anyway. He couldn't live with that.*

"You sure?" Chris asks, moving back so he can look me in the eyes. I'm struck by the depth of my feelings for him.

"Yes. My dad says it's an important case and will impact the livelihood of a lot of people. But I can ask him to keep it only if you can put up with the additional scrutiny my parents will likely put me under."

"First of all, you don't need to decide this tonight, but if you're sure that's what you want, then I'm sure we can work it out, Lindz. When are you going to believe me? I just want to be with you."

"Promise?"

"Promise." Hearing his response, I'm not sure why, but something shifts inside me. I step closer to him and briefly touch his face to pull it down toward mine with both my hands. I struggle to keep control of my emotions. I can see in his eyes that he is captivated because I have never been the one to take any kind of real initiative. I glance down for an instant to gain my composure. Chris places his hands lightly on my shoulders.

"What?" he asks, with a painful amount of concern in his voice.

"Chris, please tell me the truth right now." I look in his eyes as he slides his hands down my arms to hold my wrists.

"Lindsey, I told you, I'll always tell you the truth. Ask me anything."

"I … look, I just … if you have any …"

"What, Lindsey? Just say it. Did something else happen out there? Did those guys …" and he shifts to his dad tone.

"No, no, it's nothing like that. Okay, please don't be mad at me. But if I am just another girl in a string of dates …"

"What? What are you talking about?"

"Chris, I just ..." I close my eyes and push my hair back with one hand, nervously, while he pulls me closer and I try to finish, "I just ... I mean ... I just look at you, and I'm ... Chris, I just care for you so much—too much, I think. I just don't ... if you're going to dump me, especially after all this, I would just rather know."

"Lindsey, stop."

"No, let me finish," I say more forcefully than usual.

"Okay," he relents.

"I feel like a raw nerve right now, and if I let myself ... I don't know ... if I let myself lean on you tonight after everything you've already done and you move on ... I just think I might crack somehow. So if you would rather be dating someone else ..."

"Stop, I can't let you finish. Lindz, sweetie, look at me." He gently but firmly lifts my chin, and I'm forced to look at him. "Lindz, listen to me. Okay? It's you and me."

"Why me?"

"I fell for you the moment I first saw you. I'm *yours*, Lindsey. Please stop worrying about this. I'm not going anywhere. There's no one else I want to be with, okay? It's you and me."

"Are you sure? I just would rather know. I don't know what might happen next."

"I'm positive. Why all of a sudden are you unsure?"

"You're sure? Even with all this?"

"I'm sure; it's you and me. Okay, Lindz? I'm in this with you, okay? No matter what happens. Please tell me what I did to make you—is it because I had you ride with Mike? I just ..."

"No, no, no. I completely get that. I know that was hard for you."

"You have no idea," he admits quietly.

Looking down I continue, "It's because I'm terrified. As long as you are sure, then, please," and the tears start to fall, "please don't leave me alone tonight. I'm scared."

Surrounding me in a big hug and holding me tightly, Chris says over and over, "I've got you, Lindsey. I'm not going to let go.

Okay? *No one* will touch you tonight, okay? I am *not* going to let that happen. I'll take care of you, okay?"

Struggling against him a bit, I fight hard against the weight I feel in my chest, and pull away from him. "That's not what you want. You want a date, not someone who needs taking care of—that's what I'm worried about."

He releases his hug a bit so he can look at me, and shaking his head, he disagrees. "No, Lindsey, you're wrong. I mean, you're right that that isn't what I've wanted in the past, but with you, I *want* to take care of you. I realize now that maybe I've always wanted to take care of you." Closing his eyes for a minute and smiling at me, he adds, "I'm kind of excited you want me to be the one to take care of you. You're always so independent and busy, and you seem to rely on your dad for that—I'm so glad you called *me* tonight. *I* want to be the one to be there for you."

As we look at each other, I feel connected to Chris in a new and intimate way.

"Promise?" I say, smiling, because this has become our own term of endearment.

"Promise."

As he pulls me into him, I'm overwhelmed. I wrap my arms around his neck and bury my face in the warm nook of his neck. I finally let my mind think about the question I have been pushing out of my mind for months. Thankfully the texts were not from Chris. Or the guys. The relief in this is overwhelming.

"Okay. Now, I have to tell you something," Chris says after a brief pause.

"Oh."

"No, Lindsey. Look at me." Holding me firmly in his arms, he looks in my eyes again. "Look. All our parents know we're here, and while no one thinks these guys are coming back, we aren't taking any chances." Seeing the change in my expression, he quickly tries to remove my concerns. "No, no. I'll stay with you, but I need to stay focused. Much as I would love to curl up with you, I just can't.

Not tonight, Lindz—don't think it's because I don't want to, okay? It's just that my first priority has to be to keep you safe. Okay?"

"Okay. Ya know what's weird?"

"What?" he asks, and I'm heartened to see him smile.

"I was so looking forward to dinner and a movie with you. All day, all I could think about was how much I just wanted to be with you." Embarrassed, I look down and smile. "I know it sounds stupid, but all day I kept thinking how much I just wanted you to hold my hand."

"It's not stupid at all, Lindz. To be honest, it's nice to hear."

Buzz.

"Huh," I jump as I hear the vibration of a cell phone.

"No, no, no, it's me. Lindz, it's mine." I'm relieved it's not mine. Until I see his face shift.

"What?"

"No, it's nothing."

"Your dad?"

"Forget it. Come here."

"No, who is it, Chris?"

"Please let it go, Lindz."

Unbelievable! Apparently a Hurricane can strike even in a blizzard.

"It's her, isn't it?" And my fatigue suddenly grabs hold.

"Yes. Please don't ..."

"I can't. I'm too tired."

"It's you and me, okay?"

"I like the sound of that."

"But just in case, can you please give me your phone for tonight?"

"Sure, here."

"Now, I want you to promise me something, Lindz."

"What?"

"That if anyone or anything is ever bothering you, or scaring you, or just worrying you, I want you to come to me. I want to be there for you."

I'm overwhelmed. "Is that really what you want?"

"Yes, and I want you to know I won't let you down. Promise me."

"Promise."

"It's you and me, Lindz." And, wrapped in his arms, I finally take a deep breath.

EPILOGUE

ON SUNDAY, DAD TELLS us there had been three attorneys working with him on the case. Two of them called him early Sunday morning and requested immediate reassignment. My folks don't know I overheard them talking in his office, but it seems that ours was not the only family with some unusual activity over the weekend.

One of the two, a promising young attorney with political aspirations, agreed to talk with my dad about it. After what I imagine were some intense discussions, he offered my dad the following hypothetical: "If I had received an envelope at home, with copies of photos of me with a woman who might not resemble my wife, I would have been given all the motivation I needed to drop a case." So, without his having admitted anything, Dad knew they had gotten to him.

The second attorney advised my dad he should get off the case too. Apparently they had called his pregnant wife and convinced her to tell her husband it was time to leave the government and accept the offer he had received from a private firm. Dad could only imagine what they must have said to her. So could I.

Later that day, I told Dad I knew he had to stay on the case. After a long pause, he cracked his neck, and I knew he was thinking about the Case and the Animal. He agreed.

Now Dad is not only the lead counsel, but the only attorney working the case. The judge was sympathetic to Dad's situation. He agreed to issue the arrest warrants on Monday. Dad requested two young single attorneys to work with him. He confided to me that he would be stretched to prosecute in a timely manner, but he wanted at least to move on the arrests so that, hopefully, they would leave me alone. Mr. Kirkwood's private security firm, as well as Dad's government experts, had all come to the same conclusion—our unknown pursuers really didn't want to harm me or anyone else. They just wanted to scare the prosecutors enough not to put the subjects—very wealthy and powerful people—under arrest. They all agreed that once the arrests were made public, the threats would end.

Late Sunday afternoon Chris came over, and we ordered pizza and watched a movie. Although I know it was hard to have me out of her sight, Mom was thoughtful enough to get my dad upstairs all evening. I curled up next to Chris, and after being up for the whole night before, finally fell asleep—my hand in his, my head on his chest, and my heart wrapped around his finger.

By noon Monday, seven guys were under arrest. Mom said it is one of the largest RICO conspiracies in US history. She explained that RICO stands for Racketeer Influenced and Corrupt Organization and that basically a RICO case is one where the government can prosecute the bosses for crimes that they ordered others in their organization to commit. Dad was going after the rich guys at the top.

By Monday afternoon, their arrest and the charges had been broadcast on every local and national news channel.

Monday night, they were all out on bail.

ENDNOTE

1. Drew's Script-O-Rama, *Dracula (1979) Script*, originally transcribed by BJ Kuehl from the 1974 movie, *Dracula*. http://www.script-o-rama .com/movie_scripts/d/dracula-script-transcript-jack-palance.html.

Kimberly Kolb earned a bachelor of science degree in industrial organizational psychology from the University of Illinois. She began writing while waiting for her daughter to finish ballet and tap classes. Kolb lives with her husband and three children north of Chicago. This is her debut novel.

CPSIA information can be obtained at www.ICGtesting.com
Printed in the USA
LVOW06s0523260713

344757LV00003B/105/P